Son of Samson
and the Sword of Revenge

ZONDERVAN

The Sword of Revenge
Copyright © 2009 by Gary Martin
Illustrations copyright © 2009 by Sergio Cariello

Requests for information should be addressed to:
Zondervan, *Grand Rapids, Michigan* 49530

Library of Congress Cataloging-in-Publication Data: Applied for
ISBN 978-0-310-71285-5

Series Editor: Bud Rogers
Managing Art Director: Merit Kathan

Printed in the United States of America

09 10 11 12 13 • 10 9 8 7 6 5 4 3 2 1

Son of Samson
and the Sword of Revenge

series editor: bud rogers

story by gary martin

art by sergio cariello

letters by dave lanphear

ZONDERVAN

ZONDERVAN.com/
AUTHORTRACKER
follow your favorite authors

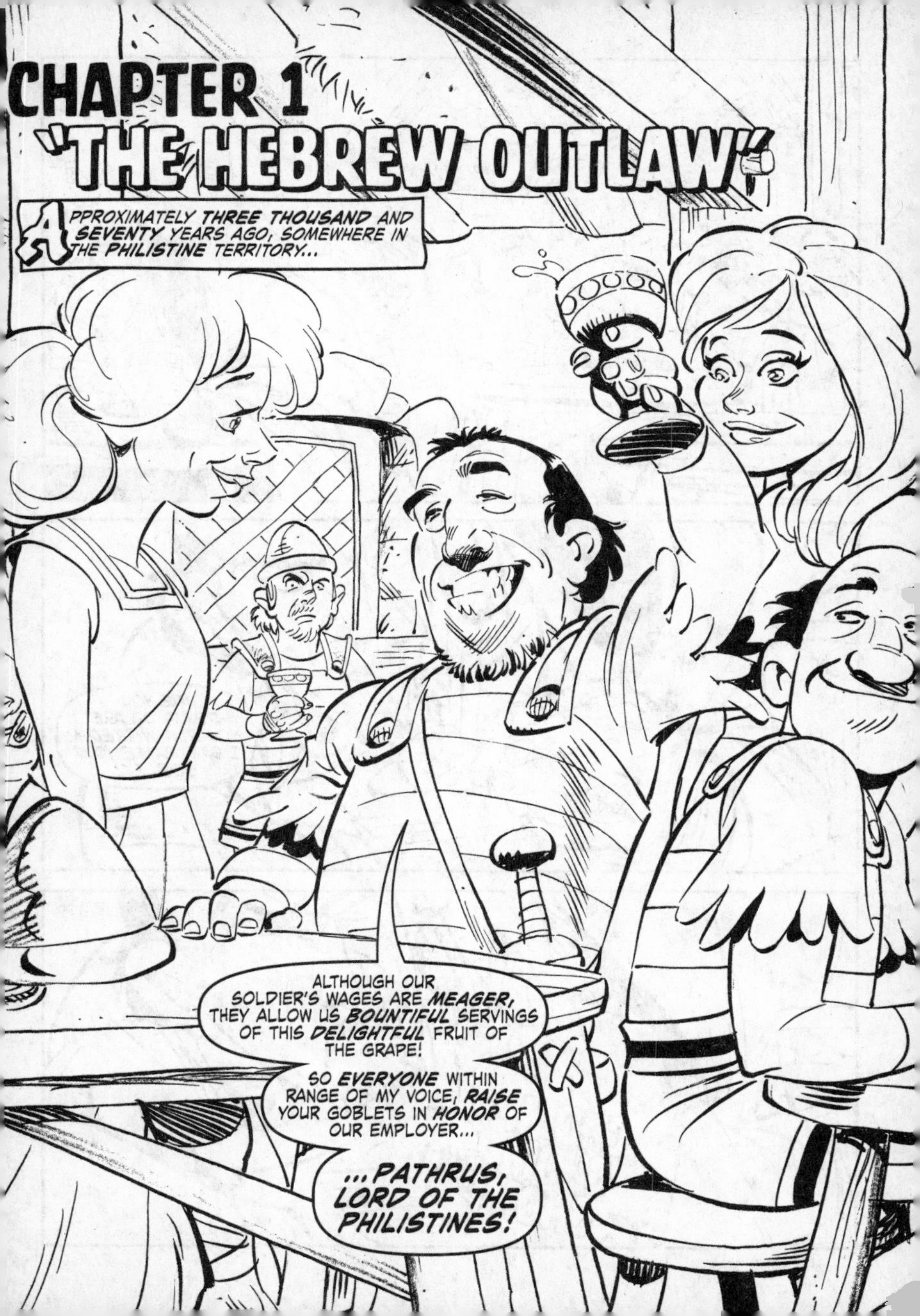
CHAPTER 1
"THE HEBREW OUTLAW"
APPROXIMATELY THREE THOUSAND AND SEVENTY YEARS AGO, SOMEWHERE IN THE PHILISTINE TERRITORY...
ALTHOUGH OUR SOLDIER'S WAGES ARE MEAGER, THEY ALLOW US BOUNTIFUL SERVINGS OF THIS DELIGHTFUL FRUIT OF THE GRAPE!
SO EVERYONE WITHIN RANGE OF MY VOICE, RAISE YOUR GOBLETS IN HONOR OF OUR EMPLOYER...
...PATHRUS, LORD OF THE PHILISTINES!

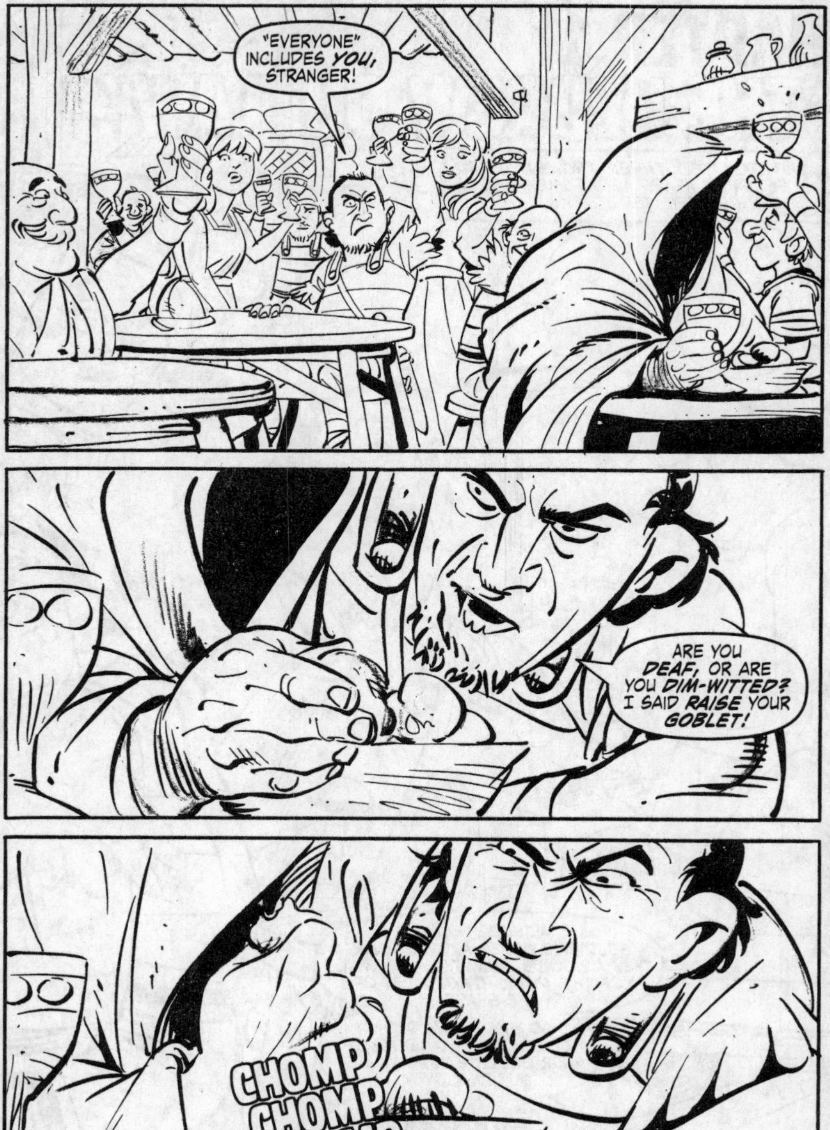
"EVERYONE" INCLUDES YOU, STRANGER!
ARE YOU DEAF, OR ARE YOU DIM-WITTED? I SAID RAISE YOUR GOBLET!
CHOMP CHOMP CHOMP

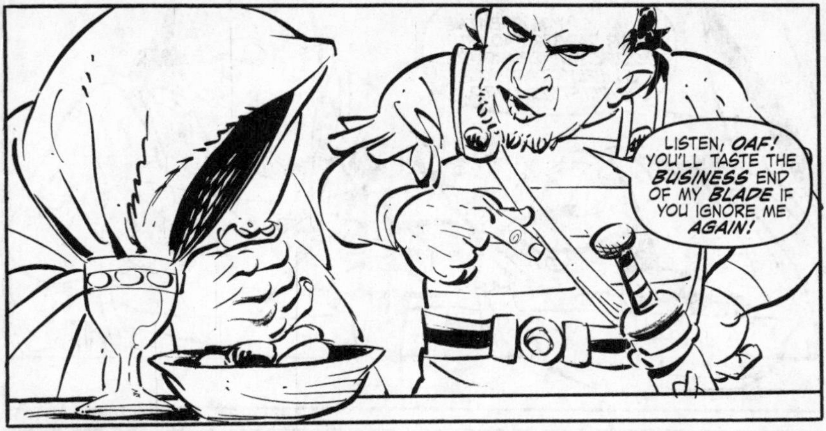
LISTEN, OAF! YOU'LL TASTE THE BUSINESS END OF MY BLADE IF YOU IGNORE ME AGAIN!

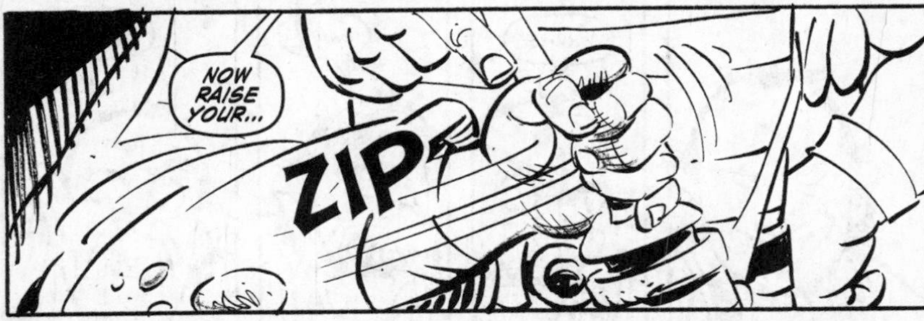
NOW RAISE YOUR...
ZIP

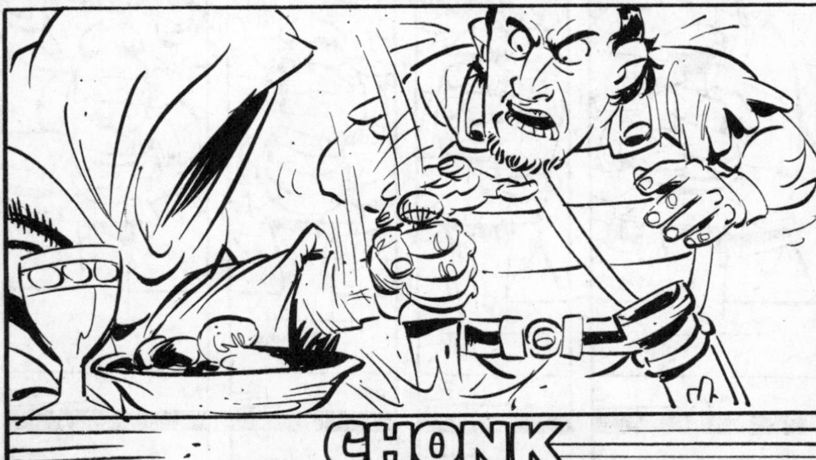
CHONK

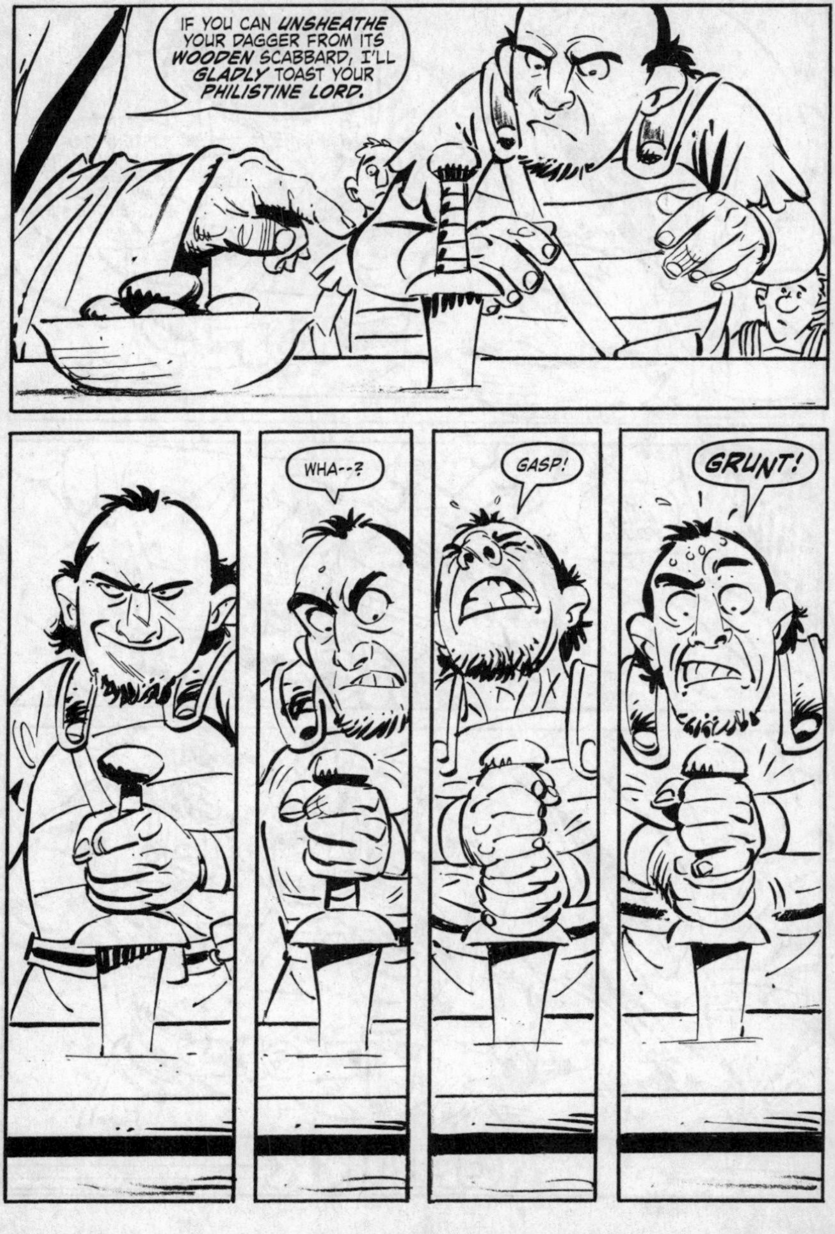
IF YOU CAN UNSHEATHE YOUR DAGGER FROM ITS WOODEN SCABBARD, I'LL GLADLY TOAST YOUR PHILISTINE LORD.
WHA--?
GASP!
GRUNT!

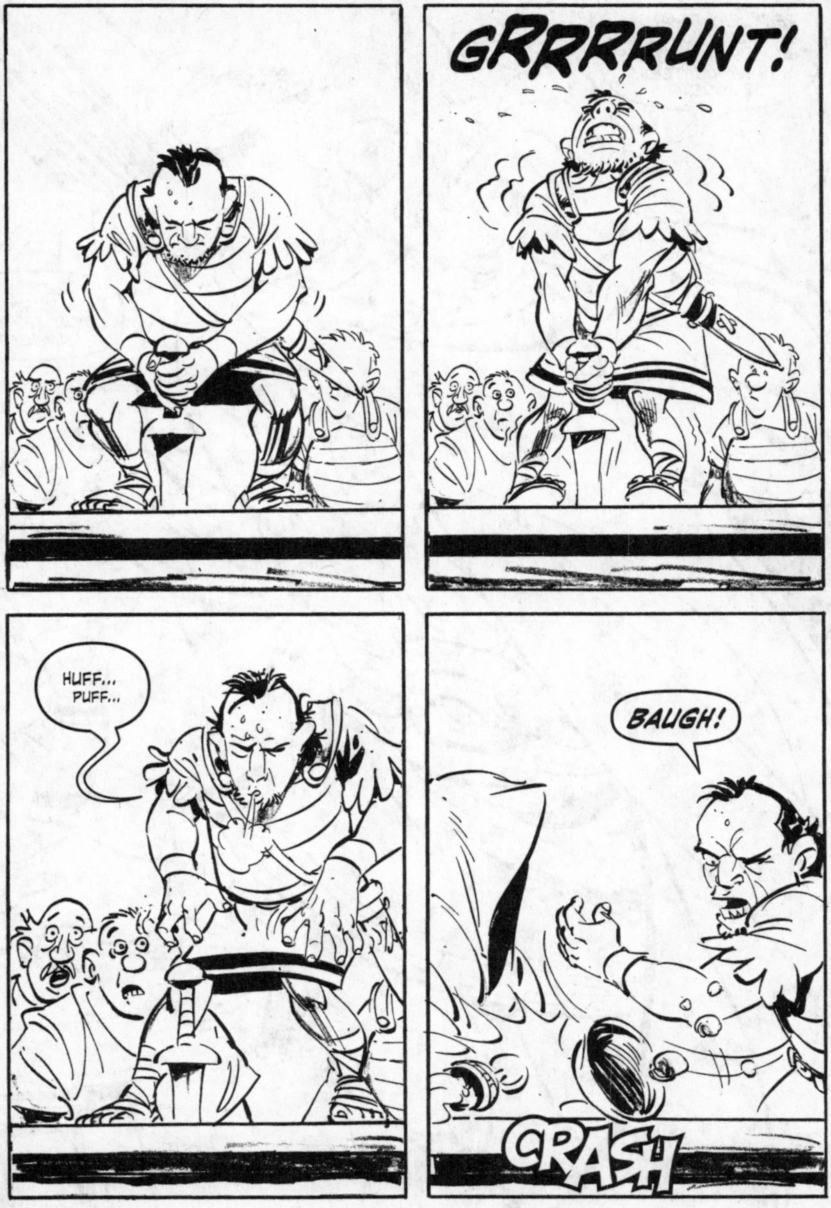
GRRRRRUNT!
HUFF... PUFF...
BAUGH!
CRASH

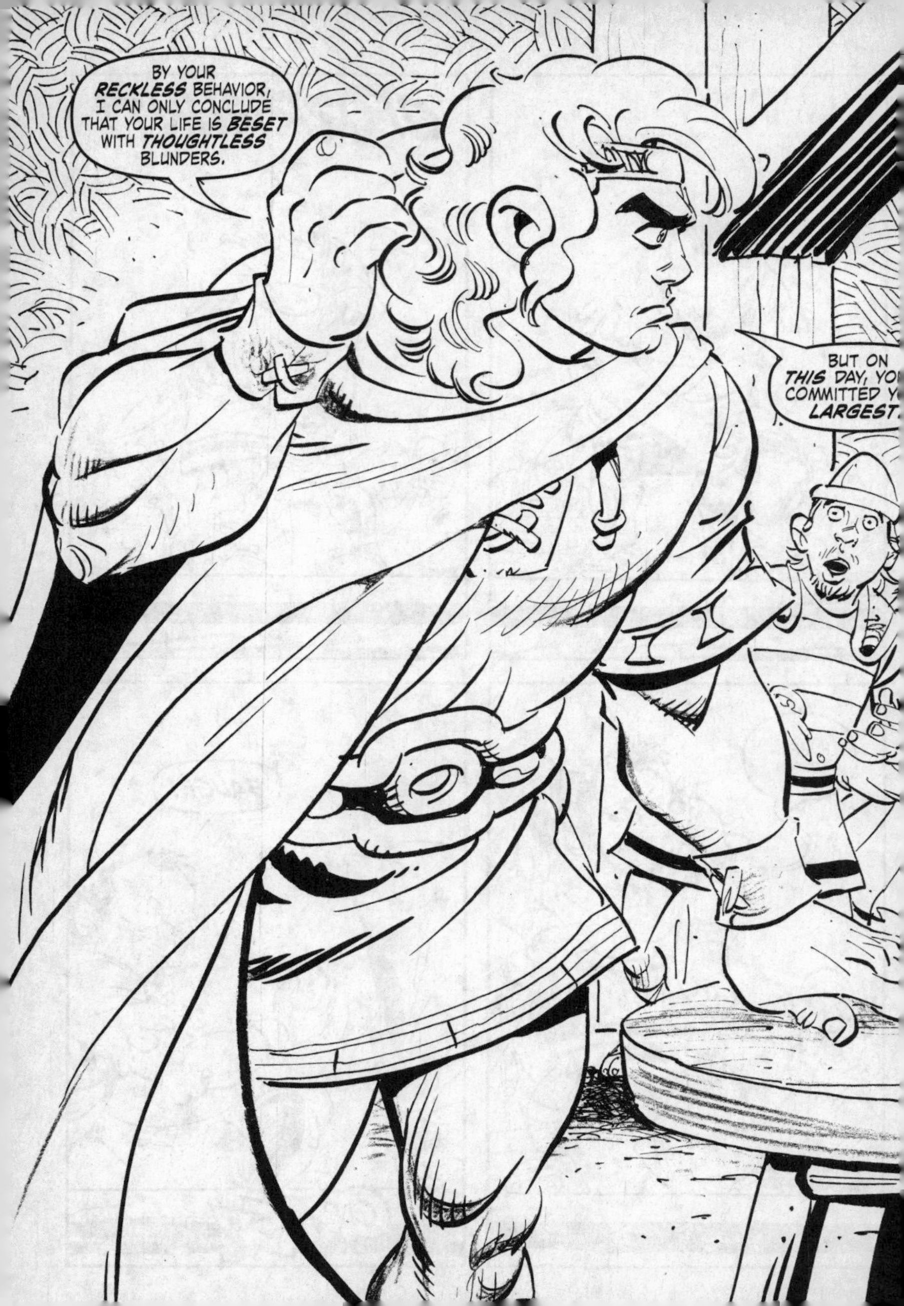
BY YOUR RECKLESS BEHAVIOR, I CAN ONLY CONCLUDE THAT YOUR LIFE IS BESET WITH THOUGHTLESS BLUNDERS.
BUT ON THIS DAY, YO COMMITTED Y LARGEST

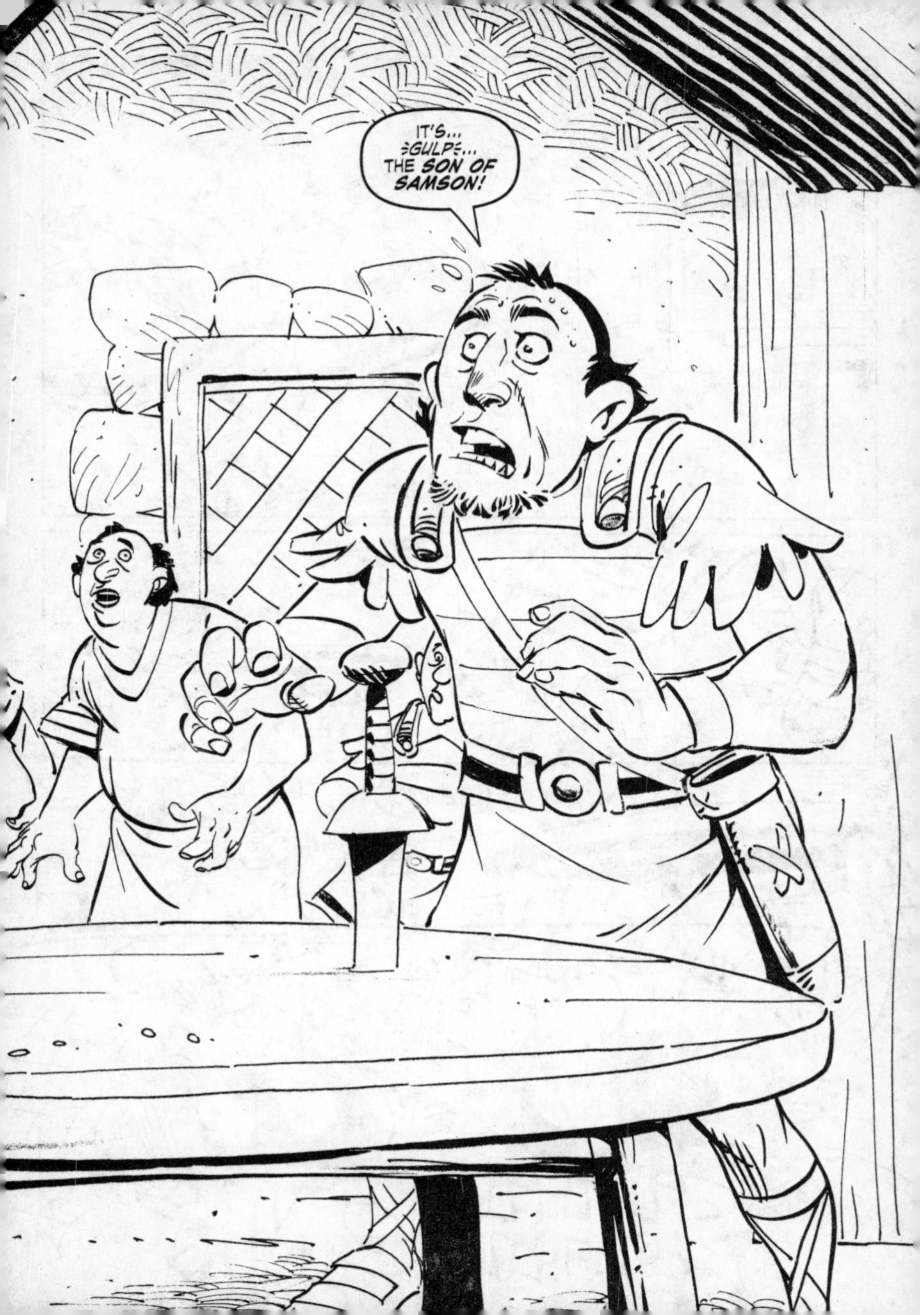

IT'S... =GULP=... THE SON OF SAMSON!

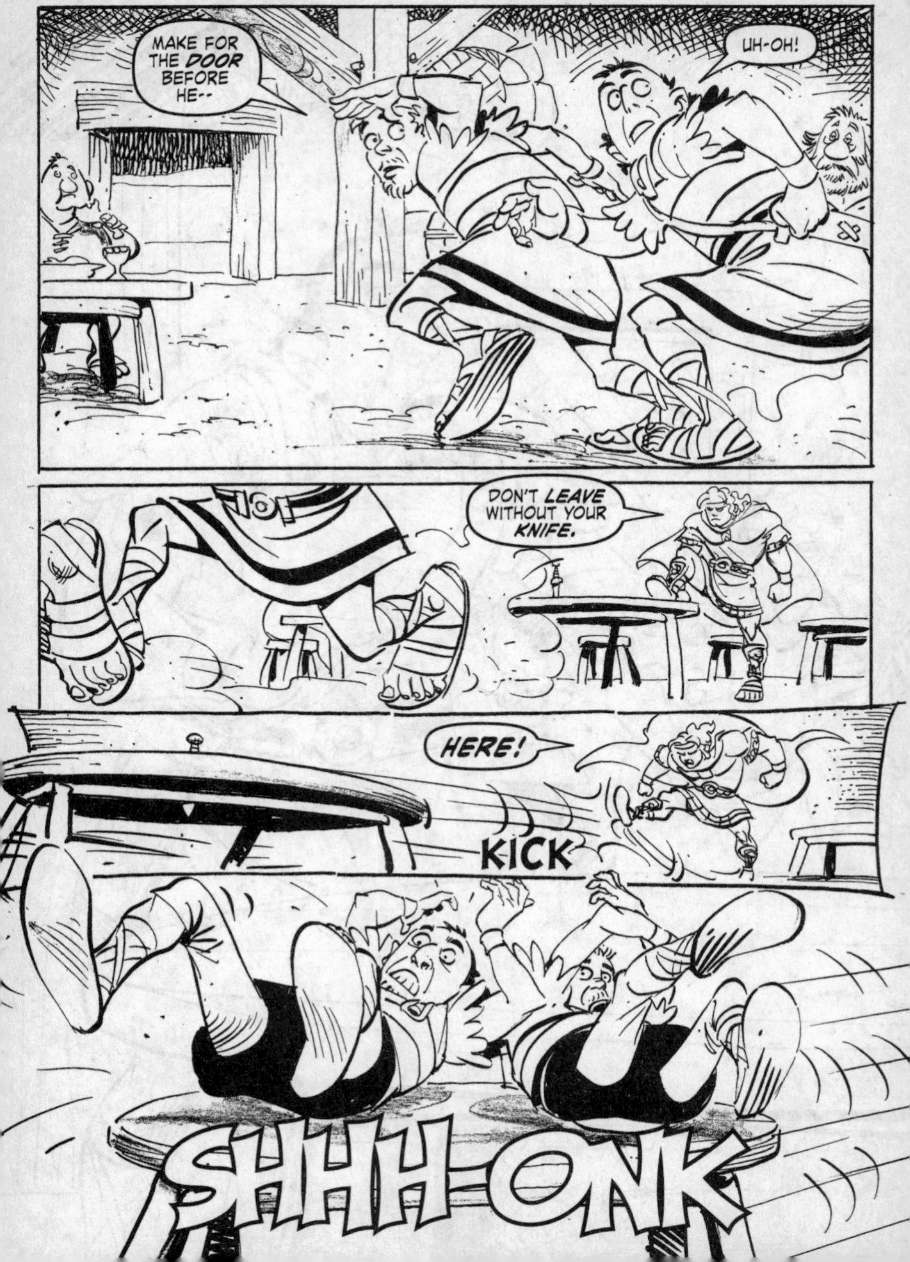
MAKE FOR THE DOOR BEFORE HE--
UH-OH!
DON'T LEAVE WITHOUT YOUR KNIFE.
HERE!
KICK
SHHH-ONK

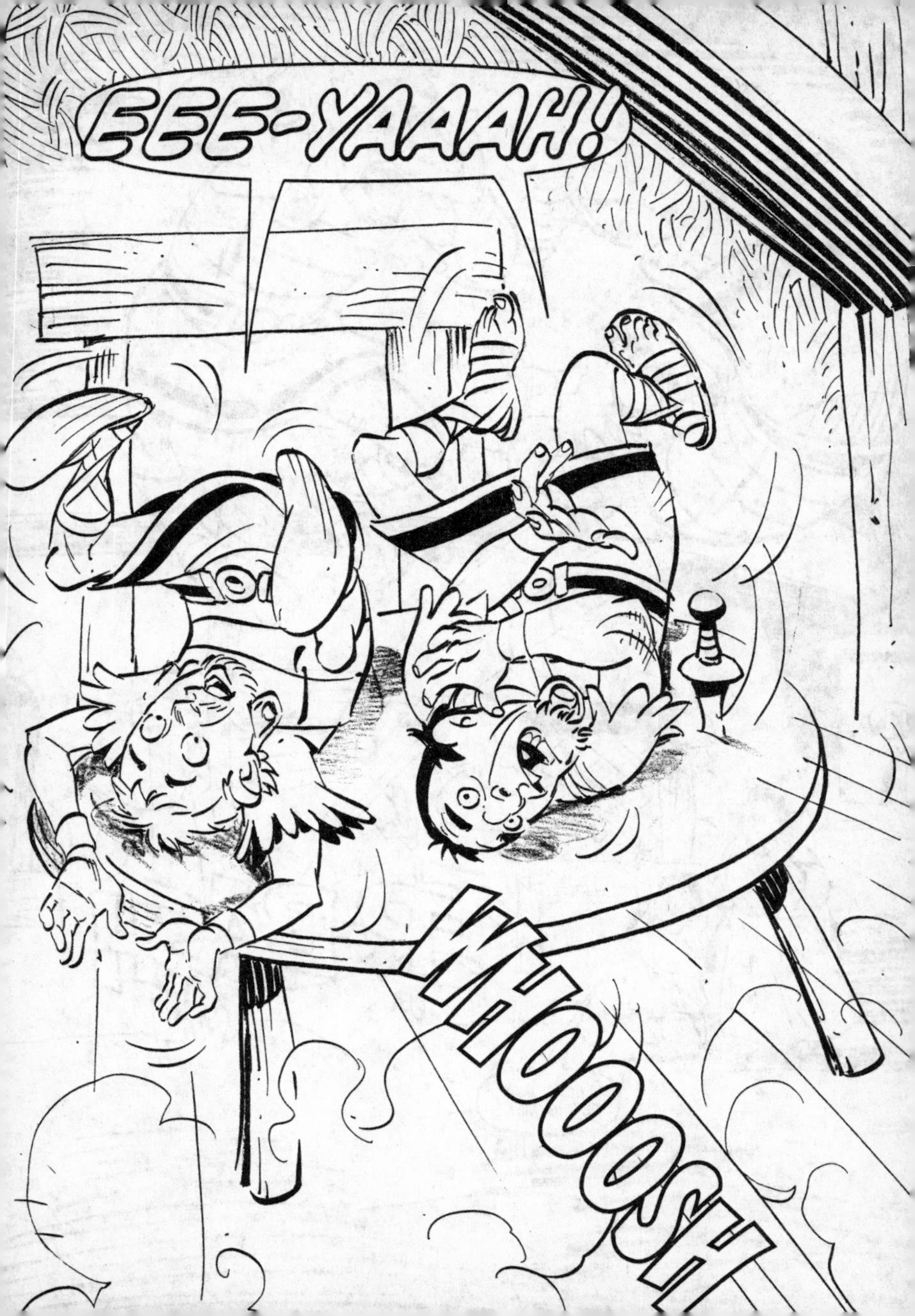
EEE-YAAAAH!
WHOOOOSH!

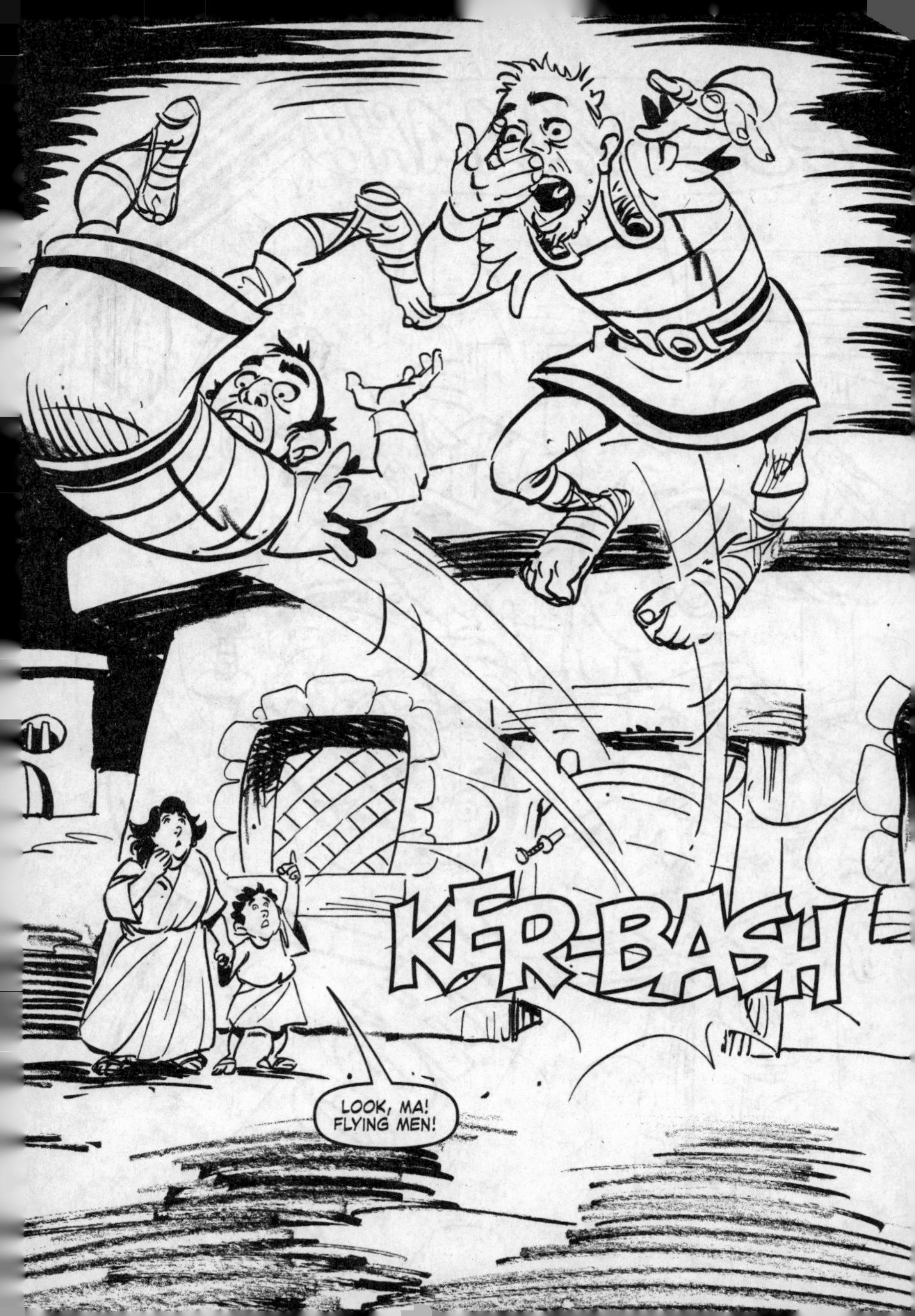
KER-BASH
LOOK, MA! FLYING MEN!

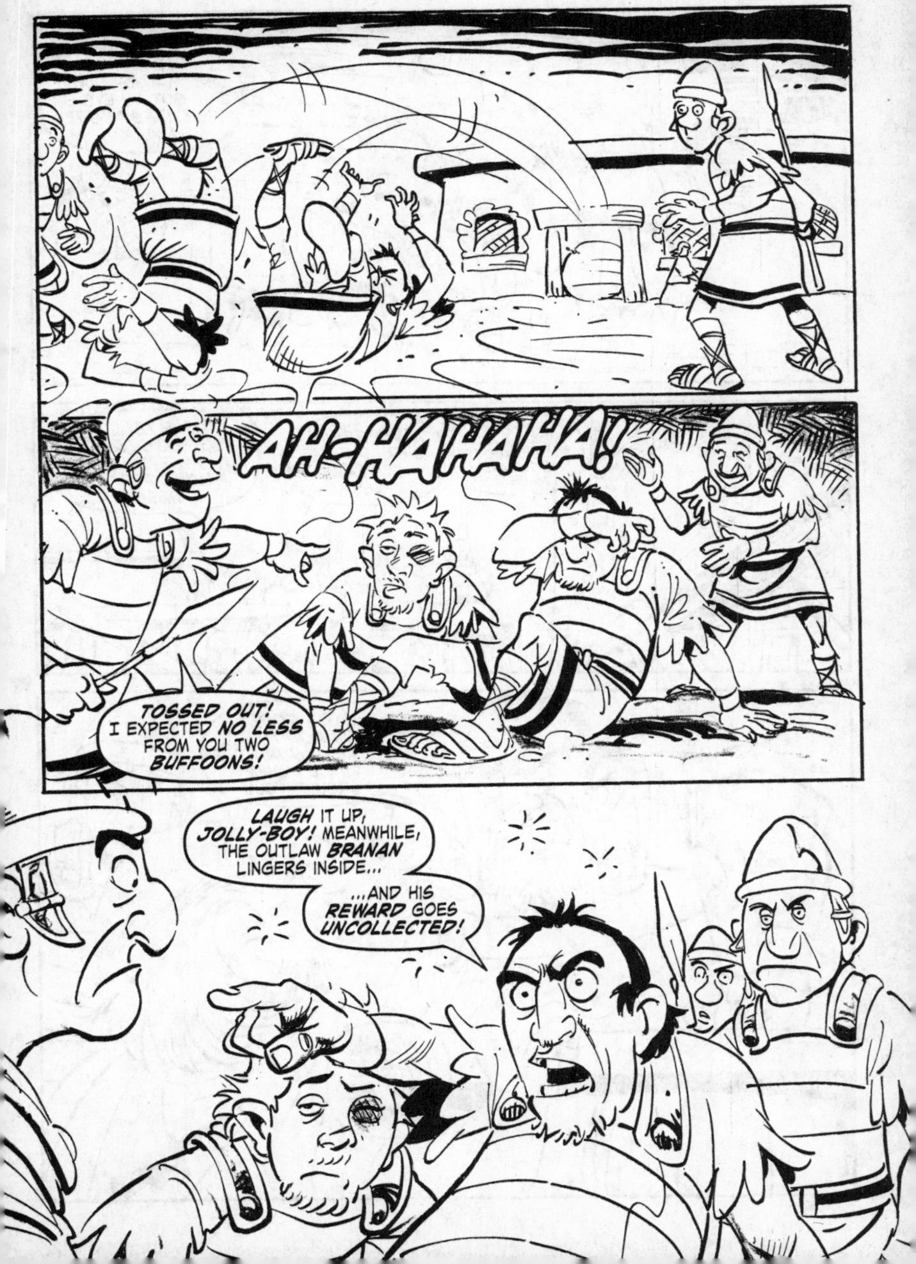
AH-HAHAHA!
TOSSED OUT! I EXPECTED NO LESS FROM YOU TWO BUFFOONS!
LAUGH IT UP, JOLLY-BOY! MEANWHILE, THE OUTLAW BRANAN LINGERS INSIDE...
...AND HIS REWARD GOES UNCOLLECTED!

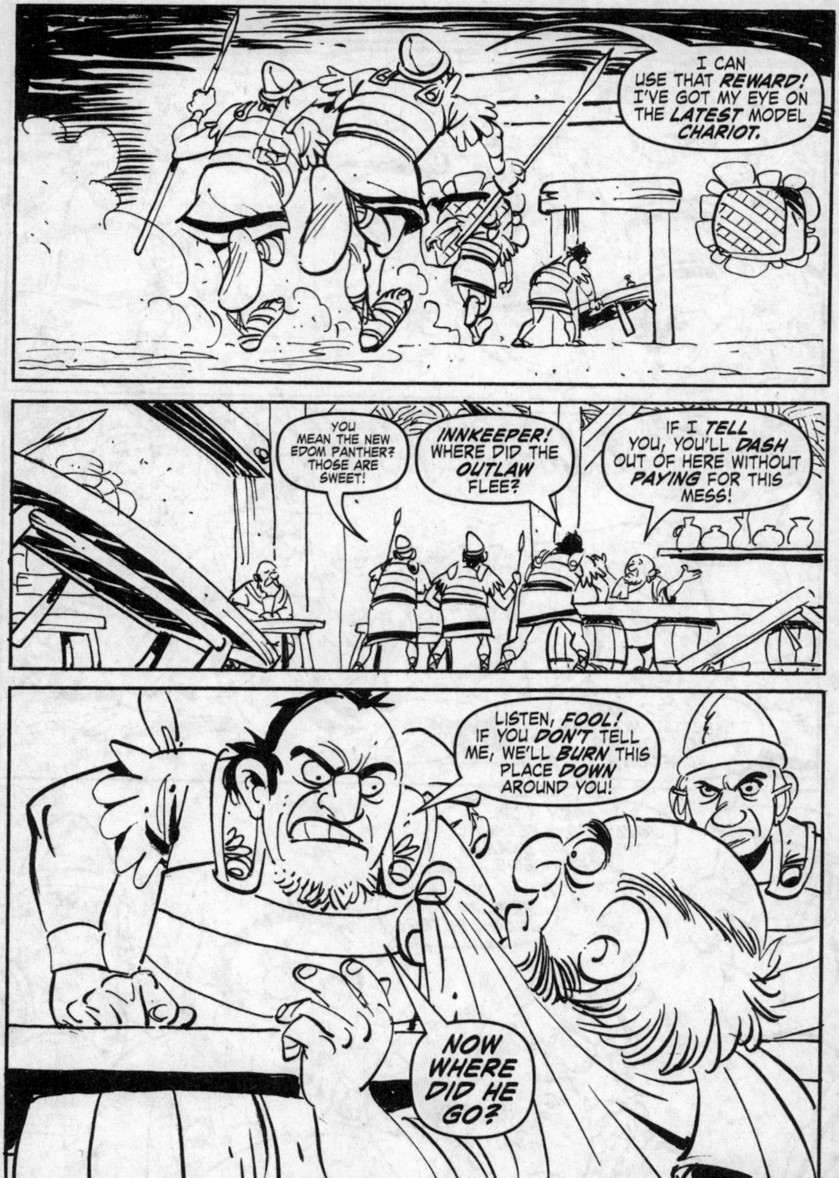
I CAN USE THAT REWARD! I'VE GOT MY EYE ON THE LATEST MODEL CHARIOT.
YOU MEAN THE NEW EDOM PANTHER? THOSE ARE SWEET!
INNKEEPER! WHERE DID THE OUTLAW FLEE?
IF I TELL YOU, YOU'LL DASH OUT OF HERE WITHOUT PAYING FOR THIS MESS!
LISTEN, FOOL! IF YOU DON'T TELL ME, WE'LL BURN THIS PLACE DOWN AROUND YOU!
NOW WHERE DID HE GO?

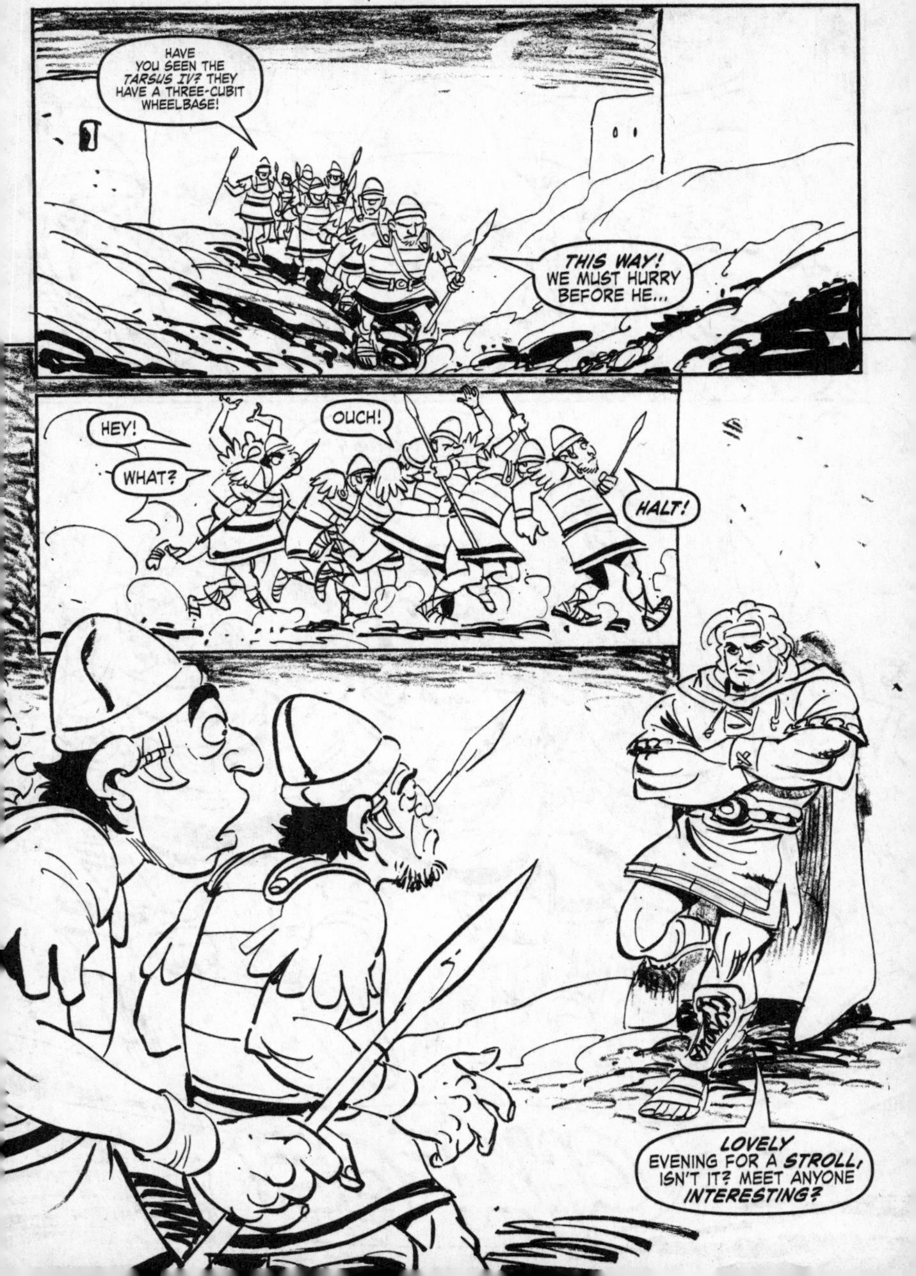
HAVE YOU SEEN THE TARSUS IV? THEY HAVE A THREE-CUBIT WHEELBASE!
THIS WAY! WE MUST HURRY BEFORE HE...
HEY!
WHAT?
OUCH!
HALT!
LOVELY EVENING FOR A STROLL, ISN'T IT? MEET ANYONE INTERESTING?

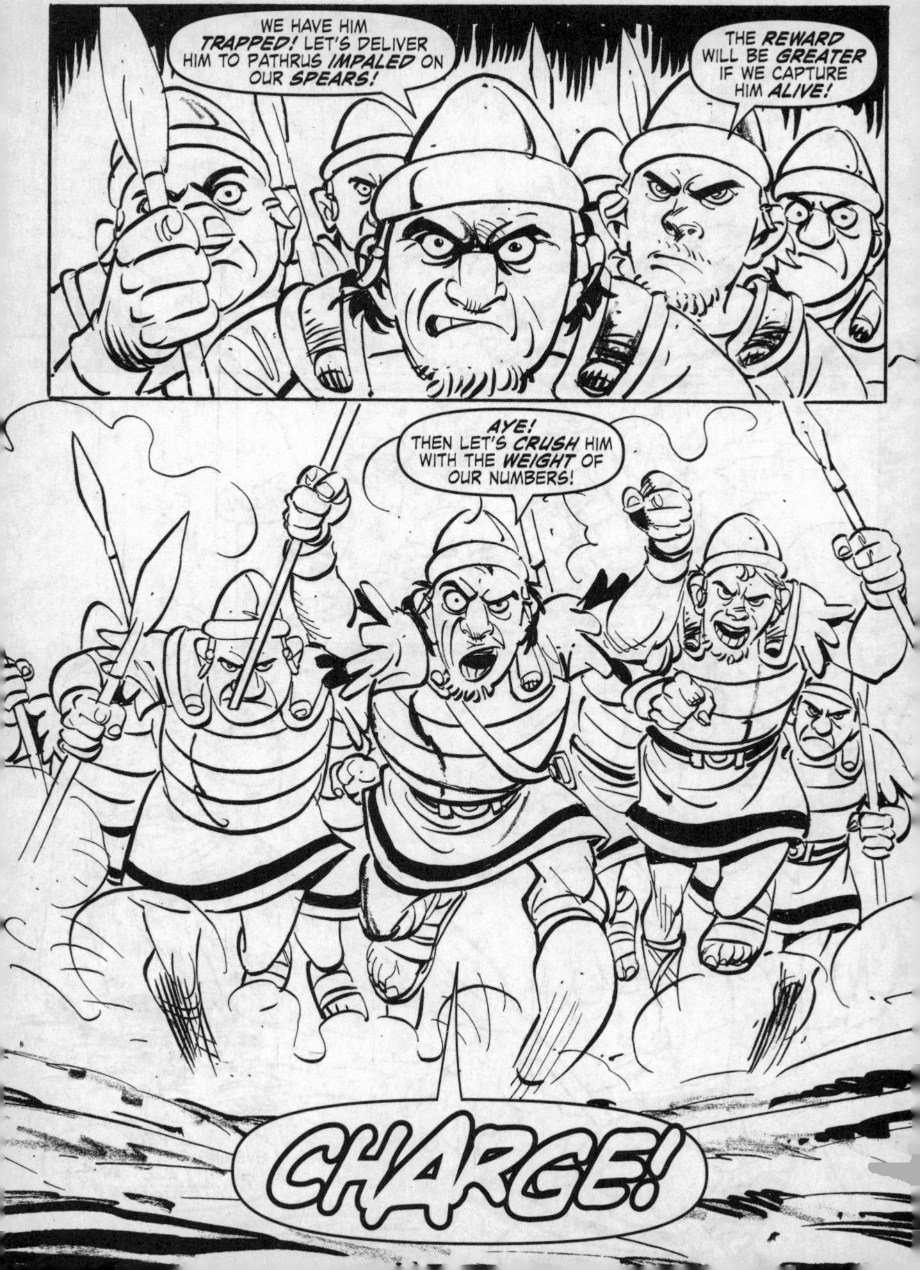
WE HAVE HIM TRAPPED! LET'S DELIVER HIM TO PATHRUS IMPALED ON OUR SPEARS!
THE REWARD WILL BE GREATER IF WE CAPTURE HIM ALIVE!
AYE! THEN LET'S CRUSH HIM WITH THE WEIGHT OF OUR NUMBERS!
CHARGE!

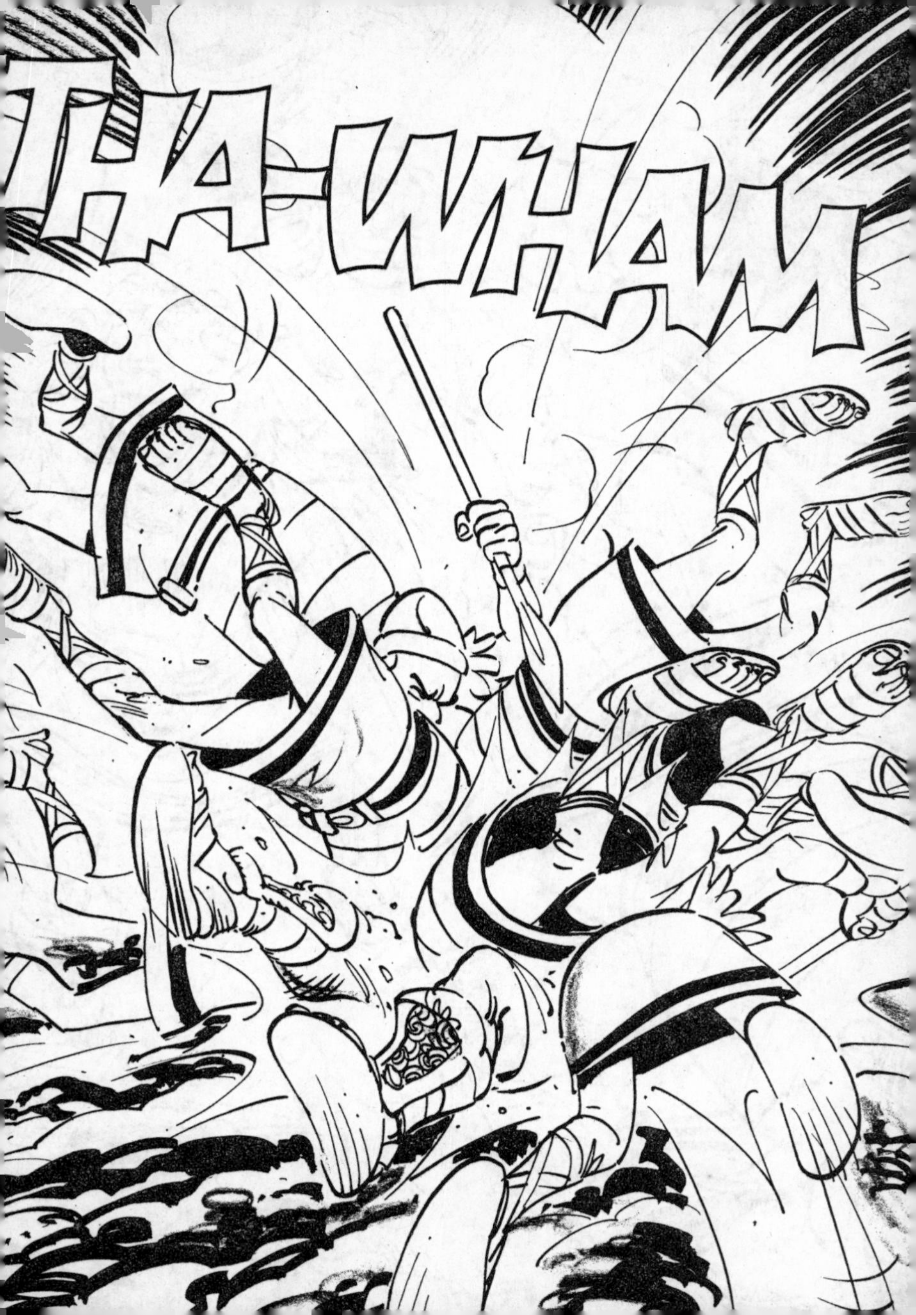
THA-WHAM

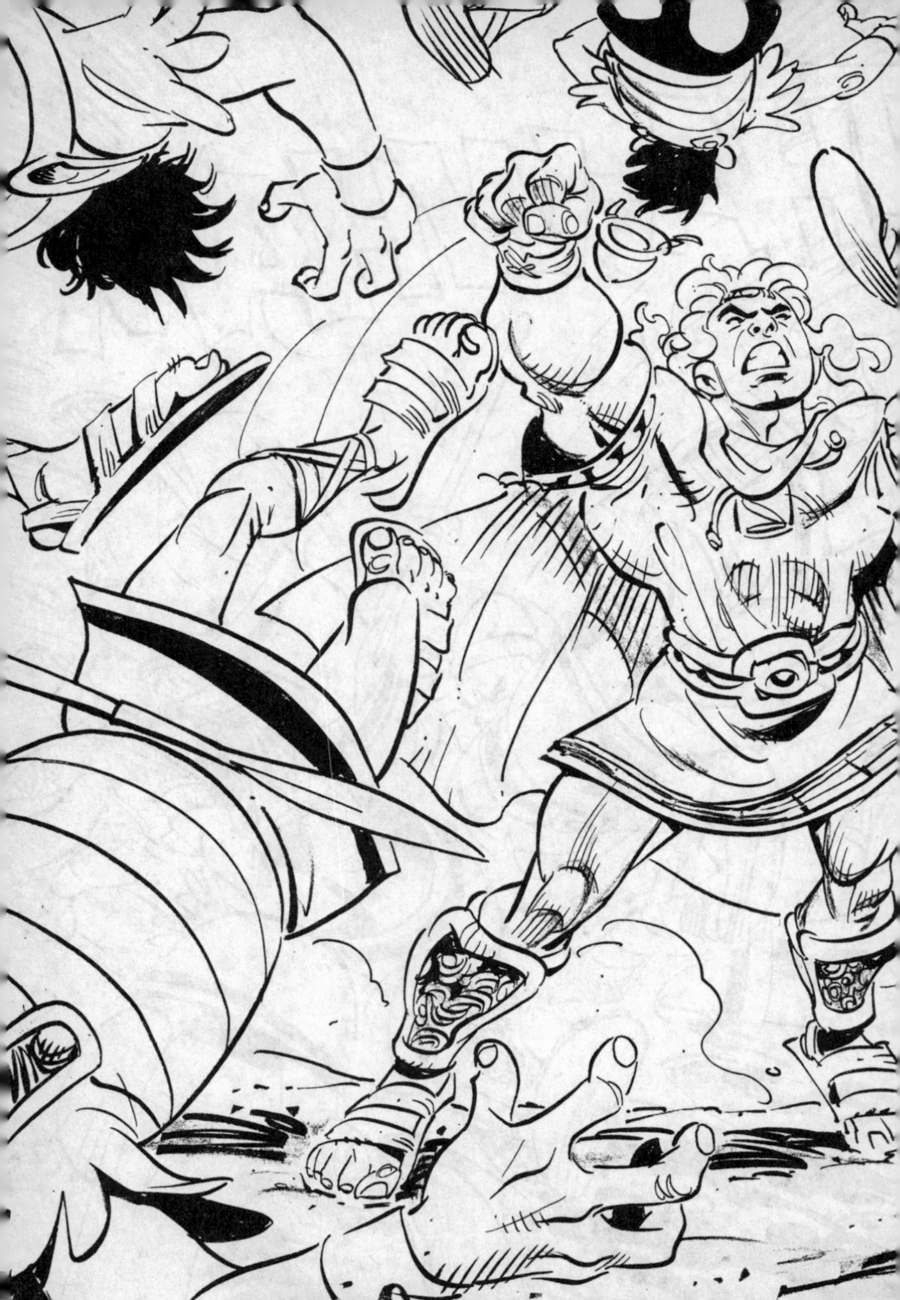

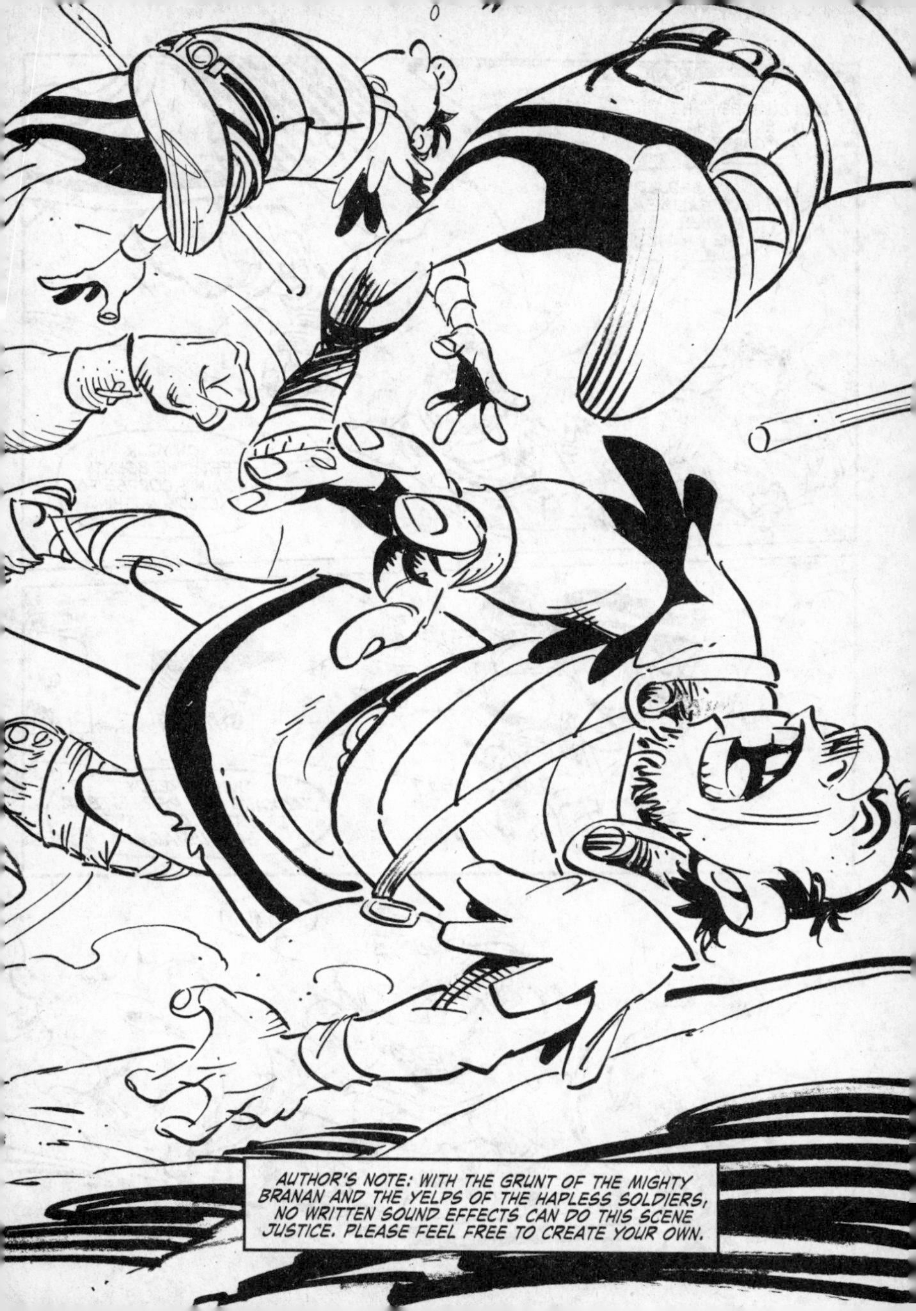
AUTHOR'S NOTE: WITH THE GRUNT OF THE MIGHTY BRANAN AND THE YELPS OF THE HAPLESS SOLDIERS, NO WRITTEN SOUND EFFECTS CAN DO THIS SCENE JUSTICE. PLEASE FEEL FREE TO CREATE YOUR OWN.

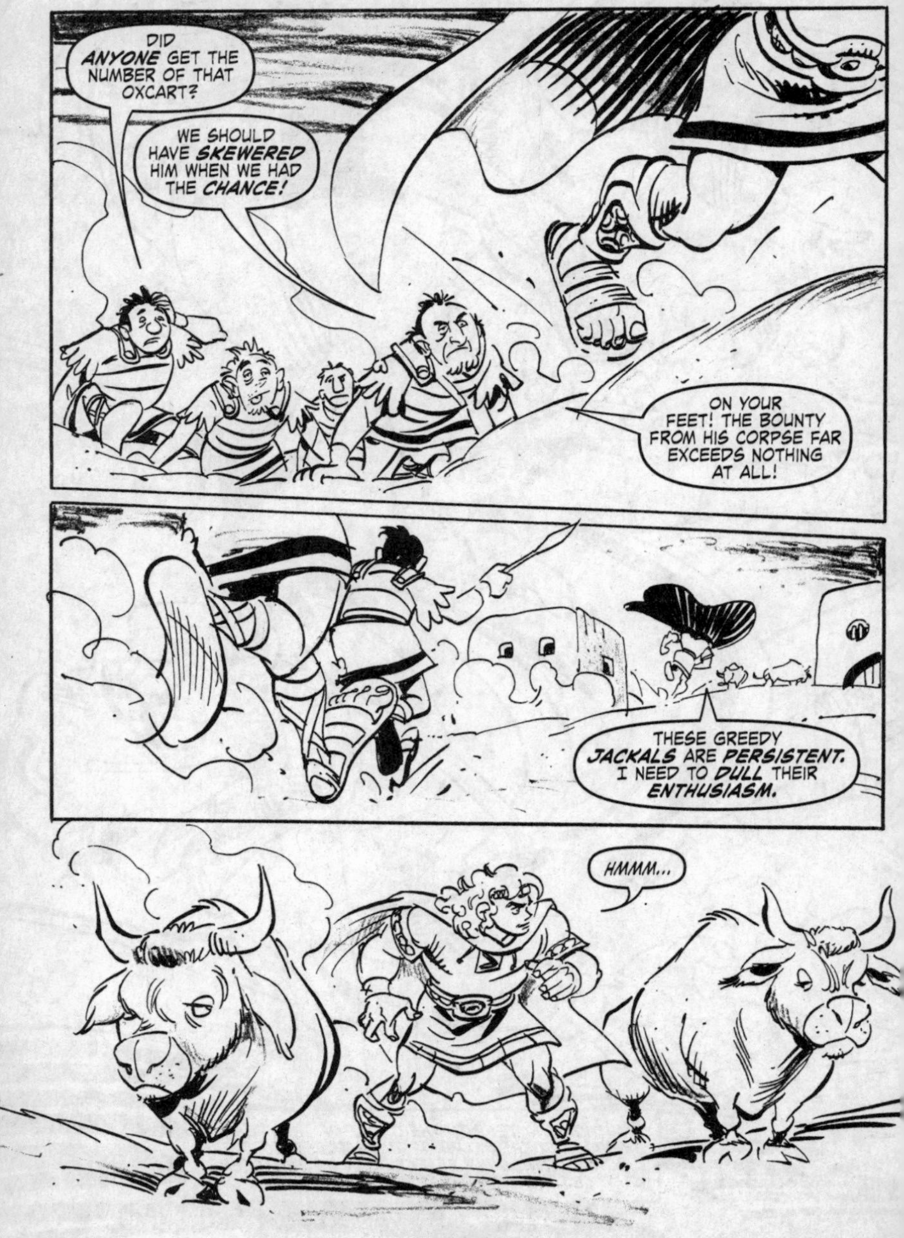
DID ANYONE GET THE NUMBER OF THAT OXCART?
WE SHOULD HAVE SKEWERED HIM WHEN WE HAD THE CHANCE!
ON YOUR FEET! THE BOUNTY FROM HIS CORPSE FAR EXCEEDS NOTHING AT ALL!
THESE GREEDY JACKALS ARE PERSISTENT. I NEED TO DULL THEIR ENTHUSIASM.
HMMM...

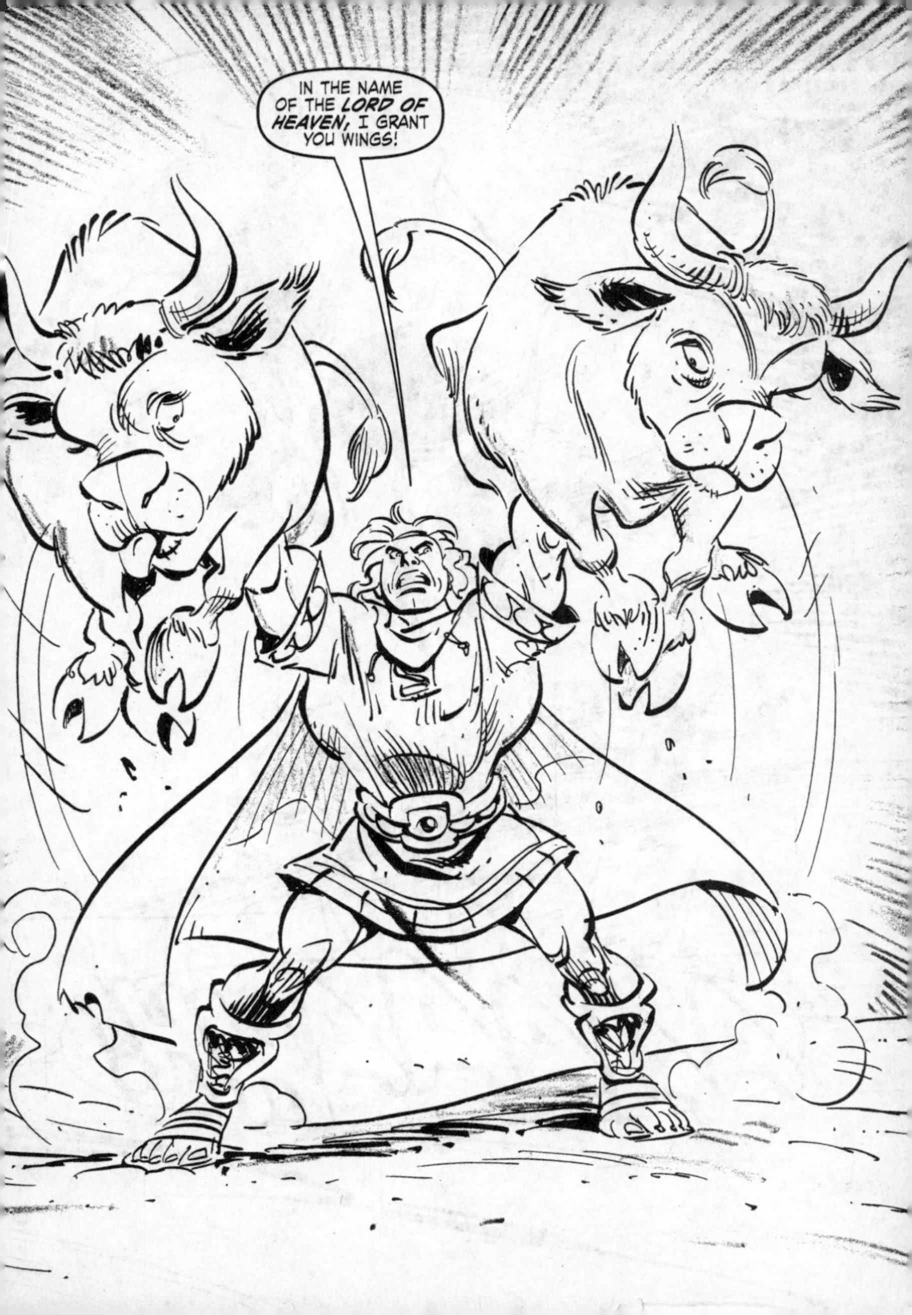
IN THE NAME OF THE LORD OF HEAVEN, I GRANT YOU WINGS!

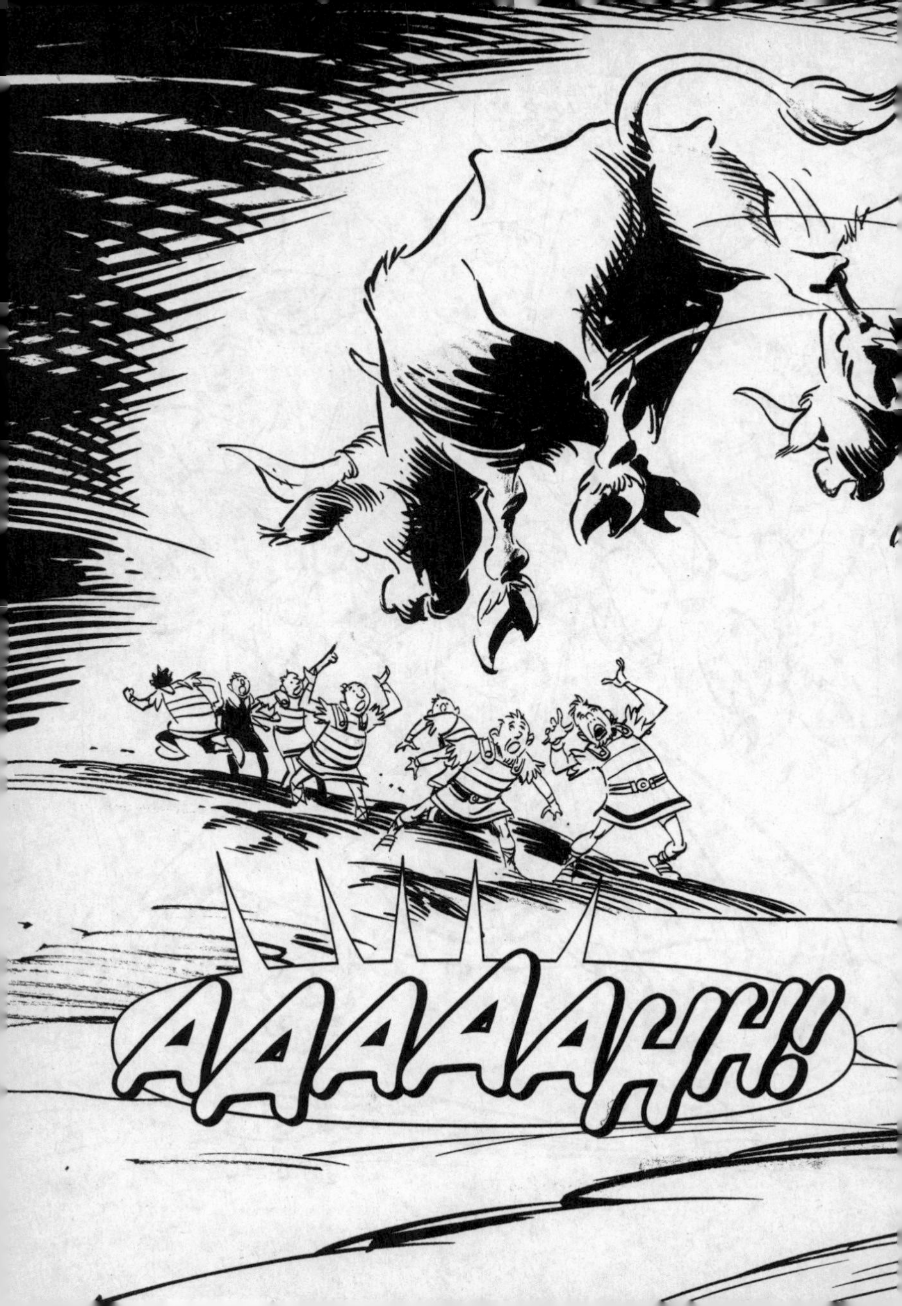
AAAAAHH!

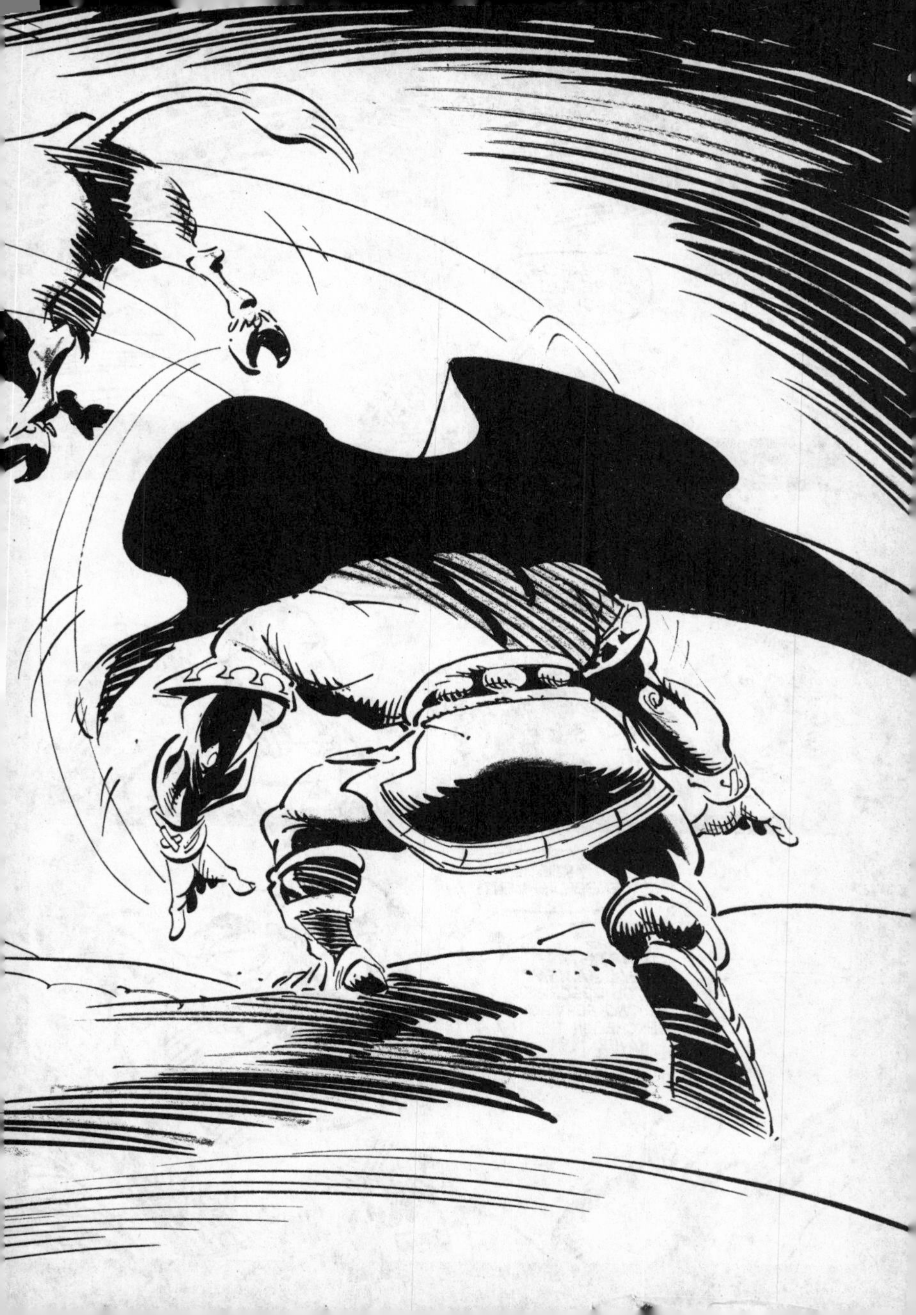

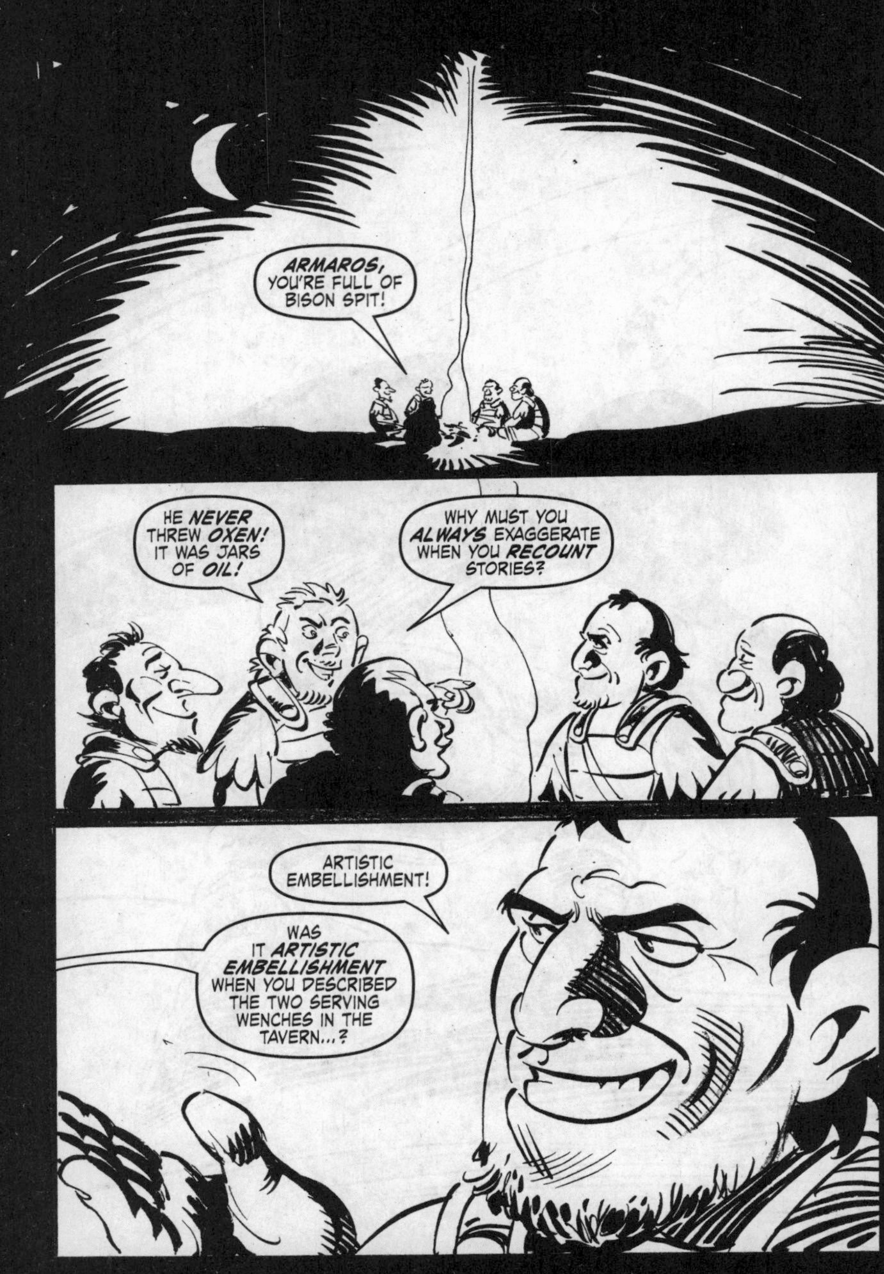
ARMAROS, YOU'RE FULL OF BISON SPIT!
HE NEVER THREW OXEN! IT WAS JARS OF OIL!
WHY MUST YOU ALWAYS EXAGGERATE WHEN YOU RECOUNT STORIES?
ARTISTIC EMBELLISHMENT!
WAS IT ARTISTIC EMBELLISHMENT WHEN YOU DESCRIBED THE TWO SERVING WENCHES IN THE TAVERN...?

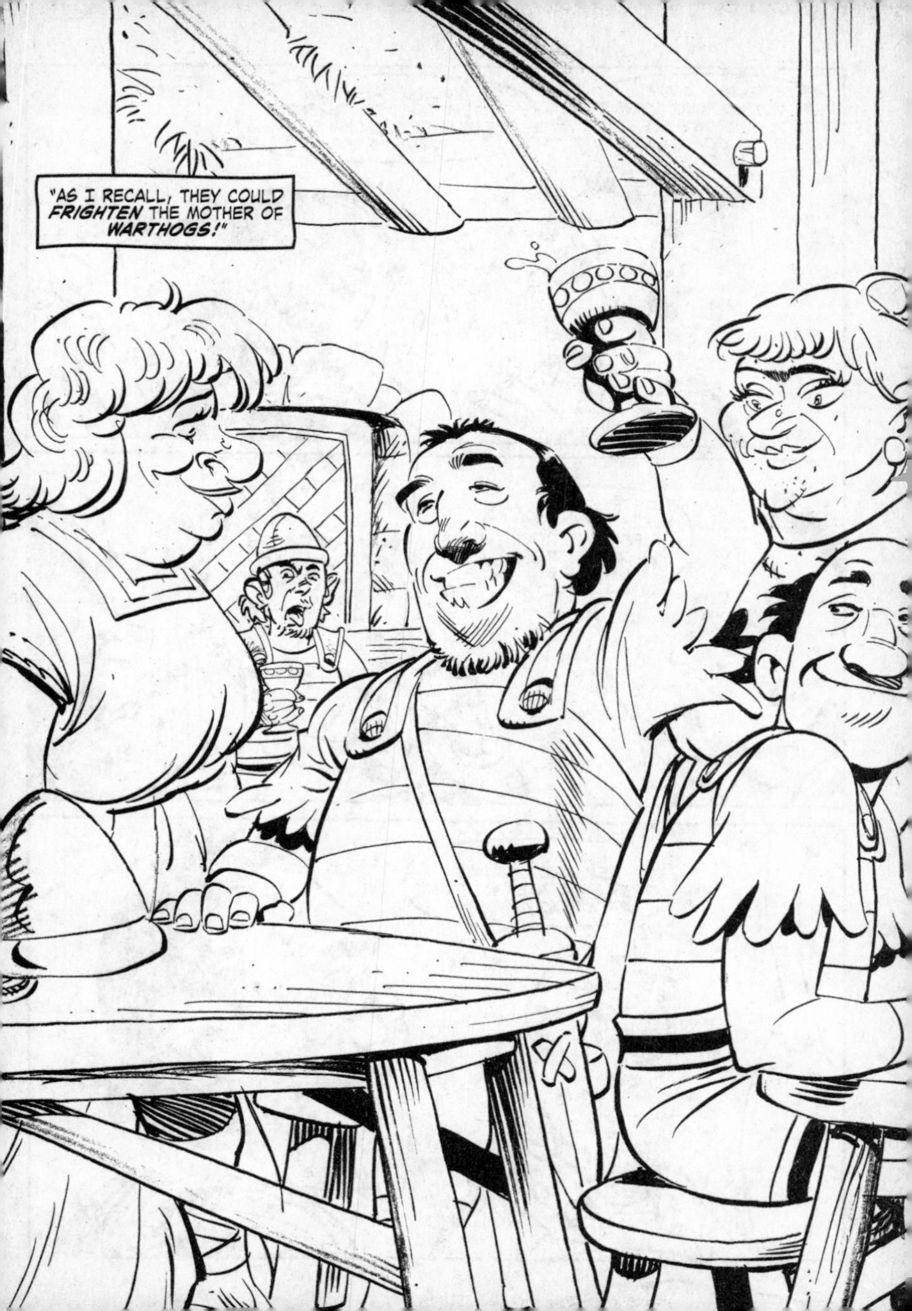
"AS I RECALL, THEY COULD FRIGHTEN THE MOTHER OF WARTHOGS!"

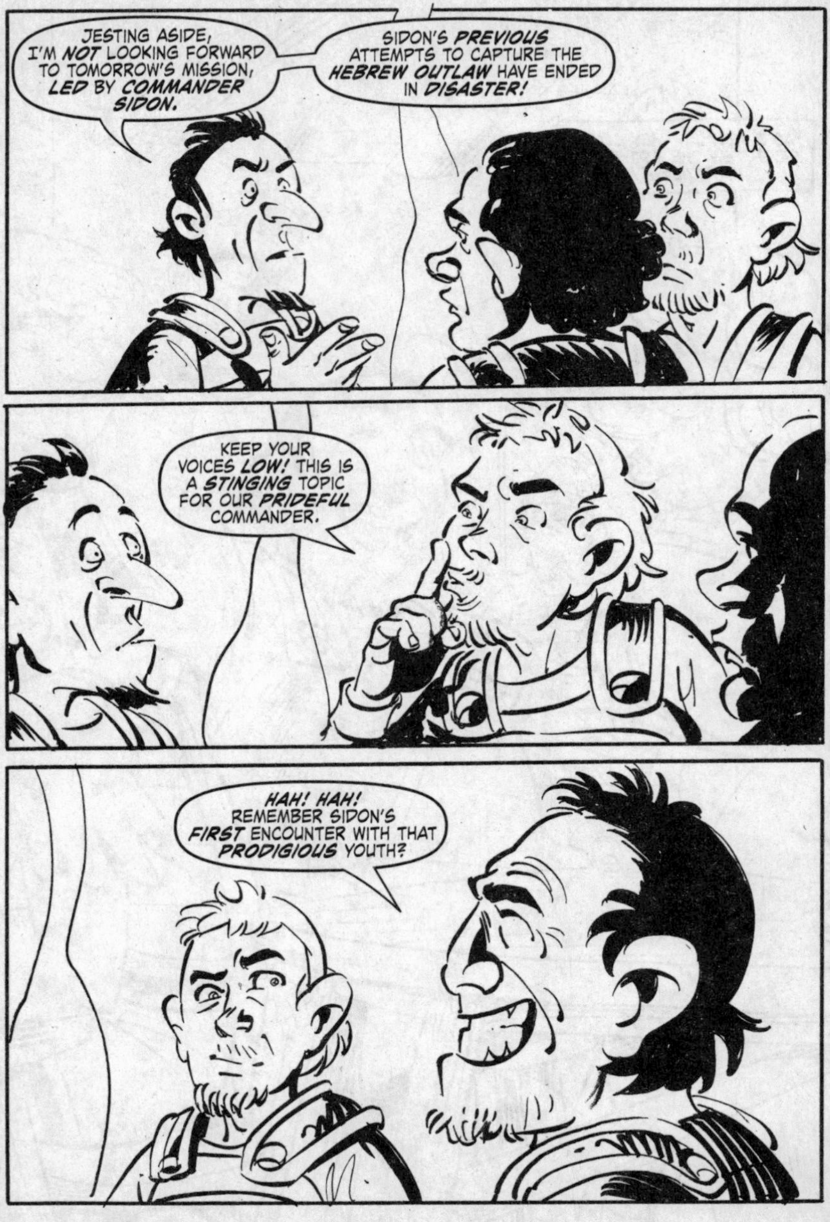
JESTING ASIDE, I'M NOT LOOKING FORWARD TO TOMORROW'S MISSION, LED BY COMMANDER SIDON.
SIDON'S PREVIOUS ATTEMPTS TO CAPTURE THE HEBREW OUTLAW HAVE ENDED IN DISASTER!
KEEP YOUR VOICES LOW! THIS IS A STINGING TOPIC FOR OUR PRIDEFUL COMMANDER.
HAH! HAH! REMEMBER SIDON'S FIRST ENCOUNTER WITH THAT PRODIGIOUS YOUTH?

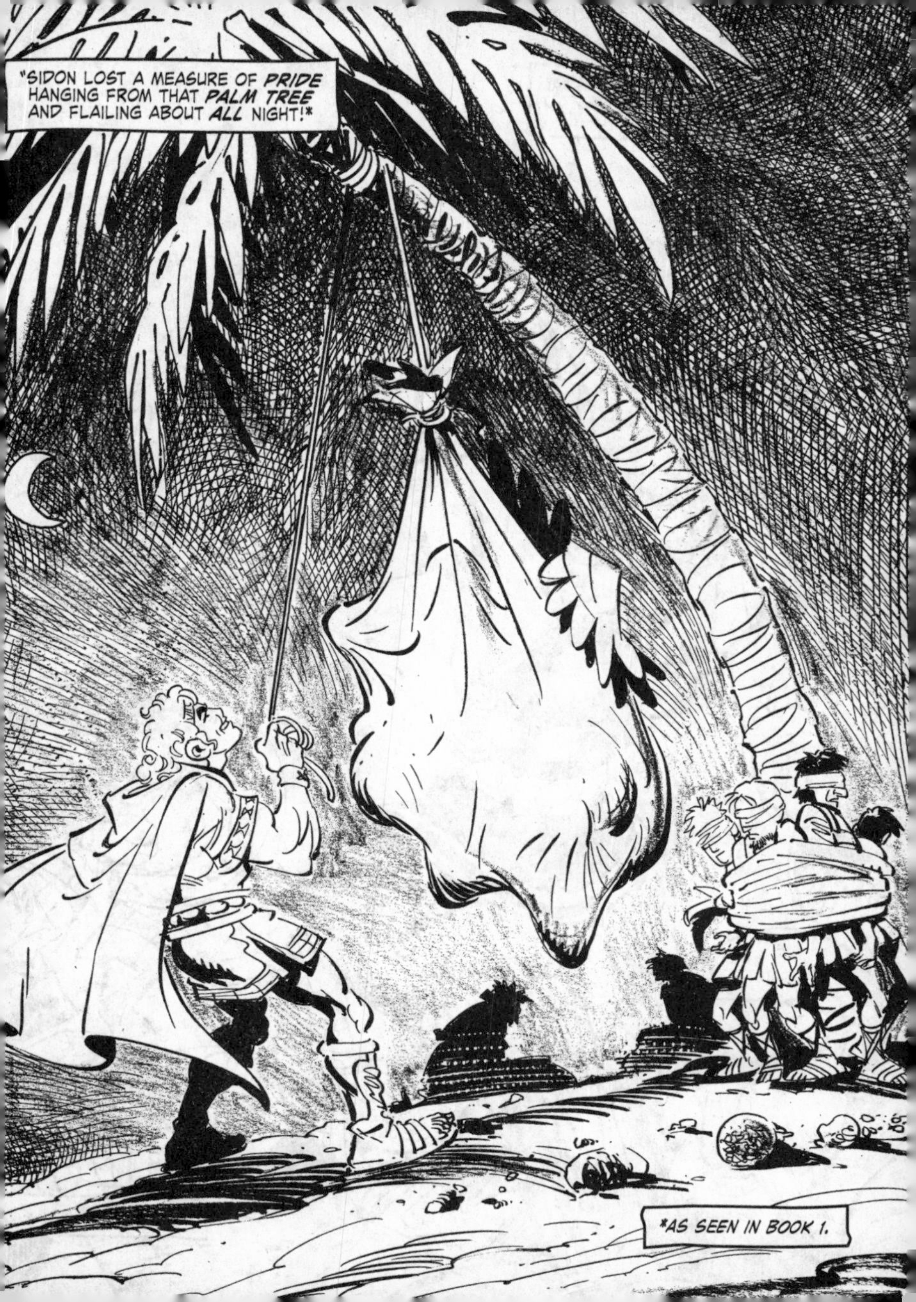
"SIDON LOST A MEASURE OF PRIDE HANGING FROM THAT PALM TREE AND FLAILING ABOUT ALL NIGHT!*
*AS SEEN IN BOOK 1.

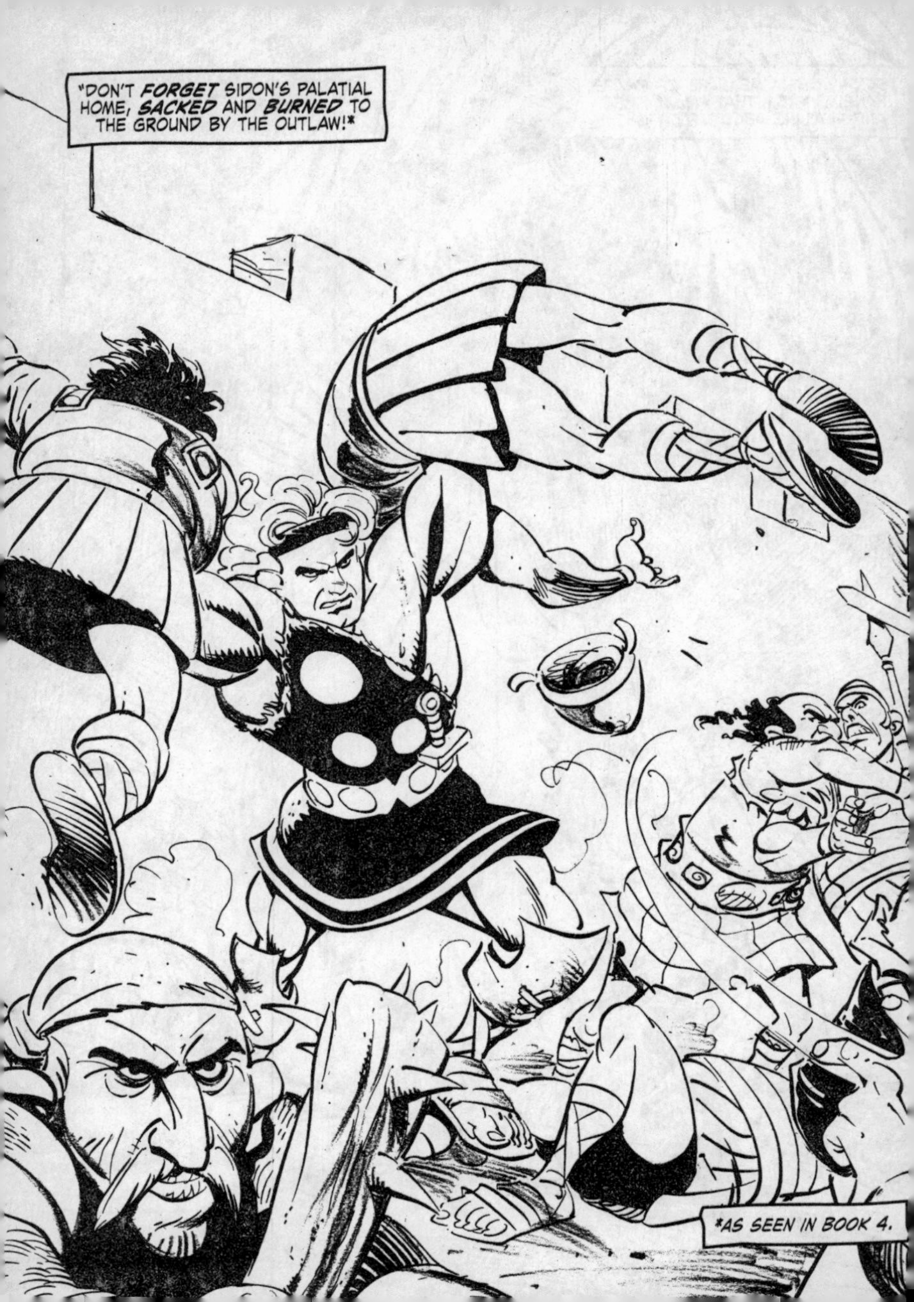
"DON'T FORGET SIDON'S PALATIAL HOME, SACKED AND BURNED TO THE GROUND BY THE OUTLAW!*
*AS SEEN IN BOOK 4.

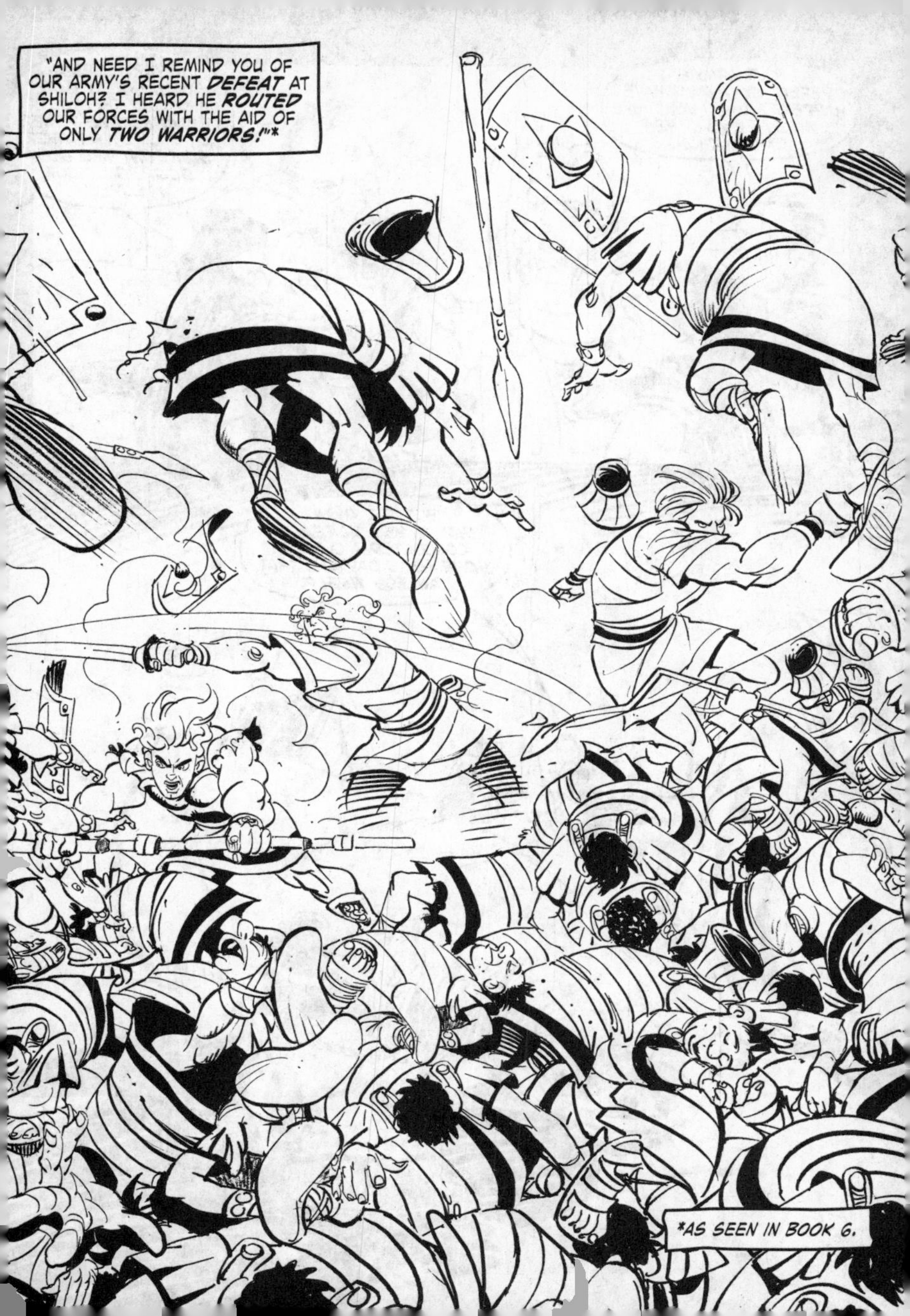
"AND NEED I REMIND YOU OF OUR ARMY'S RECENT DEFEAT AT SHILOH? I HEARD HE ROUTED OUR FORCES WITH THE AID OF ONLY TWO WARRIORS!"*
*AS SEEN IN BOOK 6.

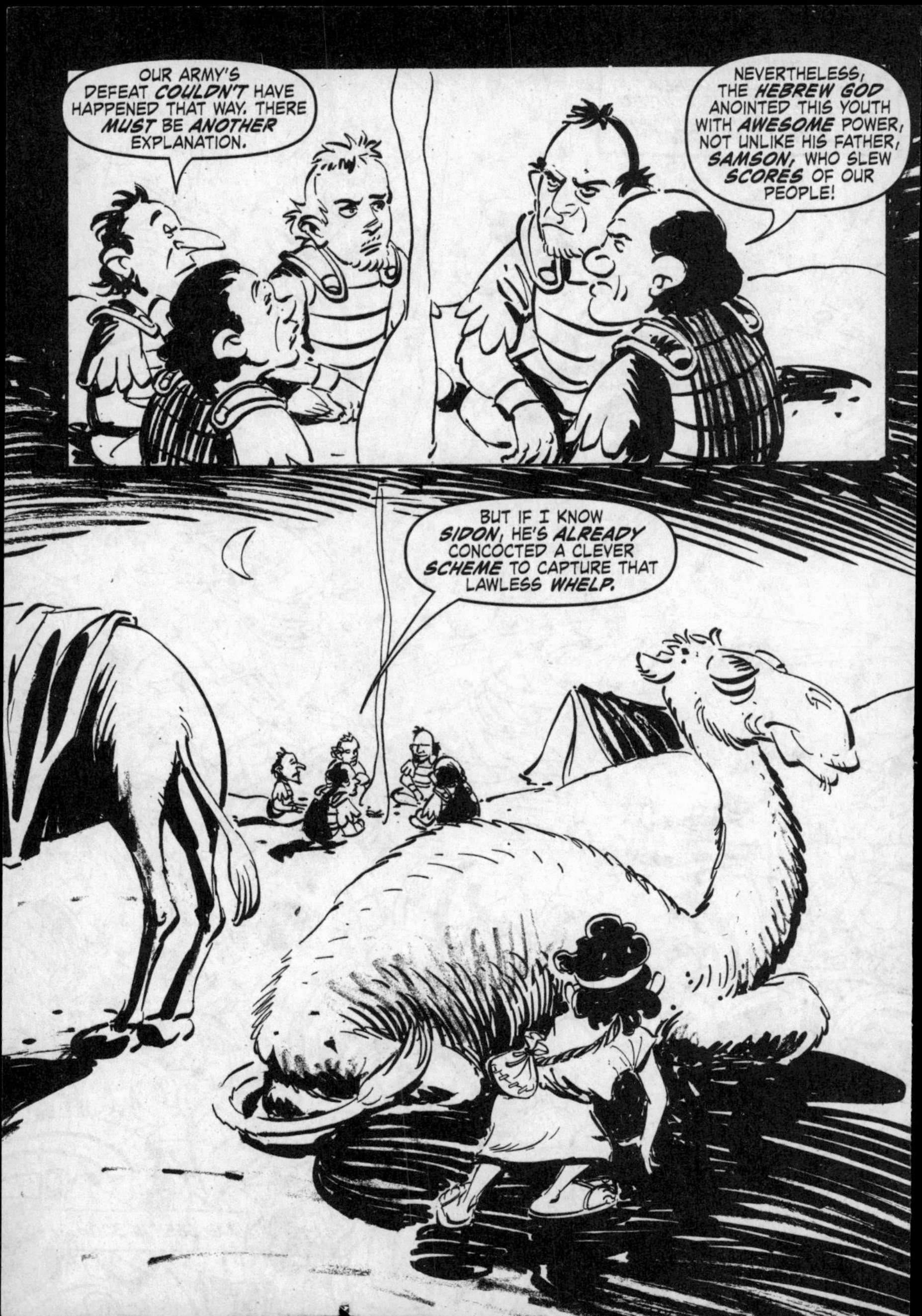
OUR ARMY'S DEFEAT COULDN'T HAVE HAPPENED THAT WAY. THERE MUST BE ANOTHER EXPLANATION.
NEVERTHELESS, THE HEBREW GOD ANOINTED THIS YOUTH WITH AWESOME POWER, NOT UNLIKE HIS FATHER, SAMSON, WHO SLEW SCORES OF OUR PEOPLE!
BUT IF I KNOW SIDON, HE'S ALREADY CONCOCTED A CLEVER SCHEME TO CAPTURE THAT LAWLESS WHELP.

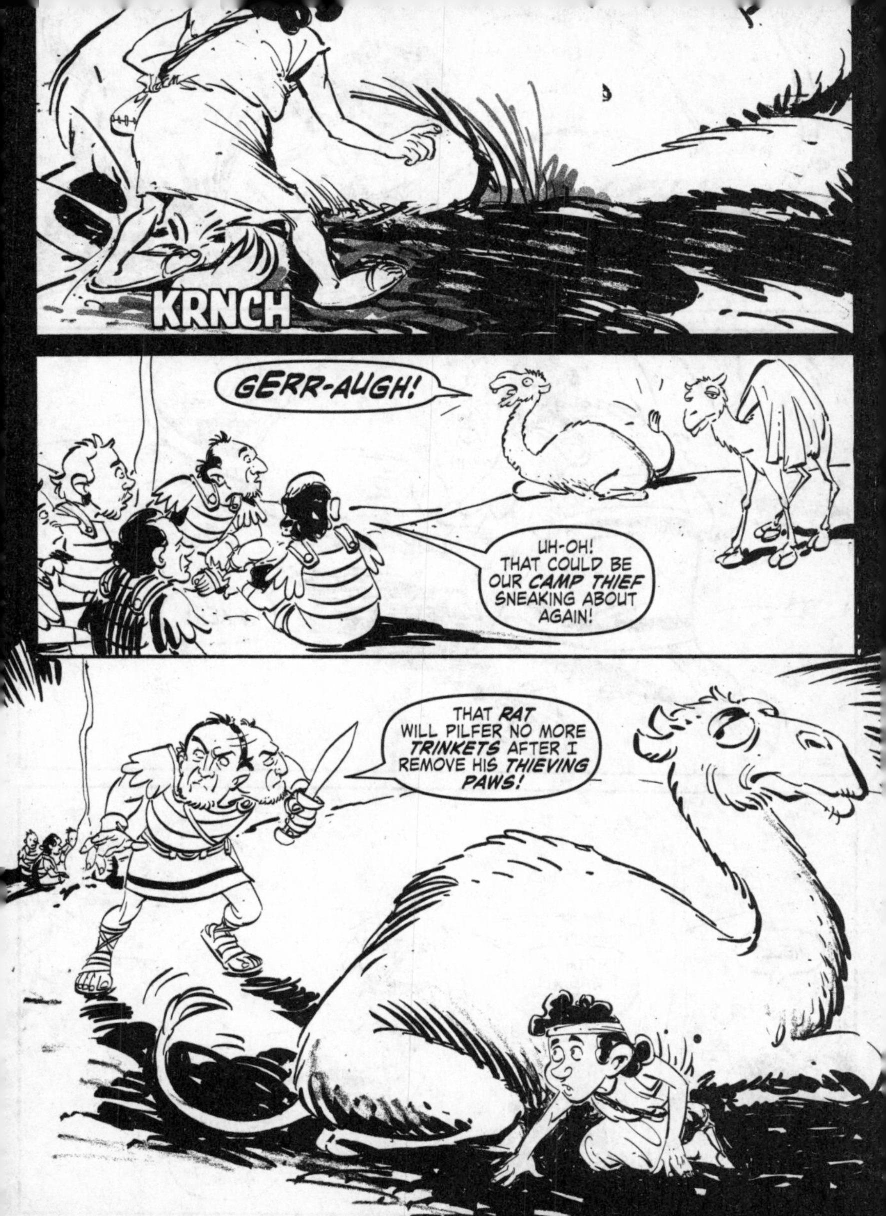
KRNCH
GERR-AUGH!
UH-OH! THAT COULD BE OUR CAMP THIEF SNEAKING ABOUT AGAIN!
THAT RAT WILL PILFER NO MORE TRINKETS AFTER I REMOVE HIS THIEVING PAWS!

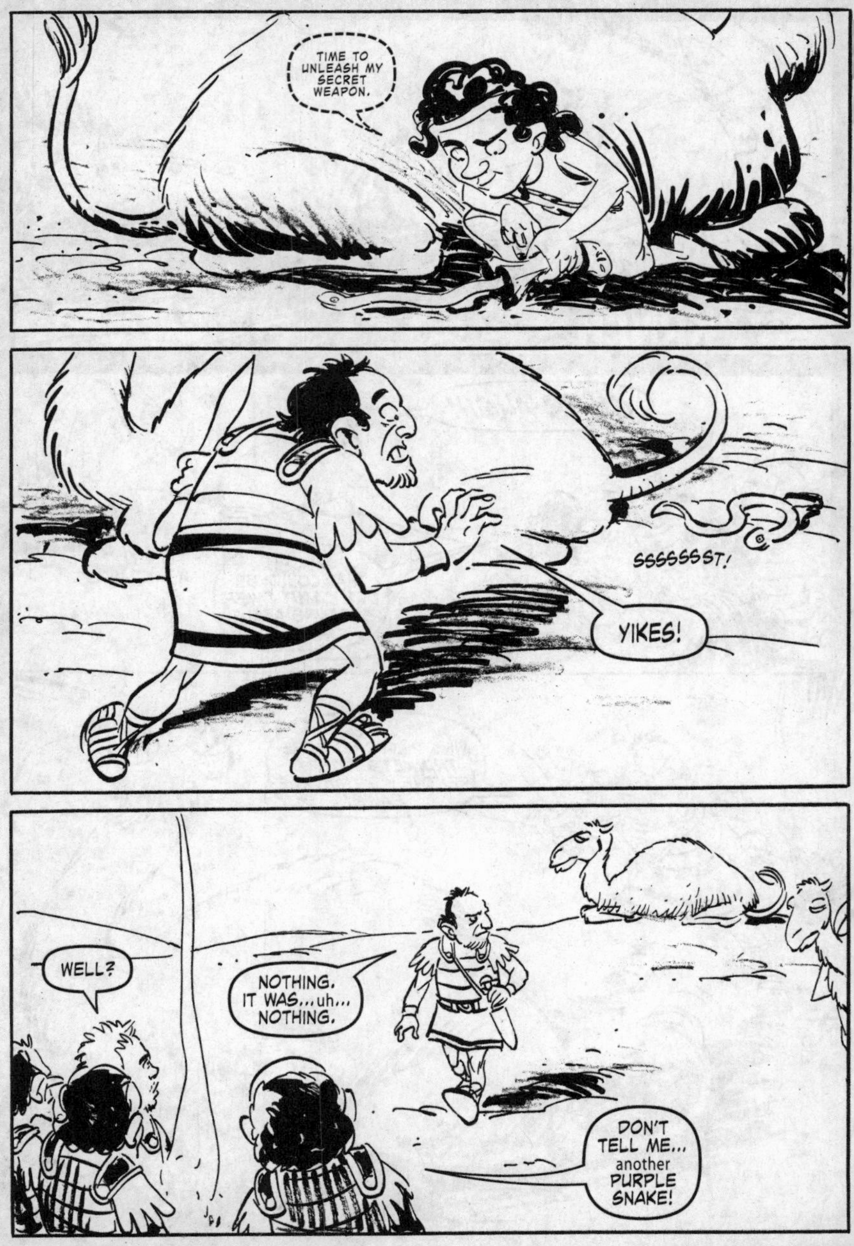
TIME TO UNLEASH MY SECRET WEAPON.
SSSSSSST!
YIKES!
WELL?
NOTHING. IT WAS...uh... NOTHING.
DON'T TELL ME... another PURPLE SNAKE!

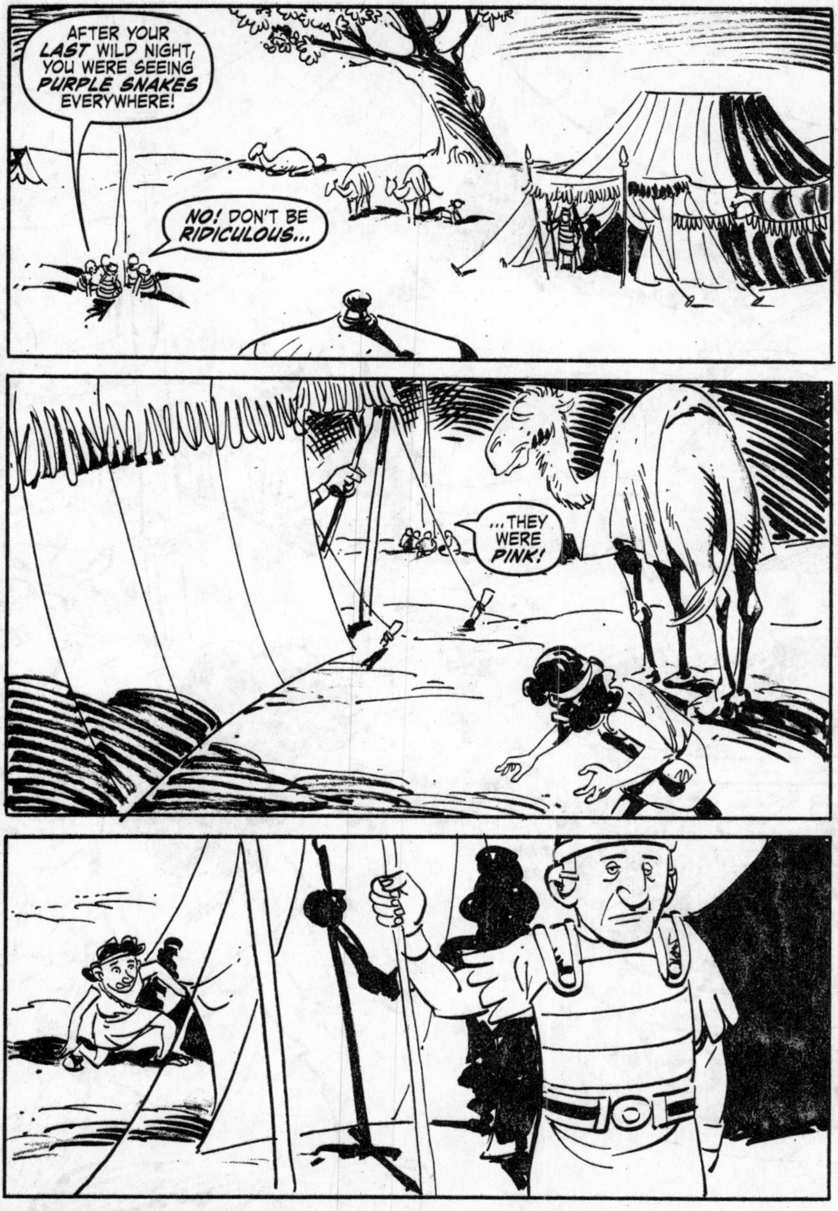
AFTER YOUR LAST WILD NIGHT, YOU WERE SEEING PURPLE SNAKES EVERYWHERE!
NO! DON'T BE RIDICULOUS...
...THEY WERE PINK!

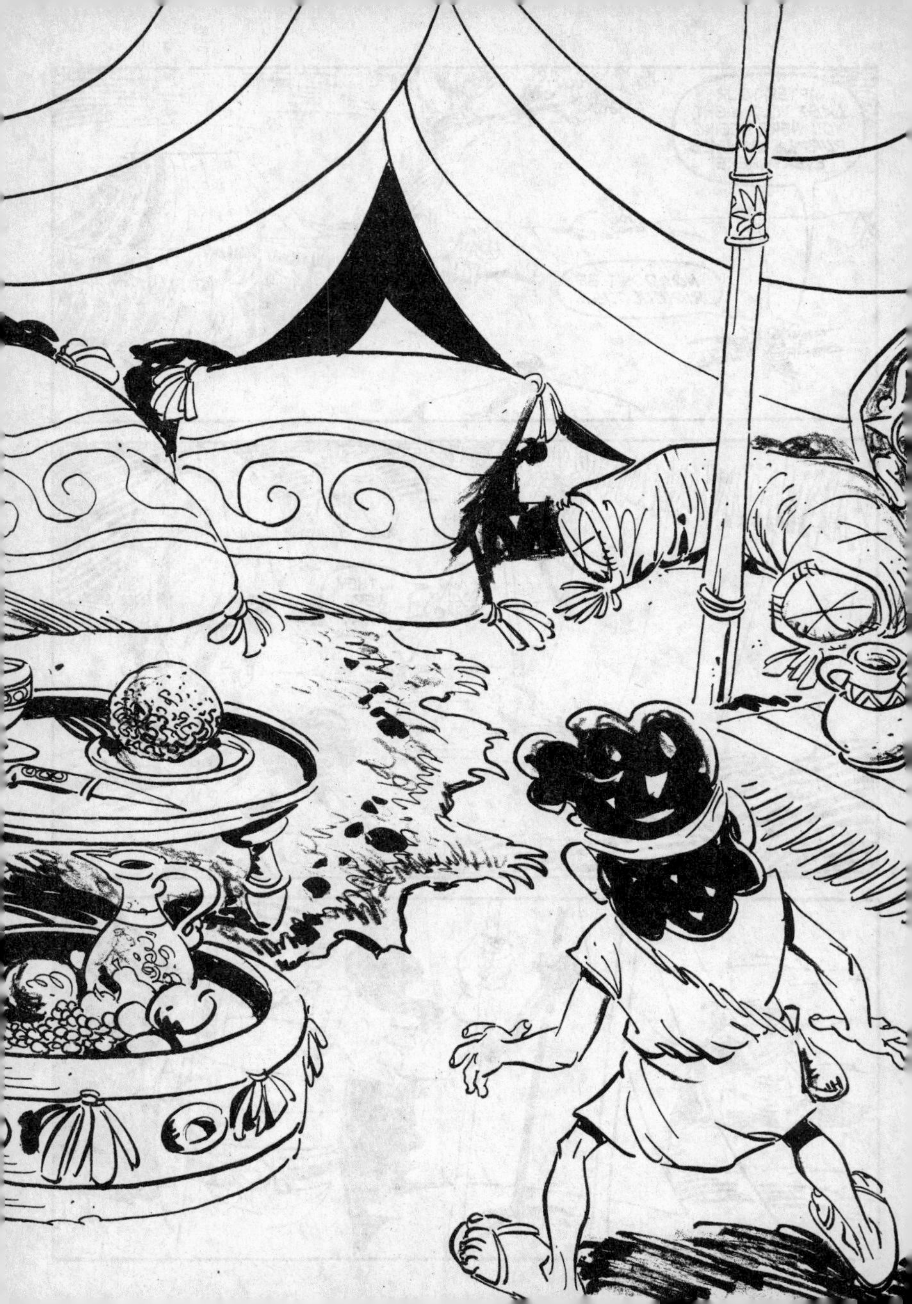

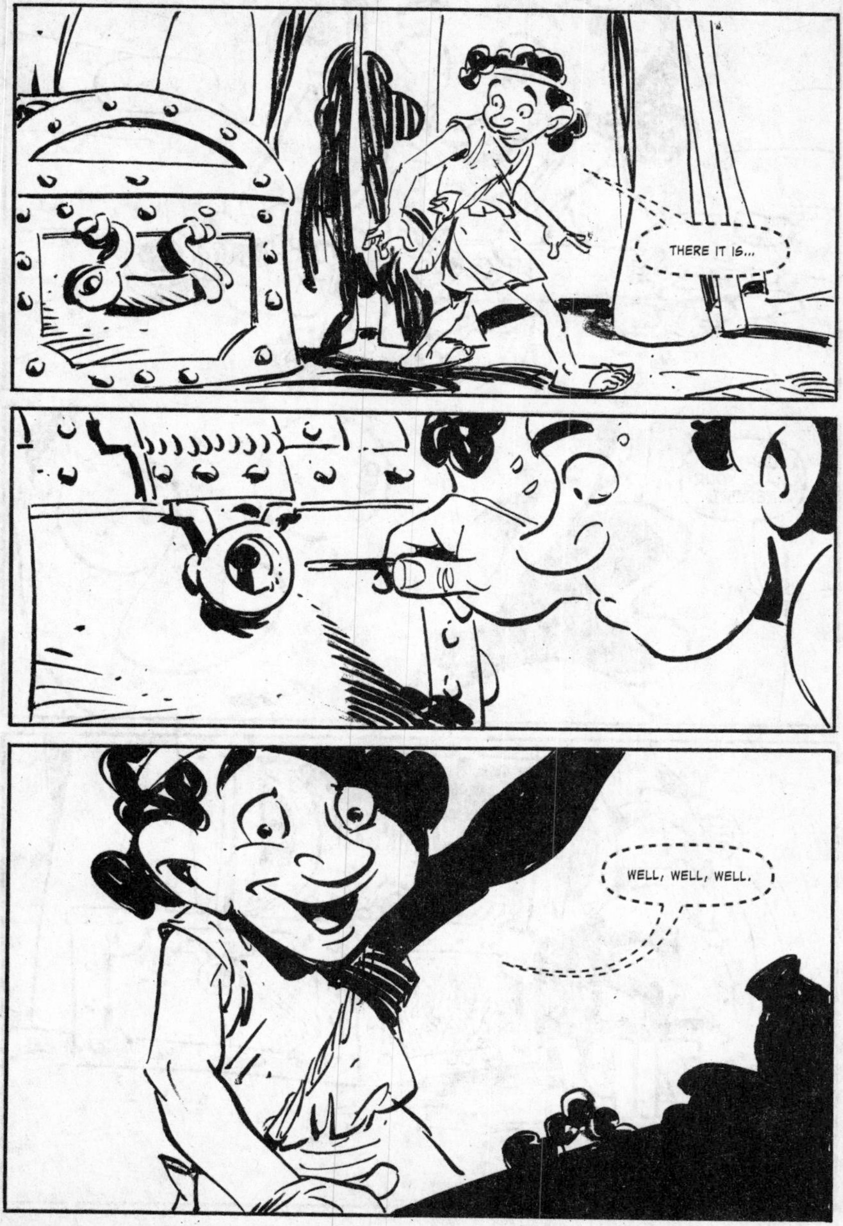
THERE IT IS...
WELL, WELL, WELL.

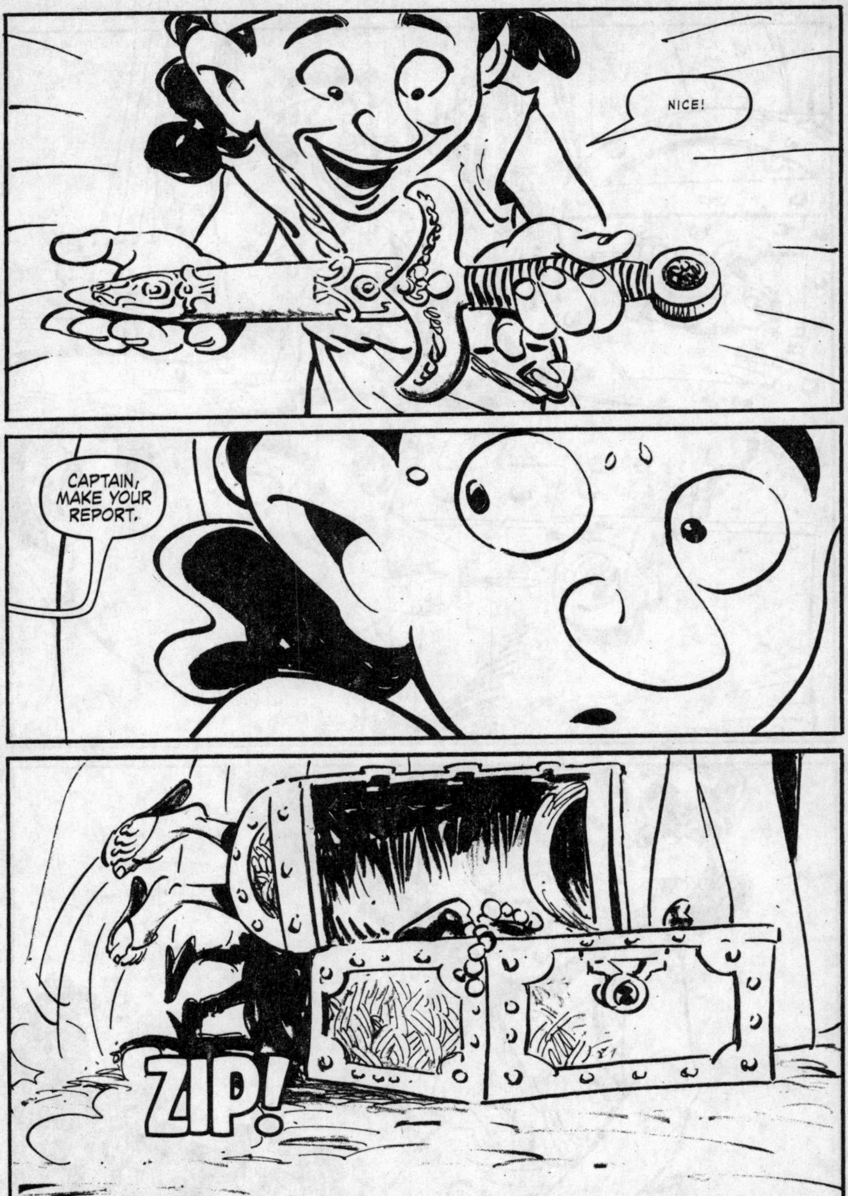
NICE!
CAPTAIN, MAKE YOUR REPORT.
ZIP!

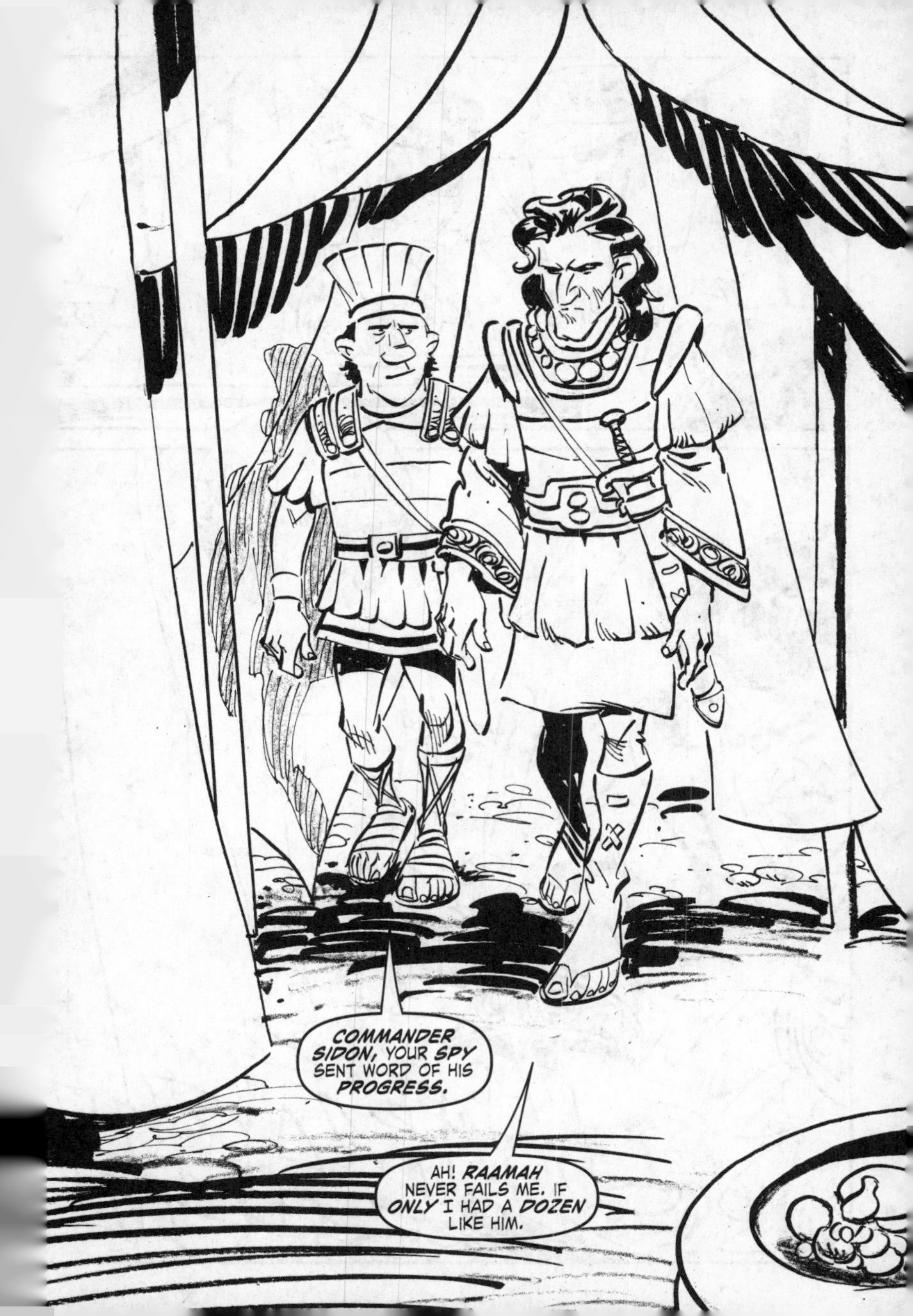
COMMANDER SIDON, YOUR SPY SENT WORD OF HIS PROGRESS.
AH! RAAMAH NEVER FAILS ME. IF ONLY I HAD A DOZEN LIKE HIM.

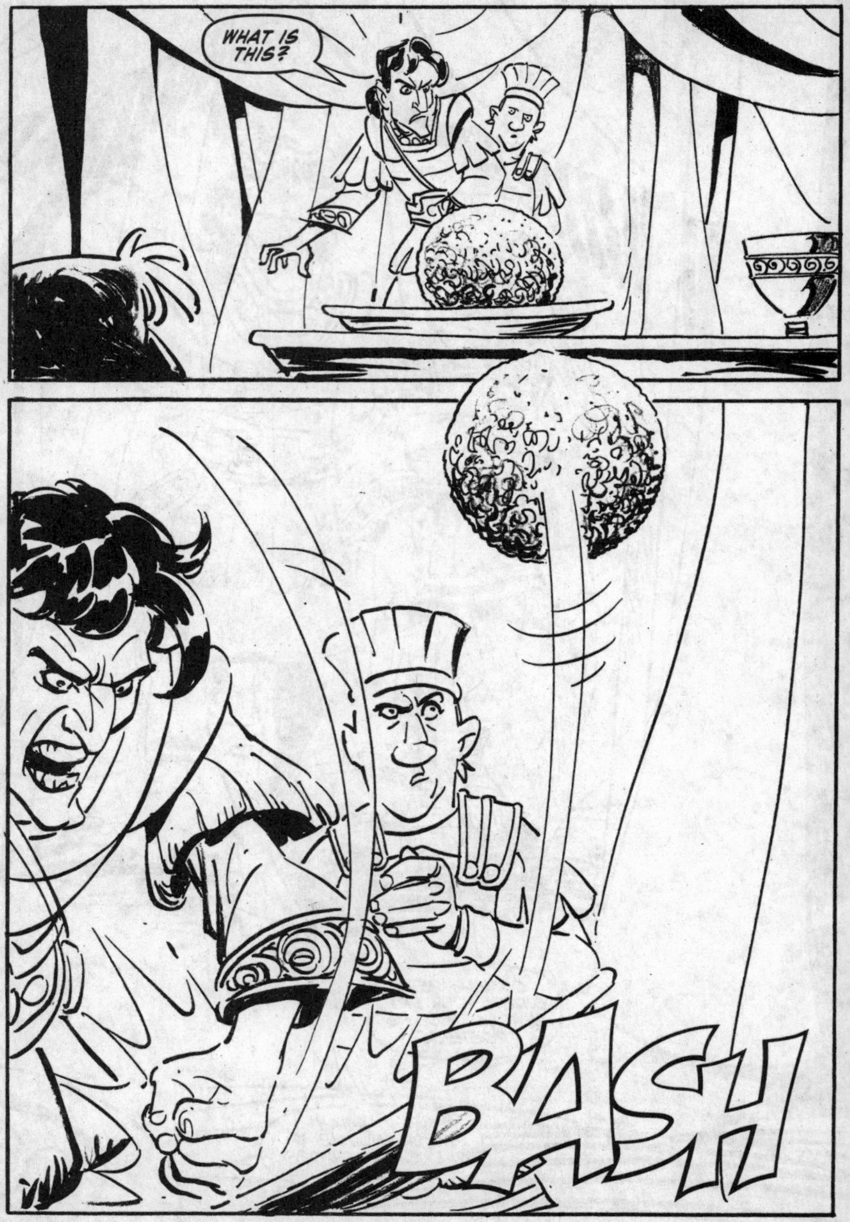
WHAT IS THIS?
BASH

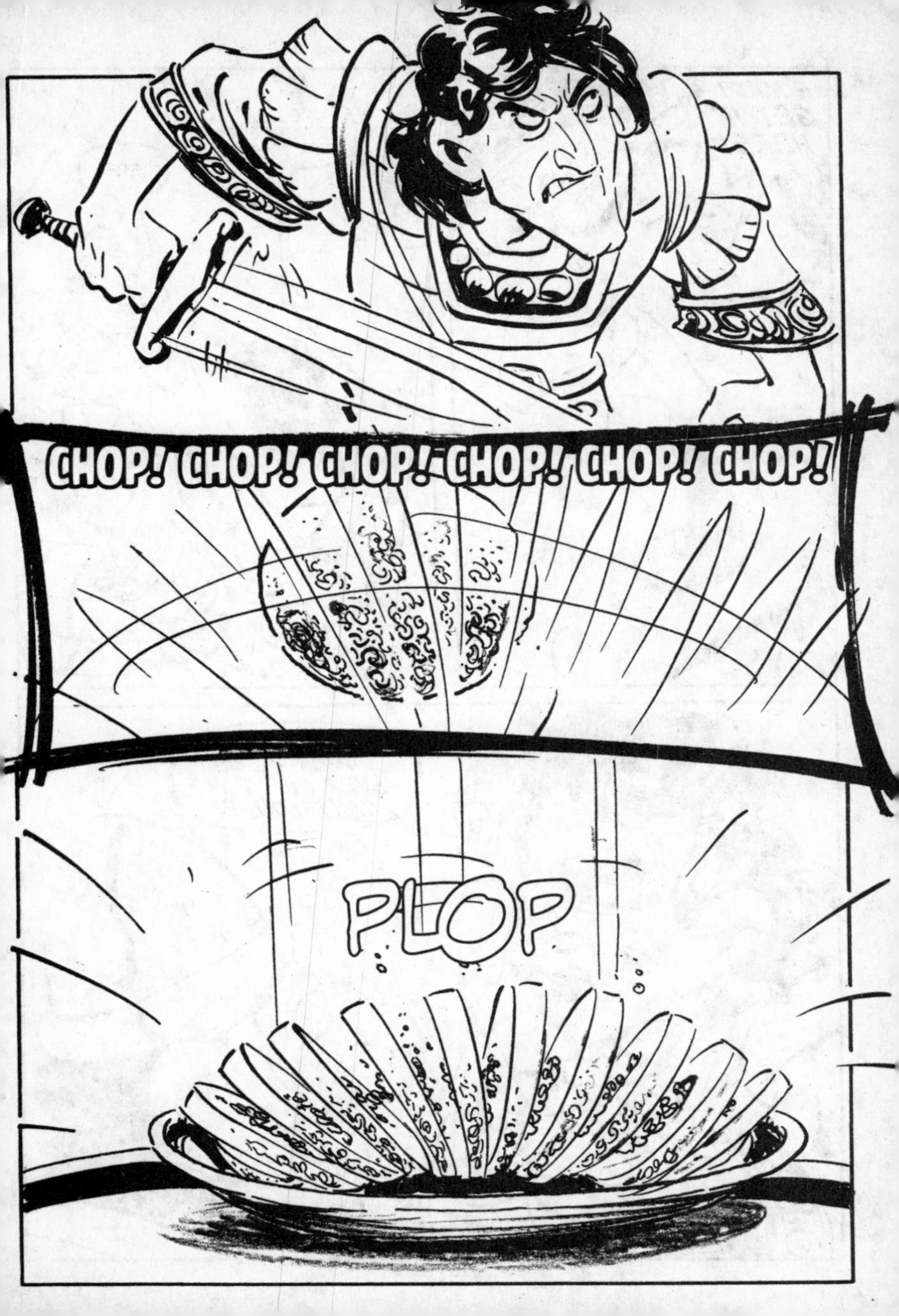
CHOP! CHOP! CHOP! CHOP! CHOP! CHOP!
PLOP

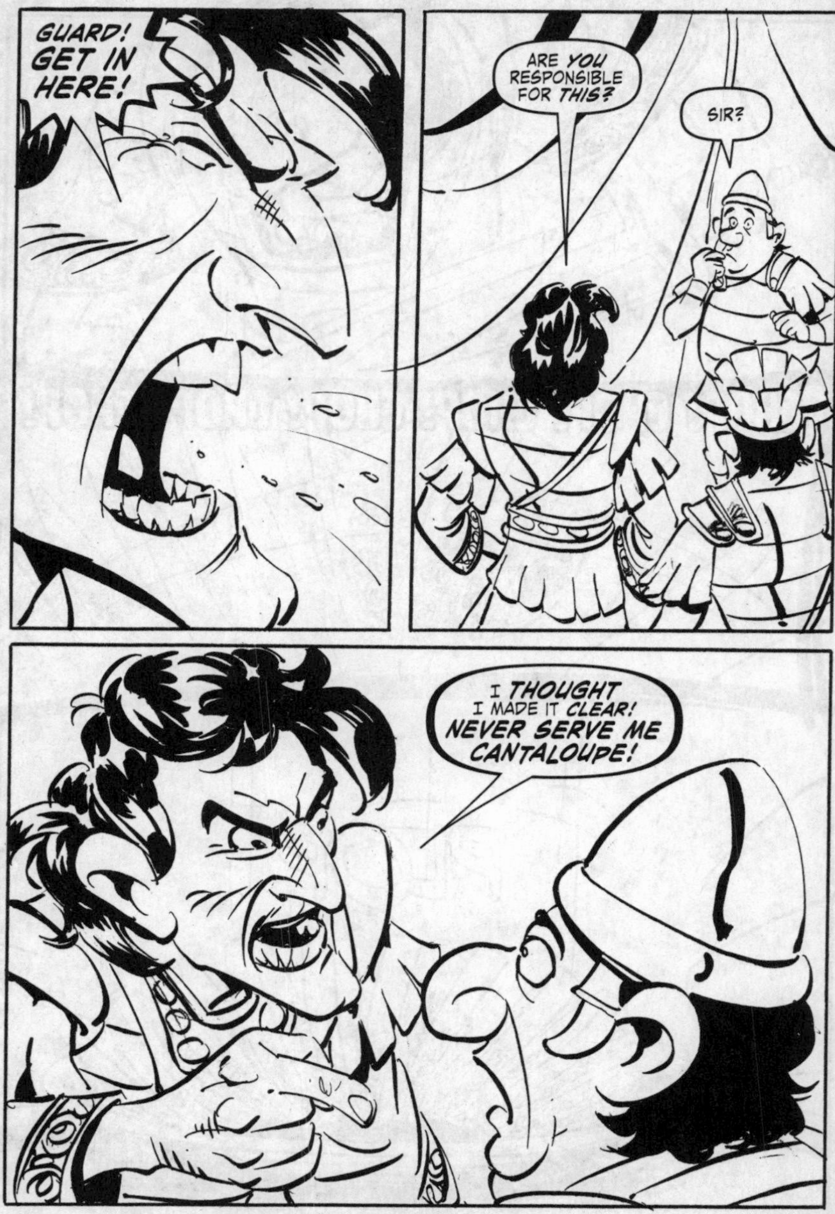
GUARD! GET IN HERE!
ARE YOU RESPONSIBLE FOR THIS?
SIR?
I THOUGHT I MADE IT CLEAR! NEVER SERVE ME CANTALOUPE!

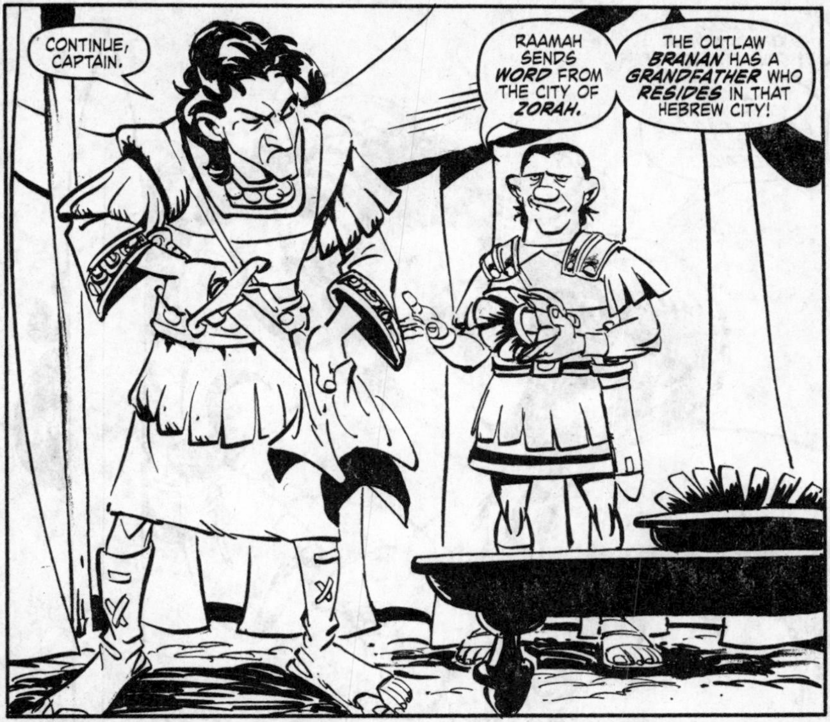

CONTINUE, CAPTAIN.
RAAMAH SENDS WORD FROM THE CITY OF ZORAH.
THE OUTLAW BRANAN HAS A GRANDFATHER WHO RESIDES IN THAT HEBREW CITY!

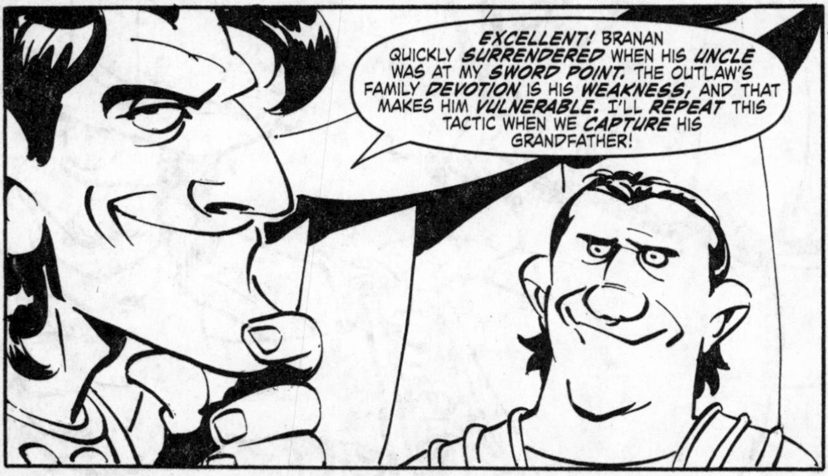

EXCELLENT! BRANAN QUICKLY SURRENDERED WHEN HIS UNCLE WAS AT MY SWORD POINT. THE OUTLAW'S FAMILY DEVOTION IS HIS WEAKNESS, AND THAT MAKES HIM VULNERABLE. I'LL REPEAT THIS TACTIC WHEN WE CAPTURE HIS GRANDFATHER!

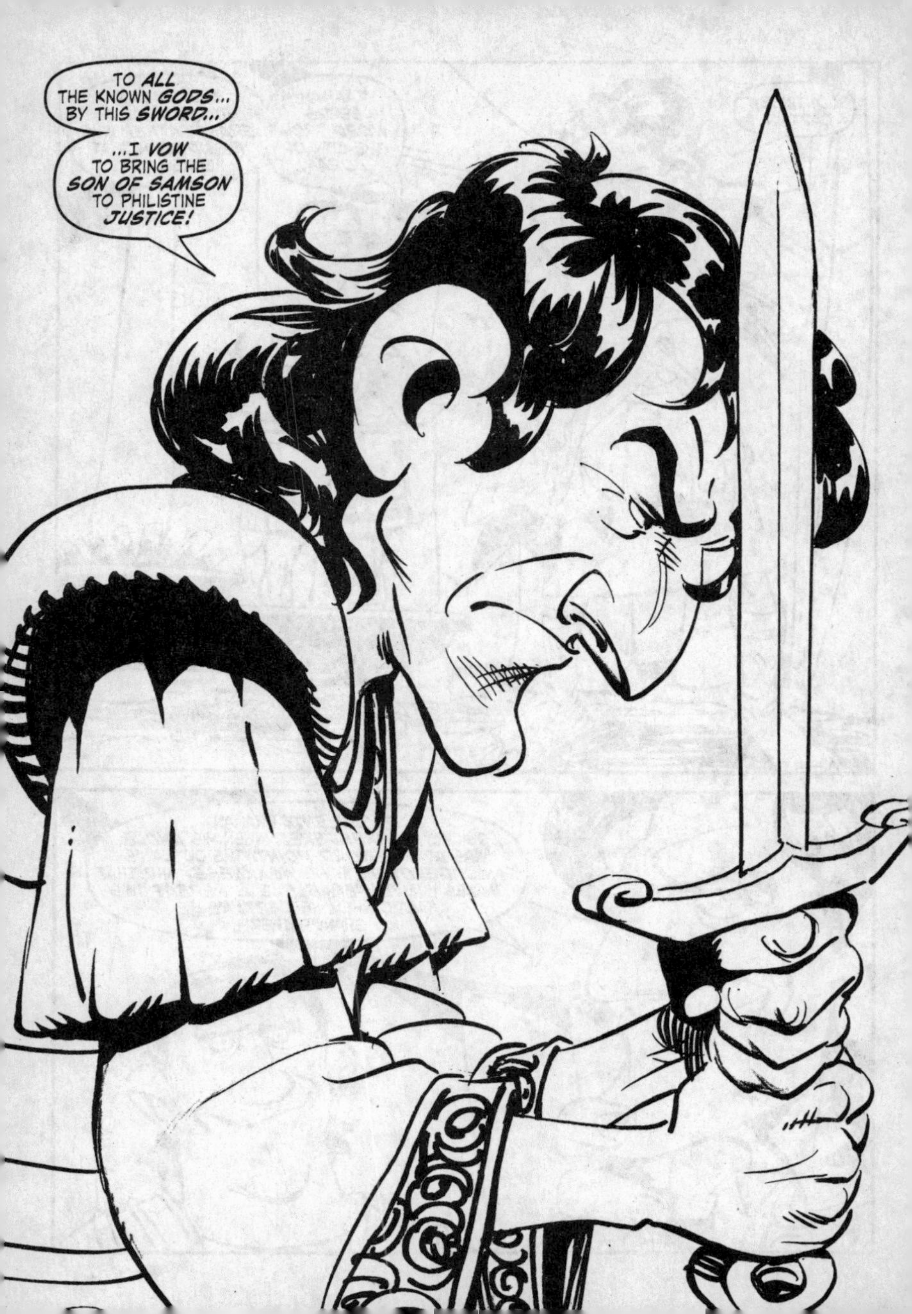
TO ALL THE KNOWN GODS... BY THIS SWORD...
...I VOW TO BRING THE SON OF SAMSON TO PHILISTINE JUSTICE!

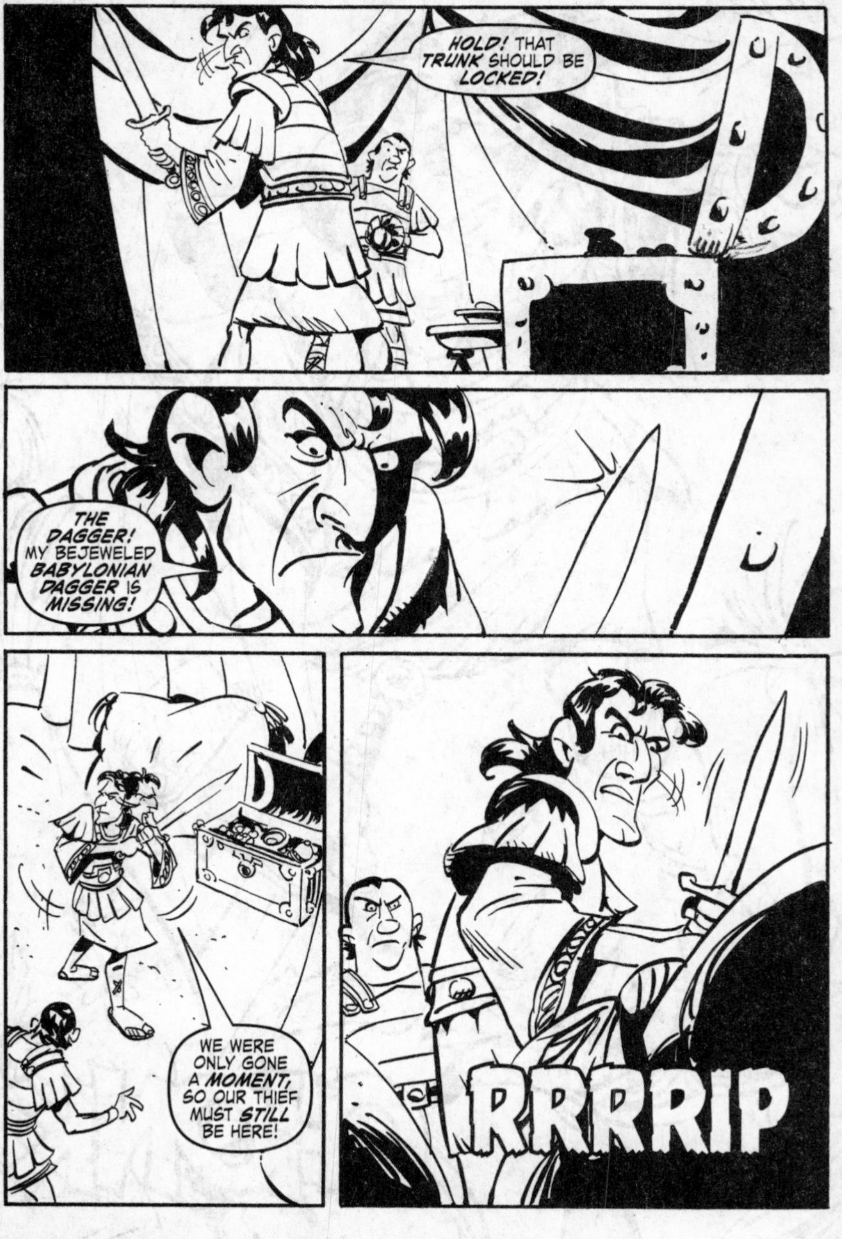
HOLD! THAT TRUNK SHOULD BE LOCKED!
THE DAGGER! MY BEJEWELED BABYLONIAN DAGGER IS MISSING!
WE WERE ONLY GONE A MOMENT, SO OUR THIEF MUST STILL BE HERE!
RRRRIP

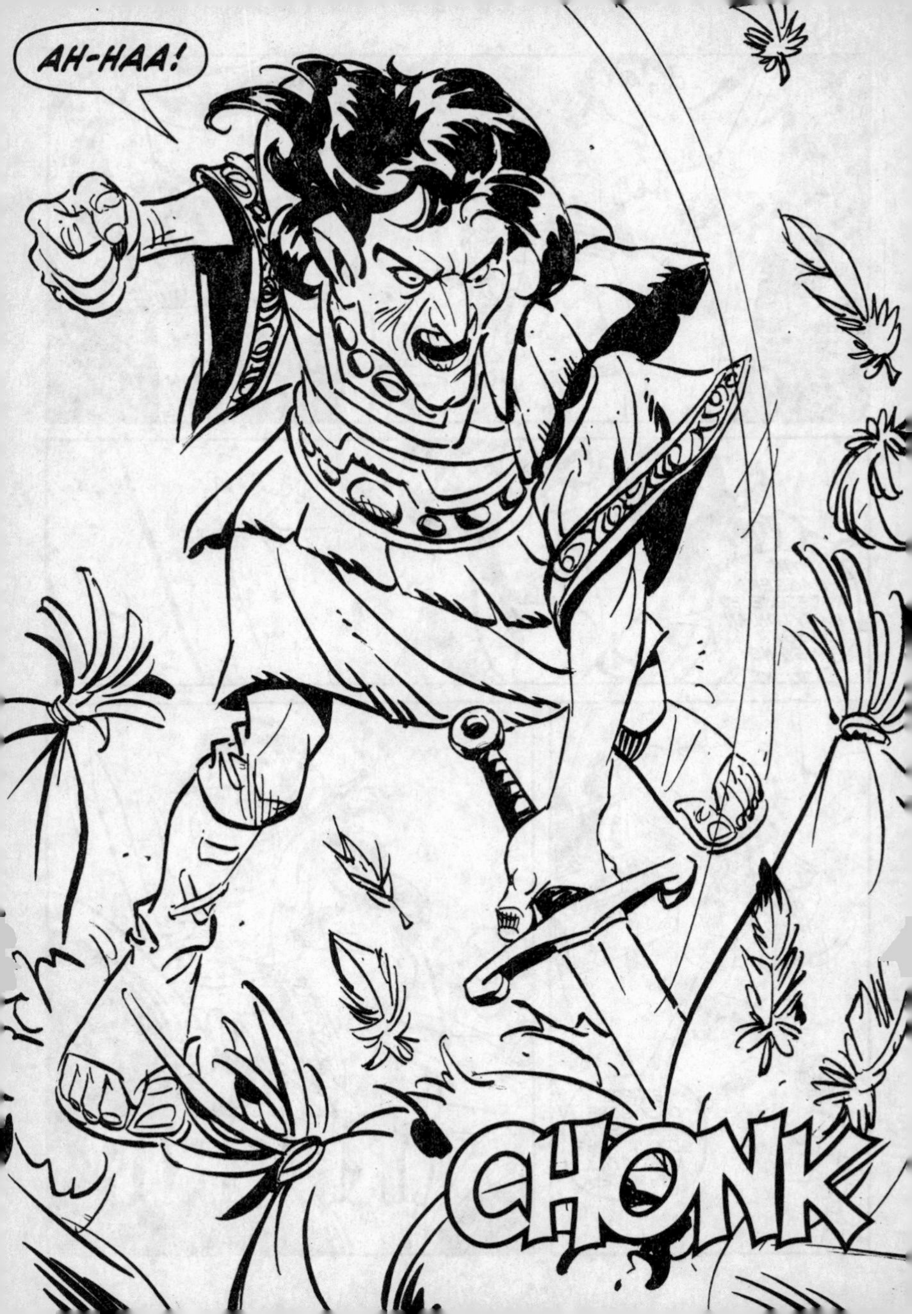
AH-HAA!
CHONK

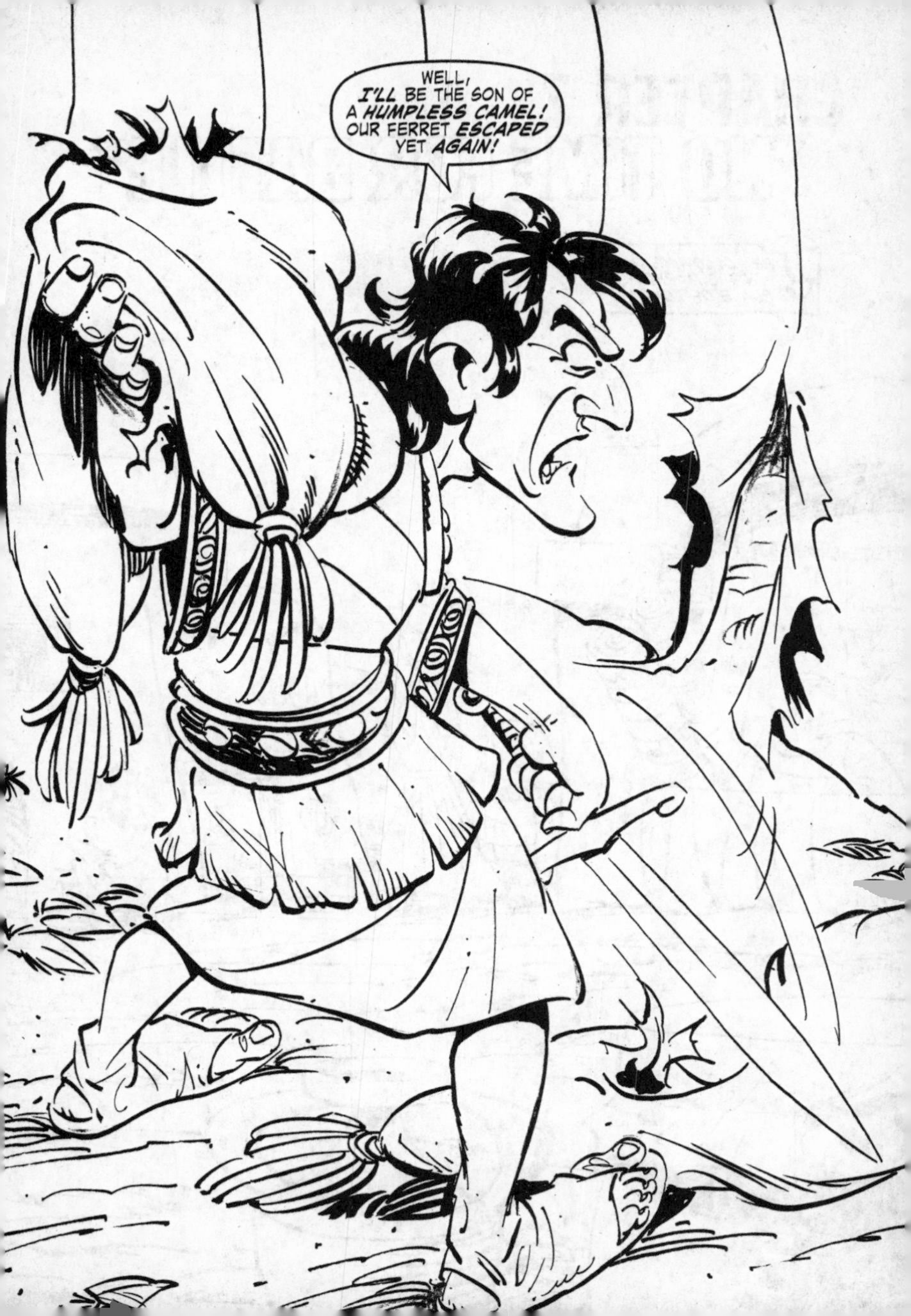
WELL, I'LL BE THE SON OF A HUMPLESS CAMEL! OUR FERRET ESCAPED YET AGAIN!

CHAPTER 2
"NO TIME FOR BATTLE"

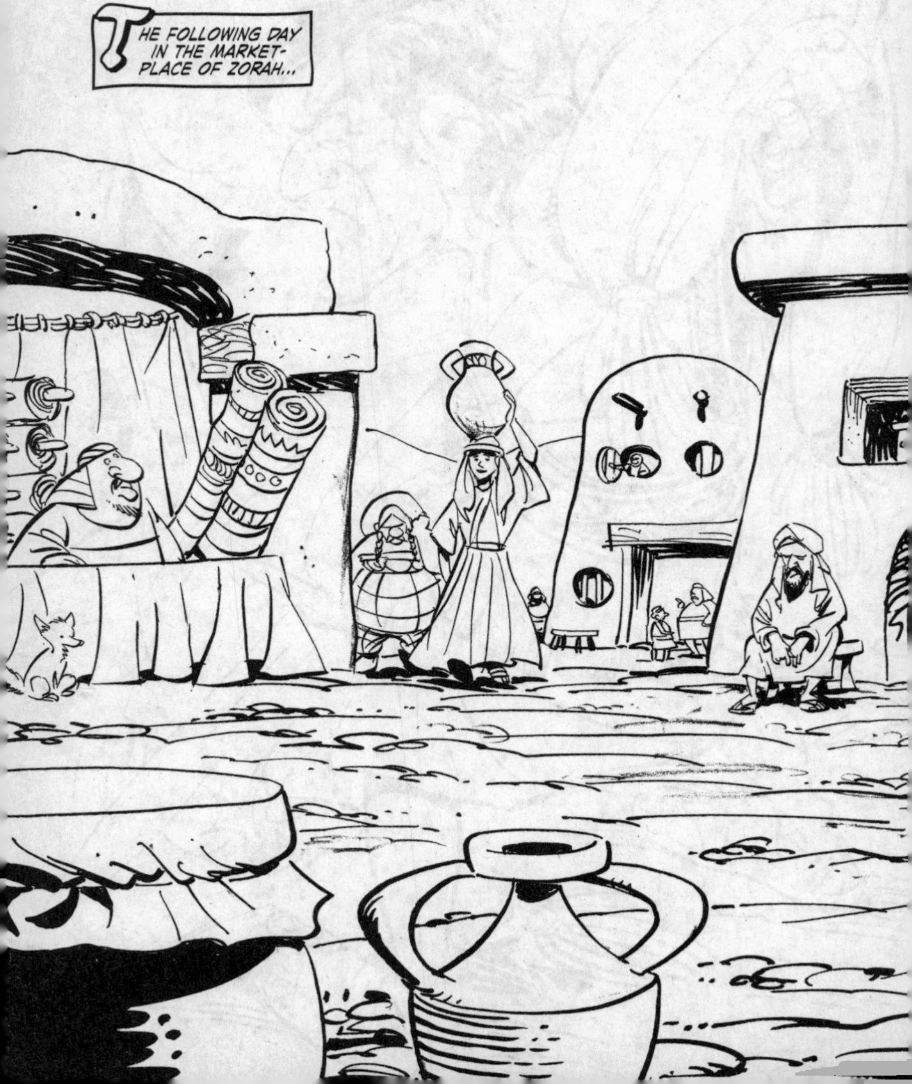
THE FOLLOWING DAY IN THE MARKET-PLACE OF ZORAH...

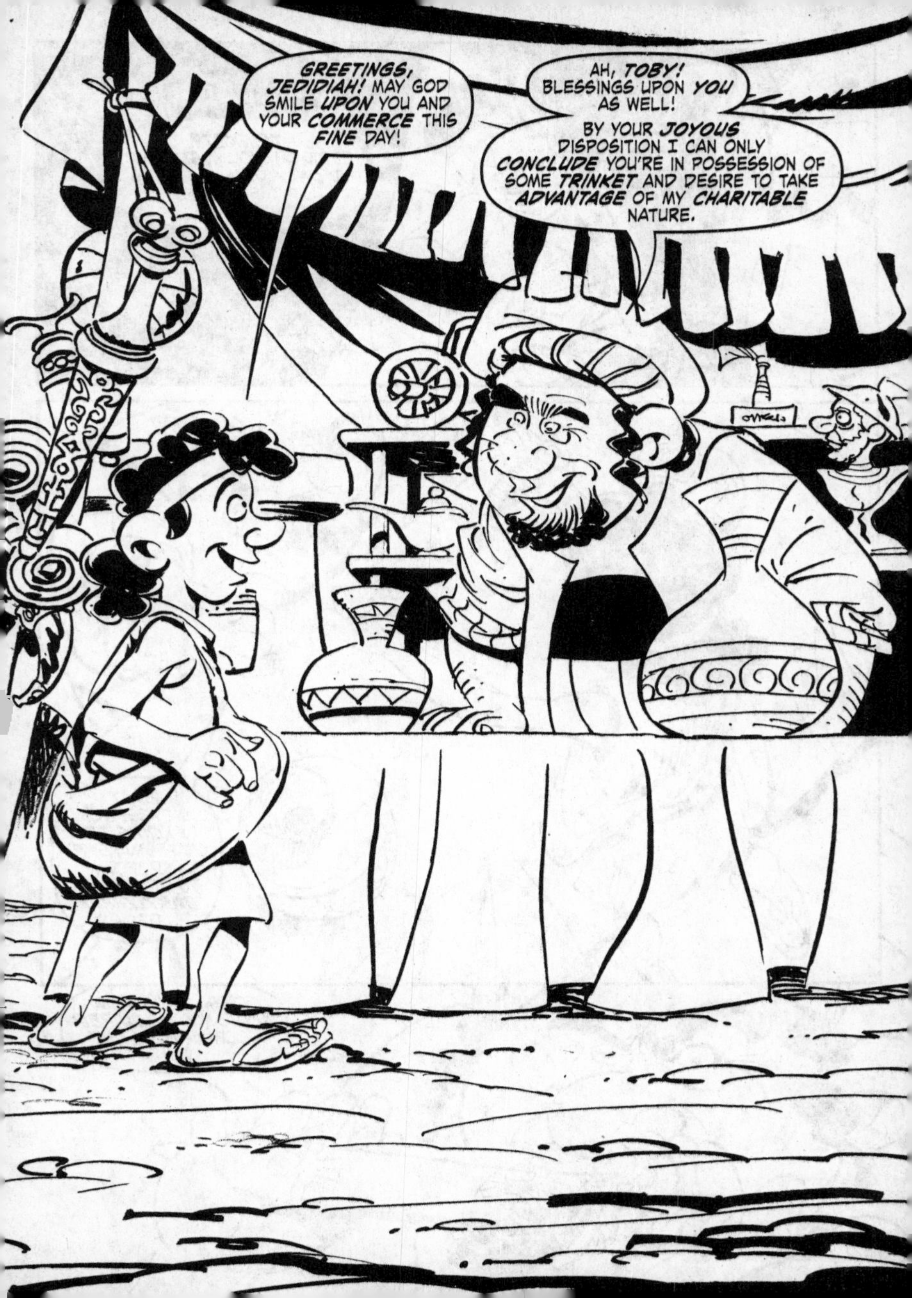
GREETINGS, JEDIDIAH! MAY GOD SMILE UPON YOU AND YOUR COMMERCE THIS FINE DAY!
AH, TOBY! BLESSINGS UPON YOU AS WELL!
BY YOUR JOYOUS DISPOSITION I CAN ONLY CONCLUDE YOU'RE IN POSSESSION OF SOME TRINKET AND DESIRE TO TAKE ADVANTAGE OF MY CHARITABLE NATURE.

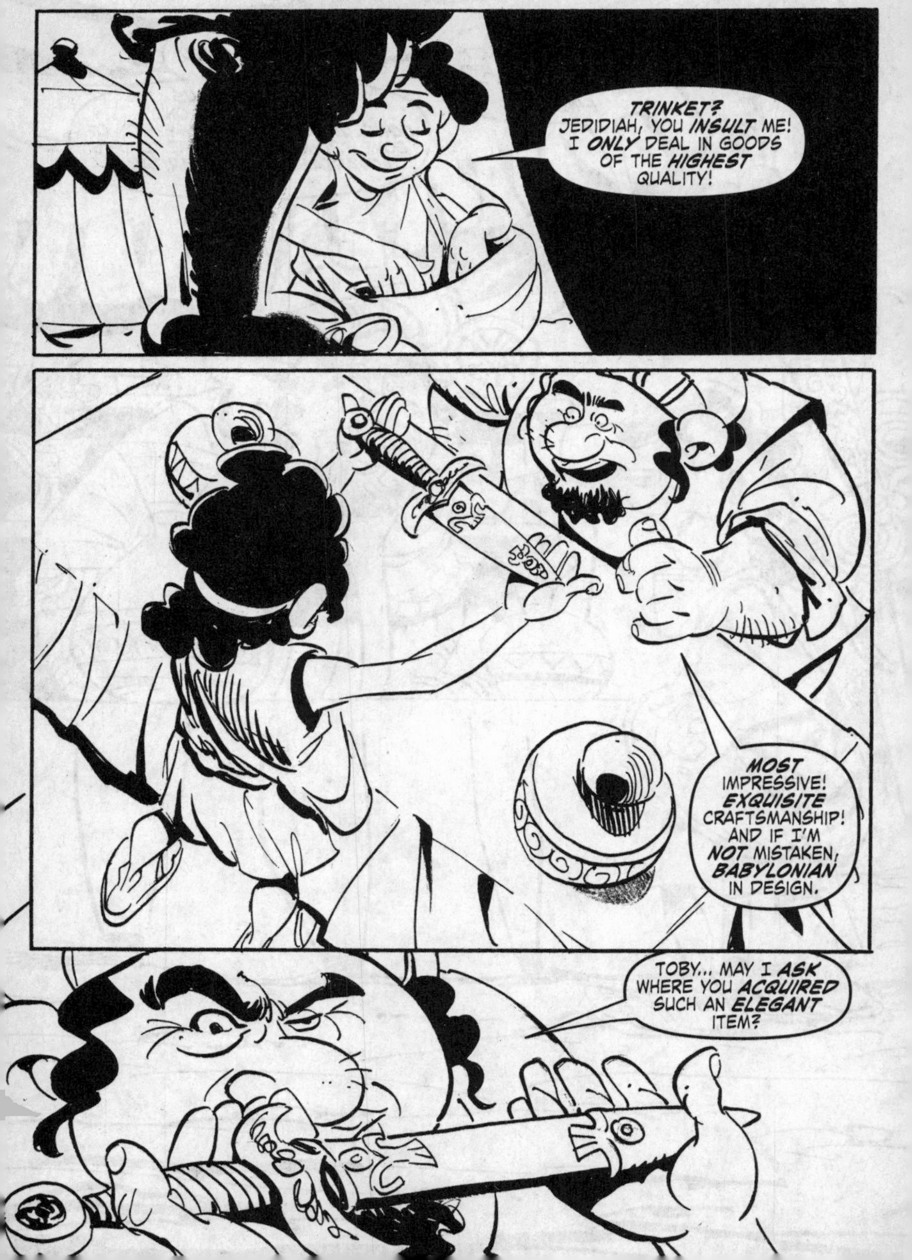
TRINKET? JEDIDIAH, YOU INSULT ME! I ONLY DEAL IN GOODS OF THE HIGHEST QUALITY!
MOST IMPRESSIVE! EXQUISITE CRAFTSMANSHIP! AND IF I'M NOT MISTAKEN, BABYLONIAN IN DESIGN.
TOBY... MAY I ASK WHERE YOU ACQUIRED SUCH AN ELEGANT ITEM?

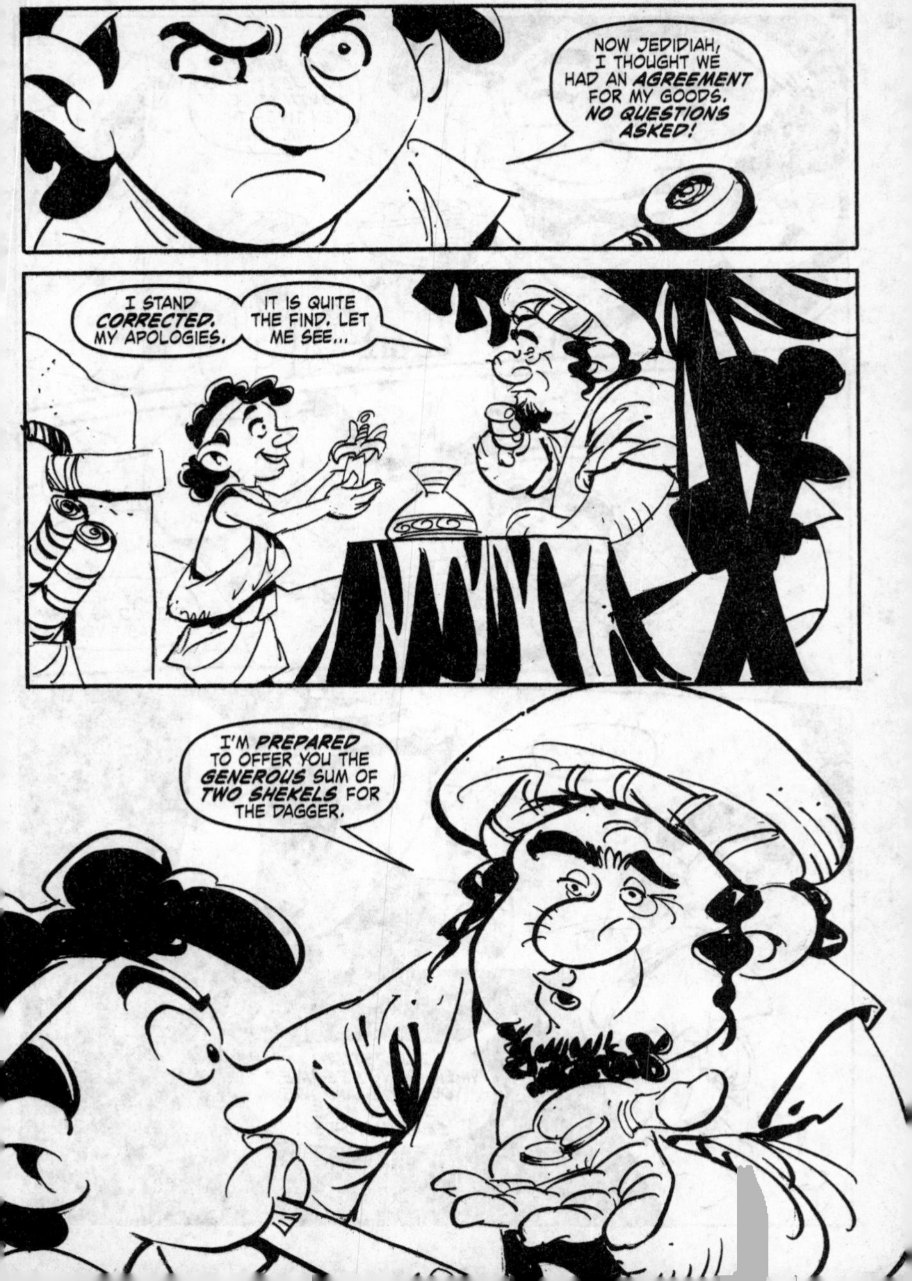
NOW JEDIDIAH, I THOUGHT WE HAD AN AGREEMENT FOR MY GOODS. NO QUESTIONS ASKED!
I STAND CORRECTED. MY APOLOGIES.
IT IS QUITE THE FIND. LET ME SEE...
I'M PREPARED TO OFFER YOU THE GENEROUS SUM OF TWO SHEKELS FOR THE DAGGER.

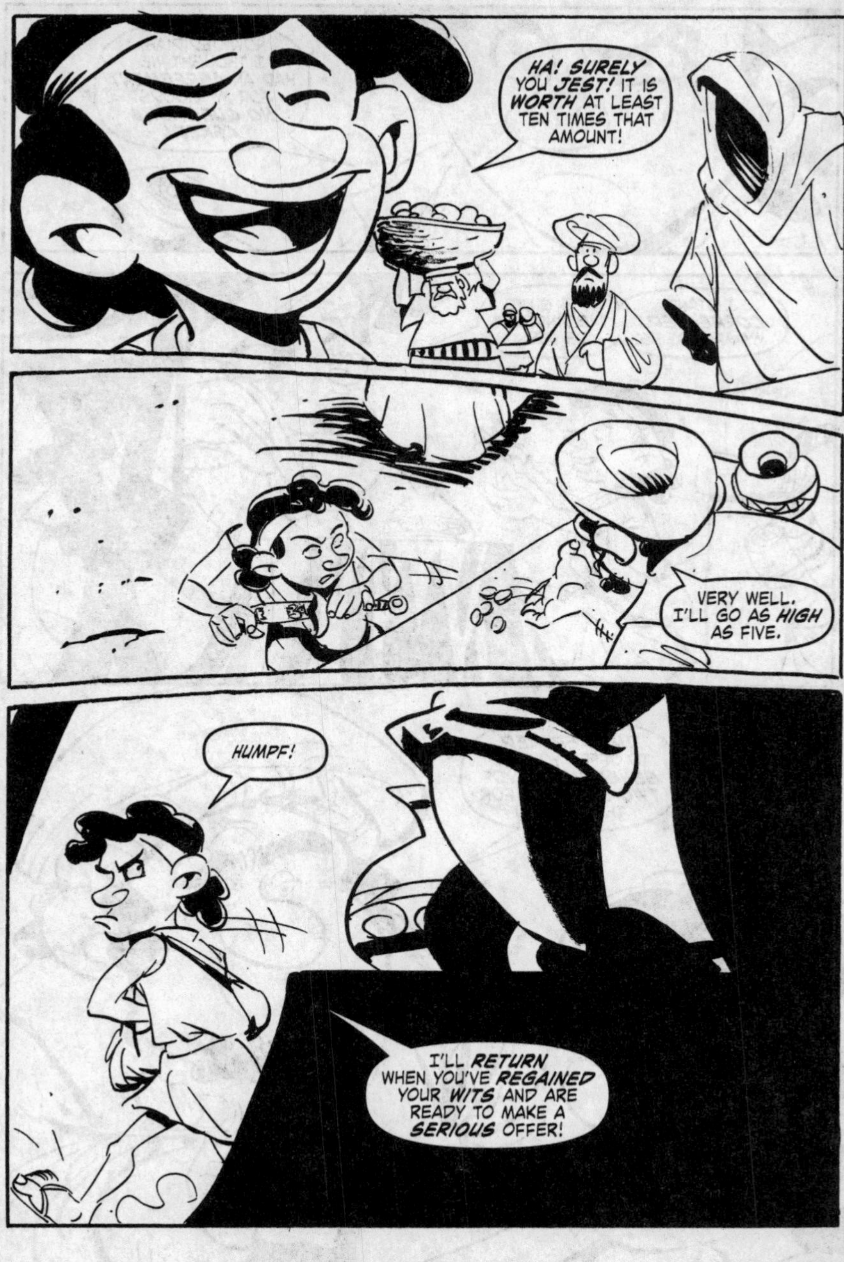
HA! SURELY YOU JEST! IT IS WORTH AT LEAST TEN TIMES THAT AMOUNT!
VERY WELL. I'LL GO AS HIGH AS FIVE.
HUMPF!
I'LL RETURN WHEN YOU'VE REGAINED YOUR WITS AND ARE READY TO MAKE A SERIOUS OFFER!

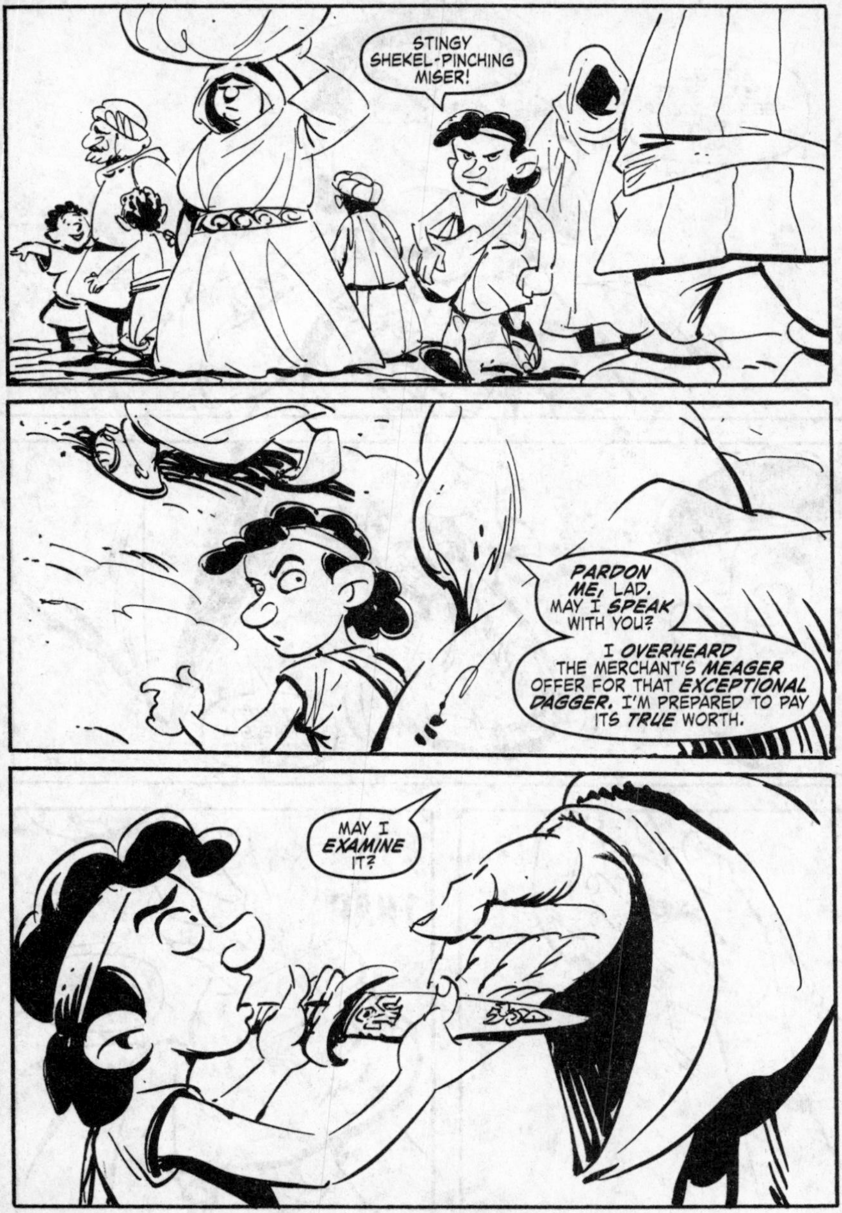
STINGY SHEKEL-PINCHING MISER!
PARDON ME, LAD. MAY I SPEAK WITH YOU?
I OVERHEARD THE MERCHANT'S MEAGER OFFER FOR THAT EXCEPTIONAL DAGGER. I'M PREPARED TO PAY ITS TRUE WORTH.
MAY I EXAMINE IT?

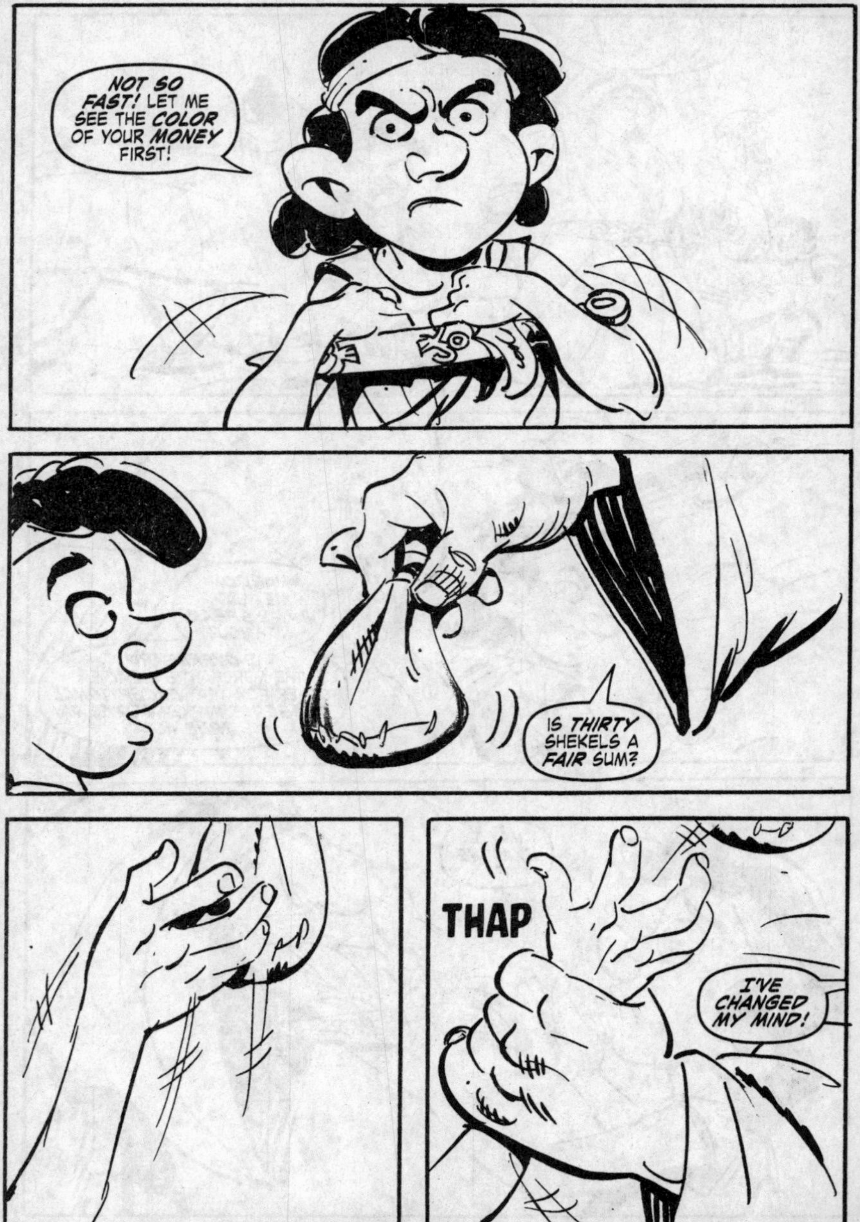
NOT SO FAST! LET ME SEE THE COLOR OF YOUR MONEY FIRST!
IS THIRTY SHEKELS A FAIR SUM?
THAP
I'VE CHANGED MY MIND!

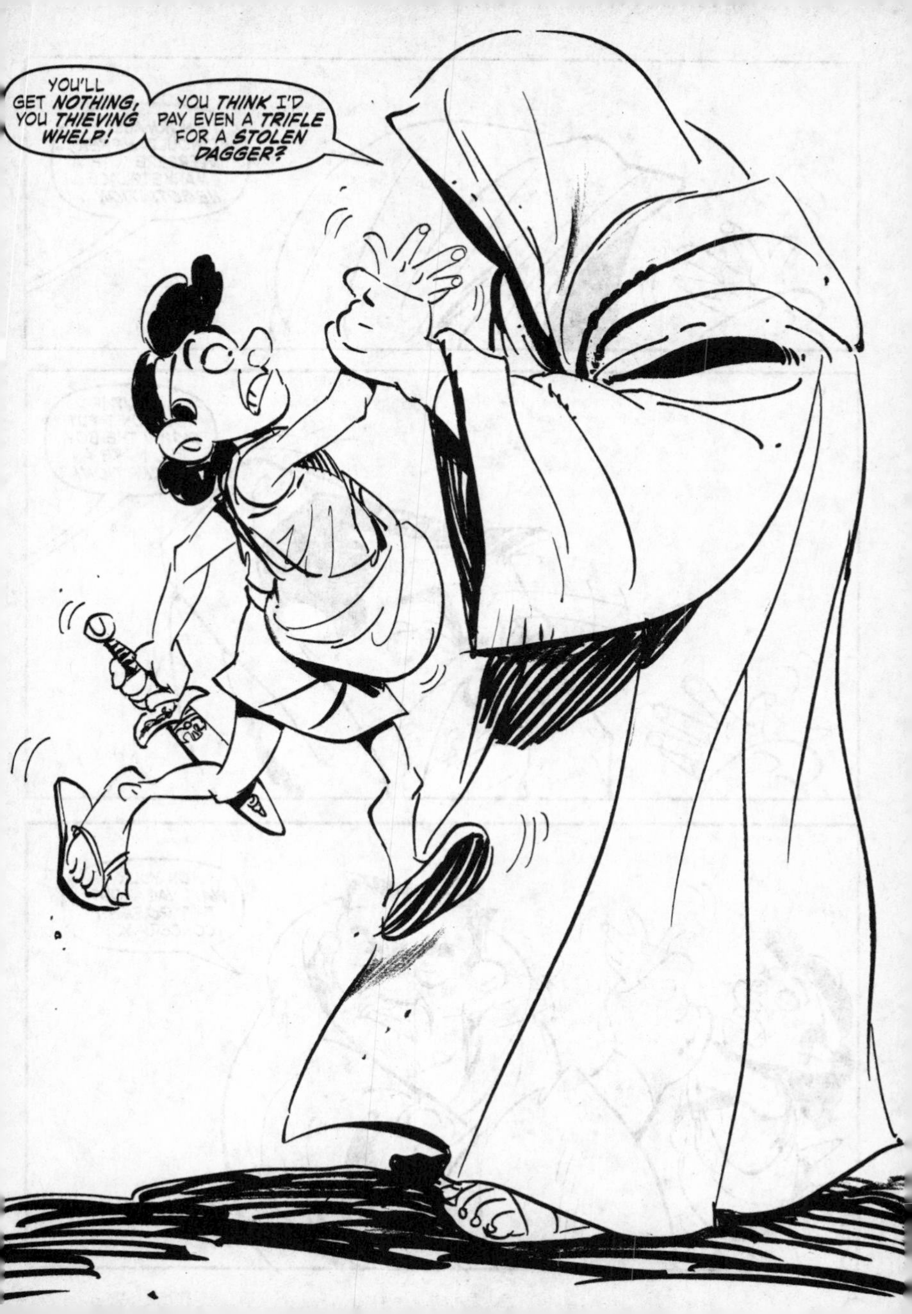
YOU'LL GET NOTHING, YOU THIEVING WHELP!
YOU THINK I'D PAY EVEN A TRIFLE FOR A STOLEN DAGGER?

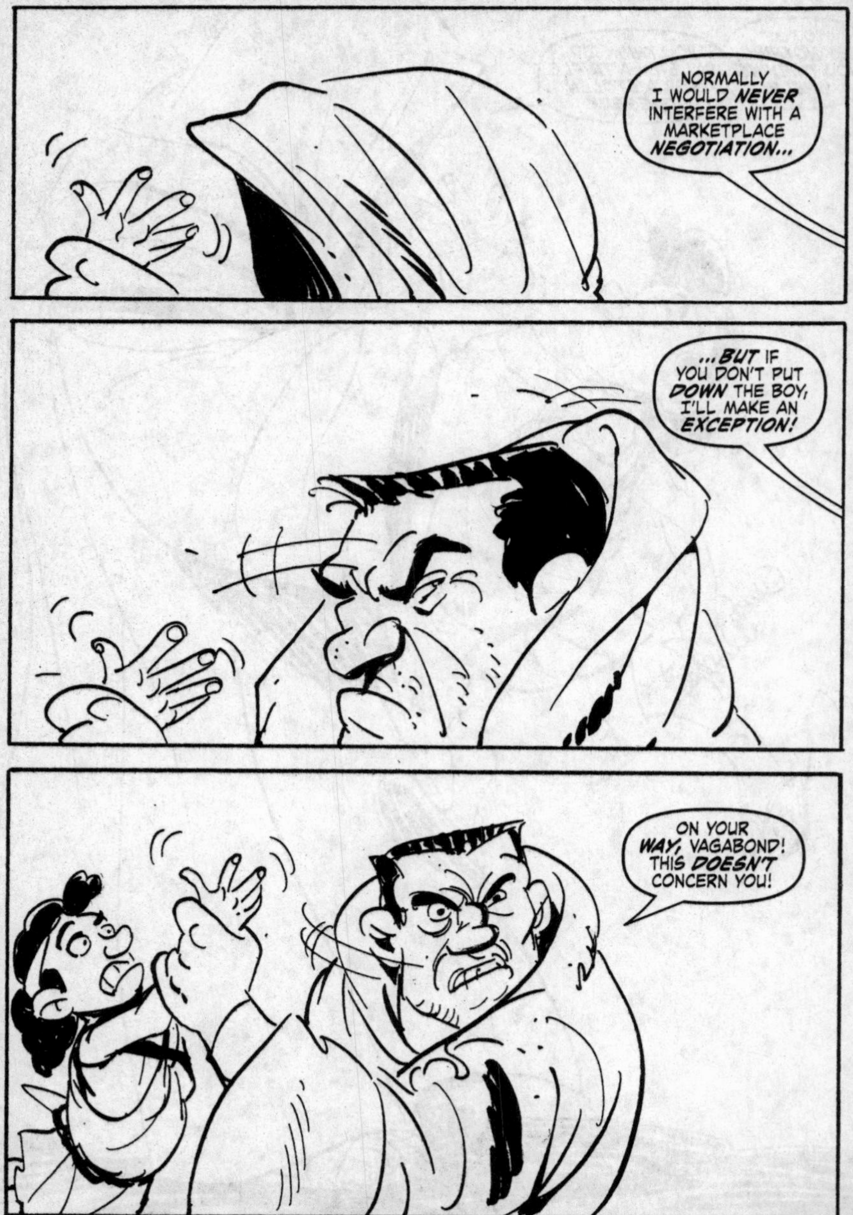
NORMALLY I WOULD NEVER INTERFERE WITH A MARKETPLACE NEGOTIATION...
...BUT IF YOU DON'T PUT DOWN THE BOY, I'LL MAKE AN EXCEPTION!
ON YOUR WAY, VAGABOND! THIS DOESN'T CONCERN YOU!

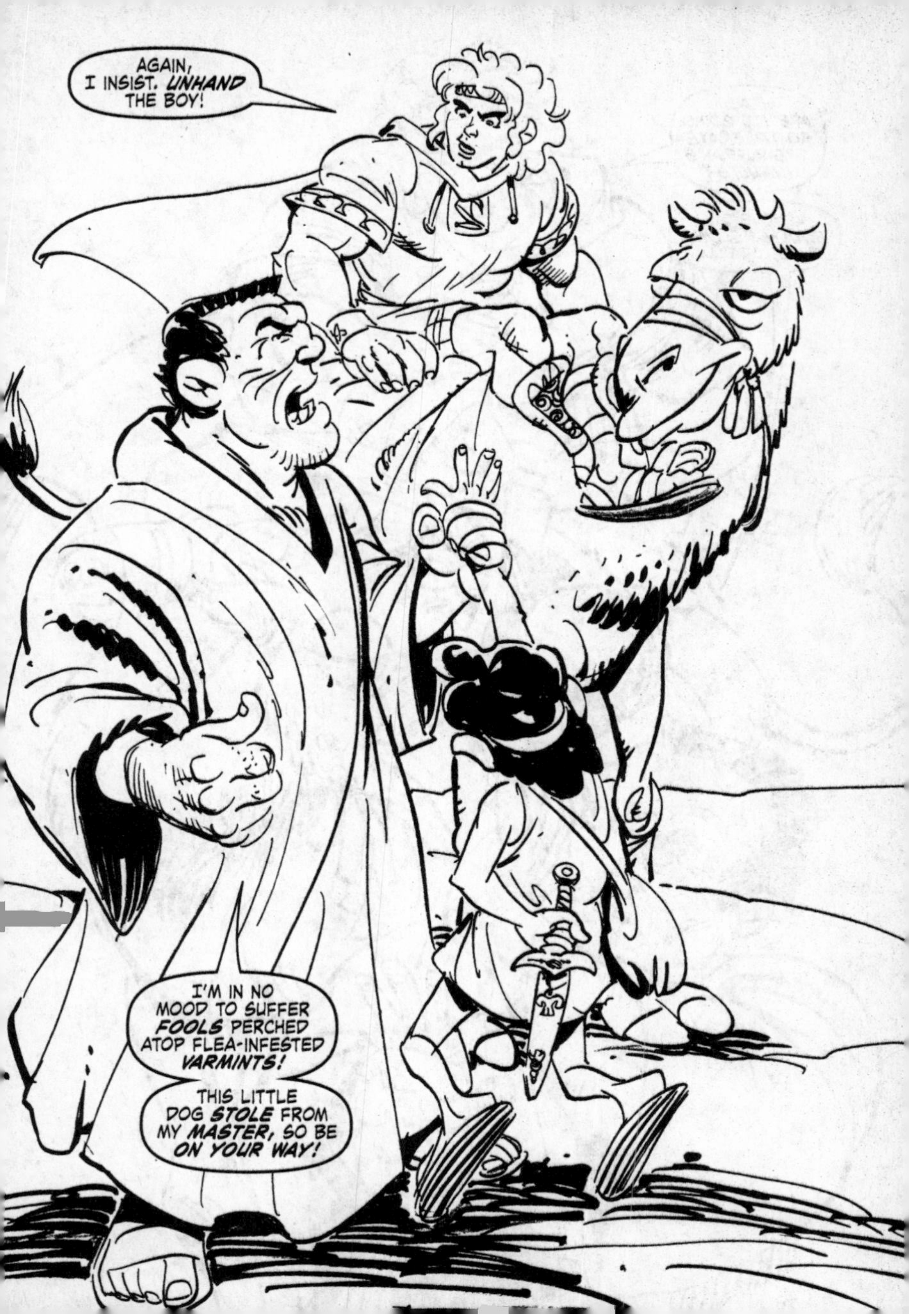
AGAIN, I INSIST. UNHAND THE BOY!
I'M IN NO MOOD TO SUFFER FOOLS PERCHED ATOP FLEA-INFESTED VARMINTS!
THIS LITTLE DOG STOLE FROM MY MASTER, SO BE ON YOUR WAY!

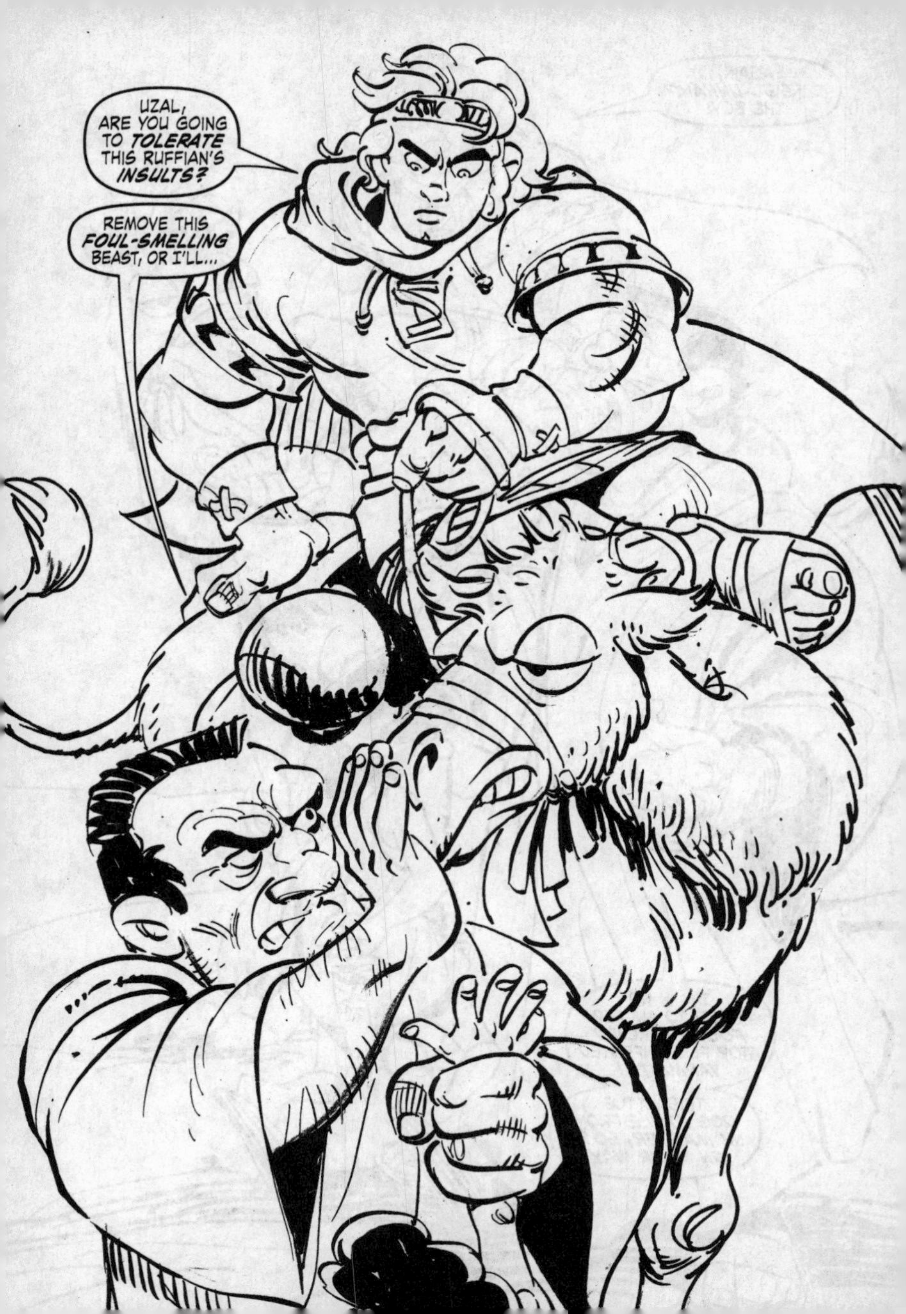
UZAL, ARE YOU GOING TO TOLERATE THIS RUFFIAN'S INSULTS?
REMOVE THIS FOUL-SMELLING BEAST, OR I'LL...

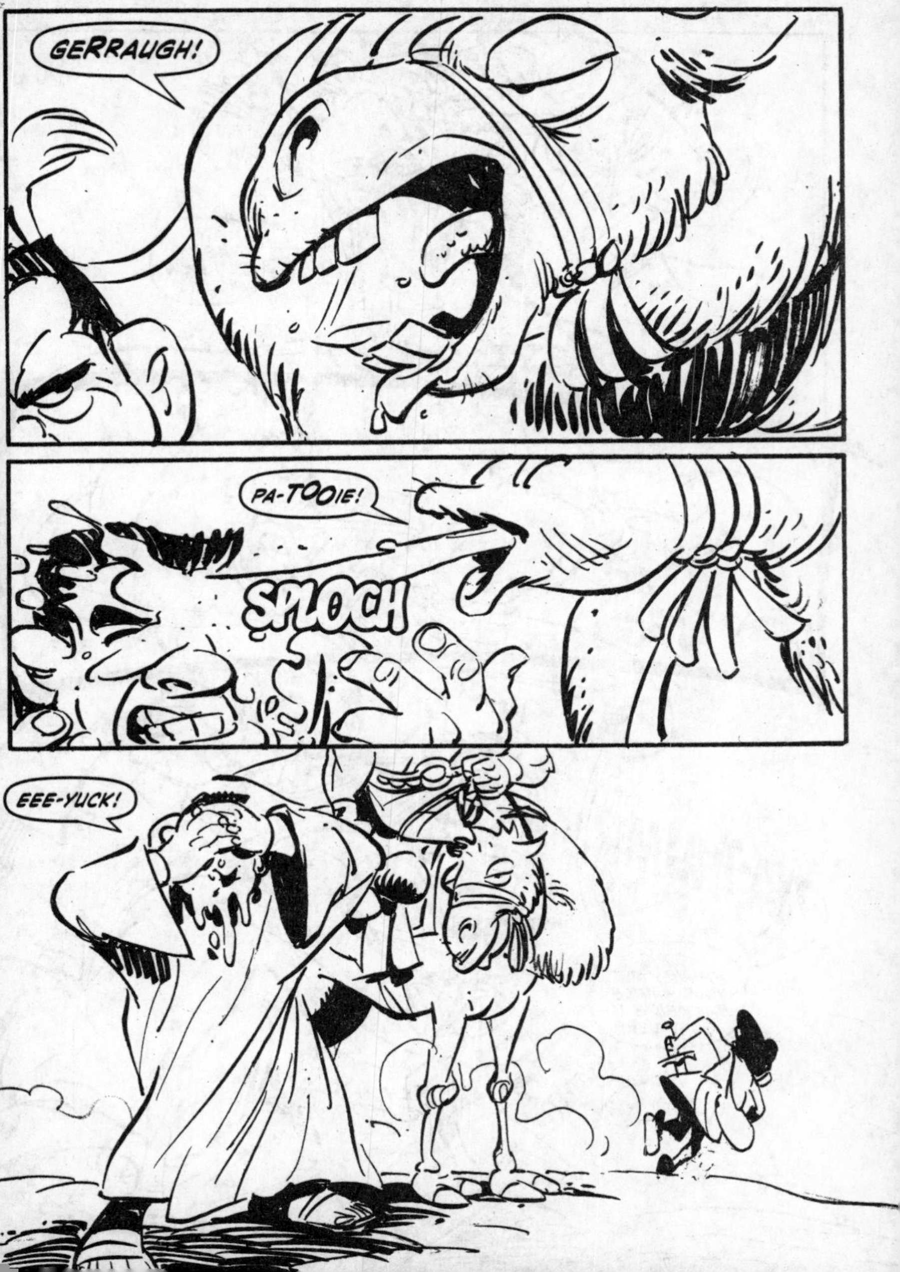
GERRAUGH!
PA-TOOIE!
SPLOCH
EEE-YUCK!

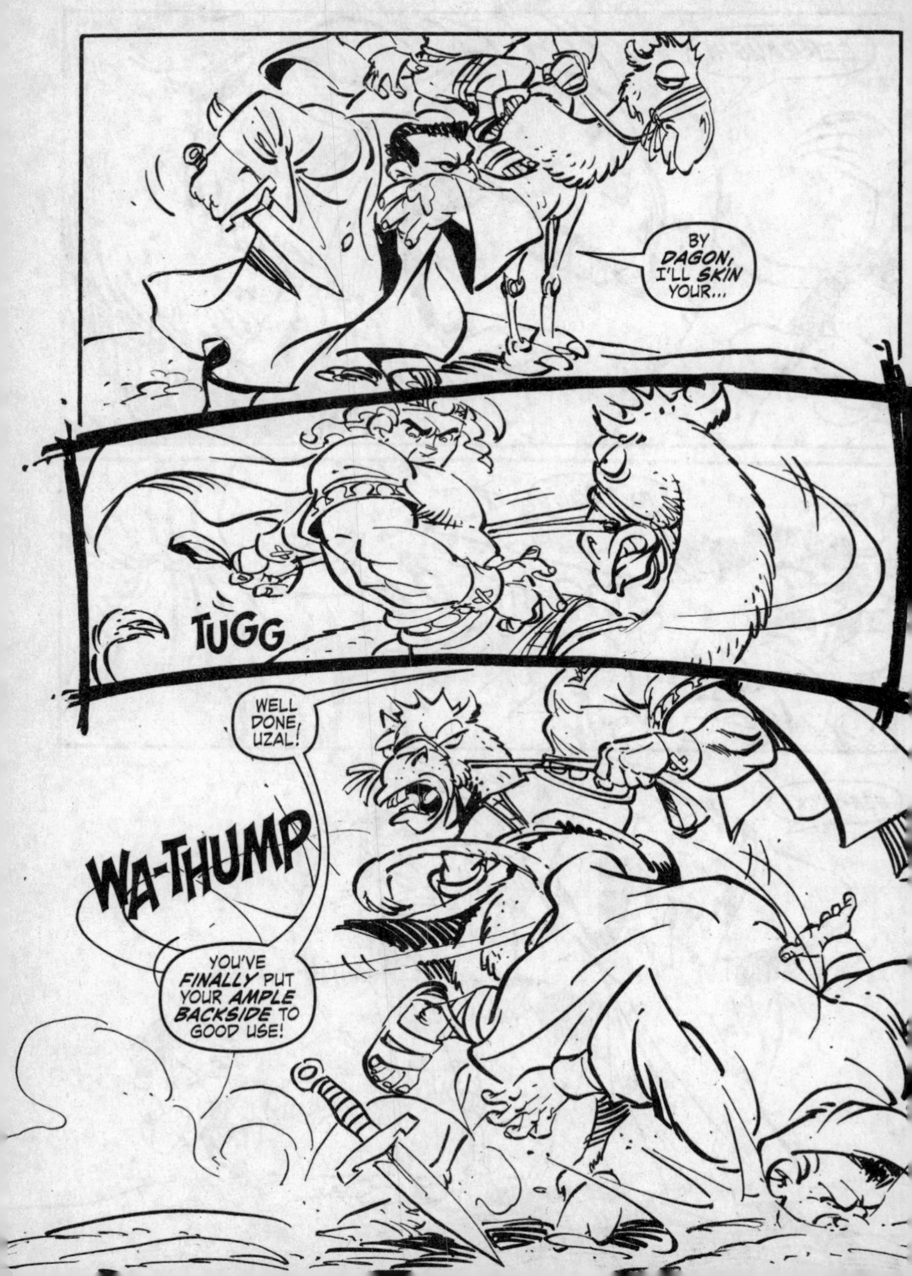
BY DAGON, I'LL SKIN YOUR...
TUGG
WELL DONE, UZAL!
WA-THUMP
YOU'VE FINALLY PUT YOUR AMPLE BACKSIDE TO GOOD USE!

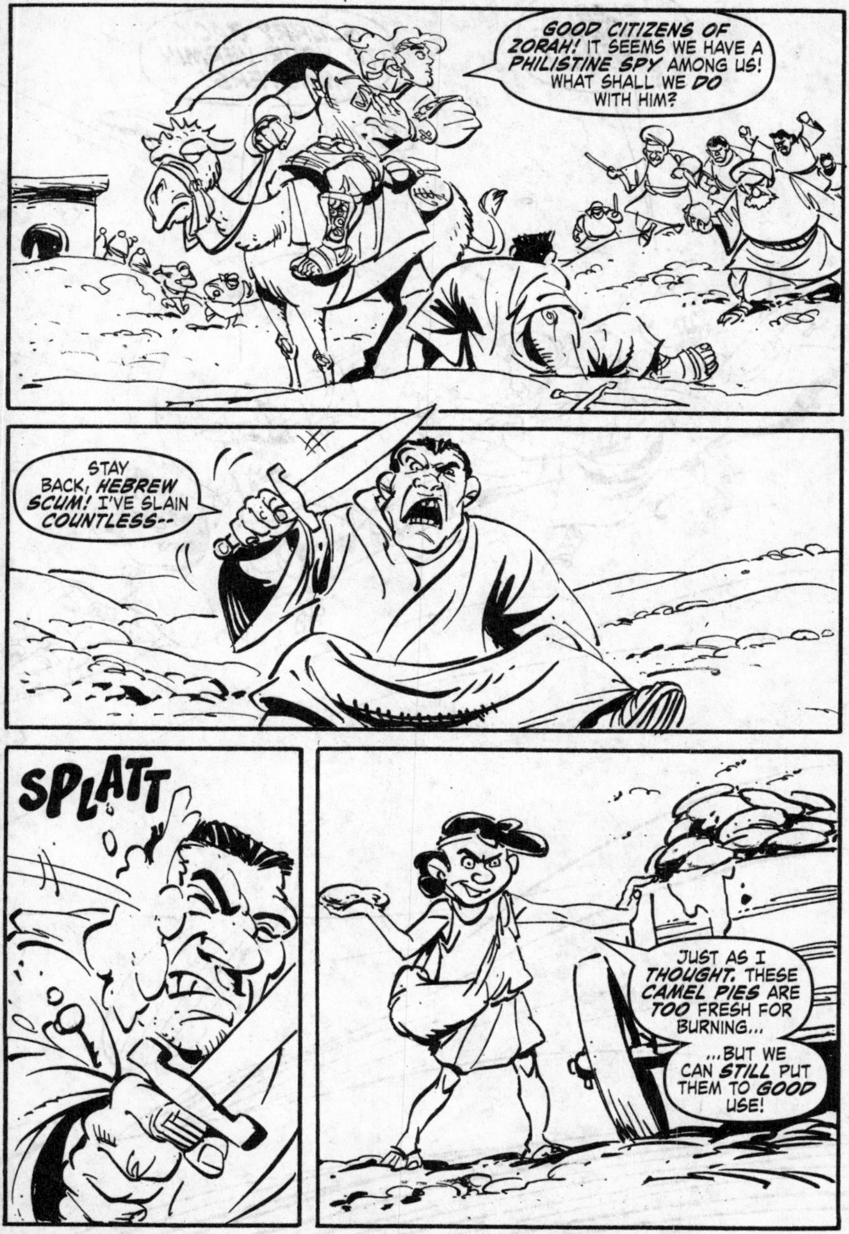
GOOD CITIZENS OF ZORAH! IT SEEMS WE HAVE A PHILISTINE SPY AMONG US! WHAT SHALL WE DO WITH HIM?
STAY BACK, HEBREW SCUM! I'VE SLAIN COUNTLESS--
SPLATT
JUST AS I THOUGHT. THESE CAMEL PIES ARE TOO FRESH FOR BURNING...
...BUT WE CAN STILL PUT THEM TO GOOD USE!

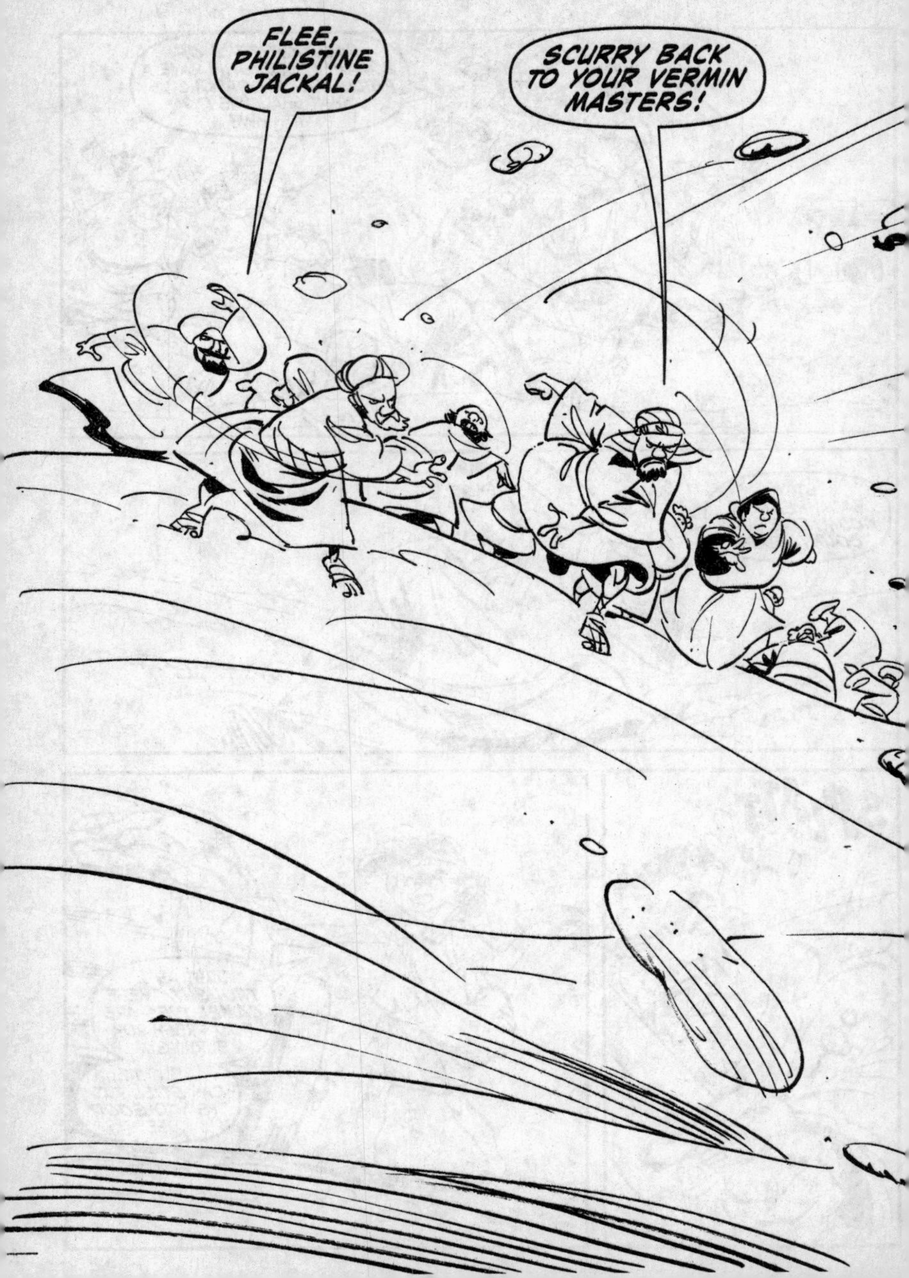
FLEE, PHILISTINE JACKAL!
SCURRY BACK TO YOUR VERMIN MASTERS!

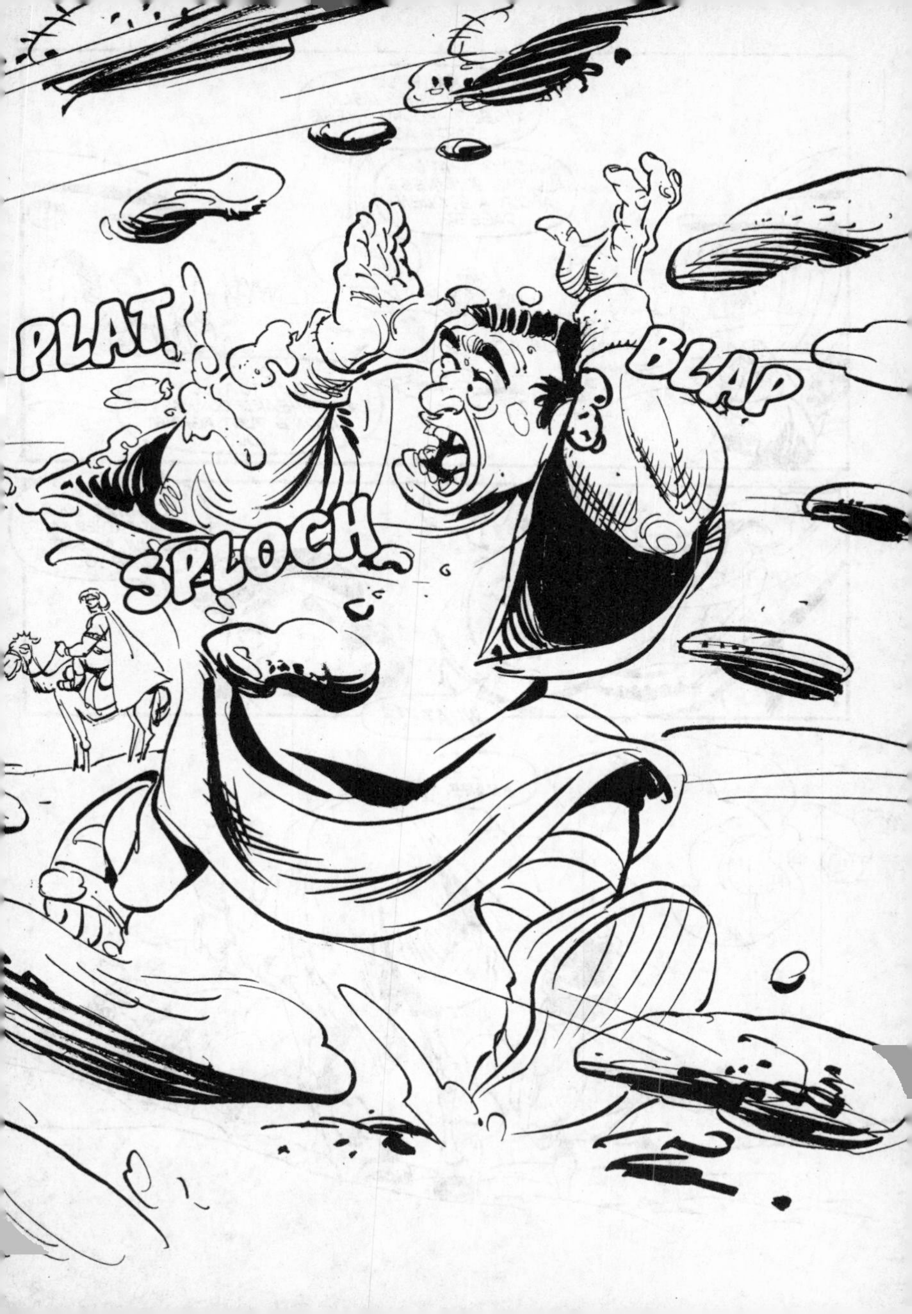
PLAT
BLAP
SPLOCH

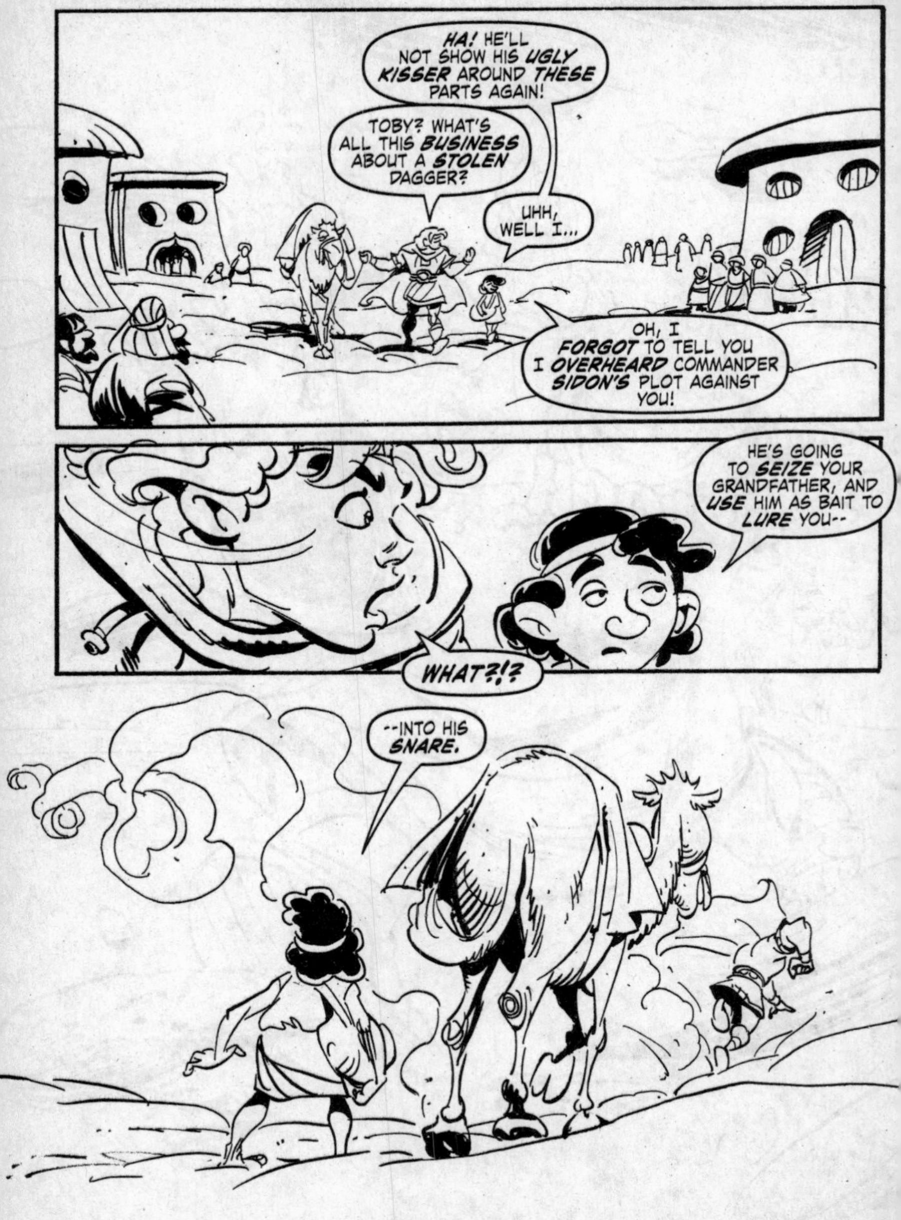

HA! HE'LL NOT SHOW HIS UGLY KISSER AROUND THESE PARTS AGAIN!
TOBY? WHAT'S ALL THIS BUSINESS ABOUT A STOLEN DAGGER?
UHH, WELL I...
OH, I FORGOT TO TELL YOU I OVERHEARD COMMANDER SIDON'S PLOT AGAINST YOU!
HE'S GOING TO SEIZE YOUR GRANDFATHER, AND USE HIM AS BAIT TO LURE YOU--
WHAT?!?
--INTO HIS SNARE.

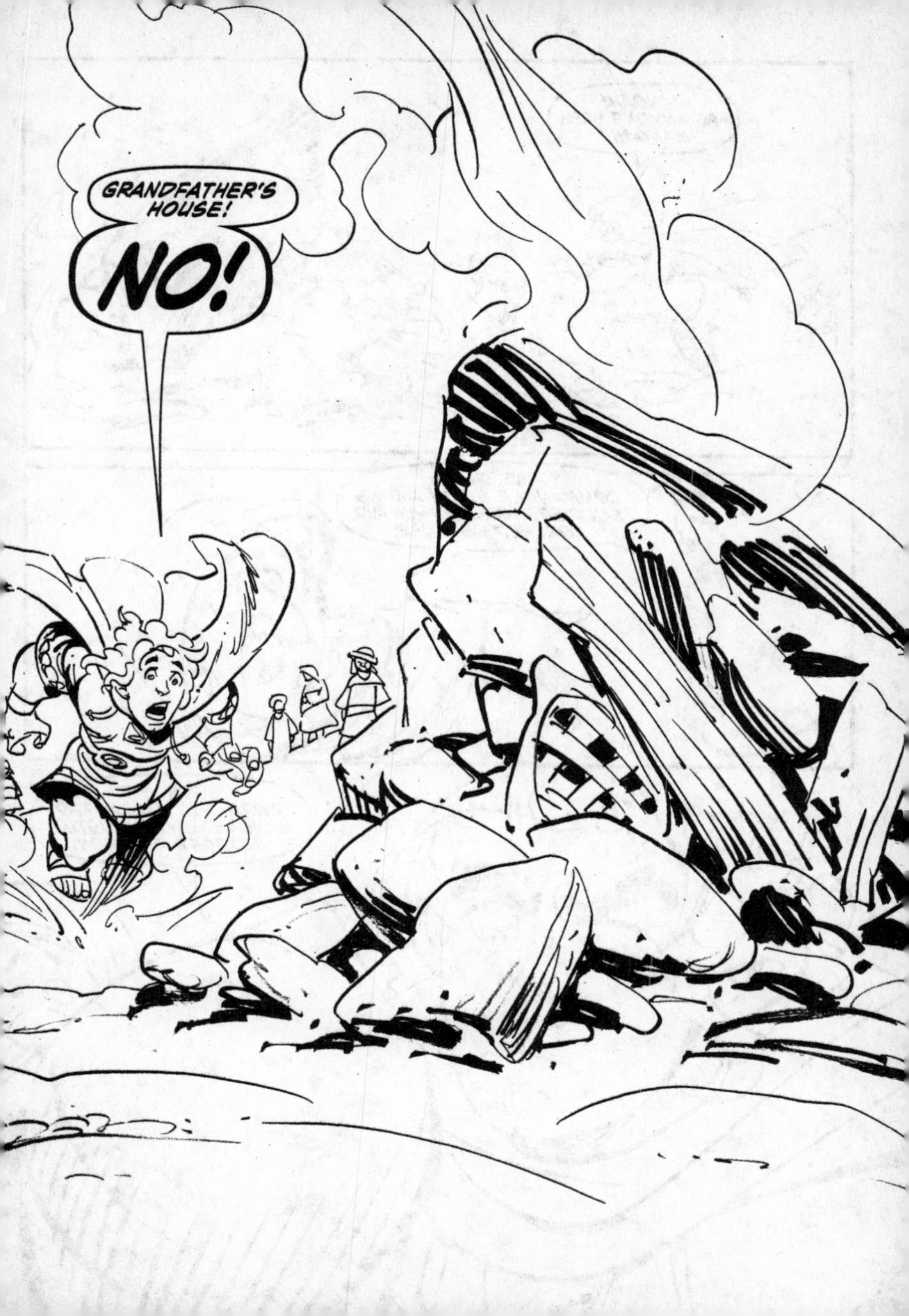
GRANDFATHER'S HOUSE!
NO!

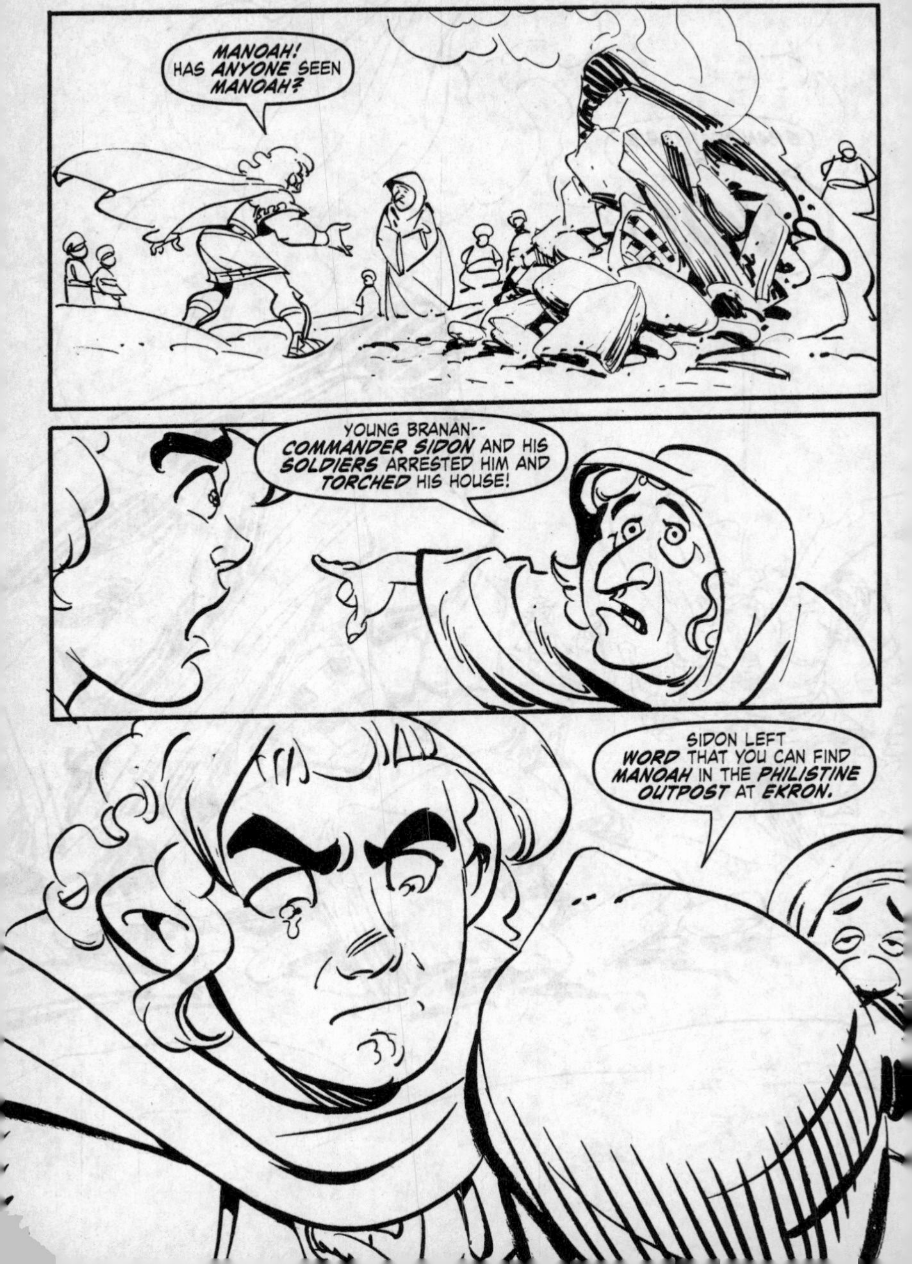
MANOAH! HAS ANYONE SEEN MANOAH?
YOUNG BRANAN-- COMMANDER SIDON AND HIS SOLDIERS ARRESTED HIM AND TORCHED HIS HOUSE!
SIDON LEFT WORD THAT YOU CAN FIND MANOAH IN THE PHILISTINE OUTPOST AT EKRON.

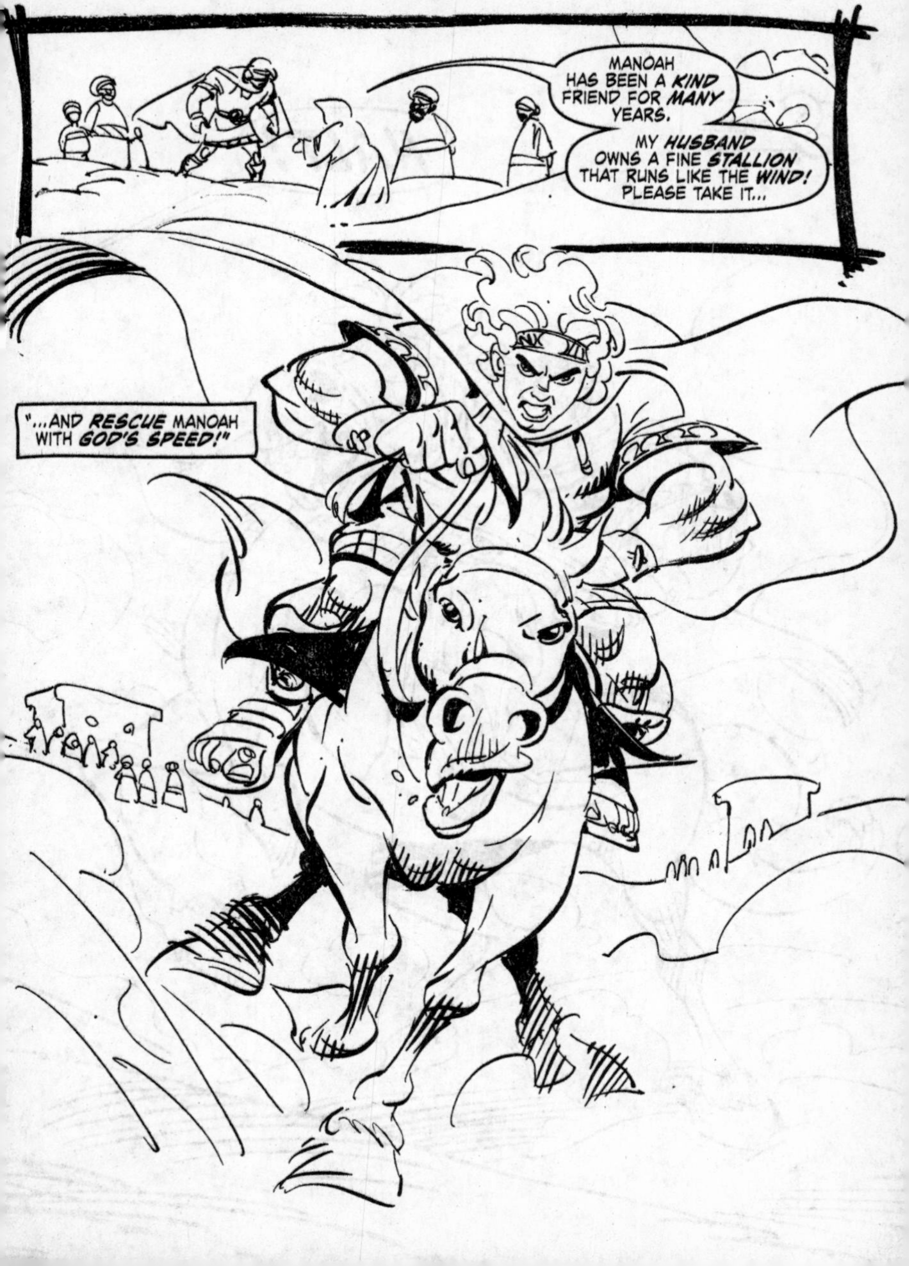
MANOAH HAS BEEN A KIND FRIEND FOR MANY YEARS.
MY HUSBAND OWNS A FINE STALLION THAT RUNS LIKE THE WIND! PLEASE TAKE IT...
"...AND RESCUE MANOAH WITH GOD'S SPEED!"

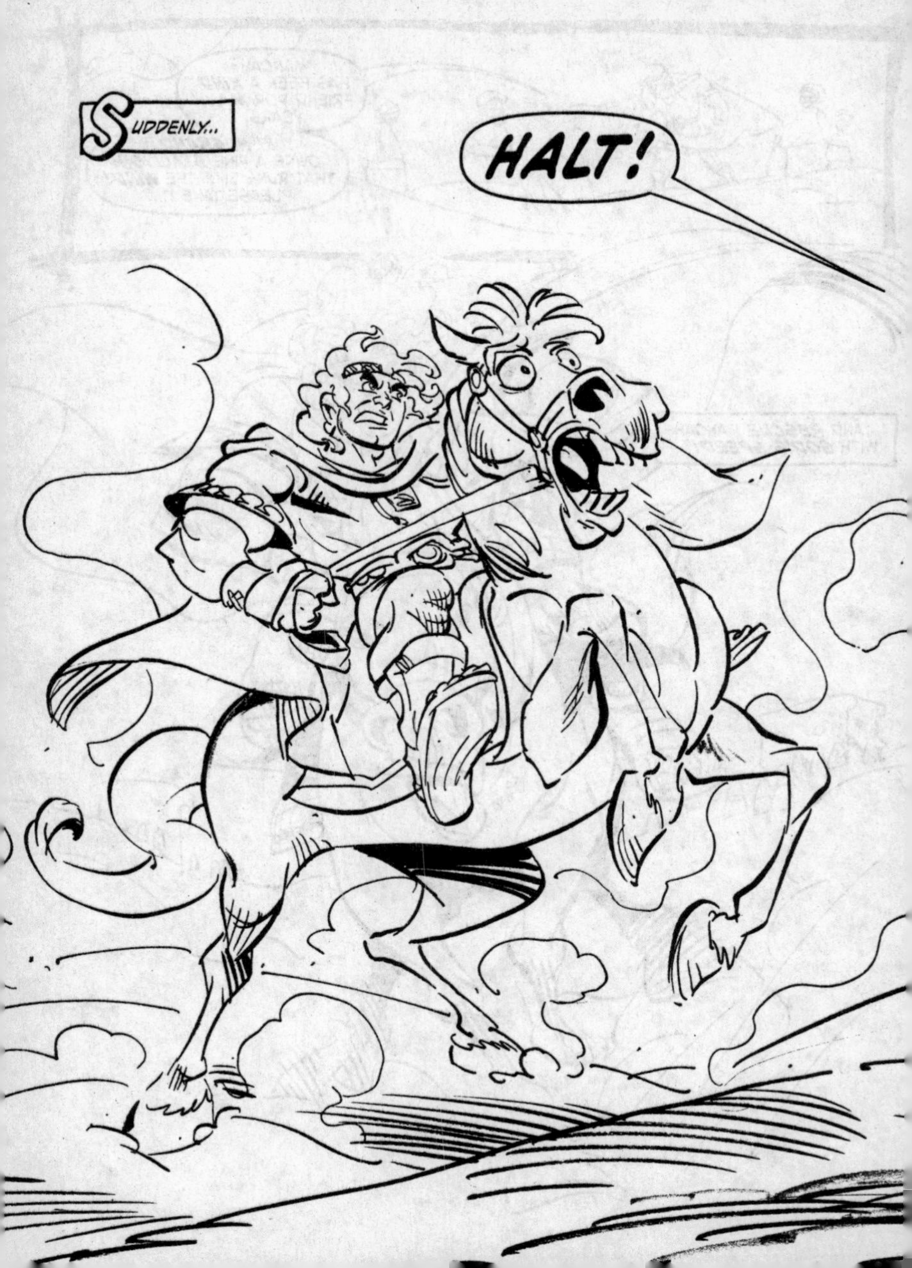
SUDDENLY...
HALT!

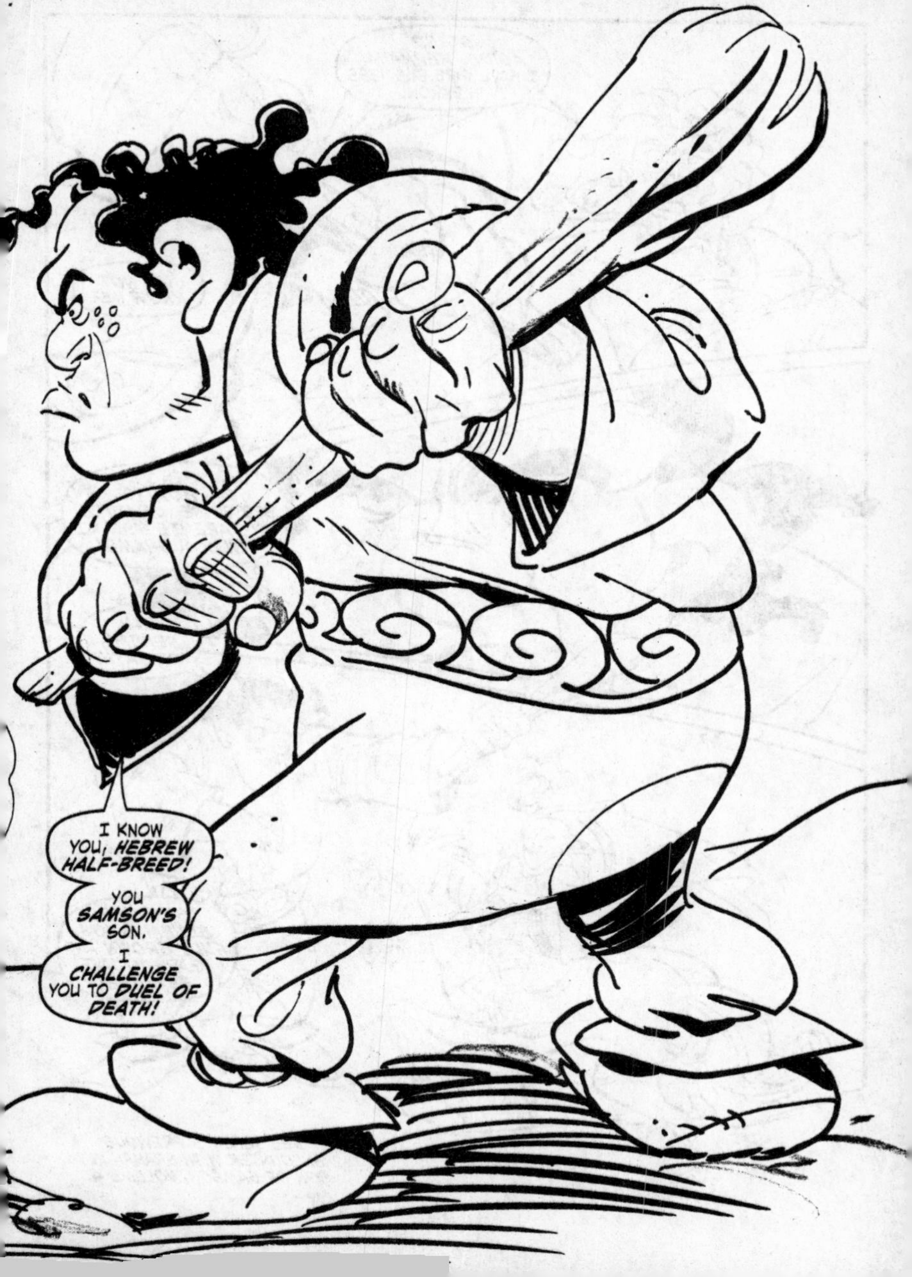
I KNOW YOU, *HEBREW HALF-BREED!*
YOU *SAMSON'S* SON.
I *CHALLENGE* YOU TO *DUEL OF DEATH!*

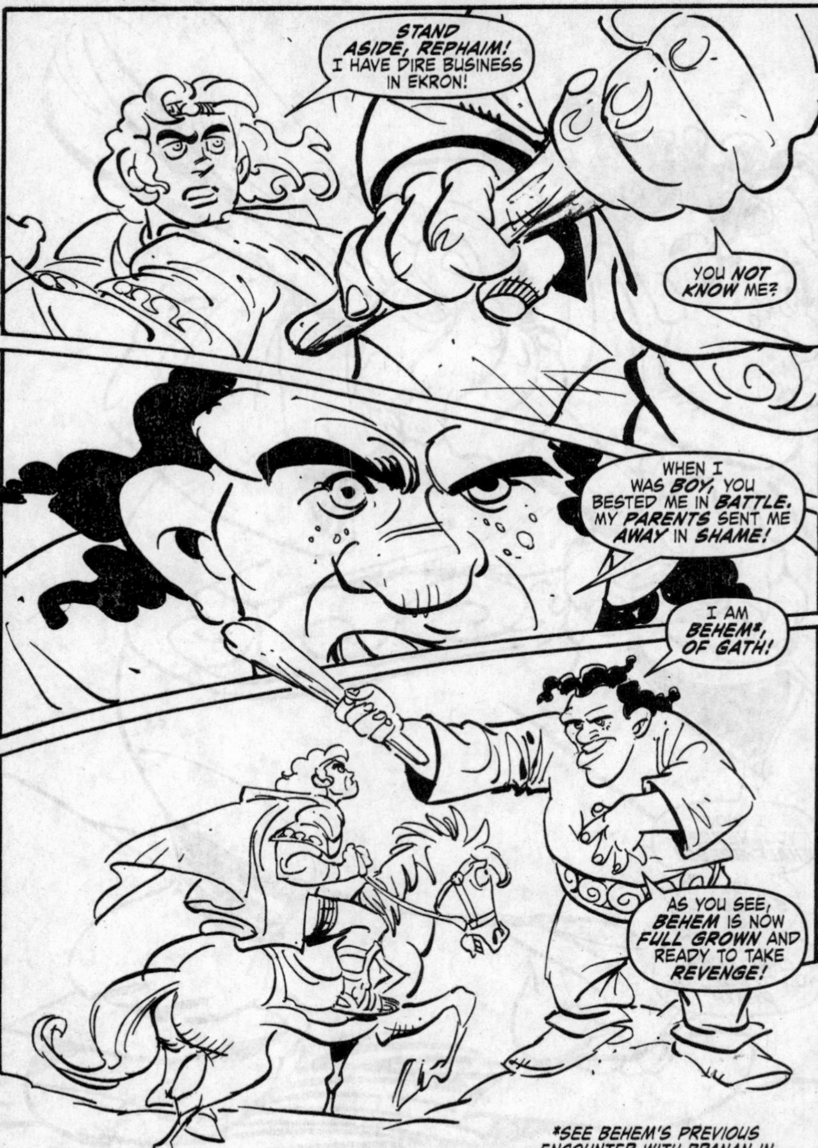
STAND ASIDE, REPHAIM! I HAVE DIRE BUSINESS IN EKRON!
YOU NOT KNOW ME?
WHEN I WAS BOY, YOU BESTED ME IN BATTLE. MY PARENTS SENT ME AWAY IN SHAME!
I AM BEHEM*, OF GATH!
AS YOU SEE, BEHEM IS NOW FULL GROWN AND READY TO TAKE REVENGE!

*SEE BEHEM'S PREVIOUS ENCOUNTER WITH BRANAN IN SON OF SAMSON, VOLUME 4.

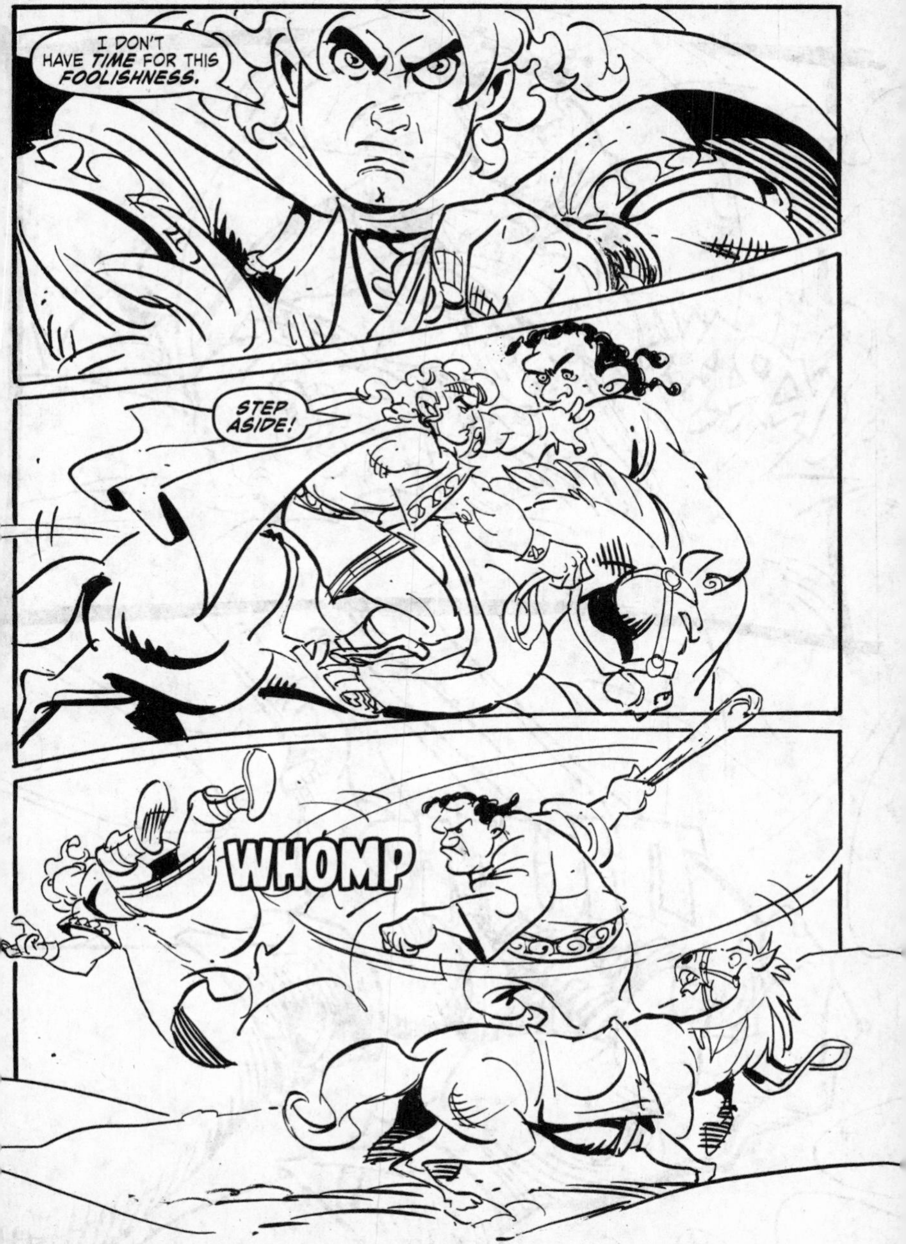
I DON'T HAVE *TIME* FOR THIS *FOOLISHNESS.*
STEP ASIDE!
WHOMP

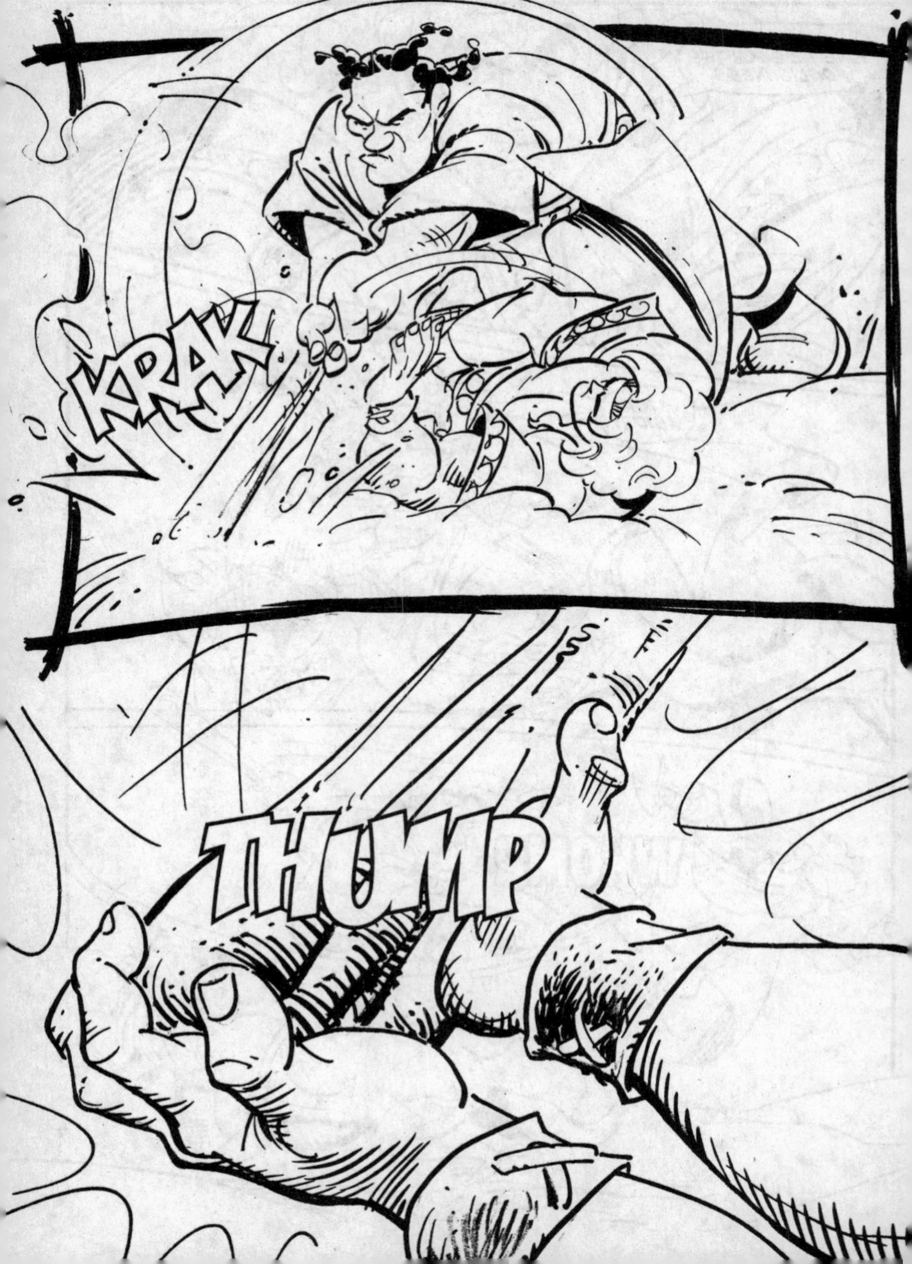
KRAK
THUMP

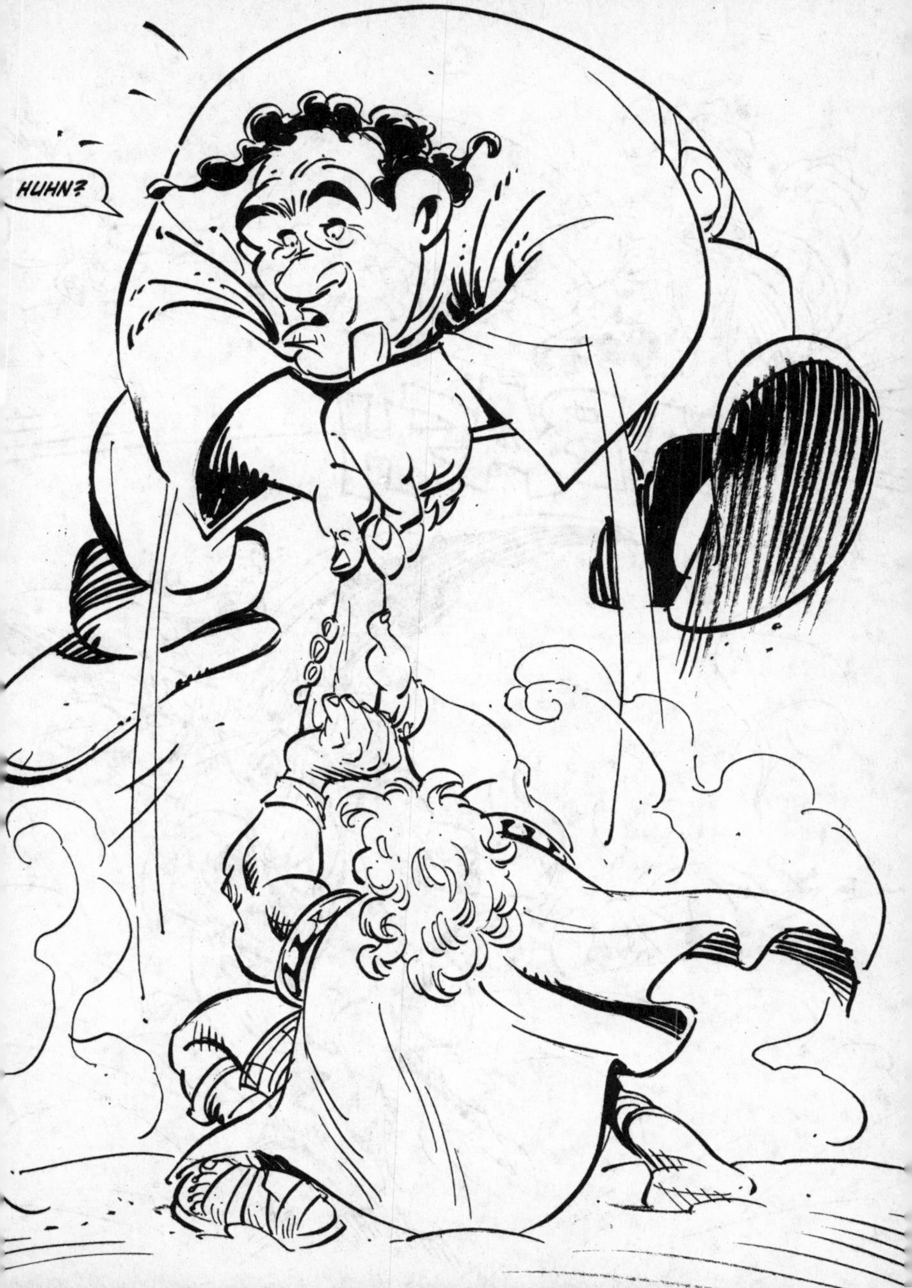
HUHN?

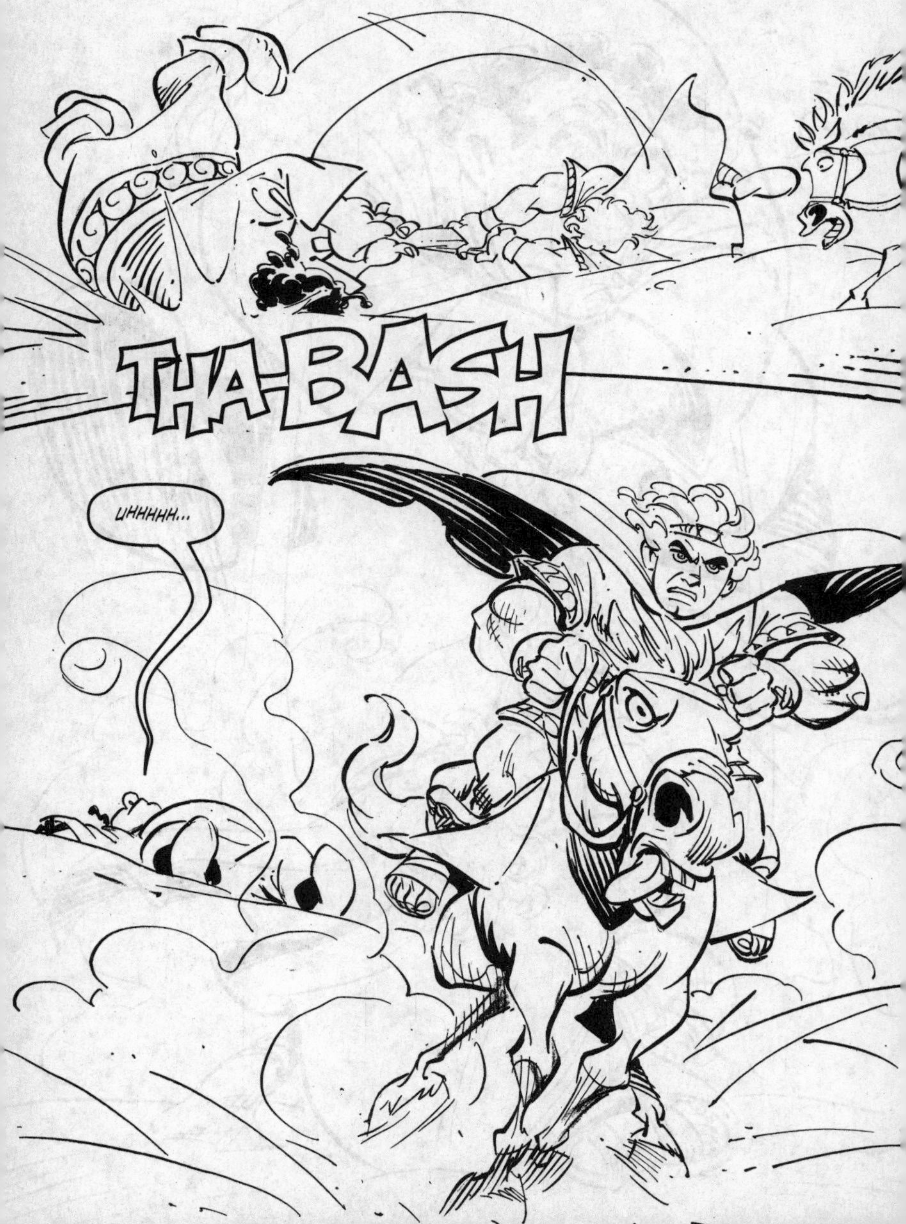
THA-BASH
UHHHHH...

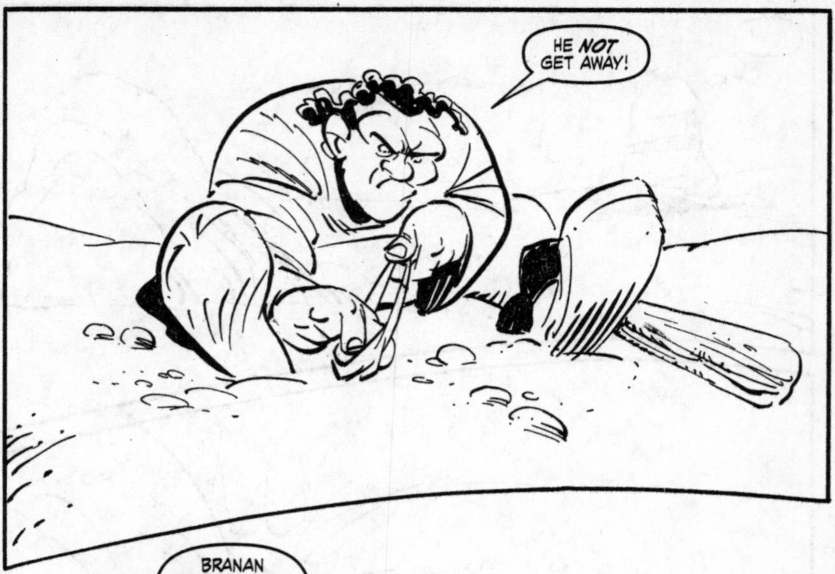
HE NOT GET AWAY!

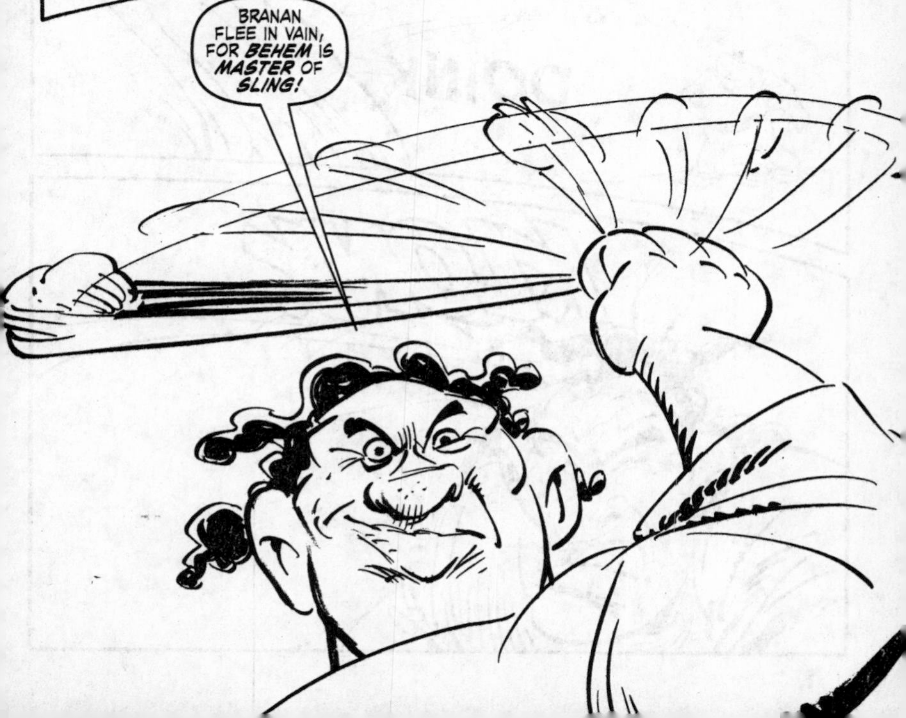
BRANAN FLEE IN VAIN, FOR BEHEM IS MASTER OF SLING!

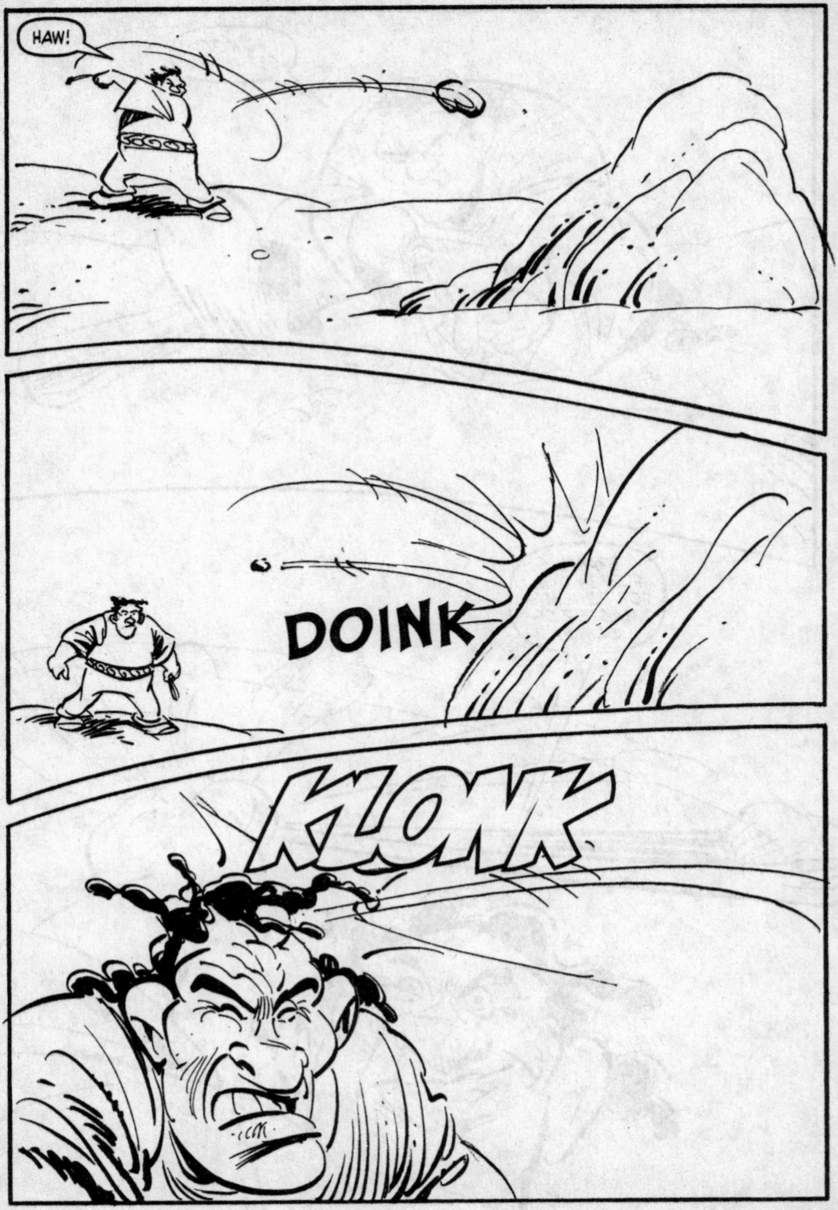
HAW!
DOINK
KLONK

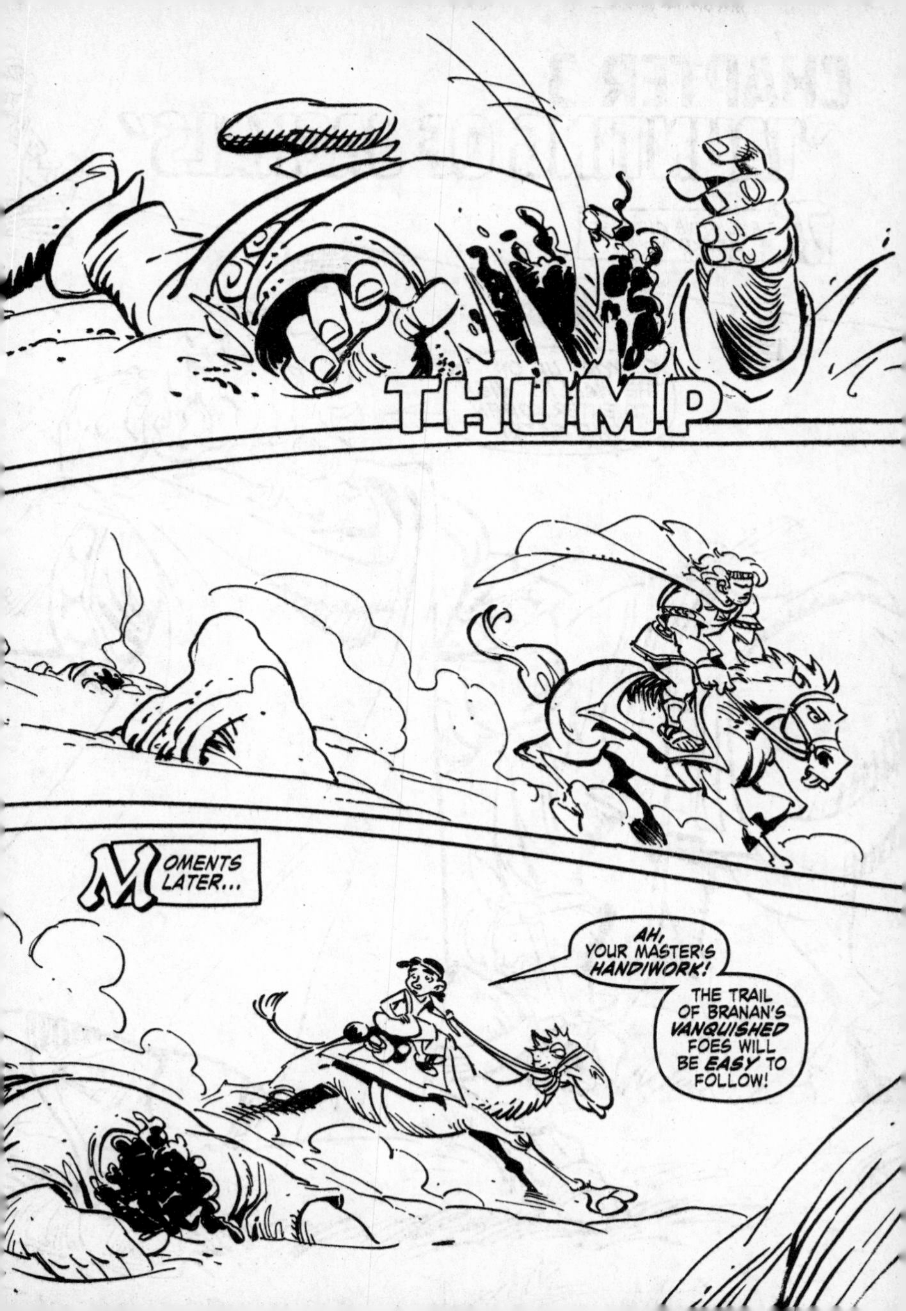
THUMP
MOMENTS LATER...
AH, YOUR MASTER'S HANDIWORK!
THE TRAIL OF BRANAN'S VANQUISHED FOES WILL BE EASY TO FOLLOW!

CHAPTER 3
"TAUNTING OF JACKALS"

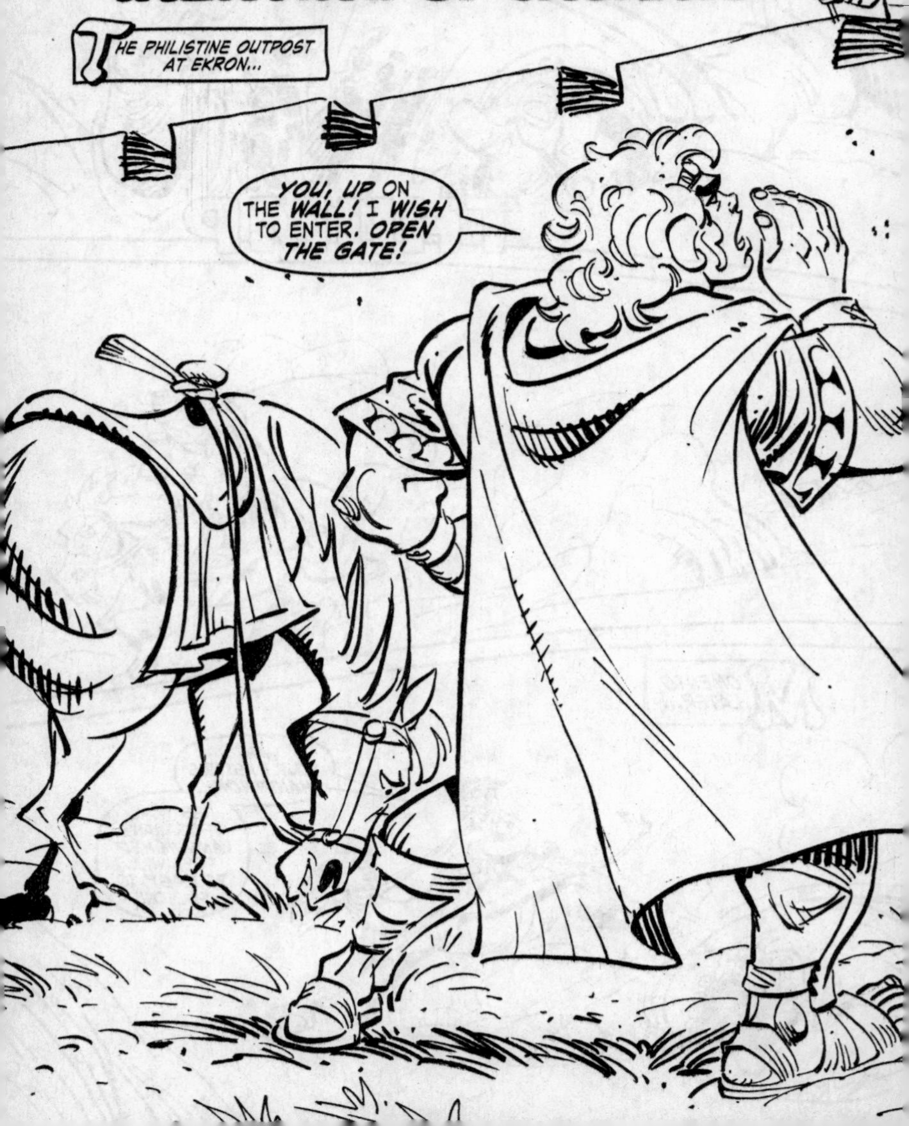
THE PHILISTINE OUTPOST AT EKRON...
YOU, UP ON THE WALL! I WISH TO ENTER. OPEN THE GATE!

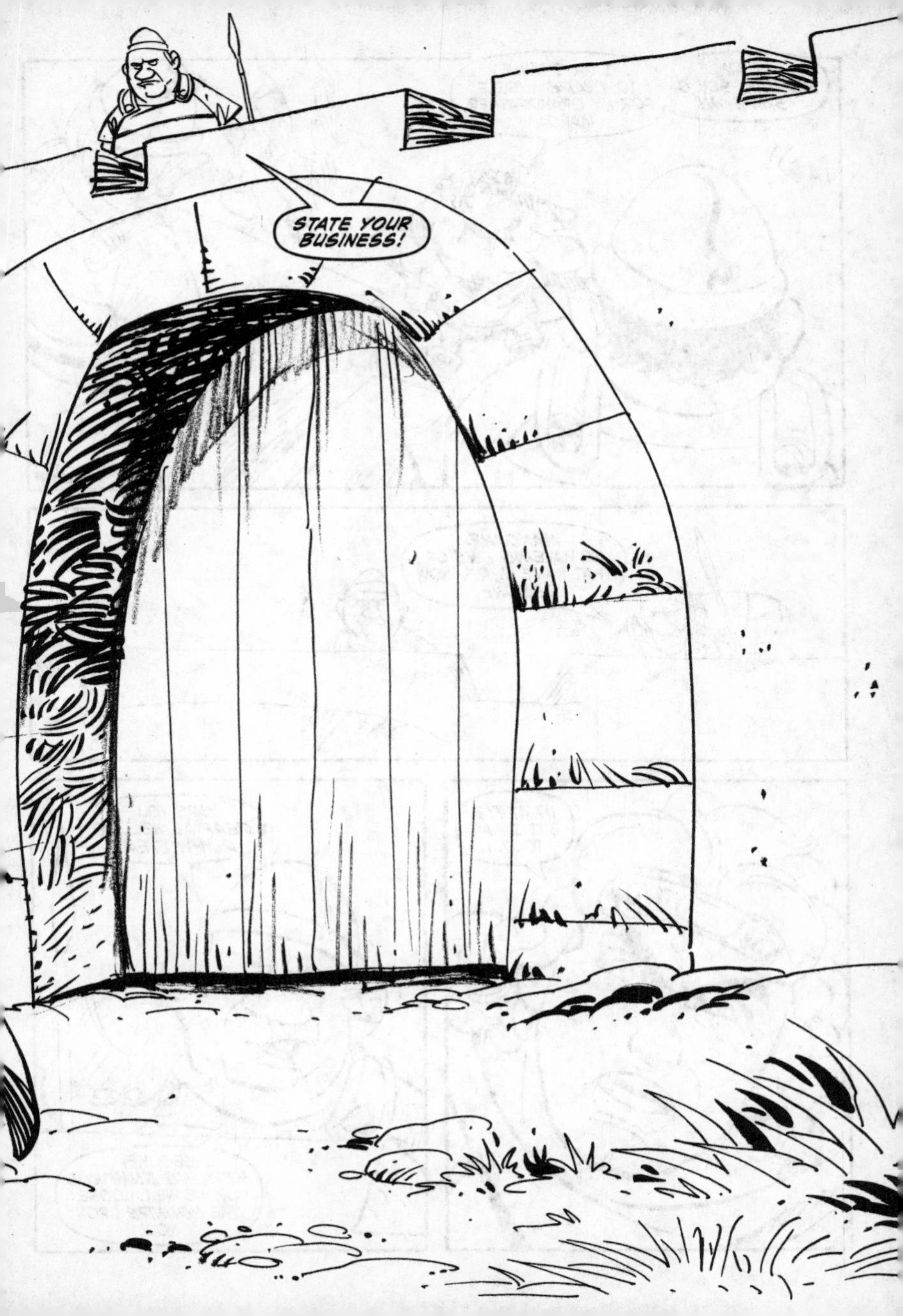
STATE YOUR BUSINESS!

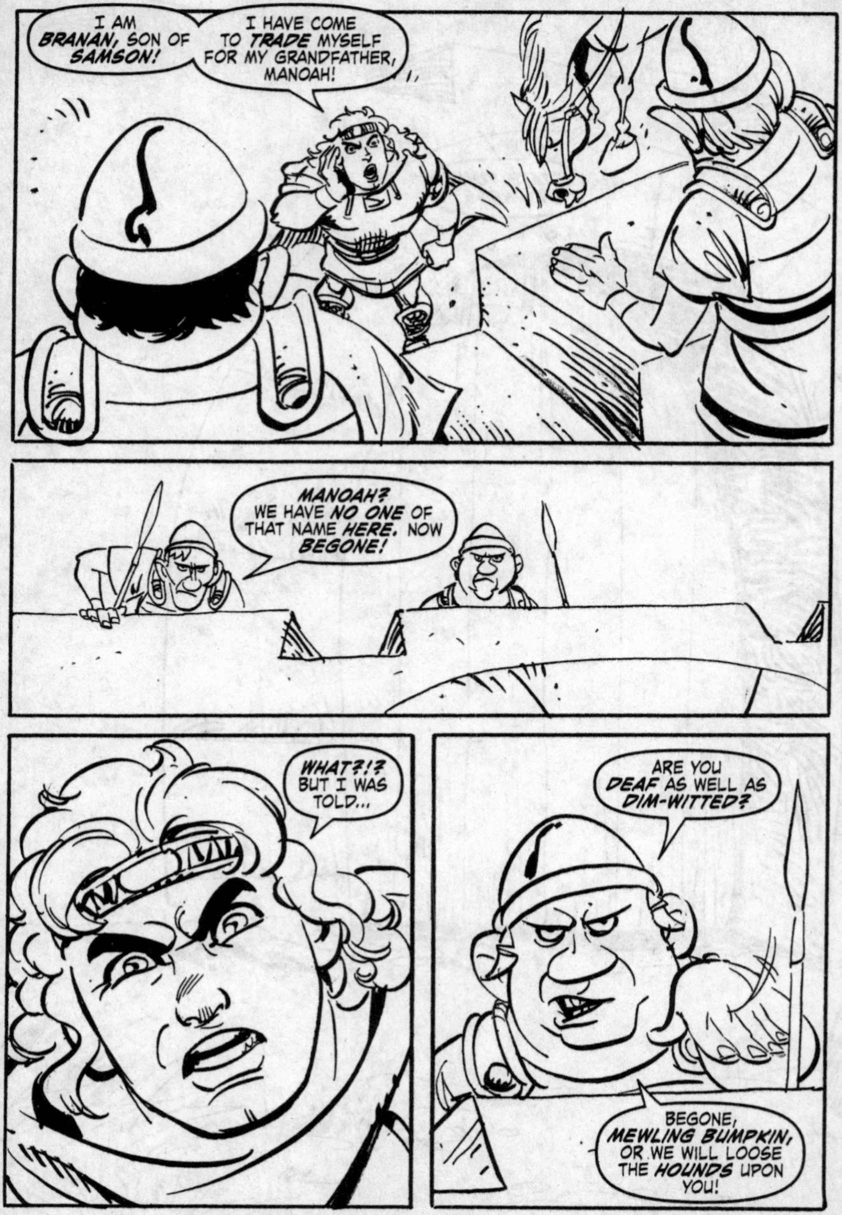
I AM BRANAN, SON OF SAMSON!
I HAVE COME TO TRADE MYSELF FOR MY GRANDFATHER, MANOAH!
MANOAH? WE HAVE NO ONE OF THAT NAME HERE. NOW BEGONE!
WHAT?!? BUT I WAS TOLD...
ARE YOU DEAF AS WELL AS DIM-WITTED?
BEGONE, MEWLING BUMPKIN, OR WE WILL LOOSE THE HOUNDS UPON YOU!

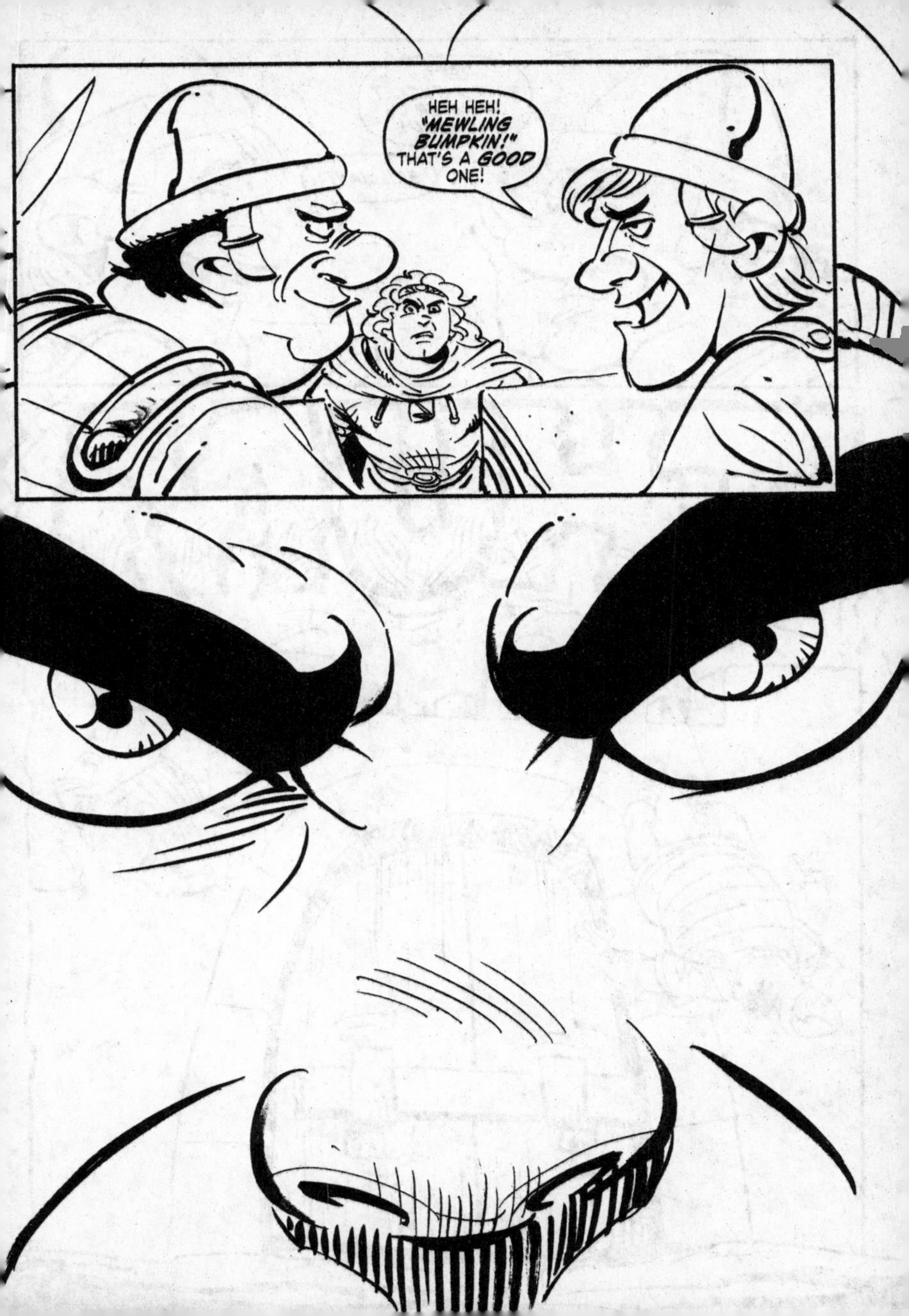
HEH HEH! "MEWLING BUMPKIN!" THAT'S A GOOD ONE!

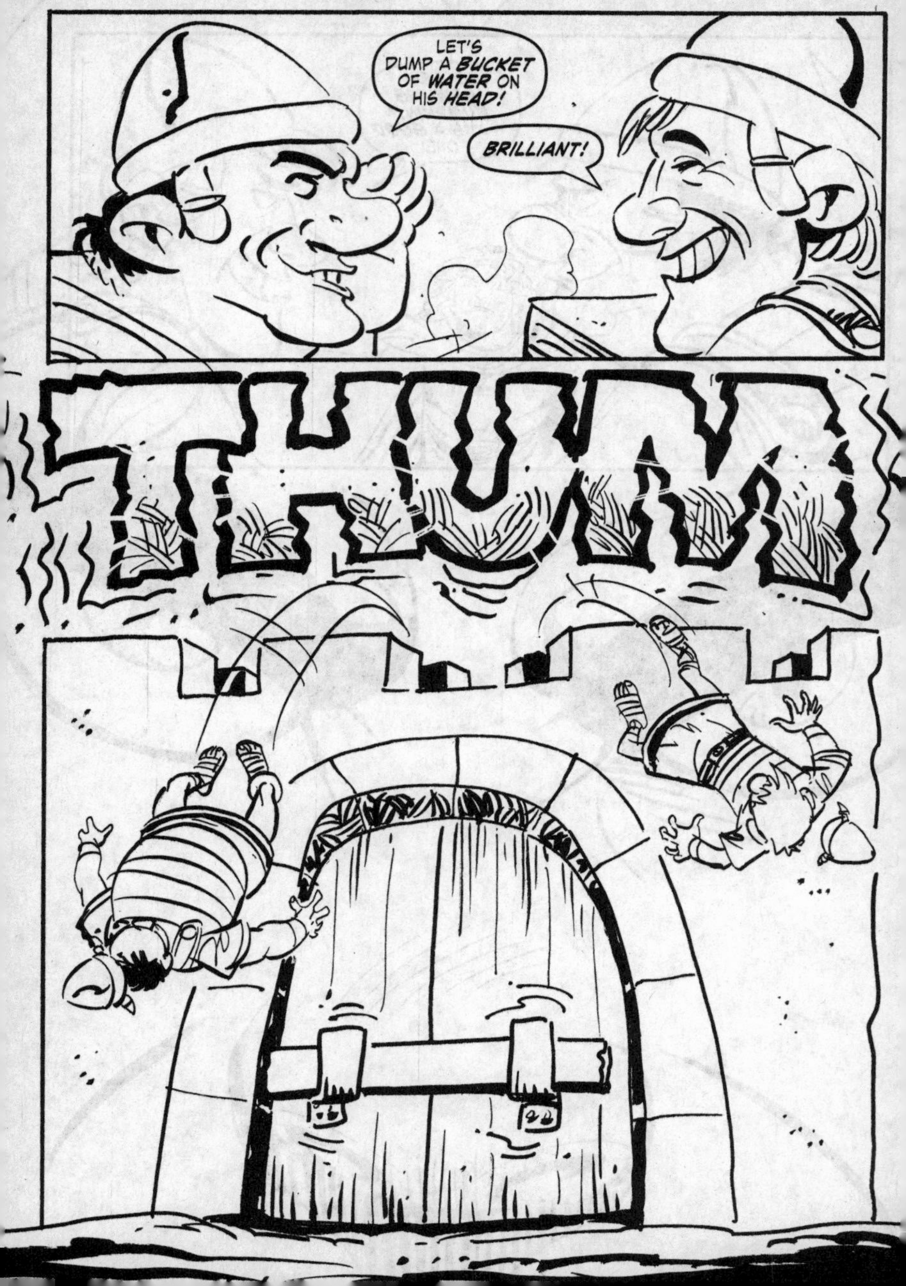

LET'S DUMP A BUCKET OF WATER ON HIS HEAD!
BRILLIANT!
THUMP

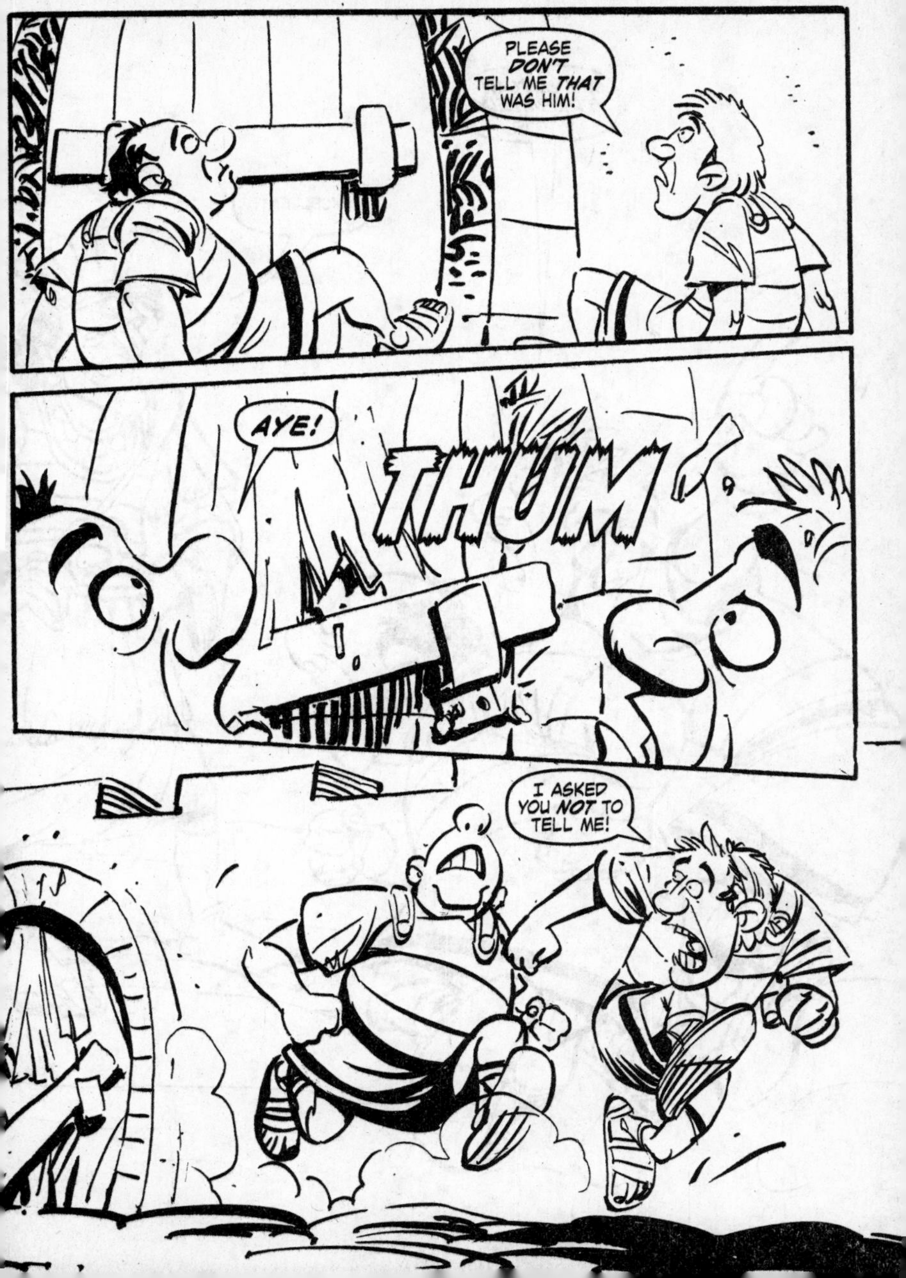
PLEASE DON'T TELL ME THAT WAS HIM!
AYE!
THUM
I ASKED YOU NOT TO TELL ME!

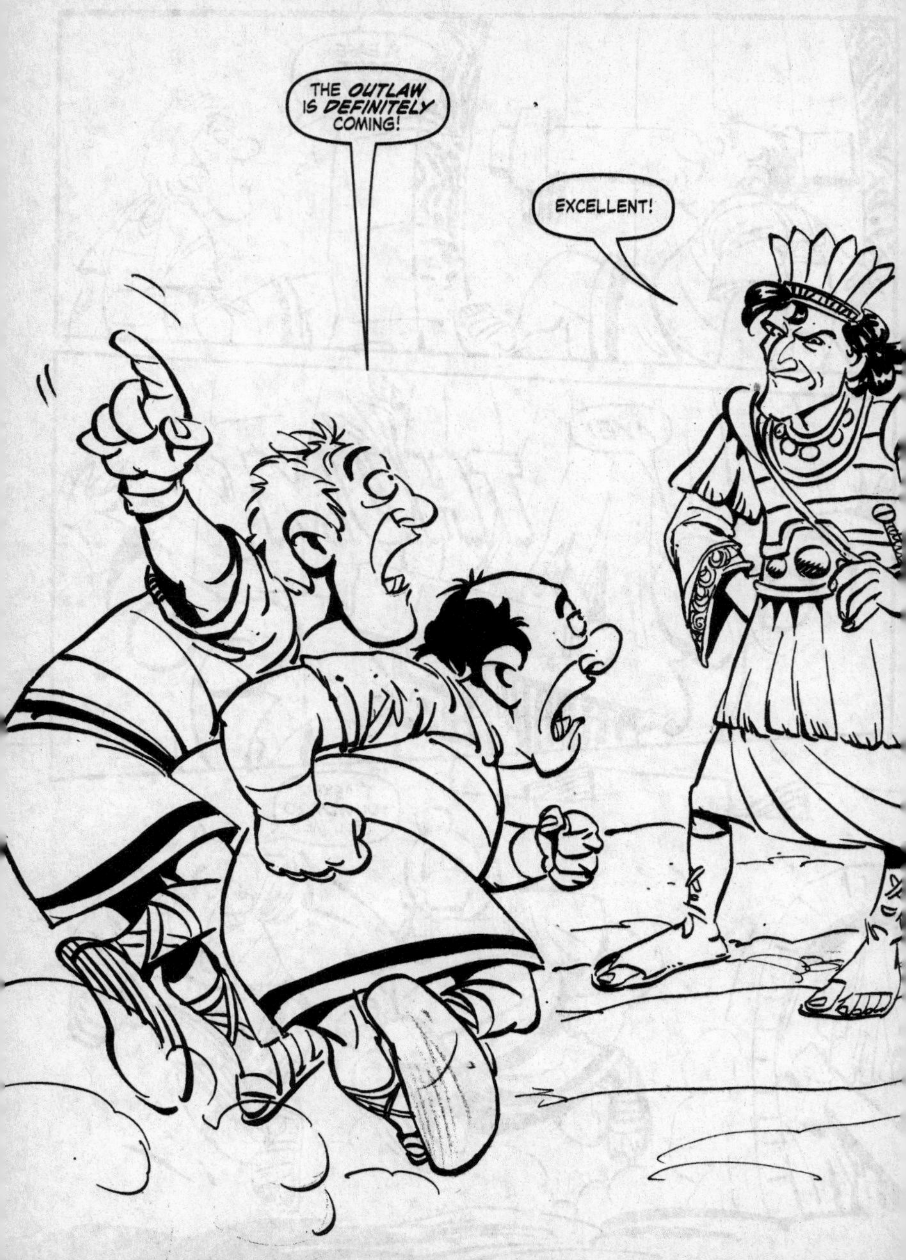
THE OUTLAW IS DEFINITELY COMING!
EXCELLENT!

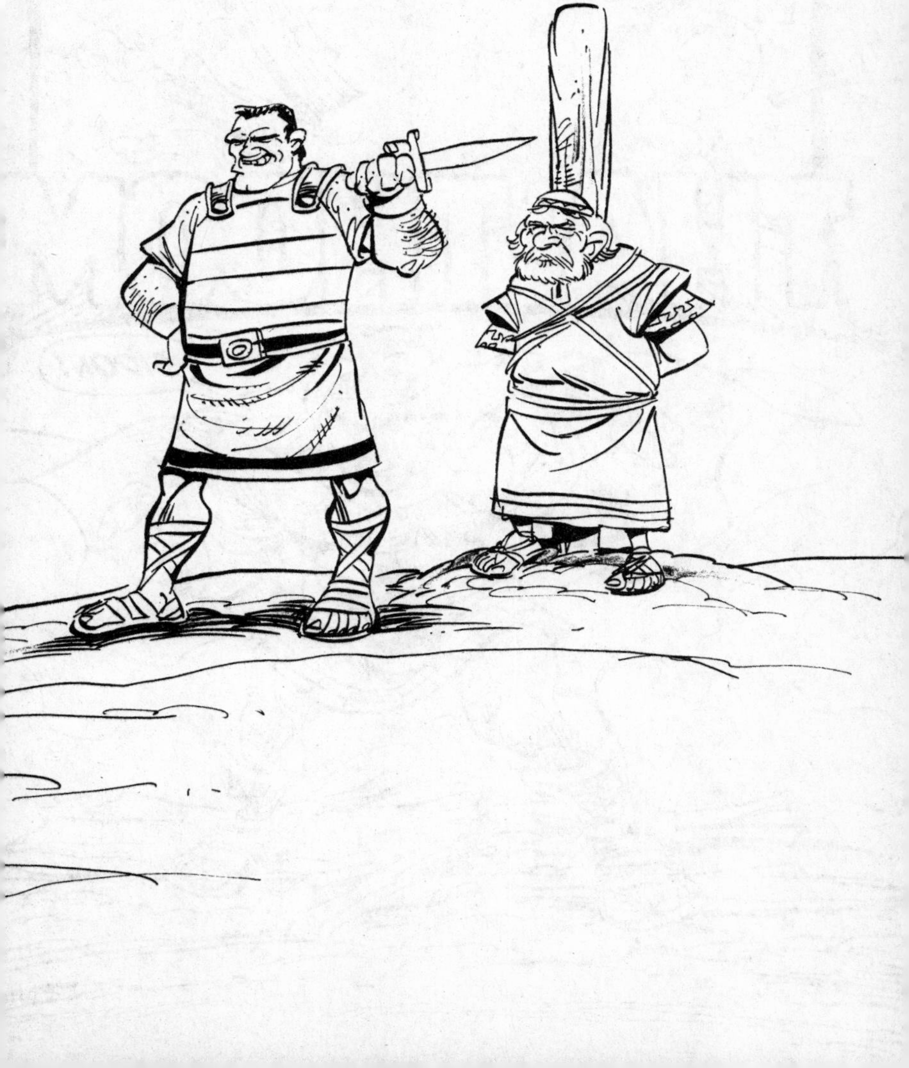

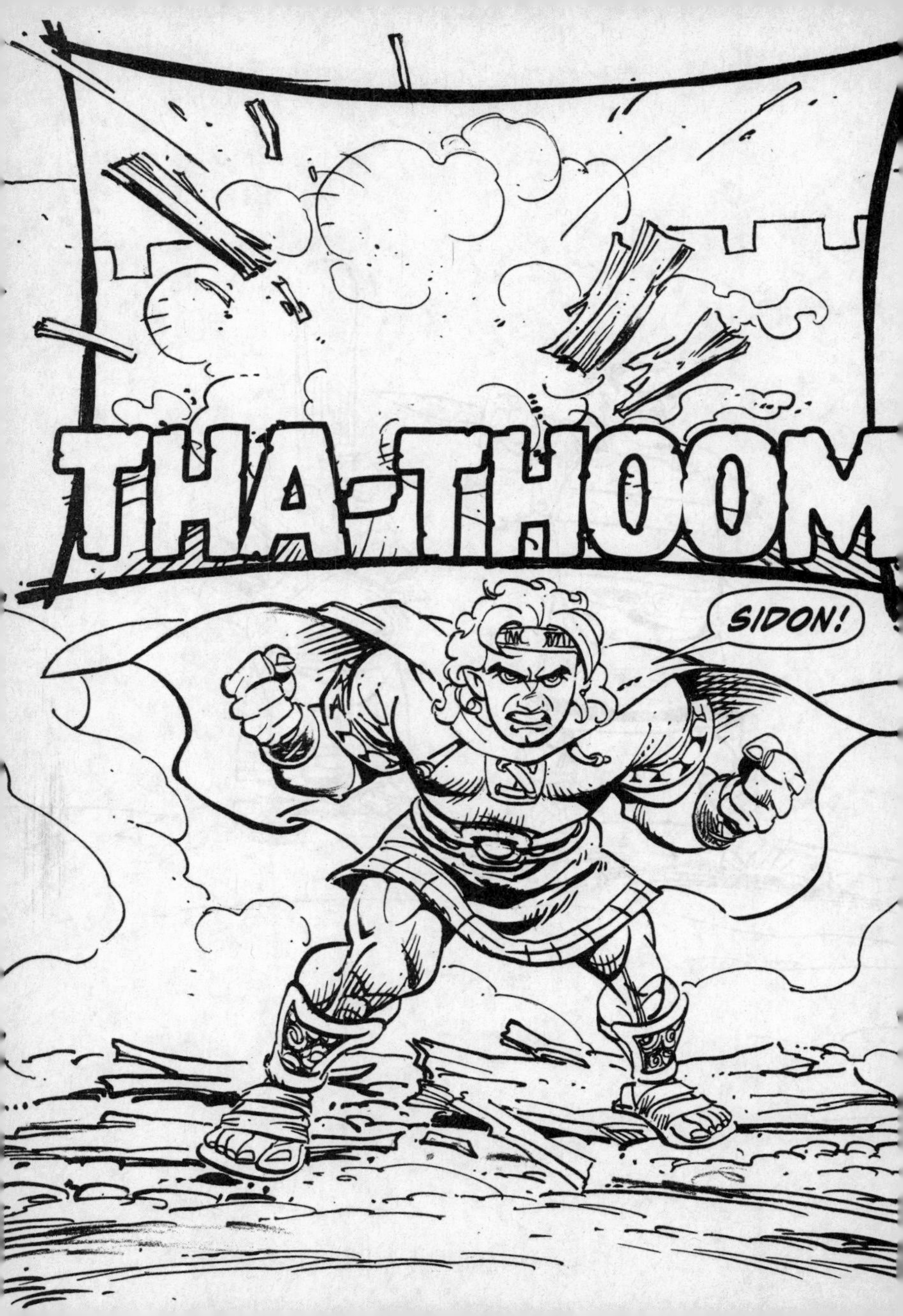
THA-THOOM
SIDON!

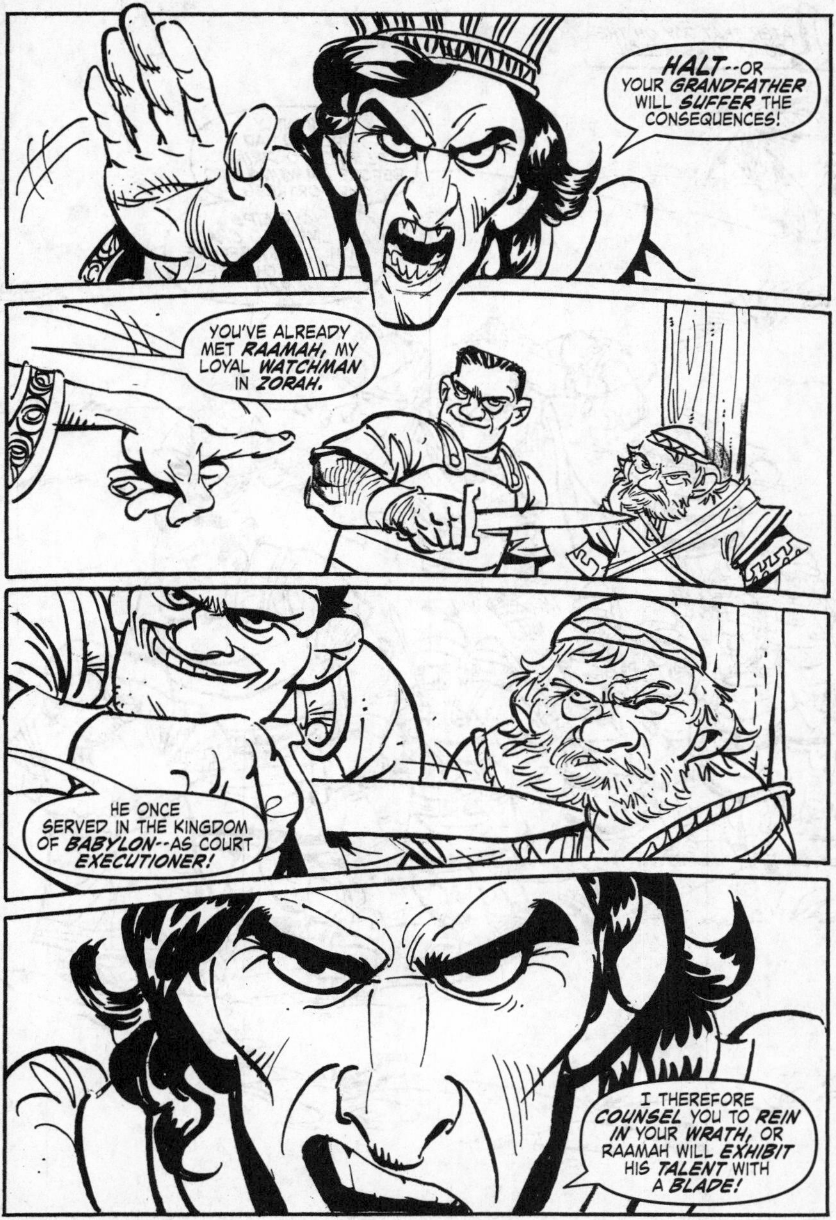
HALT--OR YOUR GRANDFATHER WILL SUFFER THE CONSEQUENCES!
YOU'VE ALREADY MET RAAMAH, MY LOYAL WATCHMAN IN ZORAH.
HE ONCE SERVED IN THE KINGDOM OF BABYLON--AS COURT EXECUTIONER!
I THEREFORE COUNSEL YOU TO REIN IN YOUR WRATH, OR RAAMAH WILL EXHIBIT HIS TALENT WITH A BLADE!

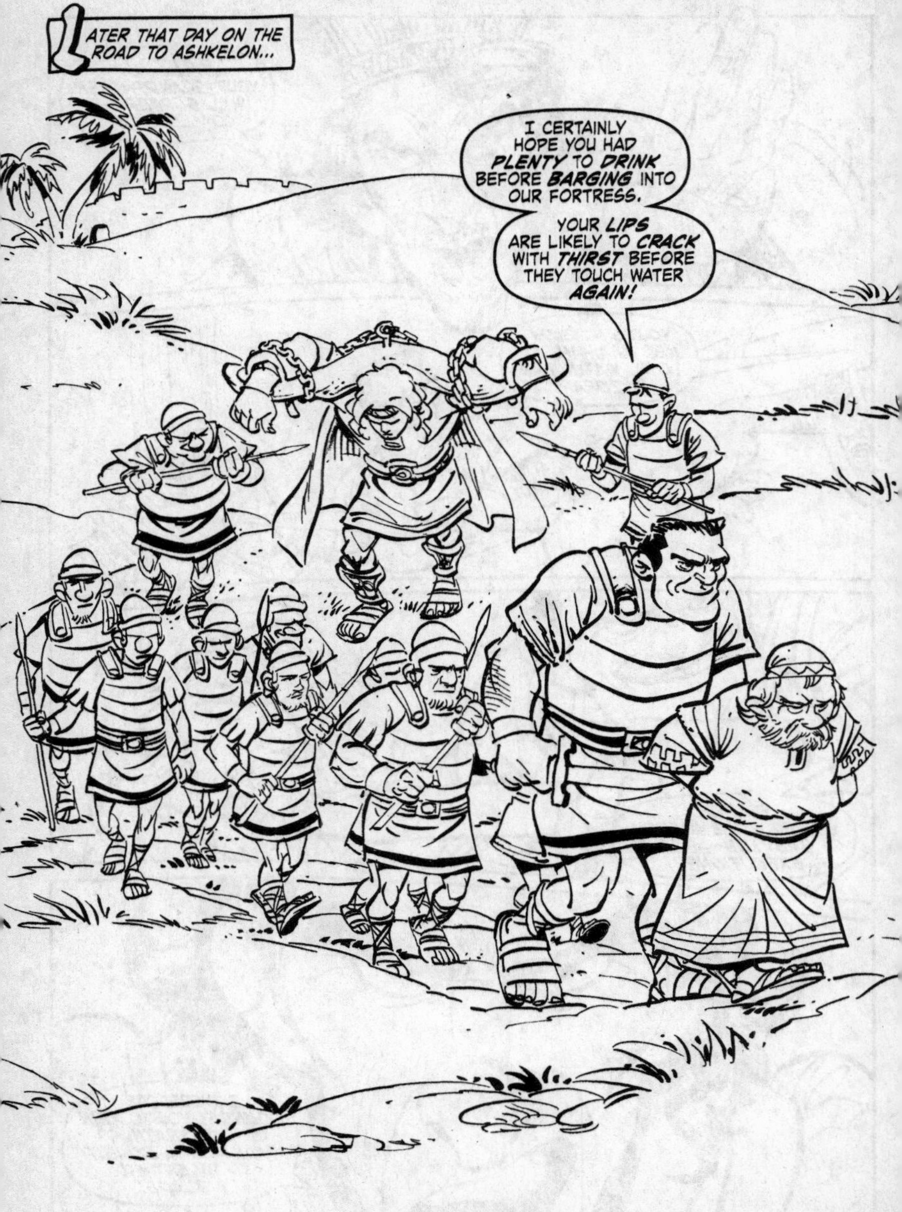
LATER THAT DAY ON THE ROAD TO ASHKELON...
I CERTAINLY HOPE YOU HAD PLENTY TO DRINK BEFORE BARGING INTO OUR FORTRESS.
YOUR LIPS ARE LIKELY TO CRACK WITH THIRST BEFORE THEY TOUCH WATER AGAIN!

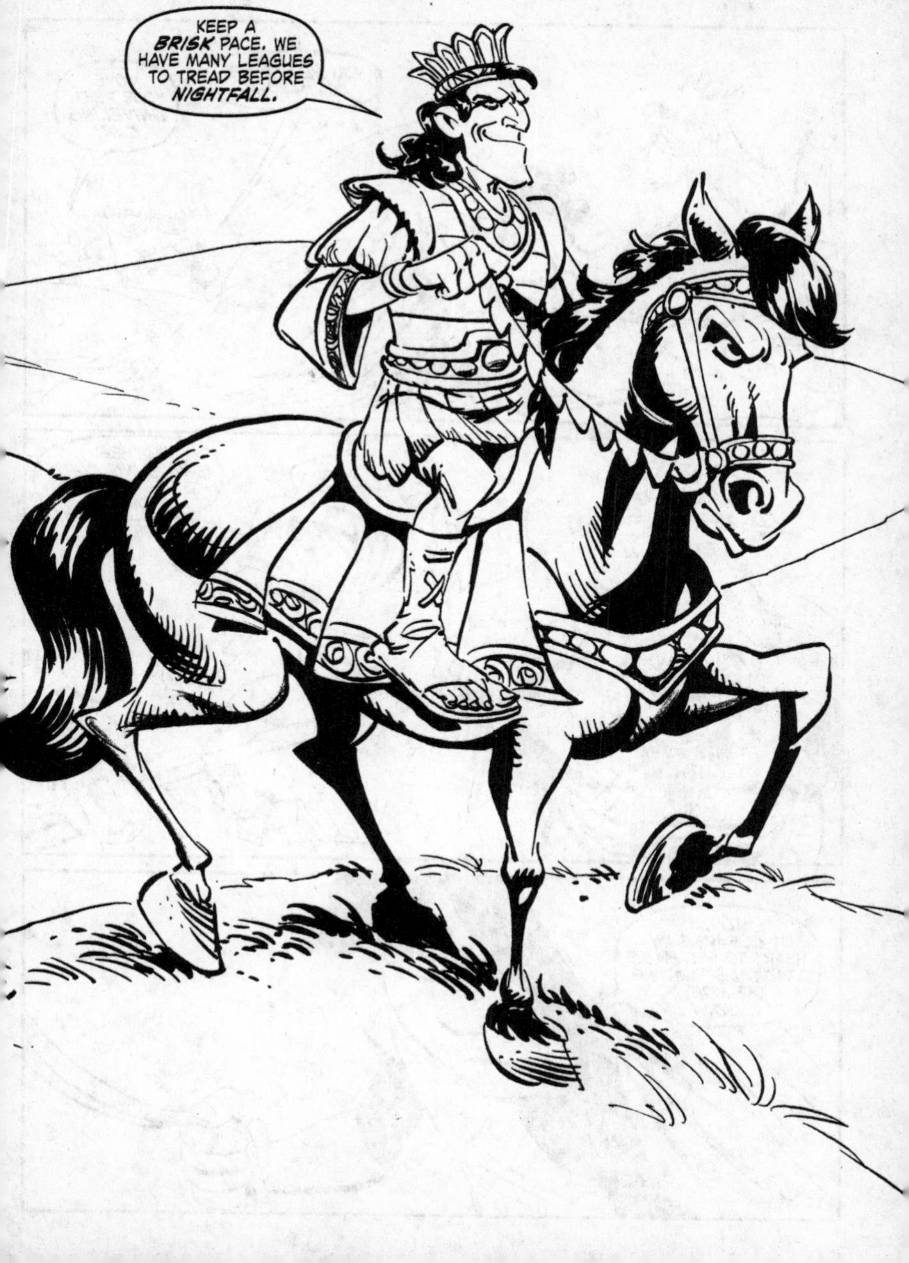
KEEP A *BRISK* PACE. WE HAVE MANY LEAGUES TO TREAD BEFORE *NIGHTFALL.*

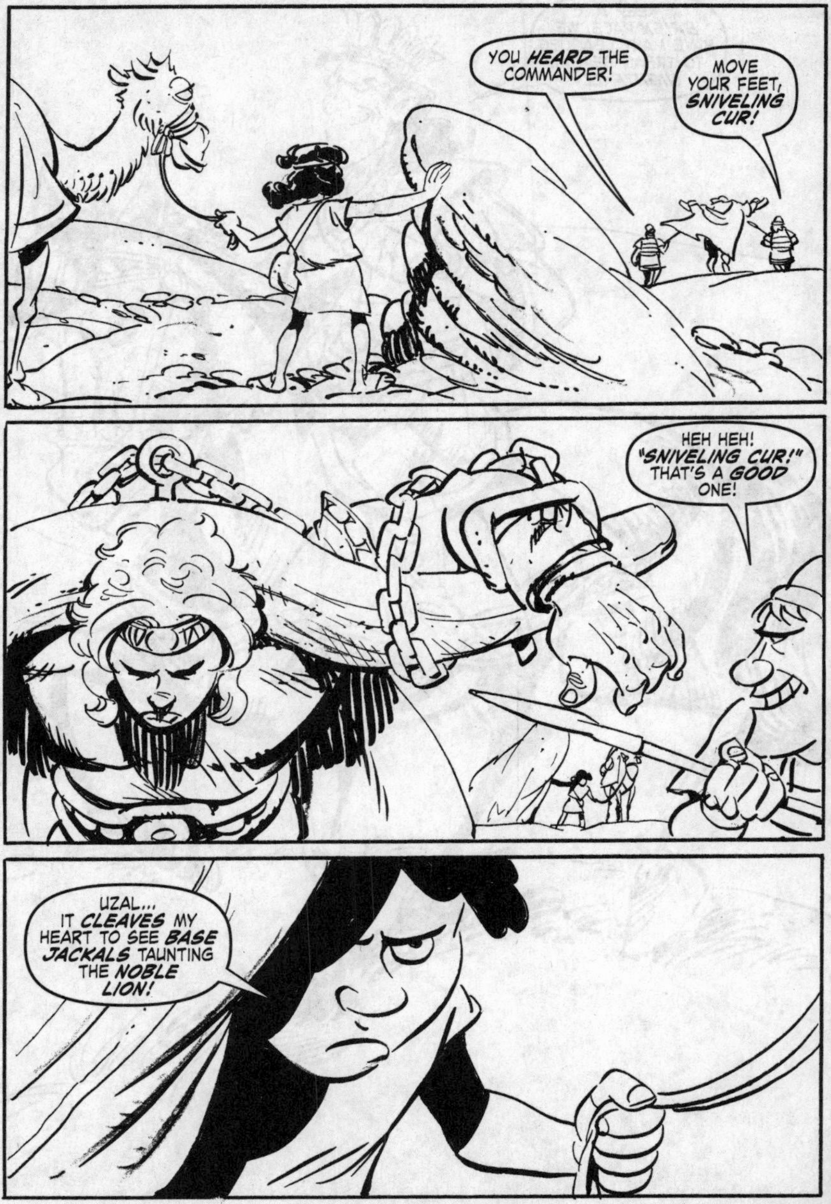
YOU HEARD THE COMMANDER!
MOVE YOUR FEET, SNIVELING CUR!
HEH HEH! "SNIVELING CUR!" THAT'S A GOOD ONE!
UZAL... IT CLEAVES MY HEART TO SEE BASE JACKALS TAUNTING THE NOBLE LION!

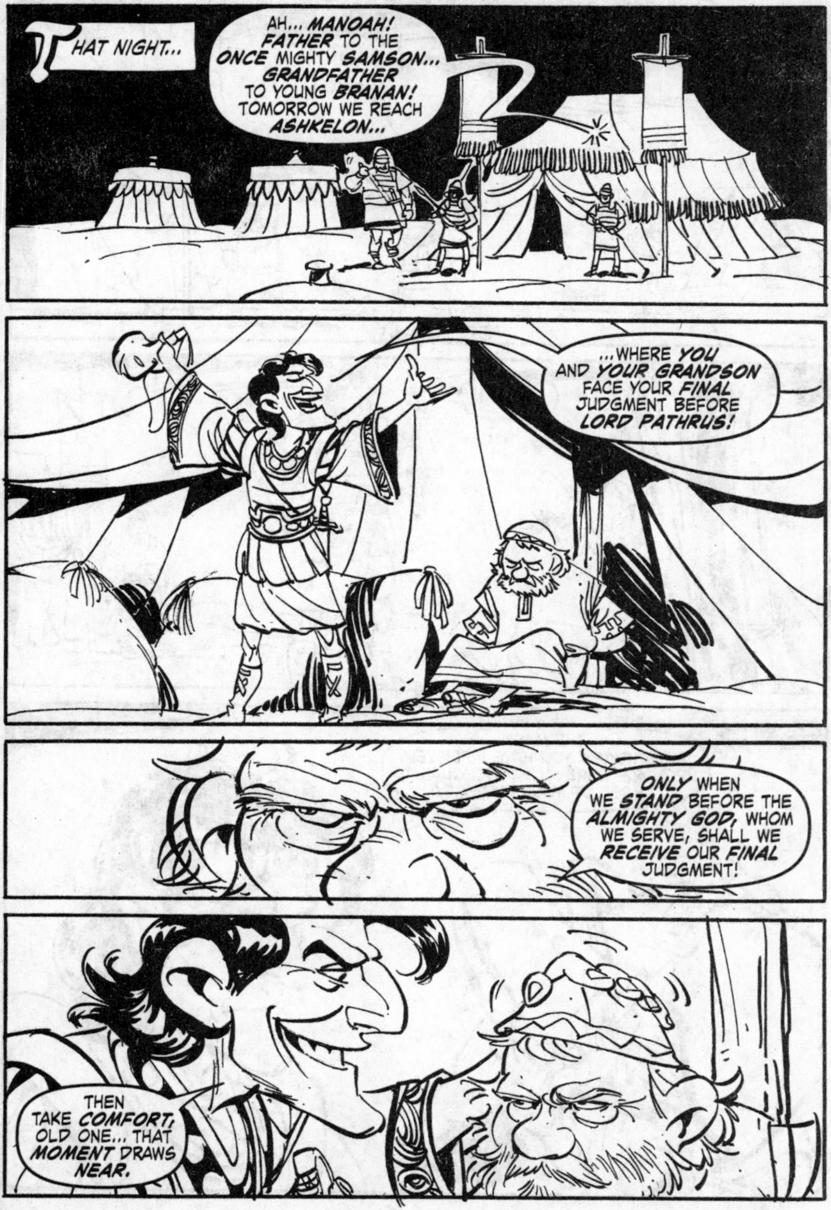
THAT NIGHT...
AH... MANOAH! FATHER TO THE ONCE MIGHTY SAMSON... GRANDFATHER TO YOUNG BRANAN! TOMORROW WE REACH ASHKELON...
...WHERE YOU AND YOUR GRANDSON FACE YOUR FINAL JUDGMENT BEFORE LORD PATHRUS!
ONLY WHEN WE STAND BEFORE THE ALMIGHTY GOD, WHOM WE SERVE, SHALL WE RECEIVE OUR FINAL JUDGMENT!
THEN TAKE COMFORT, OLD ONE... THAT MOMENT DRAWS NEAR.

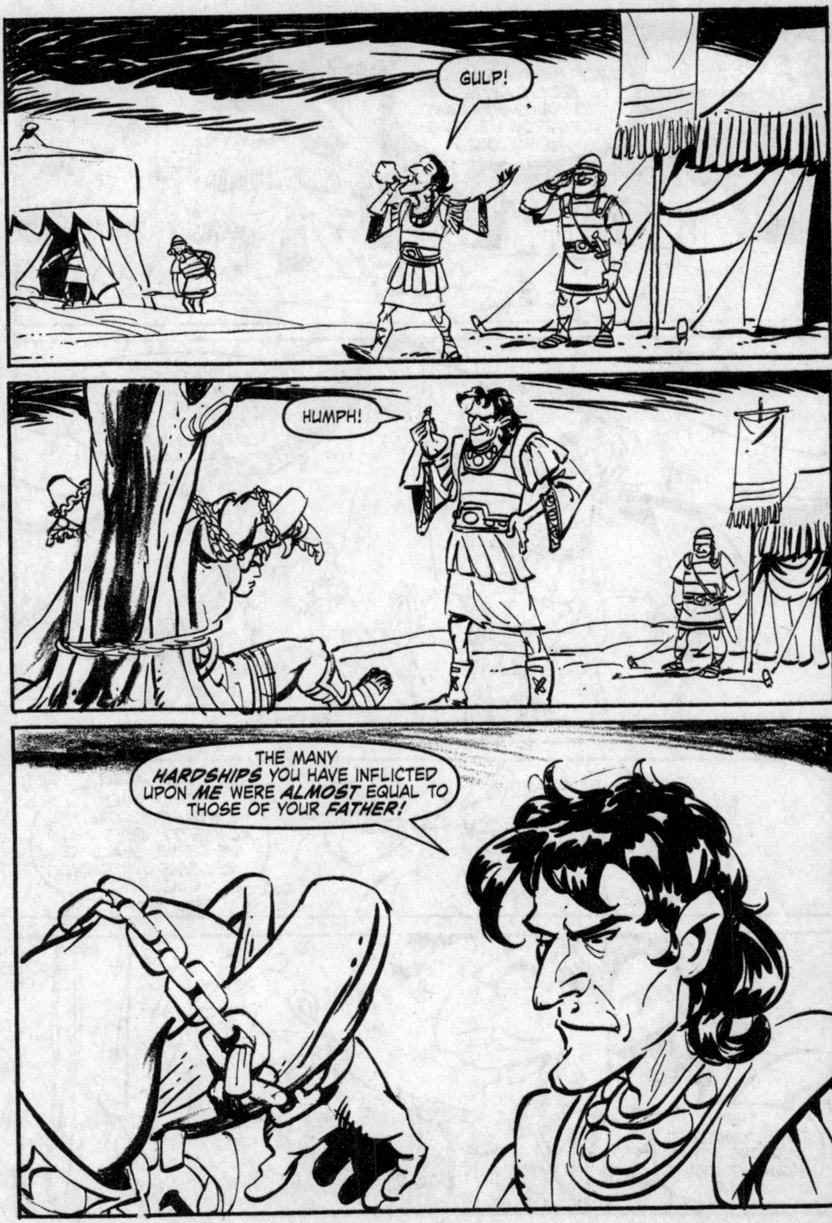
GULP!
HUMPH!
THE MANY HARDSHIPS YOU HAVE INFLICTED UPON ME WERE ALMOST EQUAL TO THOSE OF YOUR FATHER!

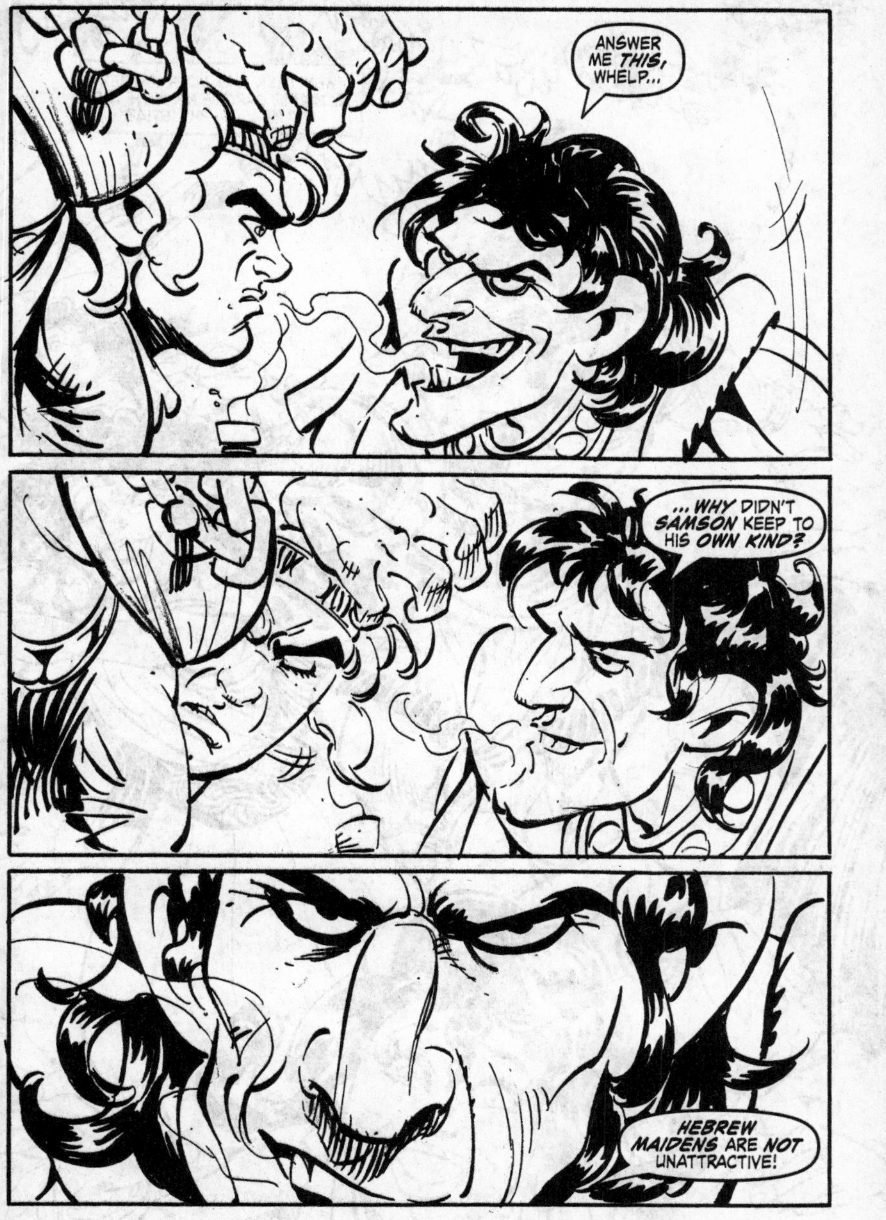
ANSWER ME *THIS*, WHELP...
...*WHY* DIDN'T *SAMSON* KEEP TO HIS *OWN KIND*?
HEBREW MAIDENS ARE *NOT* UNATTRACTIVE!

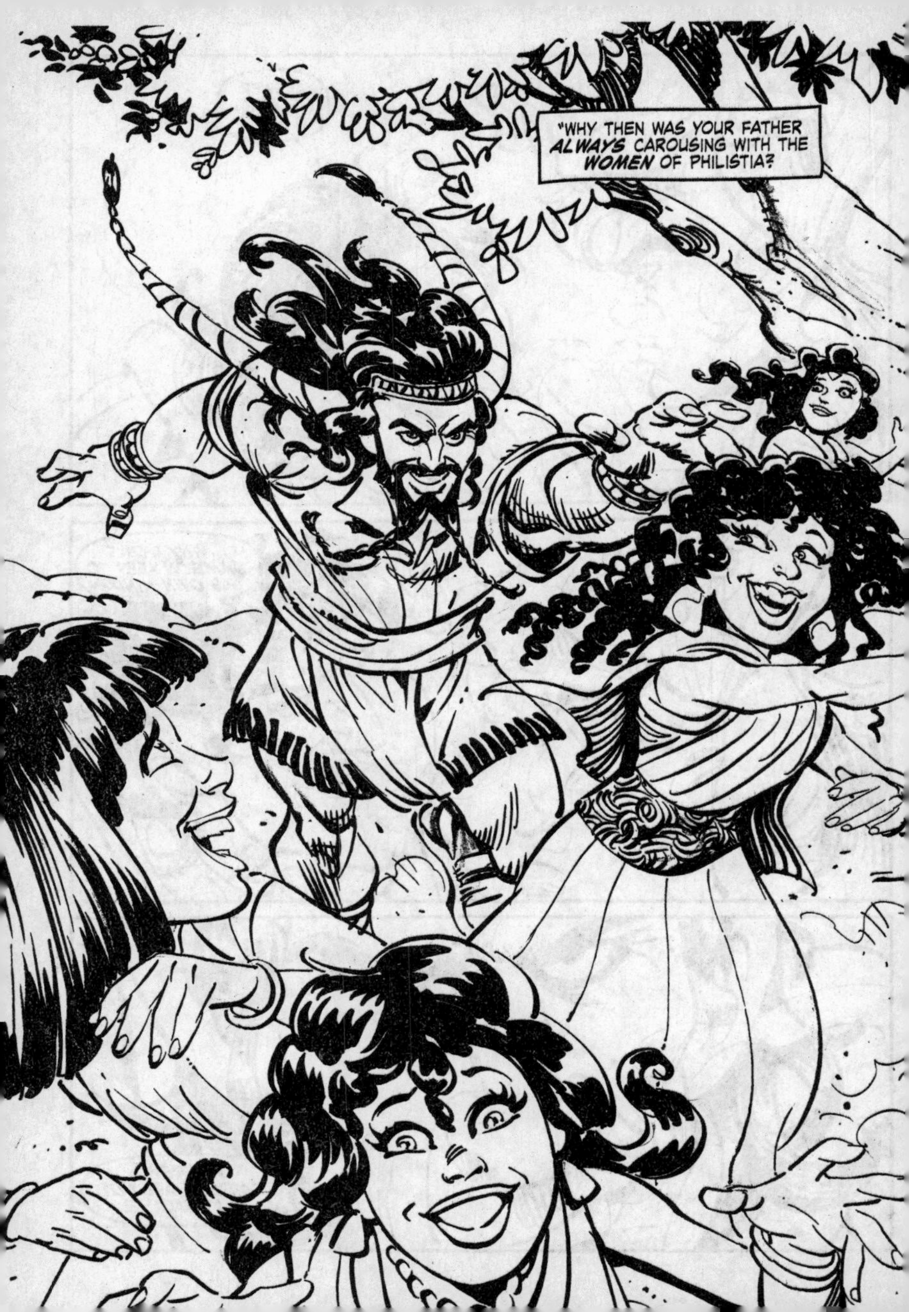
"WHY THEN WAS YOUR FATHER ALWAYS CAROUSING WITH THE WOMEN OF PHILISTIA?

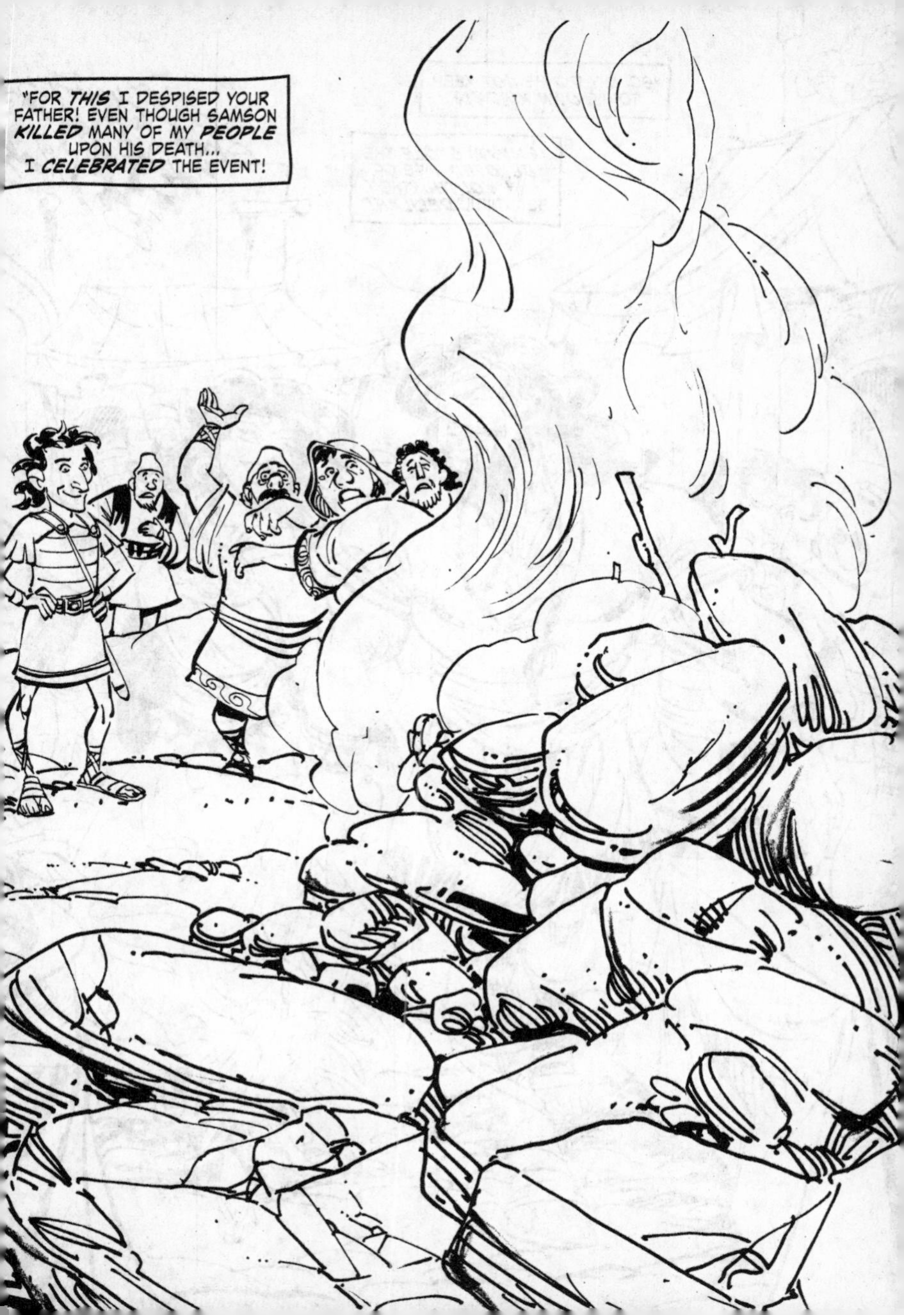
"FOR THIS I DESPISED YOUR FATHER! EVEN THOUGH SAMSON KILLED MANY OF MY PEOPLE UPON HIS DEATH... I CELEBRATED THE EVENT!

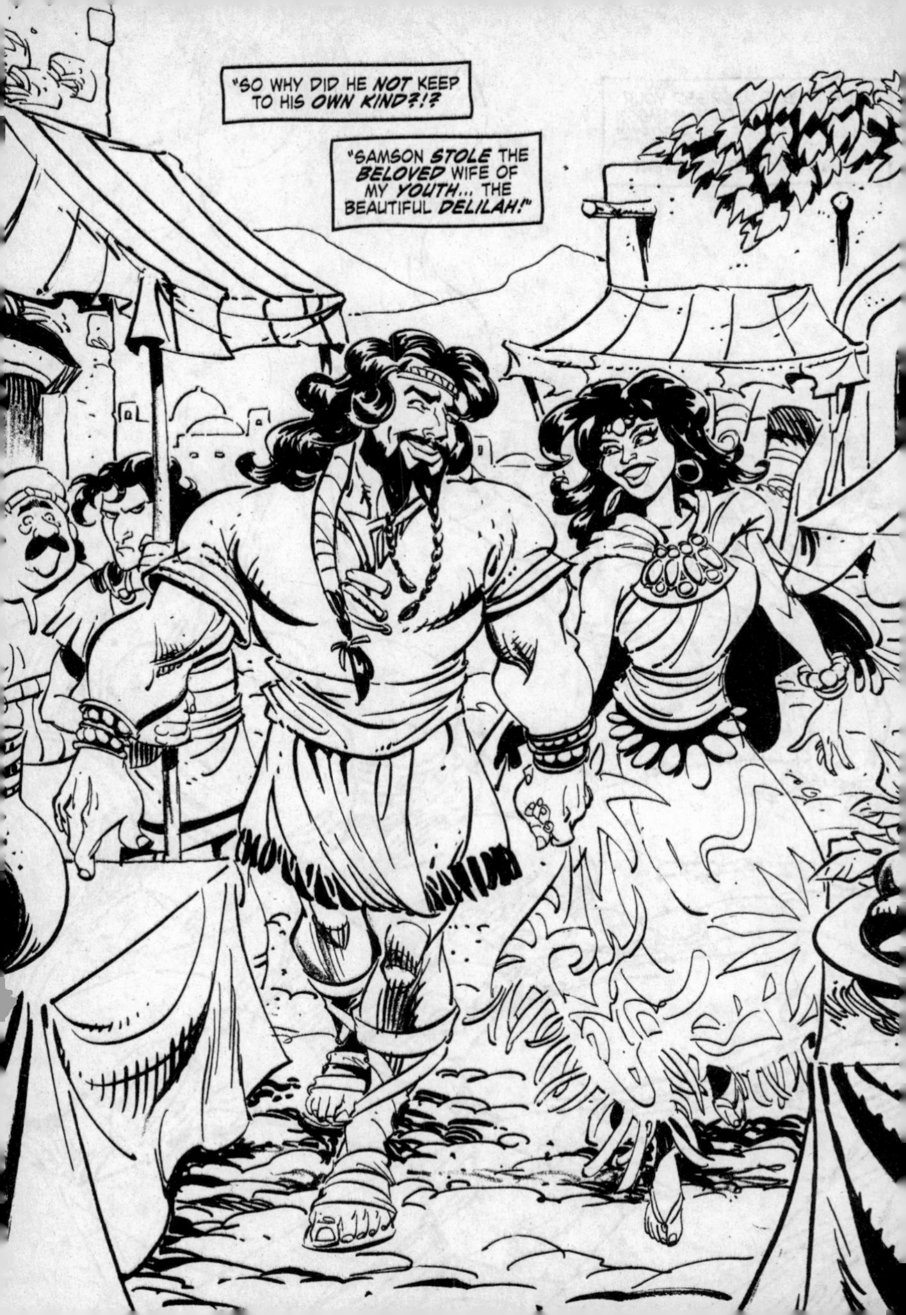
"SO WHY DID HE NOT KEEP TO HIS OWN KIND?!?
"SAMSON STOLE THE BELOVED WIFE OF MY YOUTH... THE BEAUTIFUL DELILAH!"

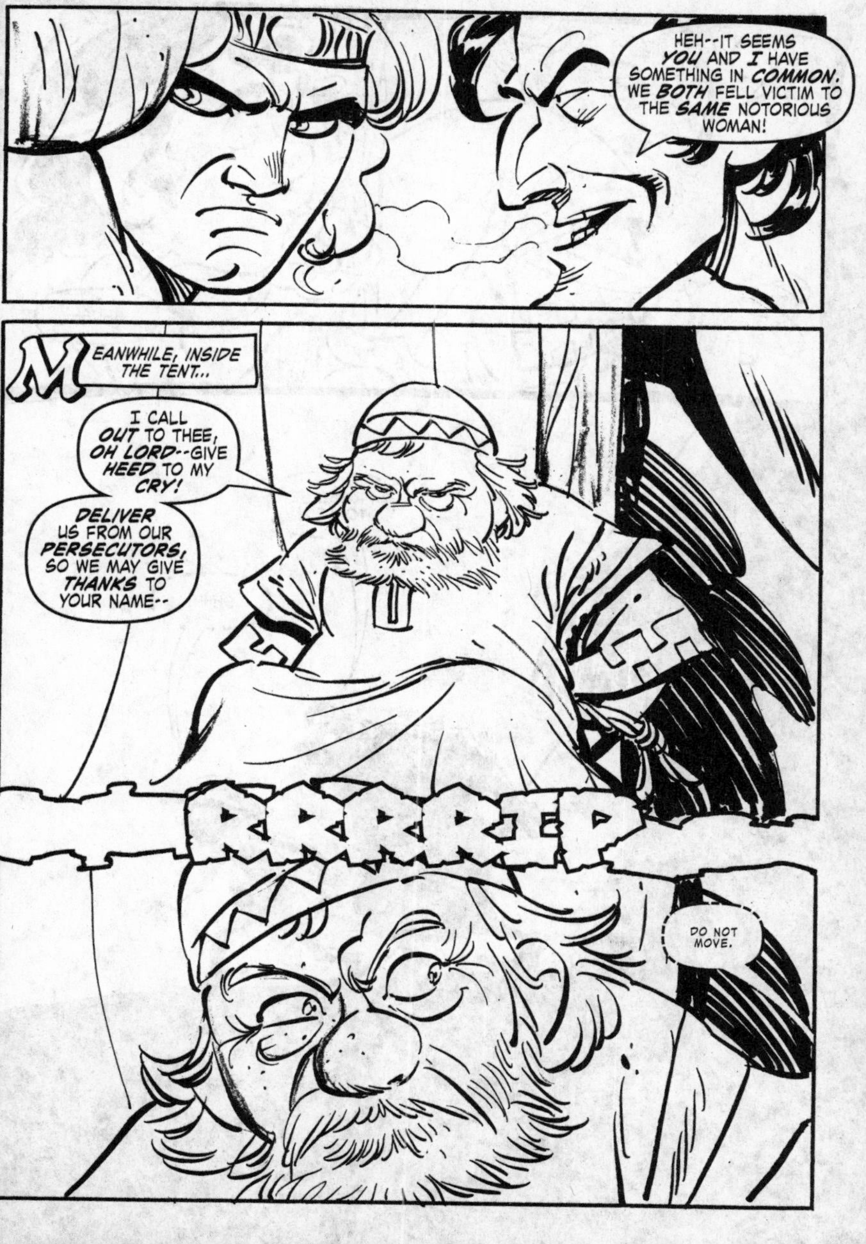
HEH--IT SEEMS YOU AND I HAVE SOMETHING IN COMMON. WE BOTH FELL VICTIM TO THE SAME NOTORIOUS WOMAN!
MEANWHILE, INSIDE THE TENT...
I CALL OUT TO THEE, OH LORD--GIVE HEED TO MY CRY!
DELIVER US FROM OUR PERSECUTORS, SO WE MAY GIVE THANKS TO YOUR NAME--
RRRRIP
DO NOT MOVE.

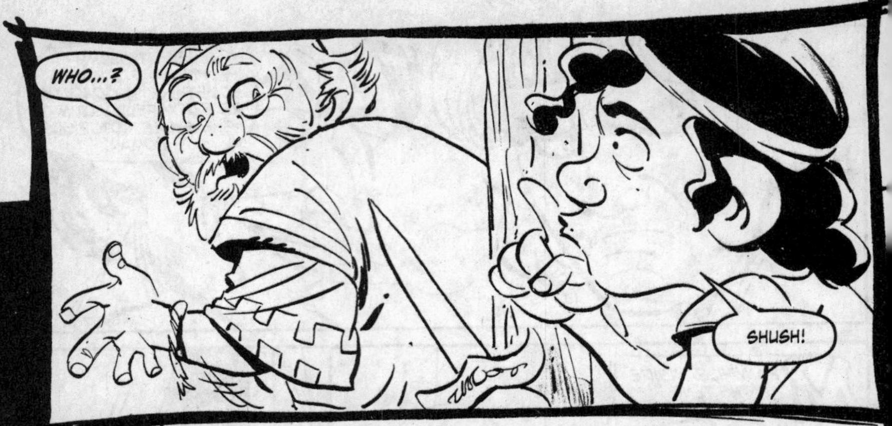
WHO...?
SHUSH!

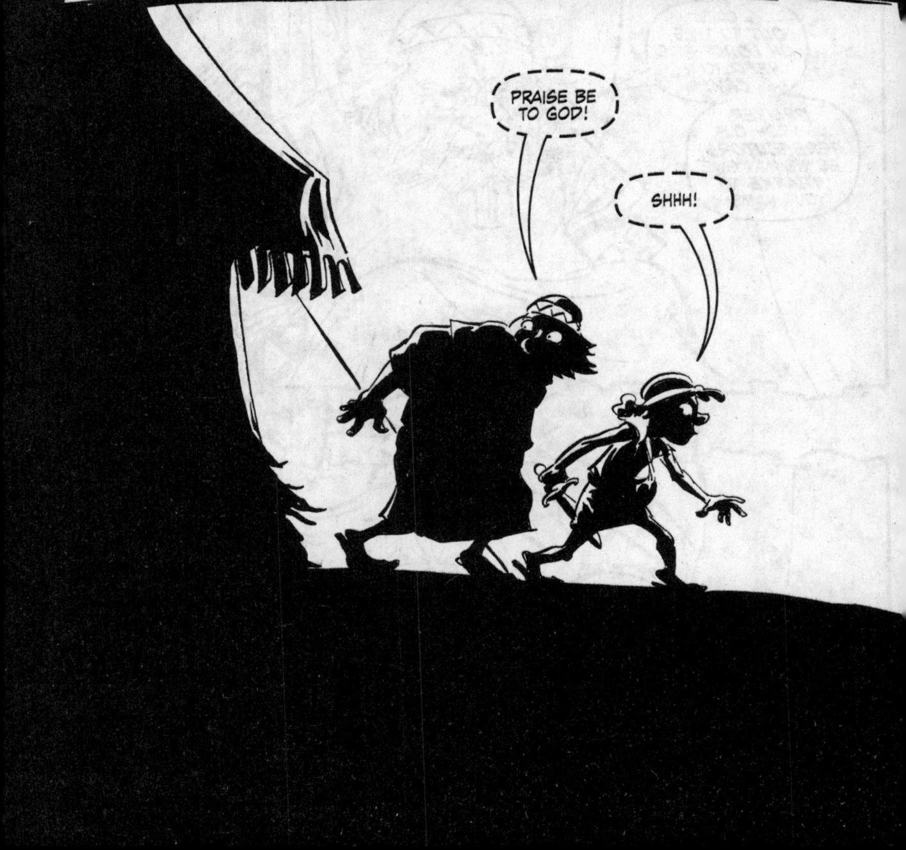
PRAISE BE TO GOD!
SHHH!

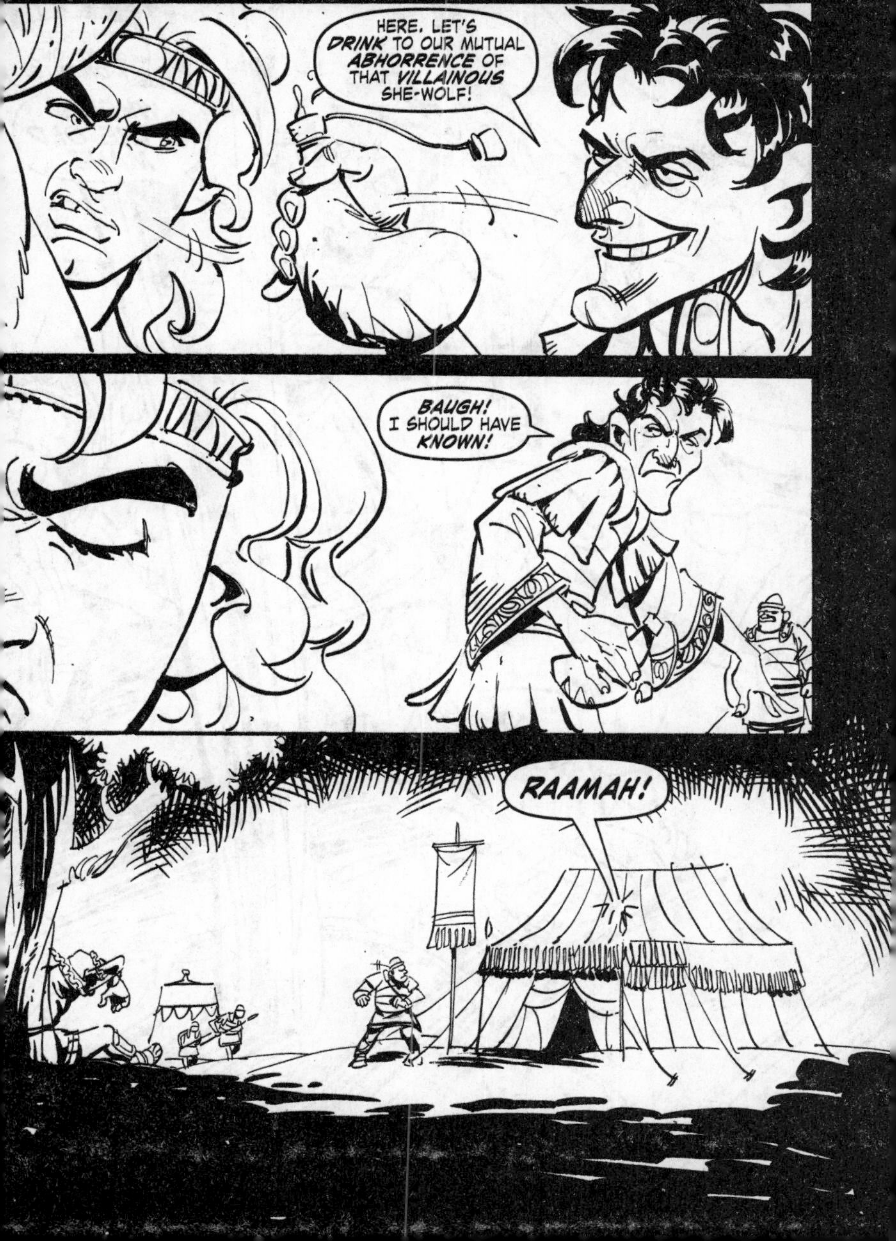
HERE. LET'S DRINK TO OUR MUTUAL ABHORRENCE OF THAT VILLAINOUS SHE-WOLF!
BAUGH! I SHOULD HAVE KNOWN!
RAAMAH!

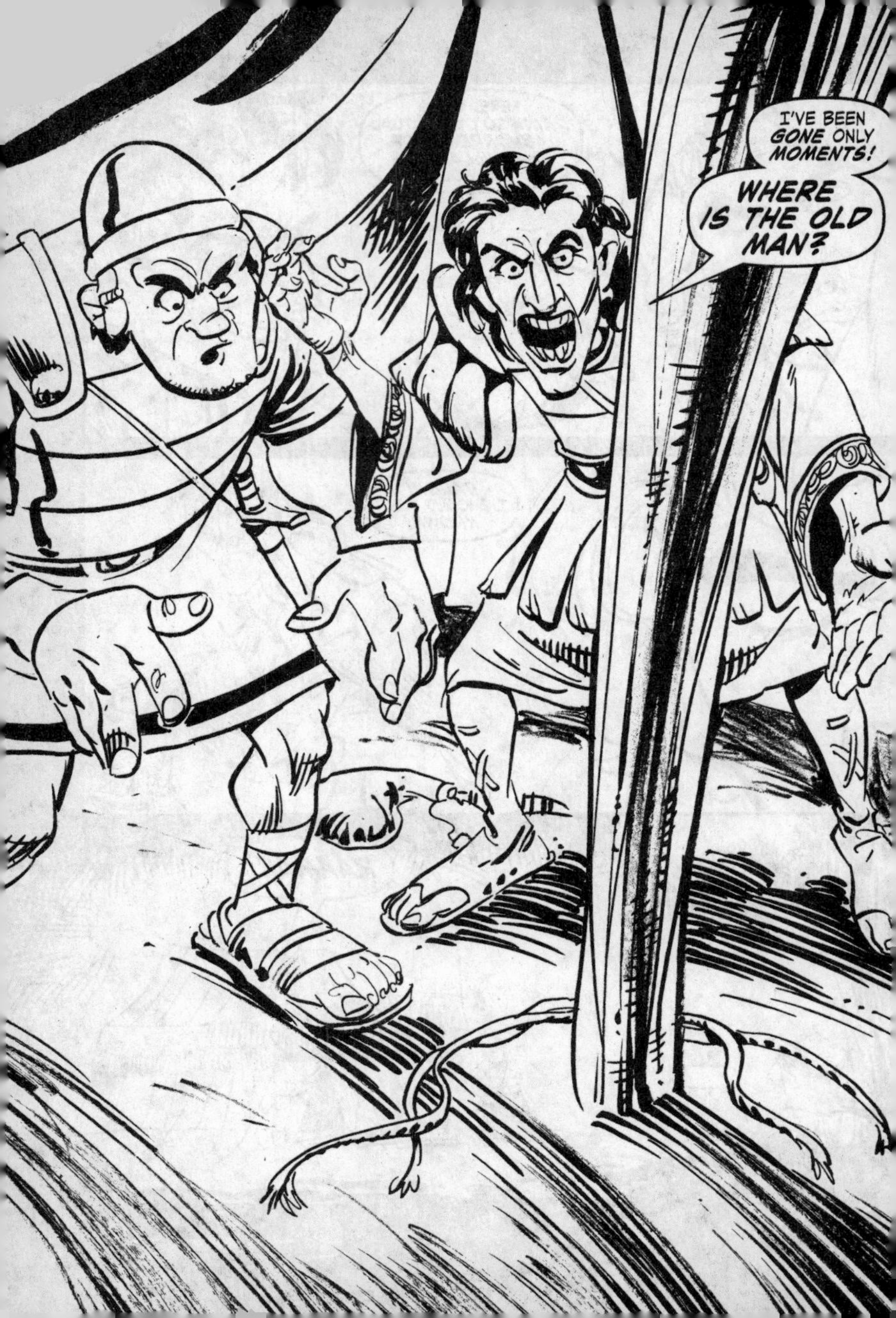
I'VE BEEN GONE ONLY MOMENTS!
WHERE IS THE OLD MAN?

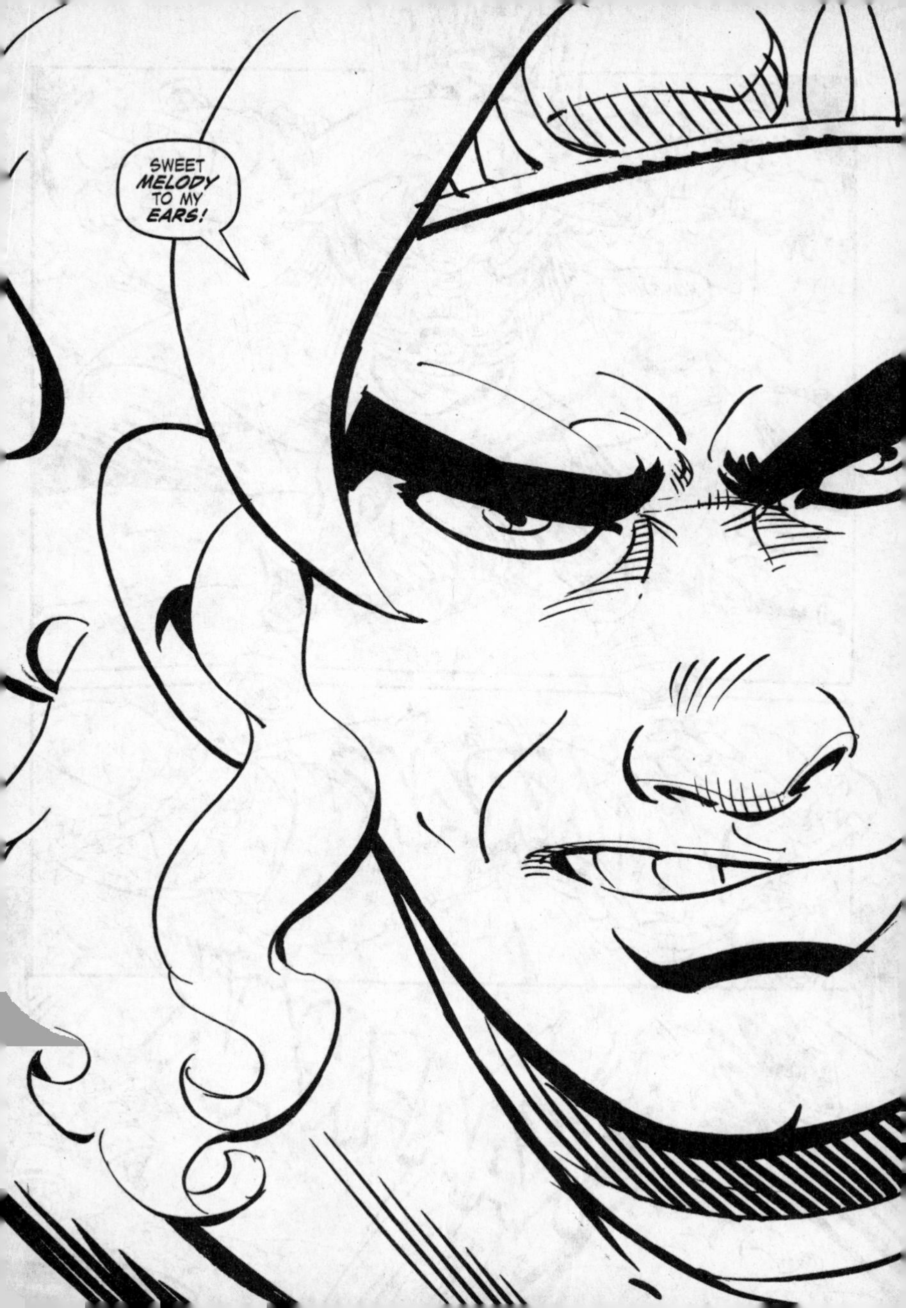
SWEET MELODY TO MY EARS!

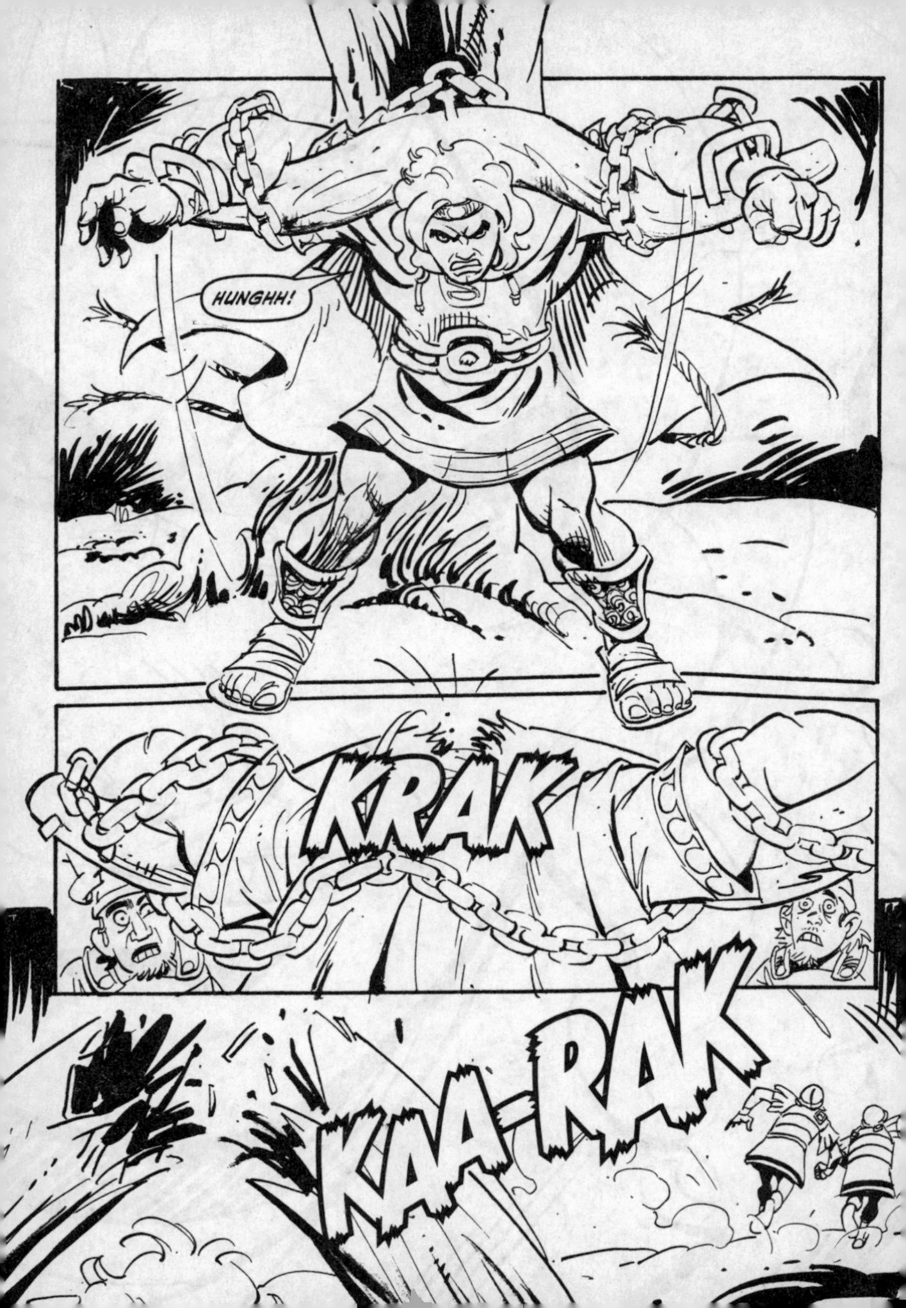
HUNGHH!
KRAK
KAA-RAK

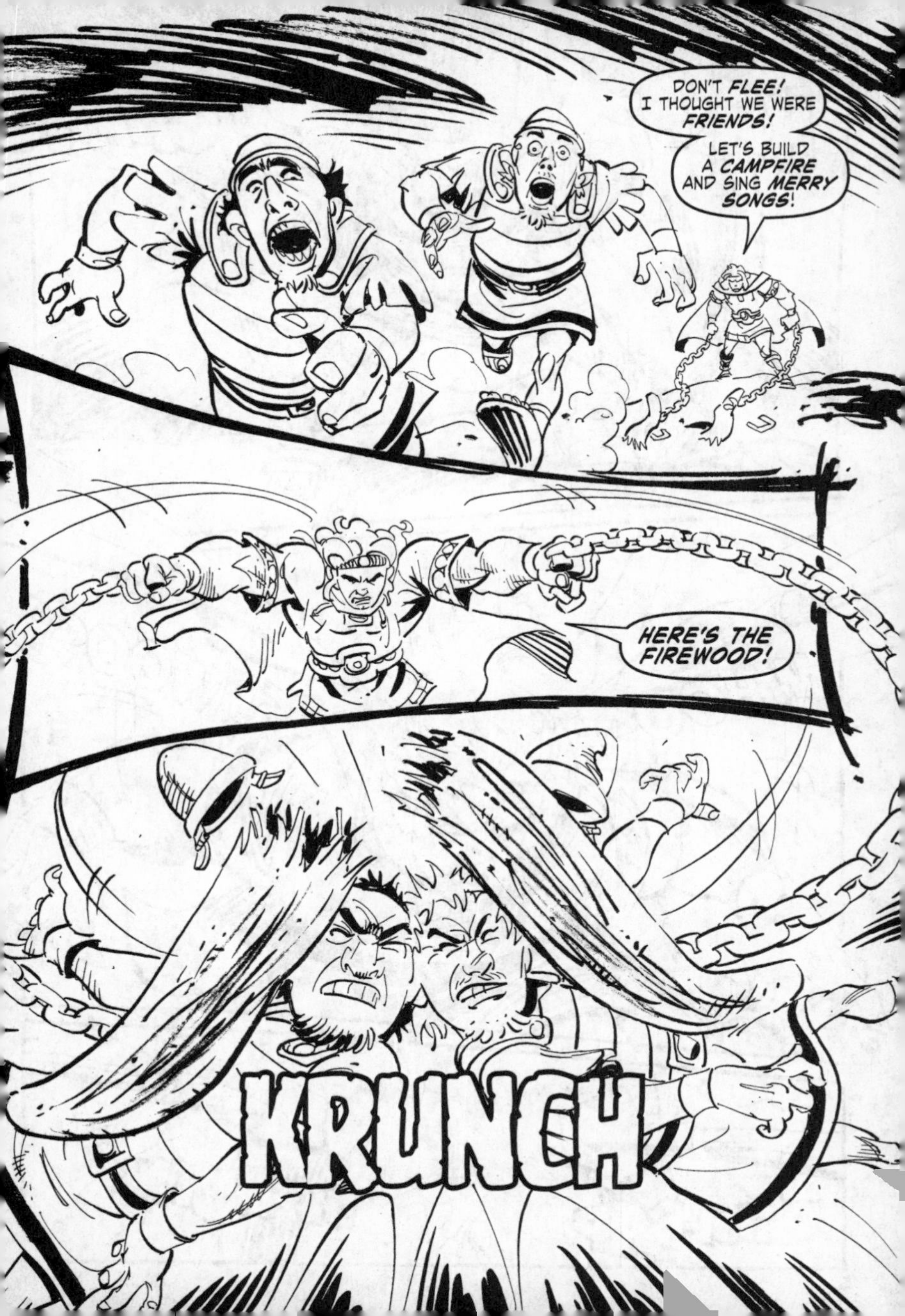
DON'T *FLEE!* I THOUGHT WE WERE *FRIENDS!*
LET'S BUILD A *CAMPFIRE* AND SING *MERRY SONGS!*
HERE'S THE FIREWOOD!
KRUNCH

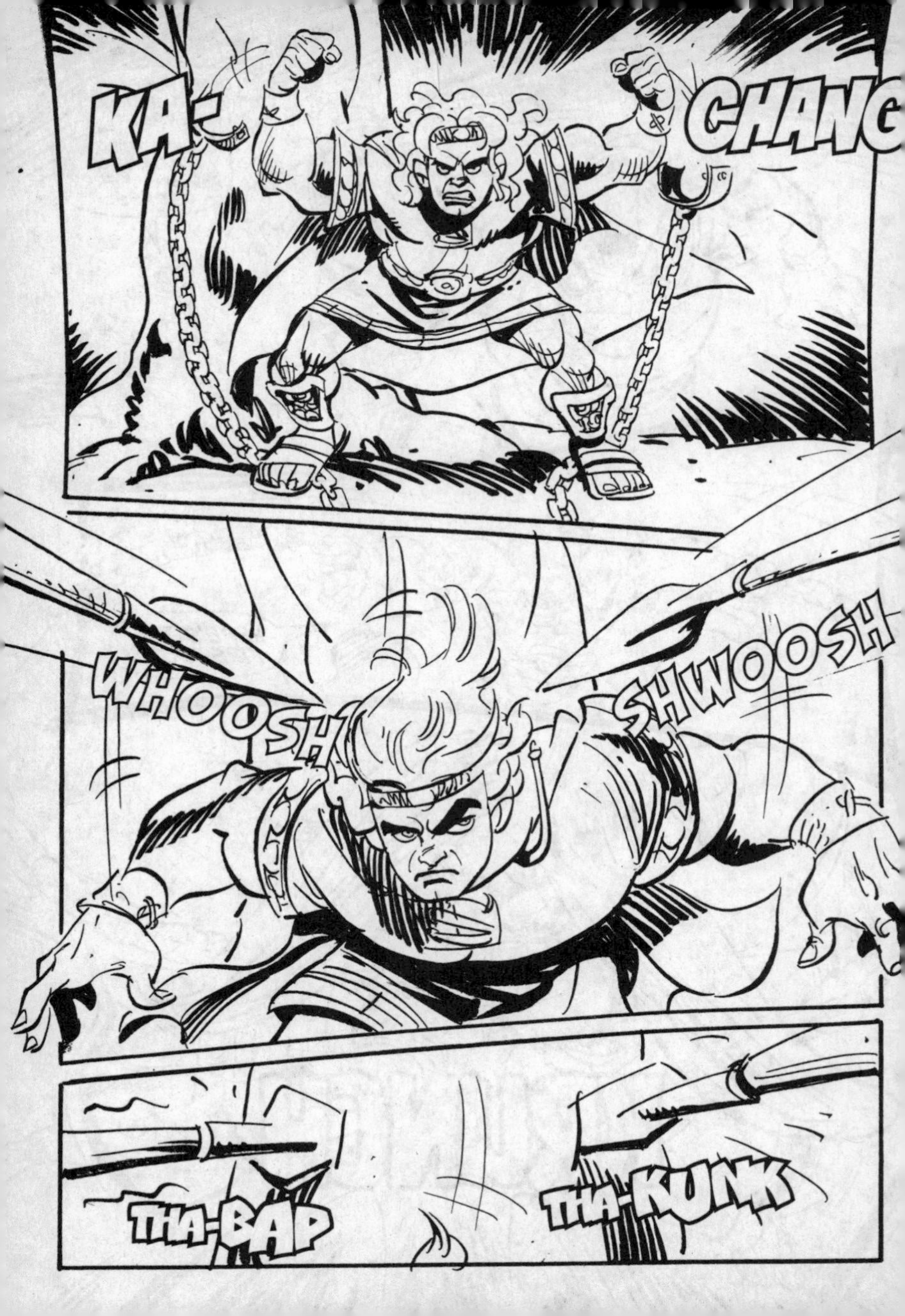
KA-
CHANG
WHOOSH
SHWOOSH
THA-BAP
THA-KUNK

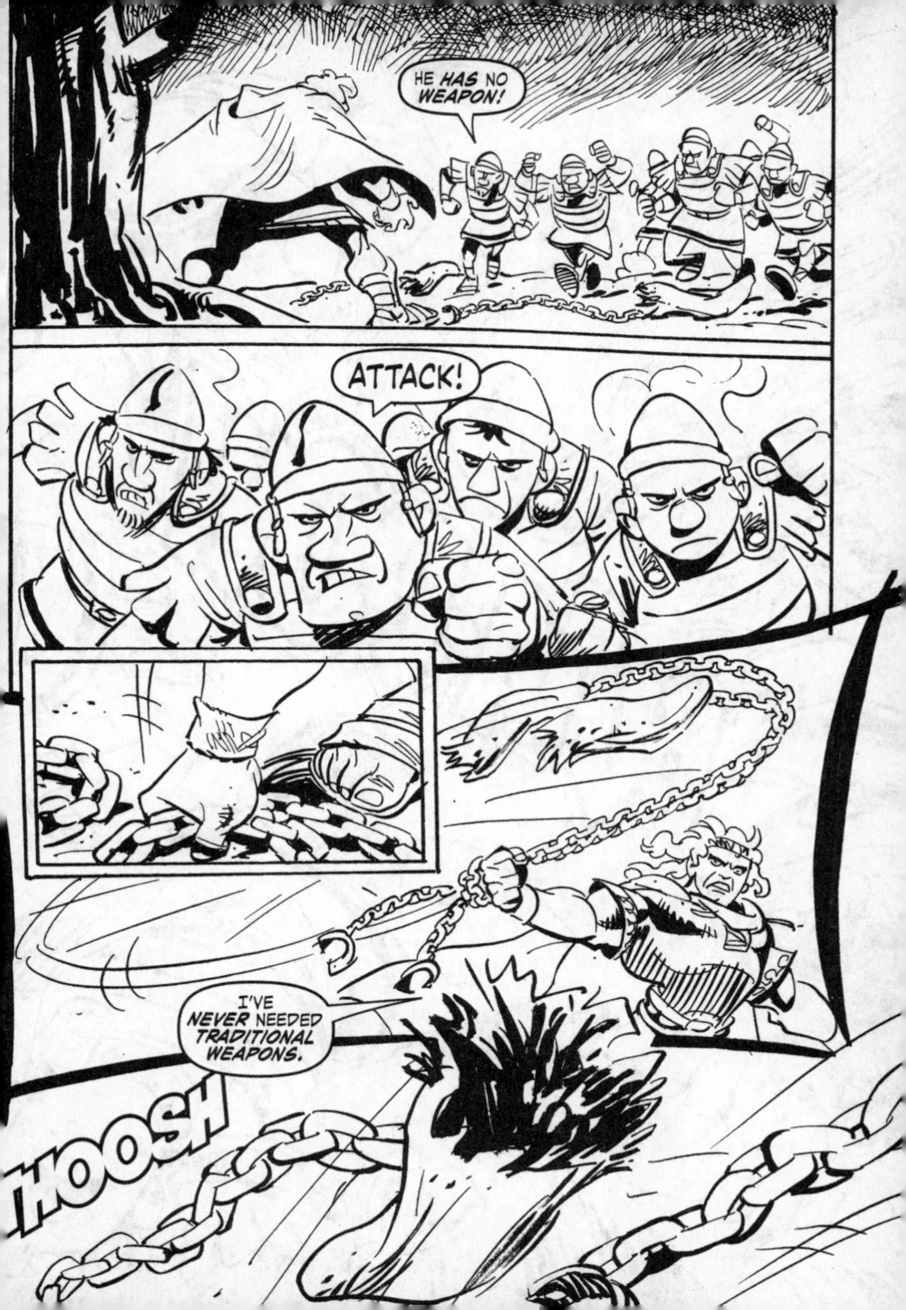
HE HAS NO WEAPON!
ATTACK!
I'VE NEVER NEEDED TRADITIONAL WEAPONS.
HOOSH

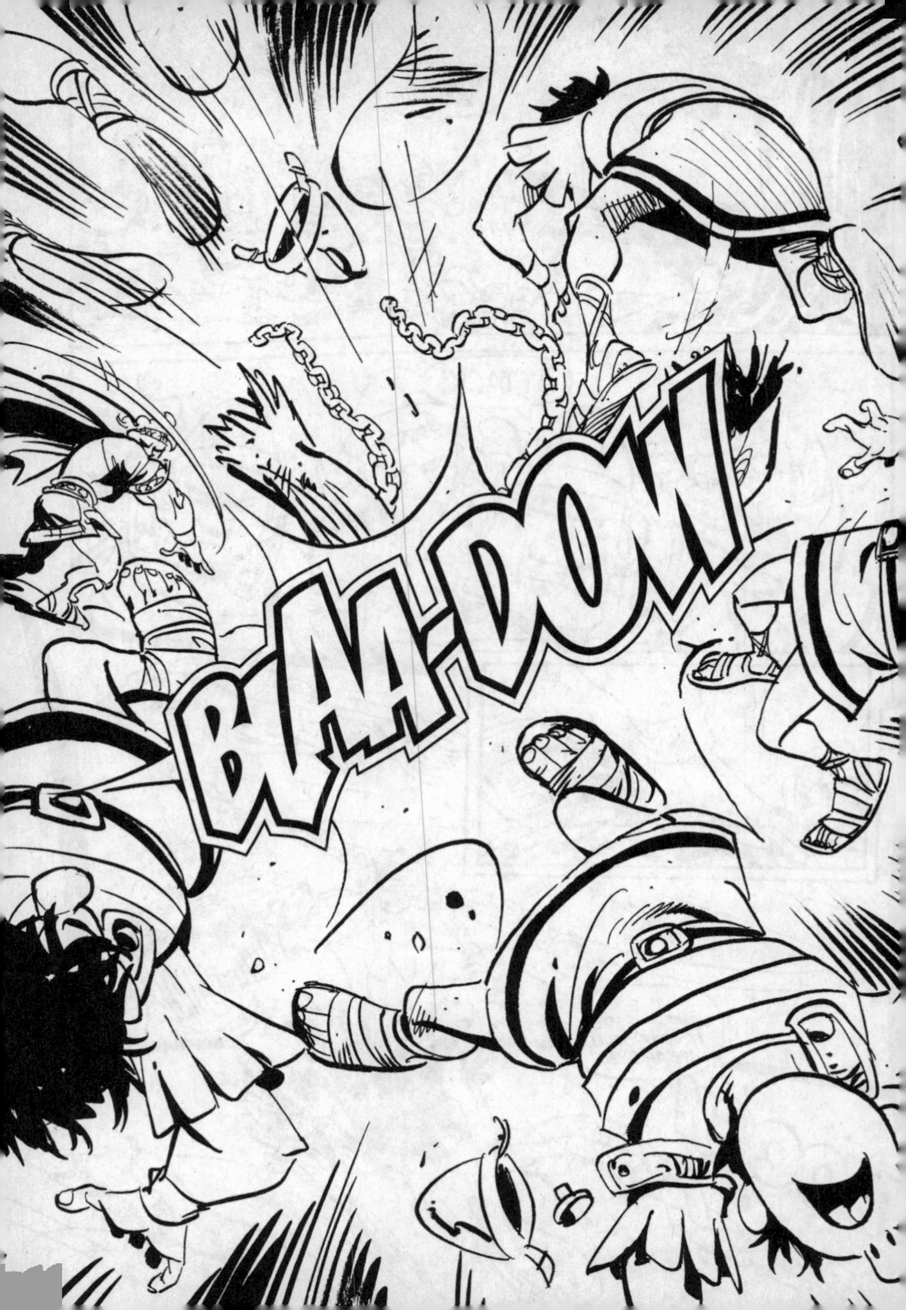
BAM-DOW

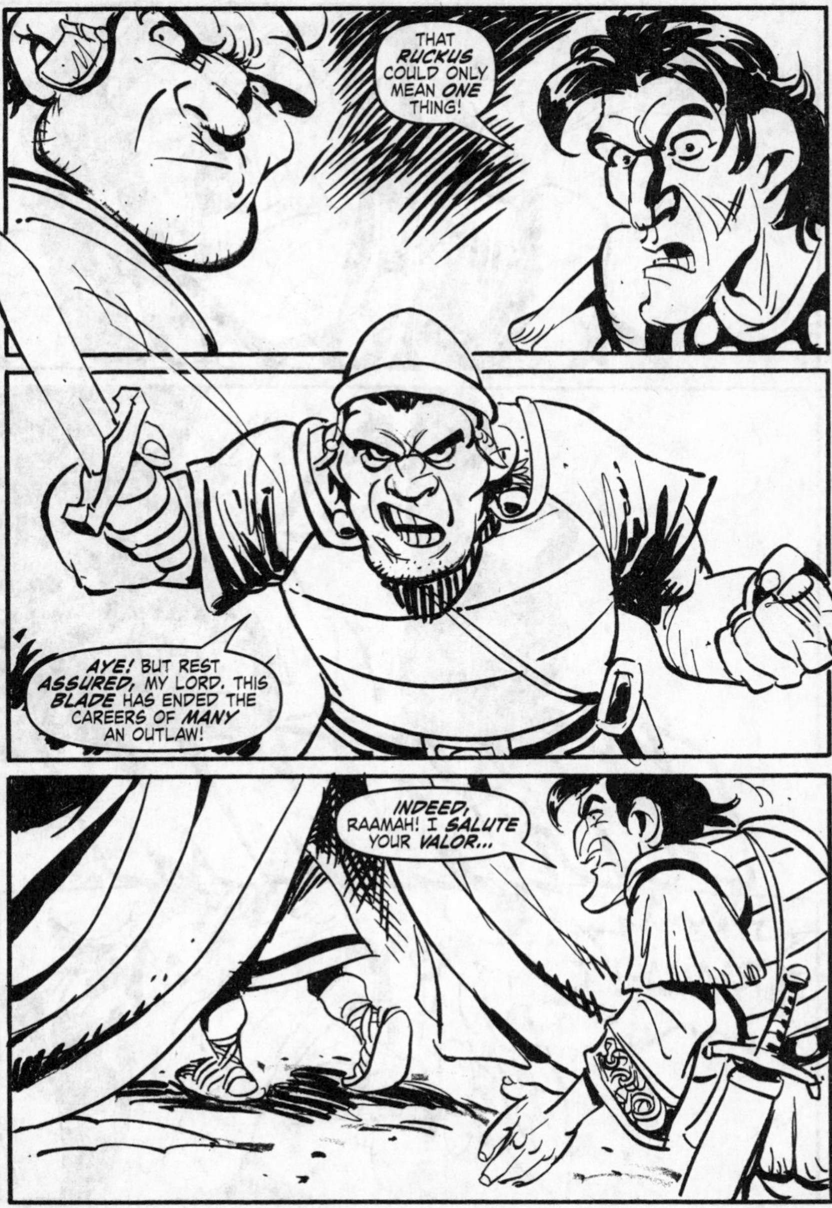
THAT RUCKUS COULD ONLY MEAN ONE THING!
AYE! BUT REST ASSURED, MY LORD. THIS BLADE HAS ENDED THE CAREERS OF MANY AN OUTLAW!
INDEED, RAAMAH! I SALUTE YOUR VALOR...

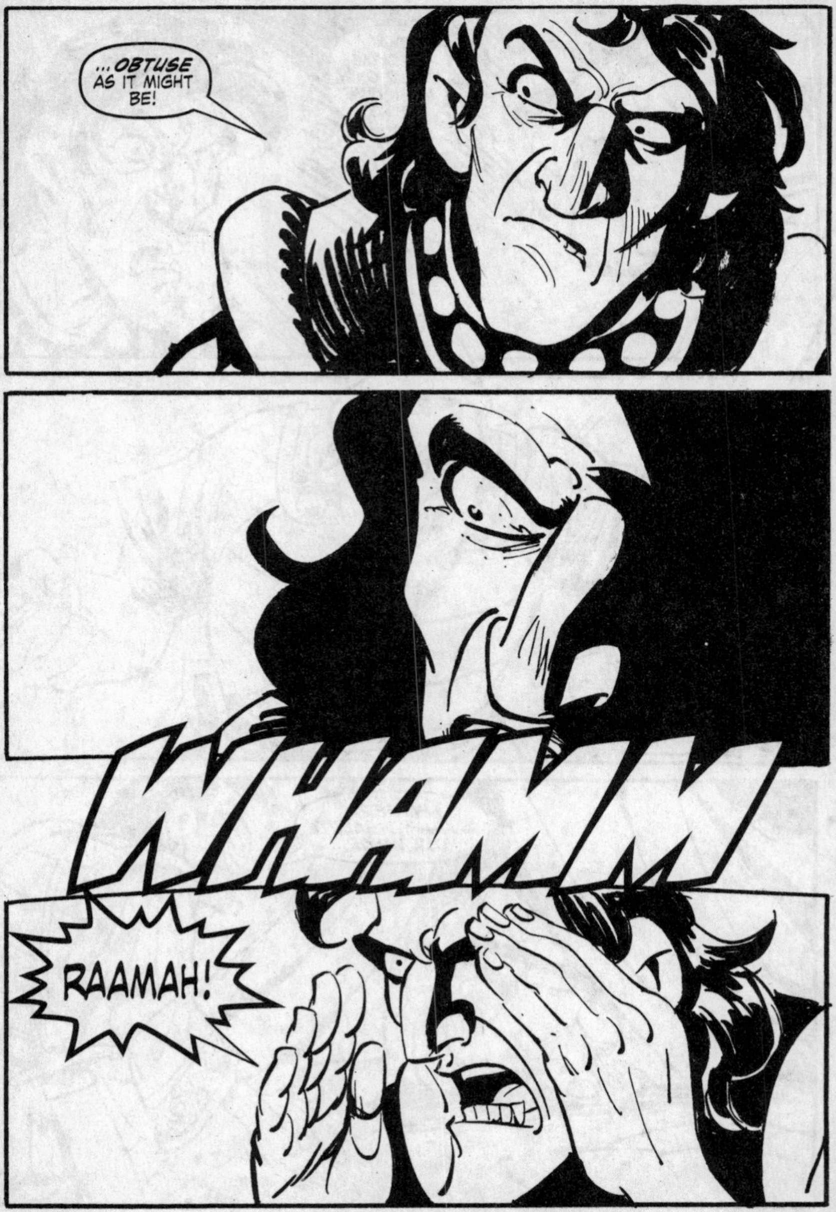
...OBTUSE AS IT MIGHT BE!
WHAM
RAAMAH!

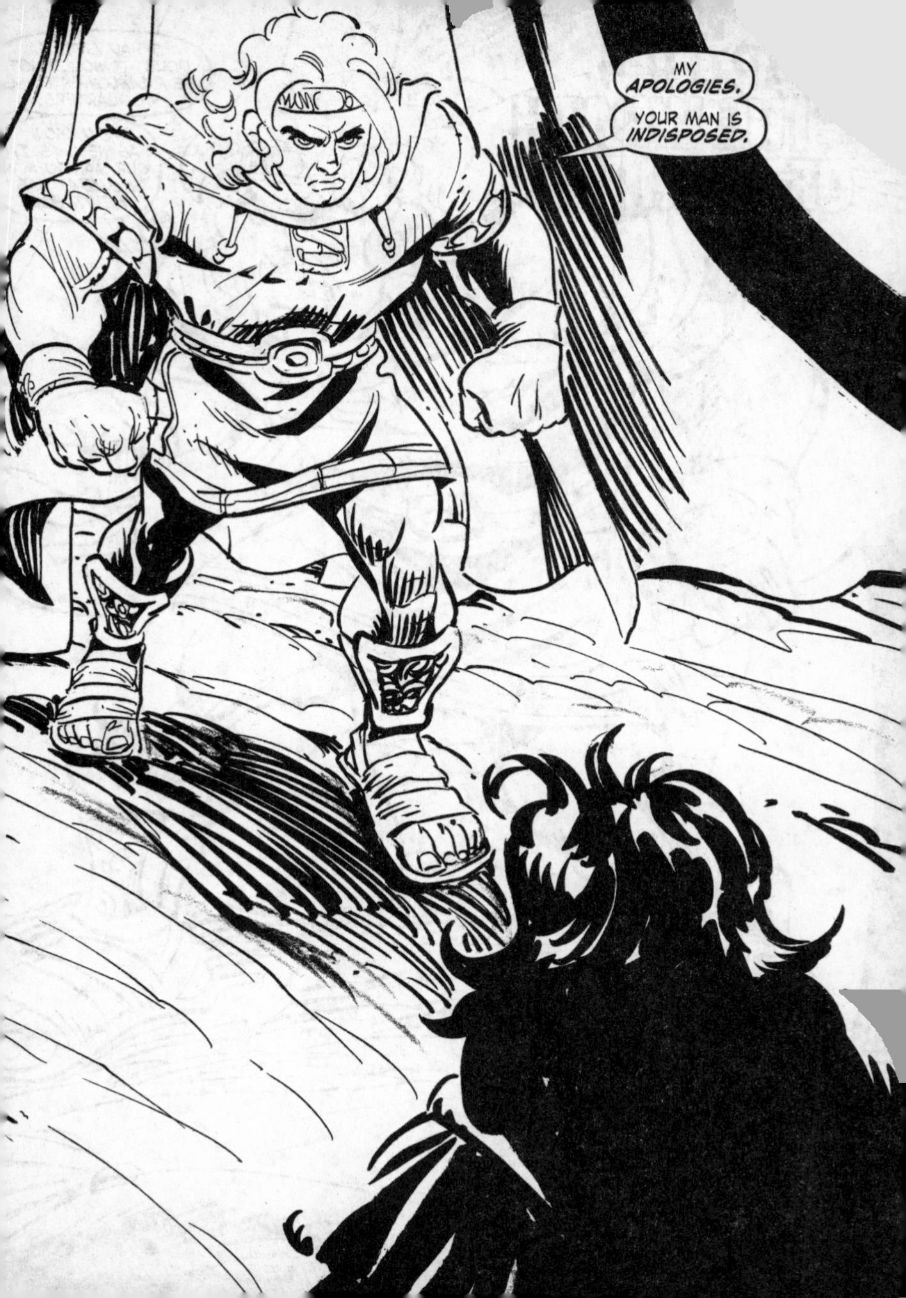
MY APOLOGIES.
YOUR MAN IS INDISPOSED.

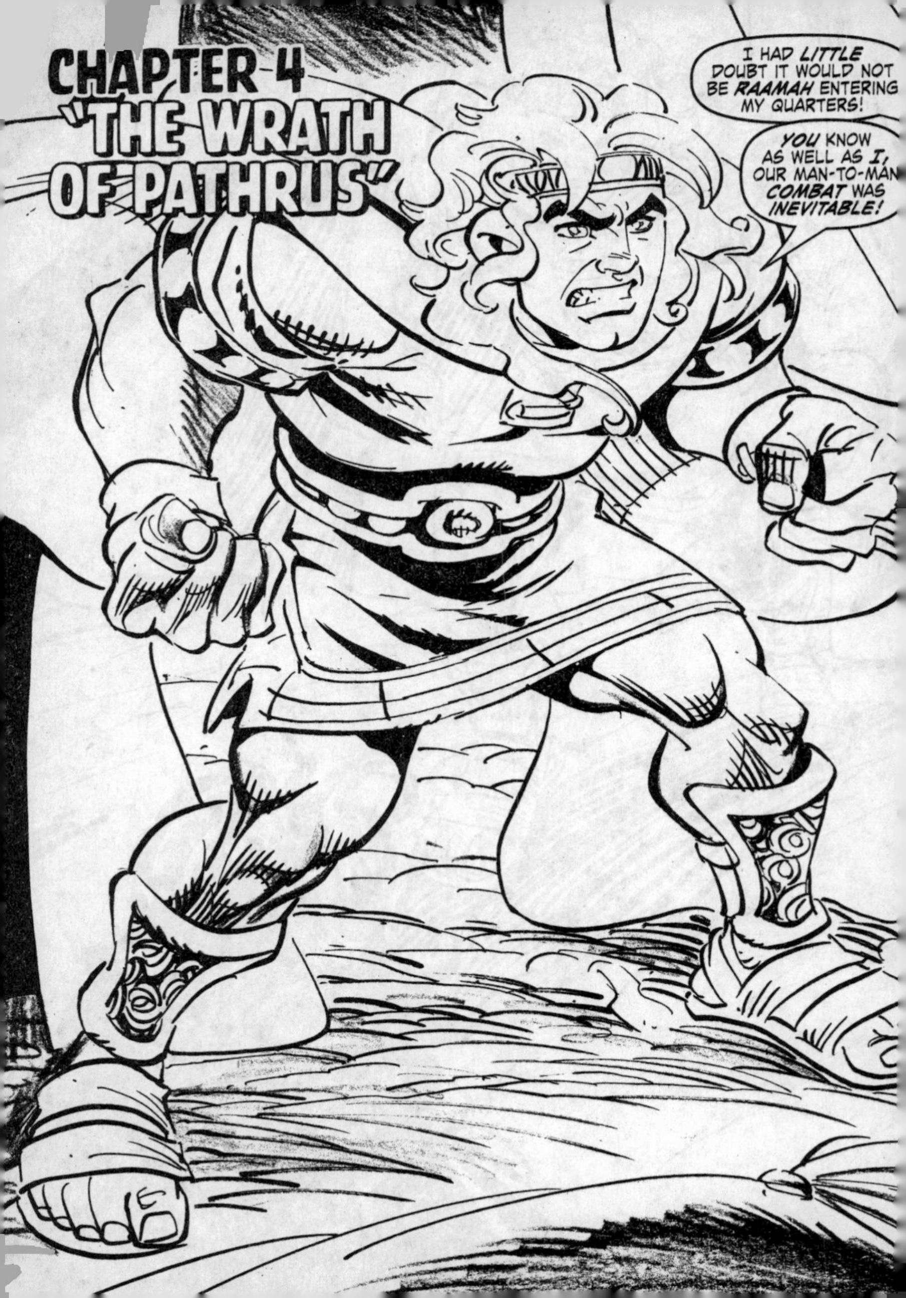
CHAPTER 4
"THE WRATH OF PATHRUS"
I HAD LITTLE DOUBT IT WOULD NOT BE RAAMAH ENTERING MY QUARTERS!
YOU KNOW AS WELL AS I, OUR MAN-TO-MAN COMBAT WAS INEVITABLE!

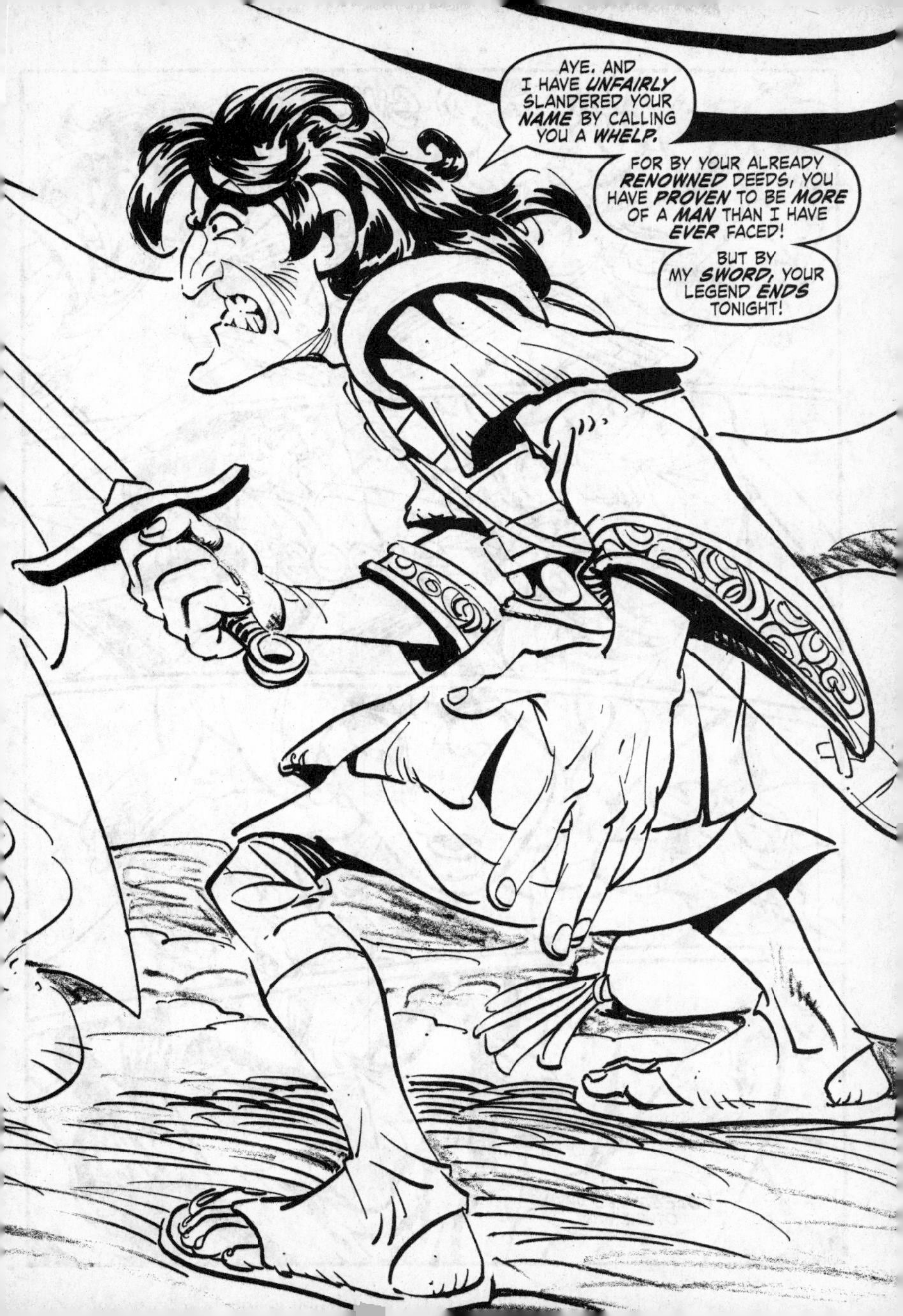
AYE. AND I HAVE UNFAIRLY SLANDERED YOUR NAME BY CALLING YOU A WHELP.
FOR BY YOUR ALREADY RENOWNED DEEDS, YOU HAVE PROVEN TO BE MORE OF A MAN THAN I HAVE EVER FACED!
BUT BY MY SWORD, YOUR LEGEND ENDS TONIGHT!

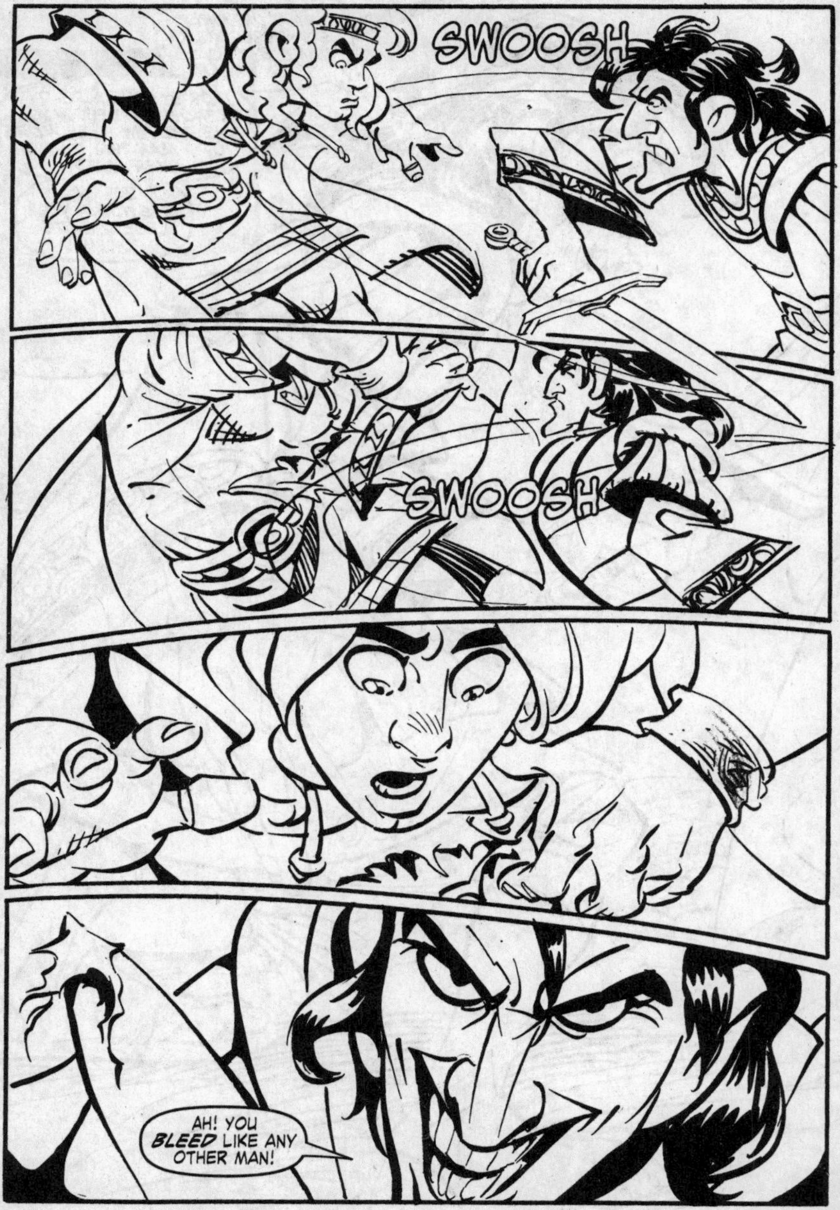
SWOOSH
SWOOSH
AH! YOU *BLEED* LIKE ANY OTHER MAN!

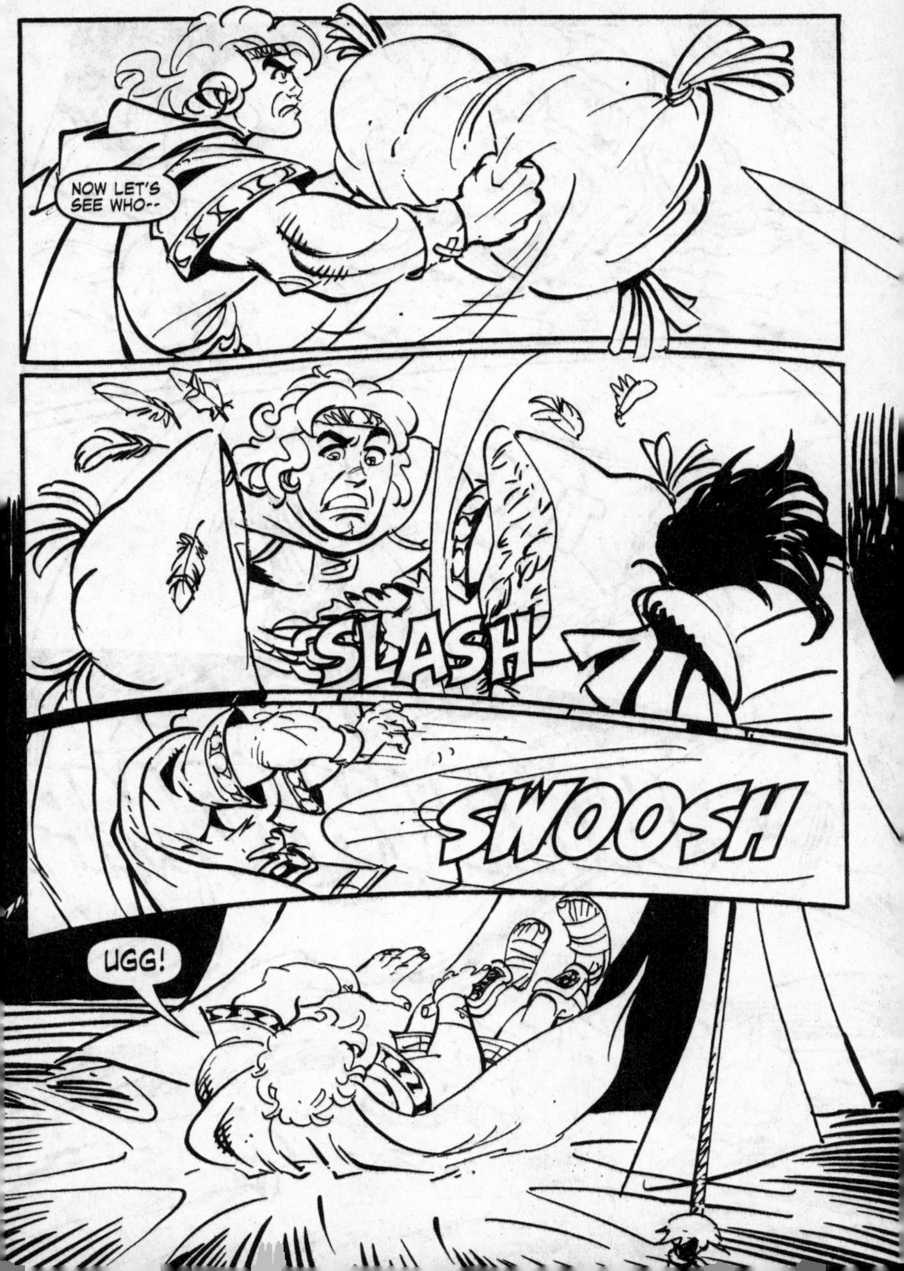
NOW LET'S SEE WHO--
SLASH
SWOOSH
UGG!

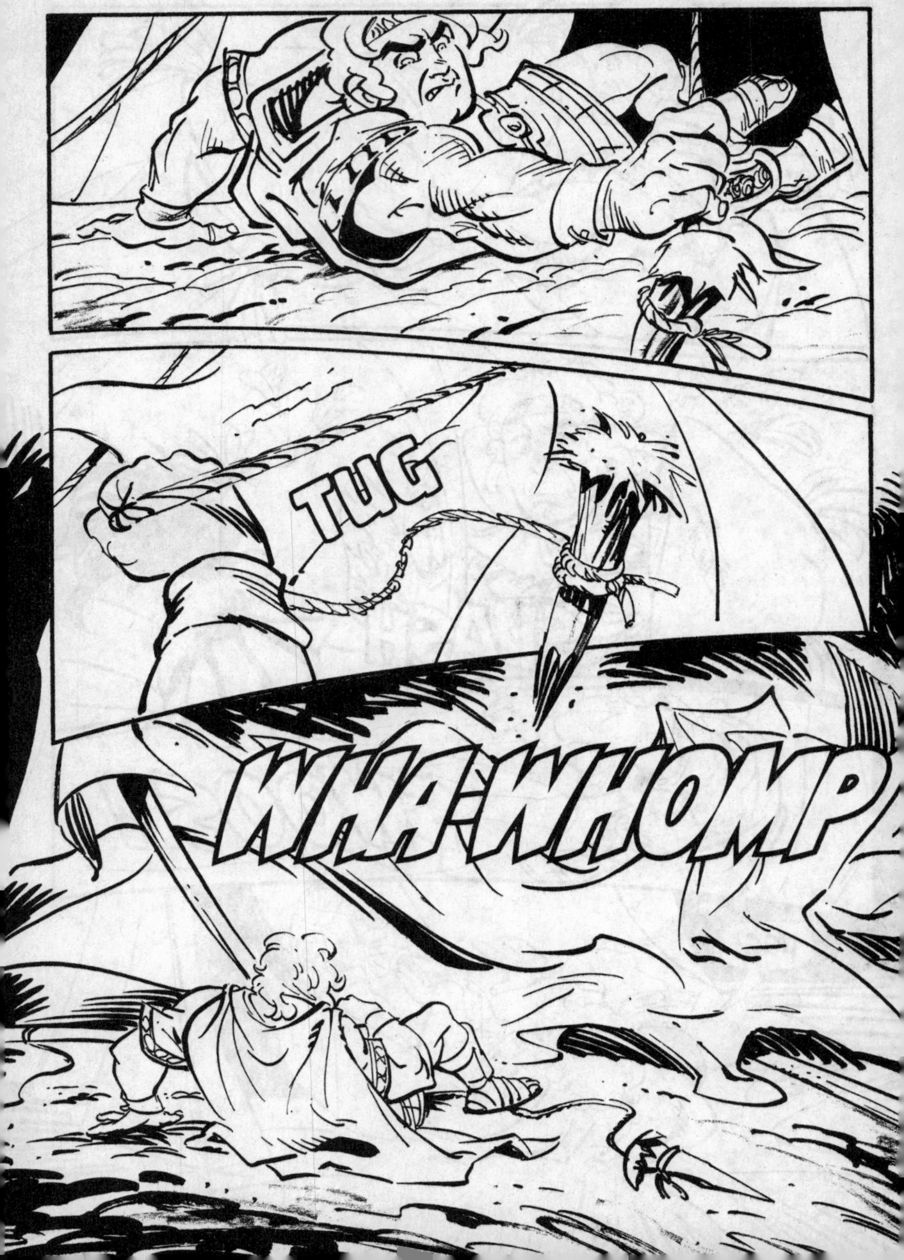
TUG
WHA-WHOMP

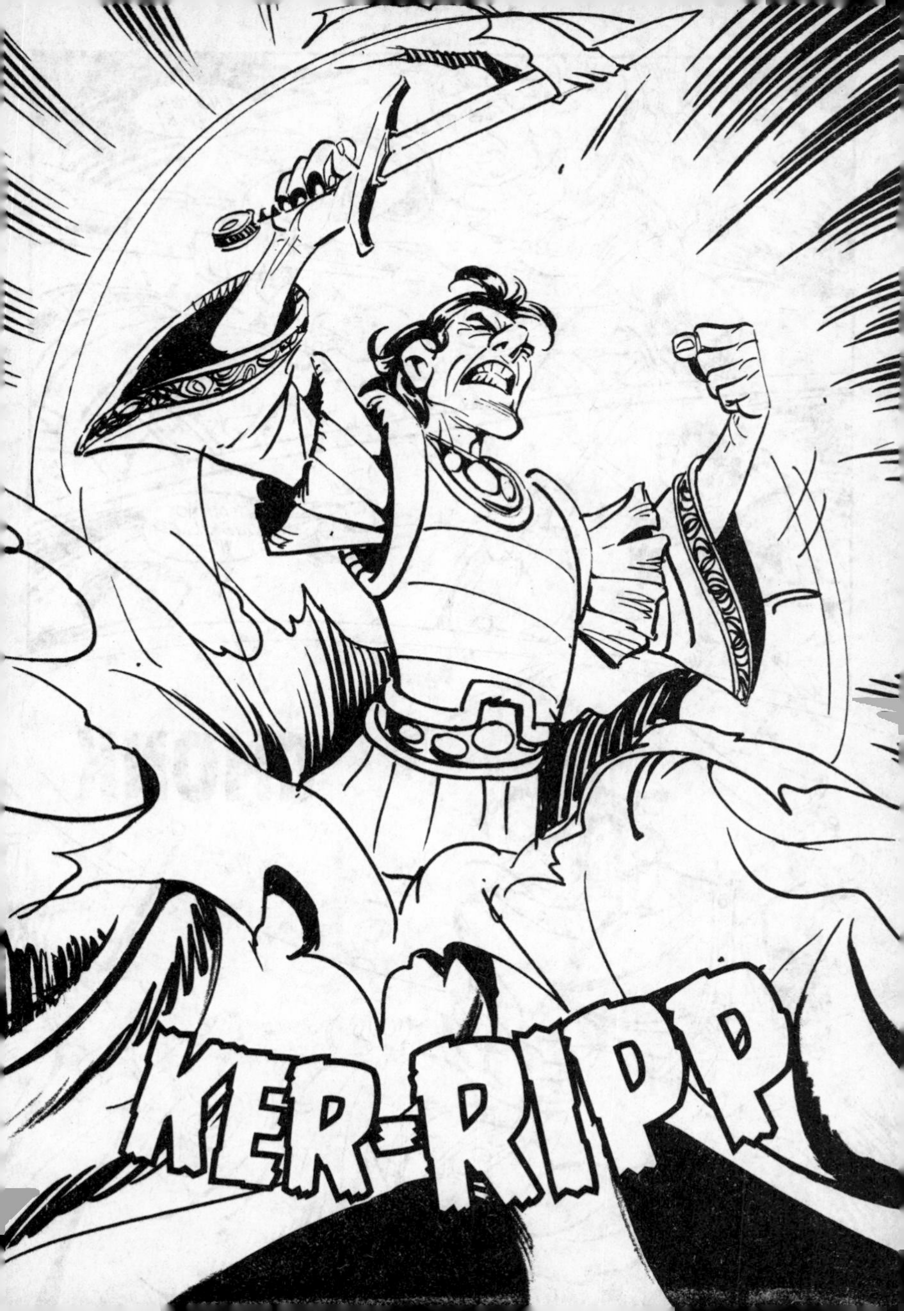
KER-RIPP

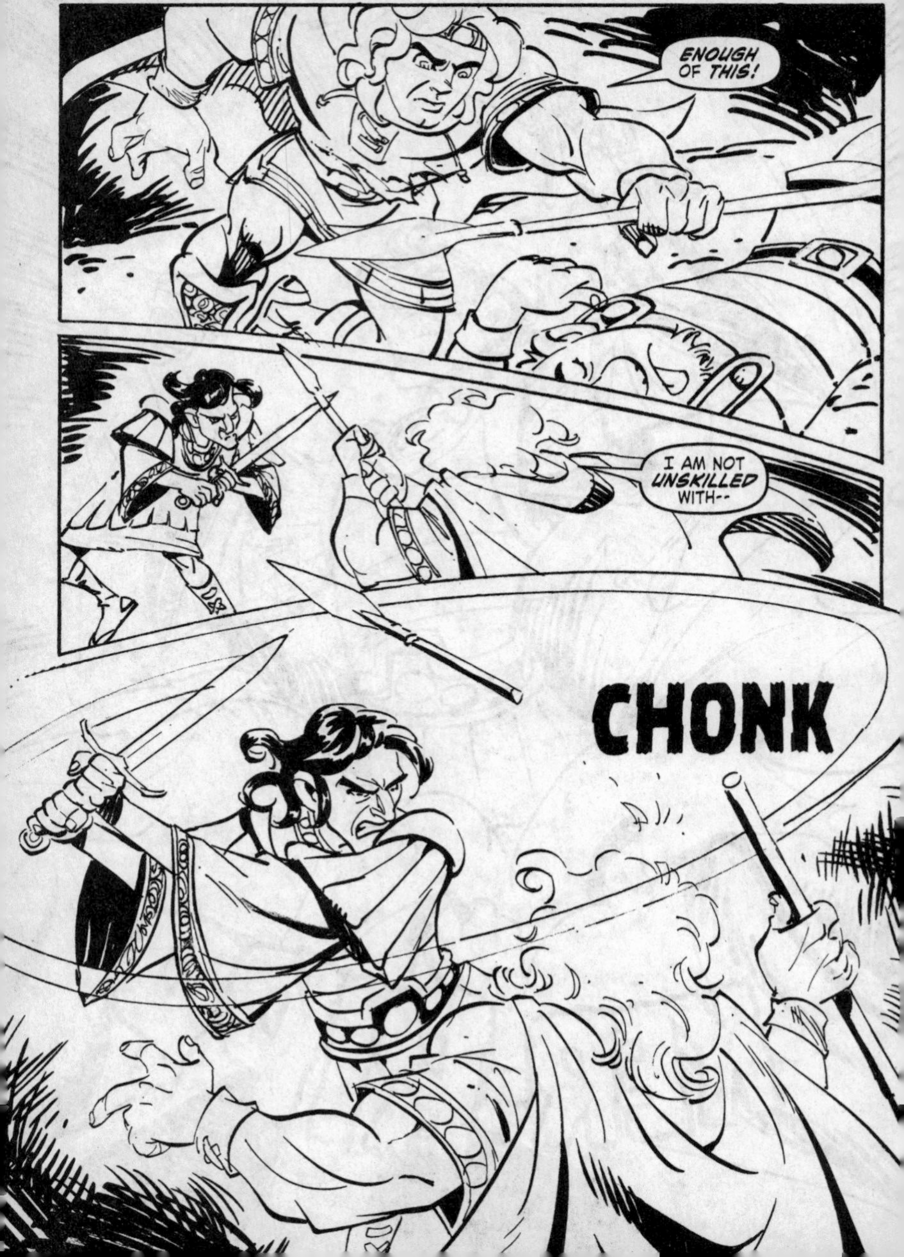
ENOUGH OF THIS!
I AM NOT UNSKILLED WITH--
CHONK

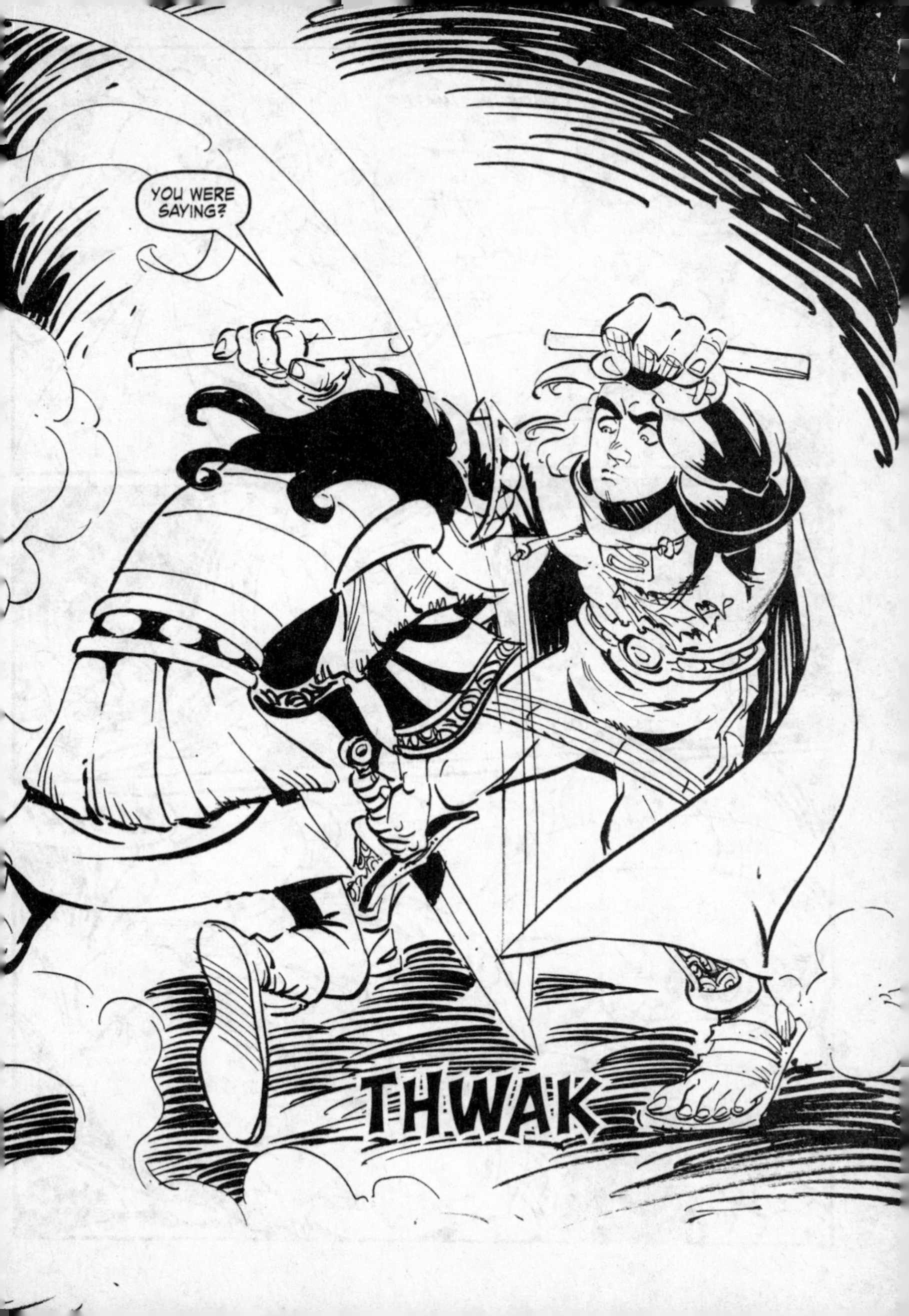
YOU WERE SAYING?
THWAK

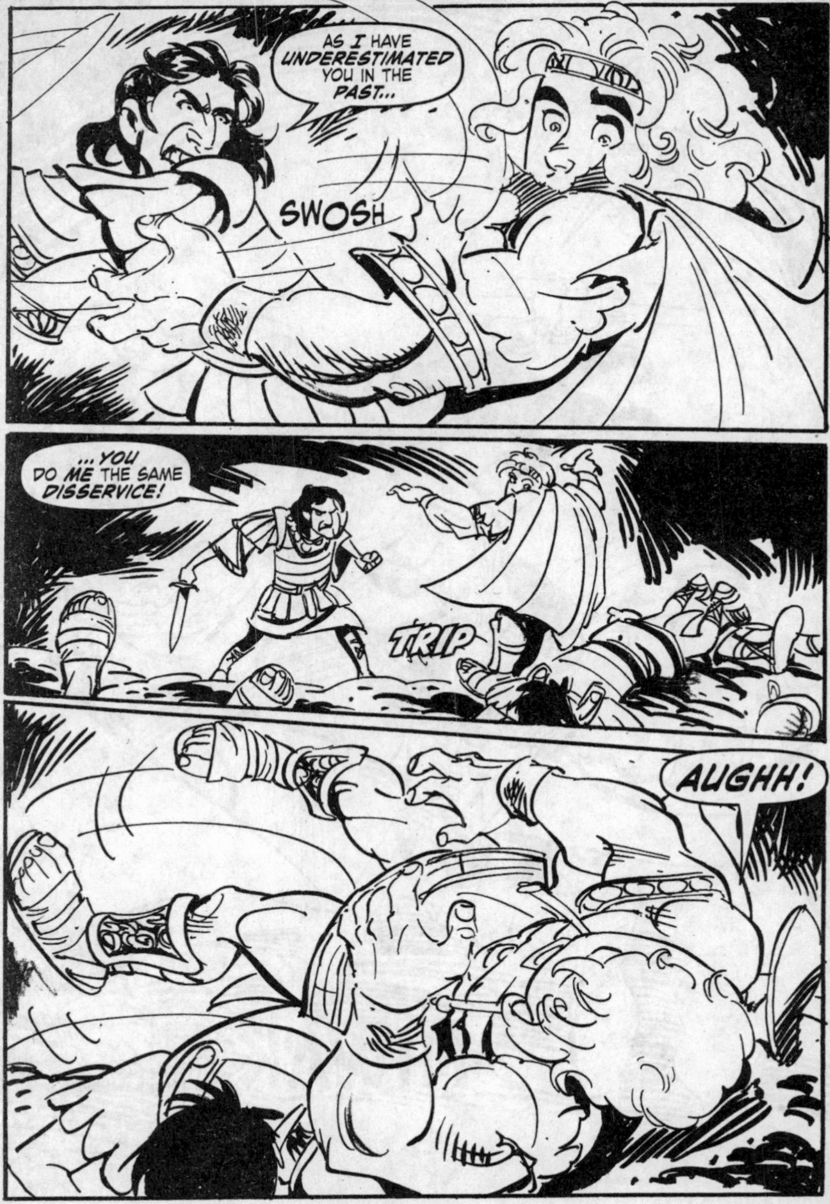
AS I HAVE UNDERESTIMATED YOU IN THE PAST...
SWOSH
...YOU DO ME THE SAME DISSERVICE!
TRIP
AUGHH!

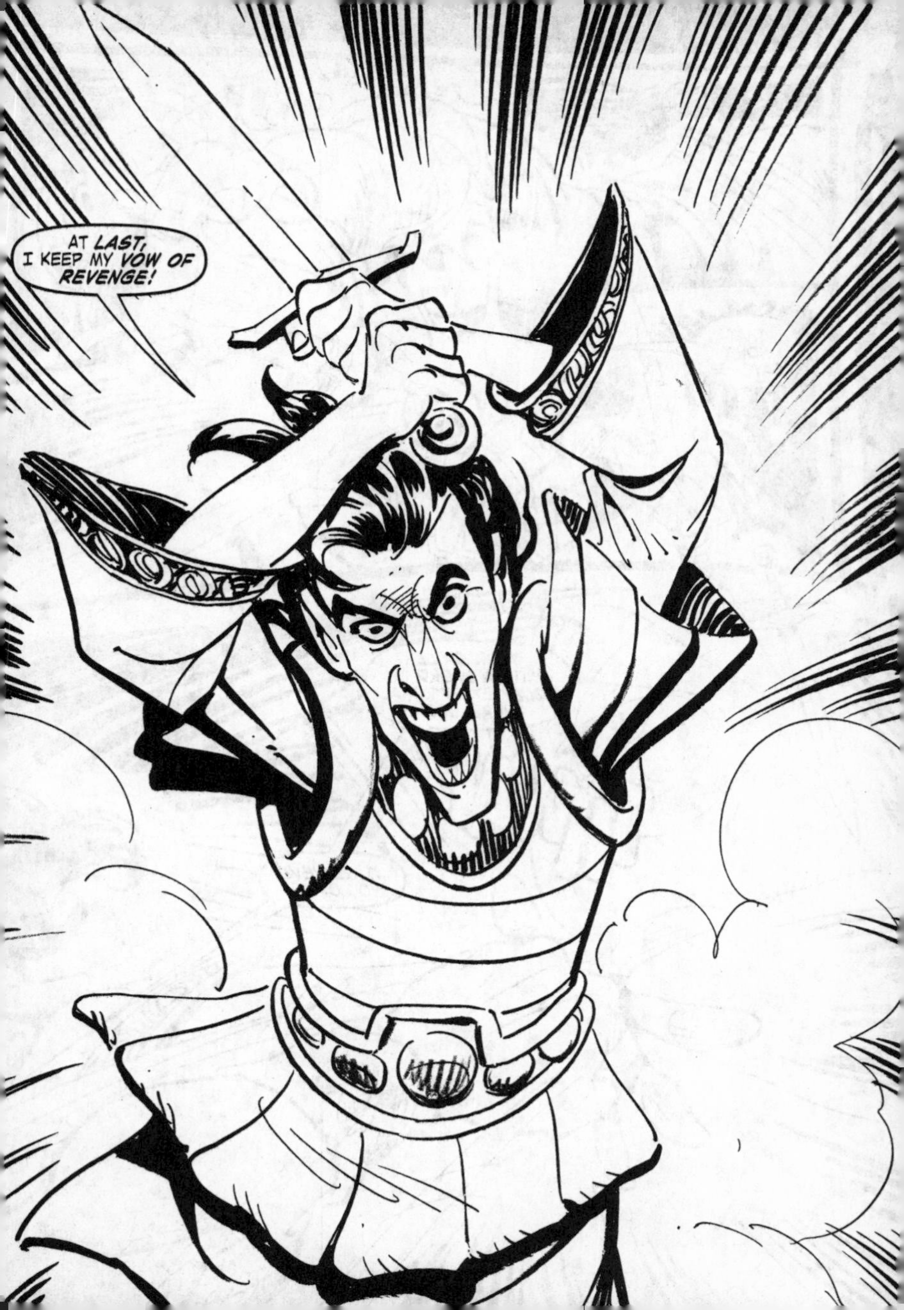
AT LAST, I KEEP MY VOW OF REVENGE!

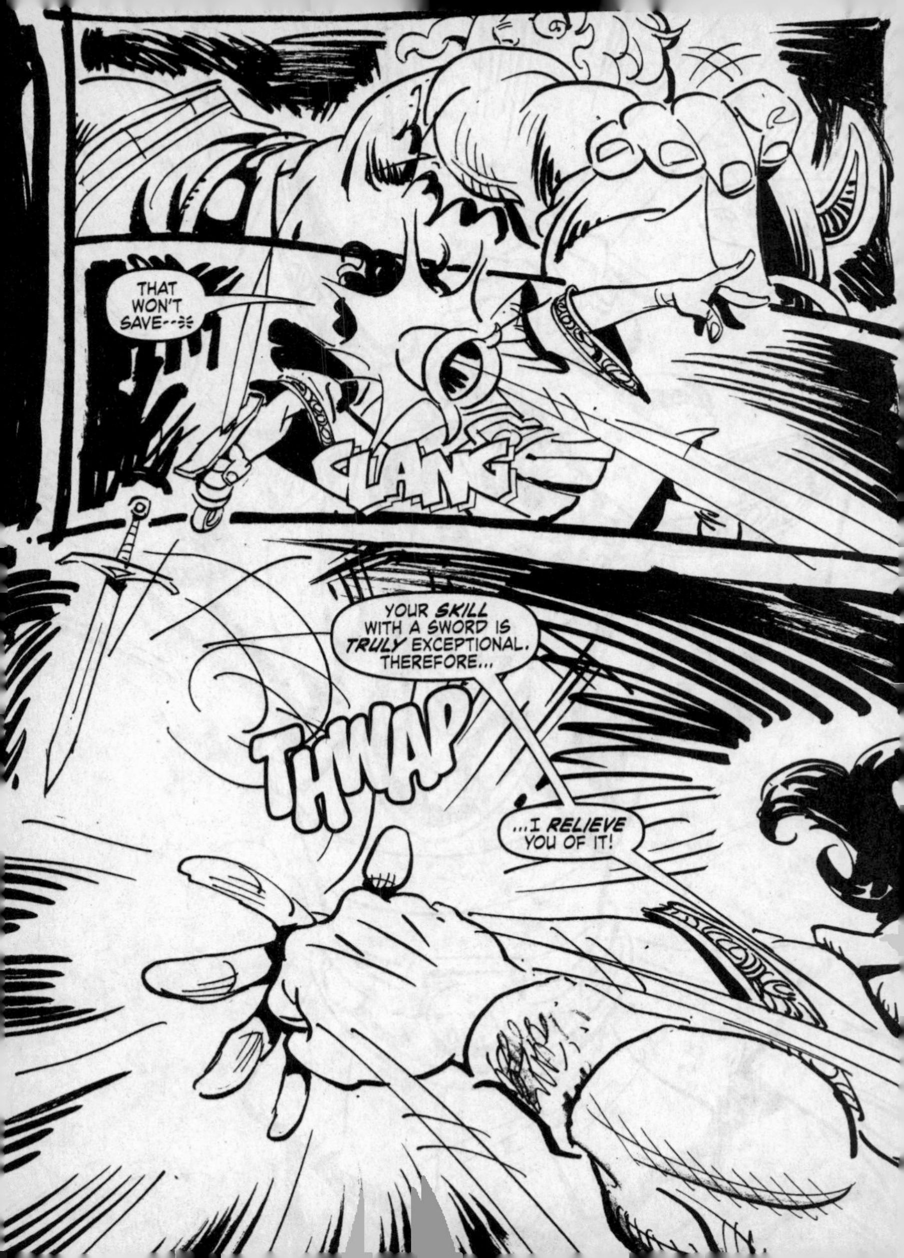
THAT WON'T SAVE--
CLANG
YOUR SKILL WITH A SWORD IS TRULY EXCEPTIONAL. THEREFORE...
THWAP
...I RELIEVE YOU OF IT!

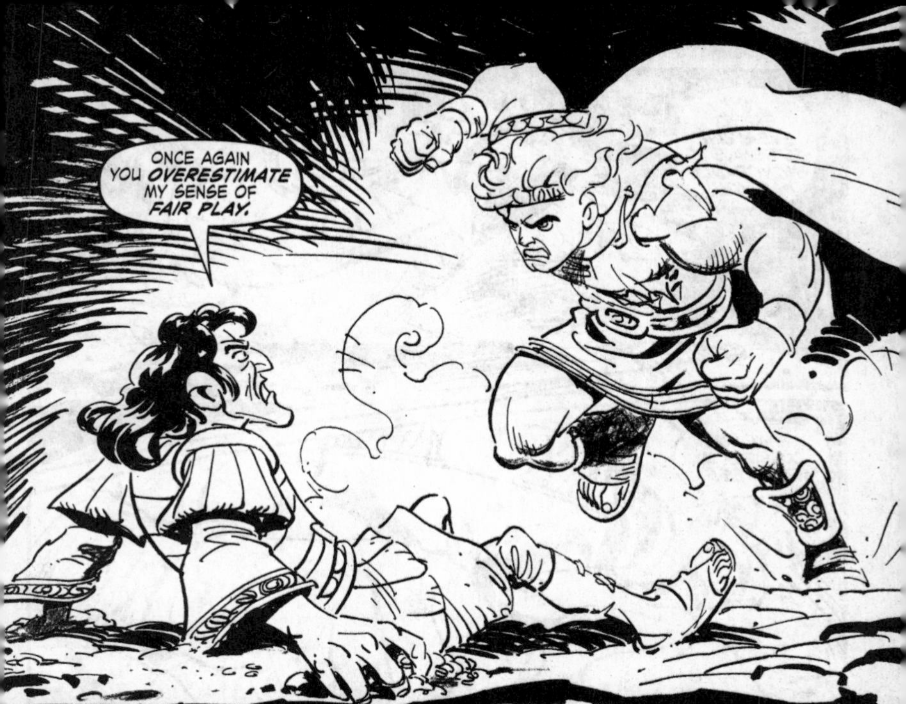
ONCE AGAIN YOU *OVERESTIMATE* MY SENSE OF *FAIR PLAY.*

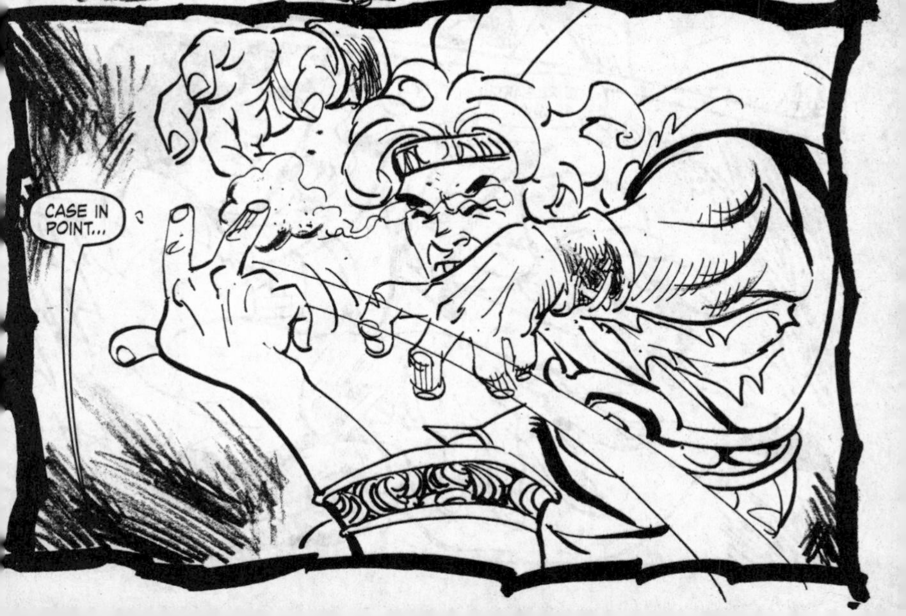
CASE IN POINT...

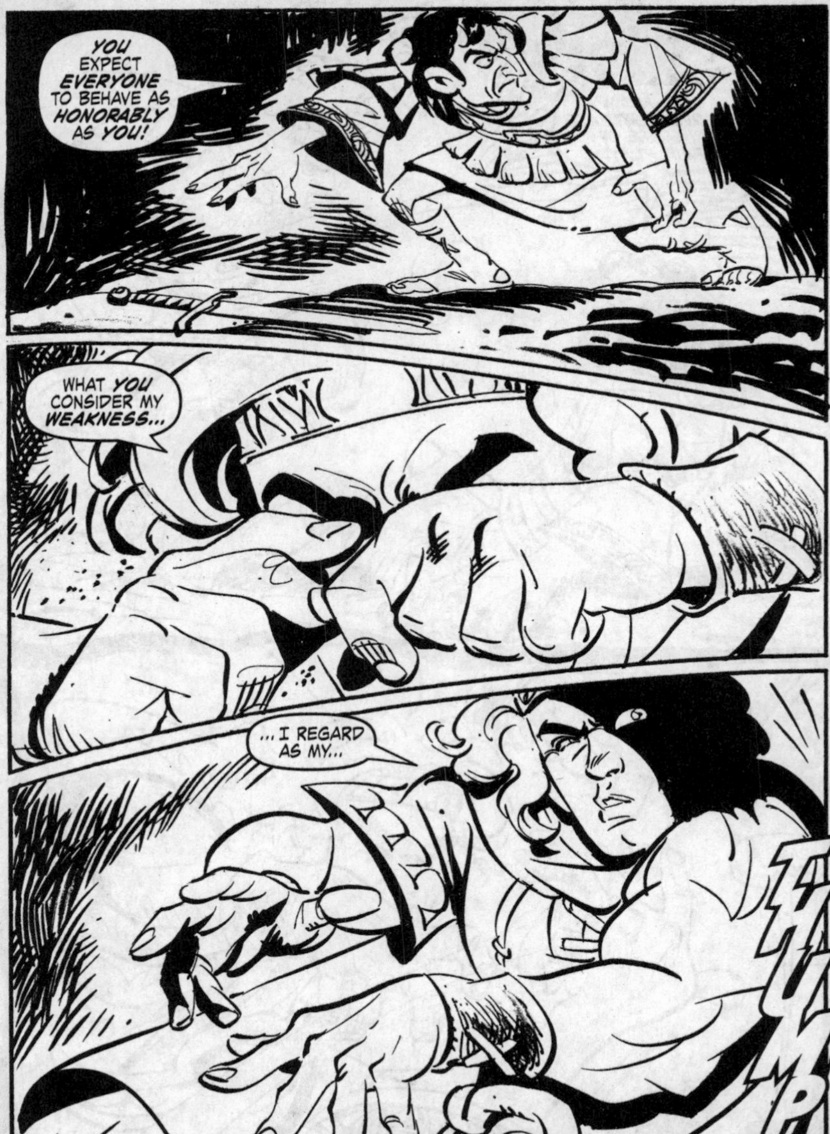
YOU EXPECT EVERYONE TO BEHAVE AS HONORABLY AS YOU!
WHAT YOU CONSIDER MY WEAKNESS...
...I REGARD AS MY...
THUMP

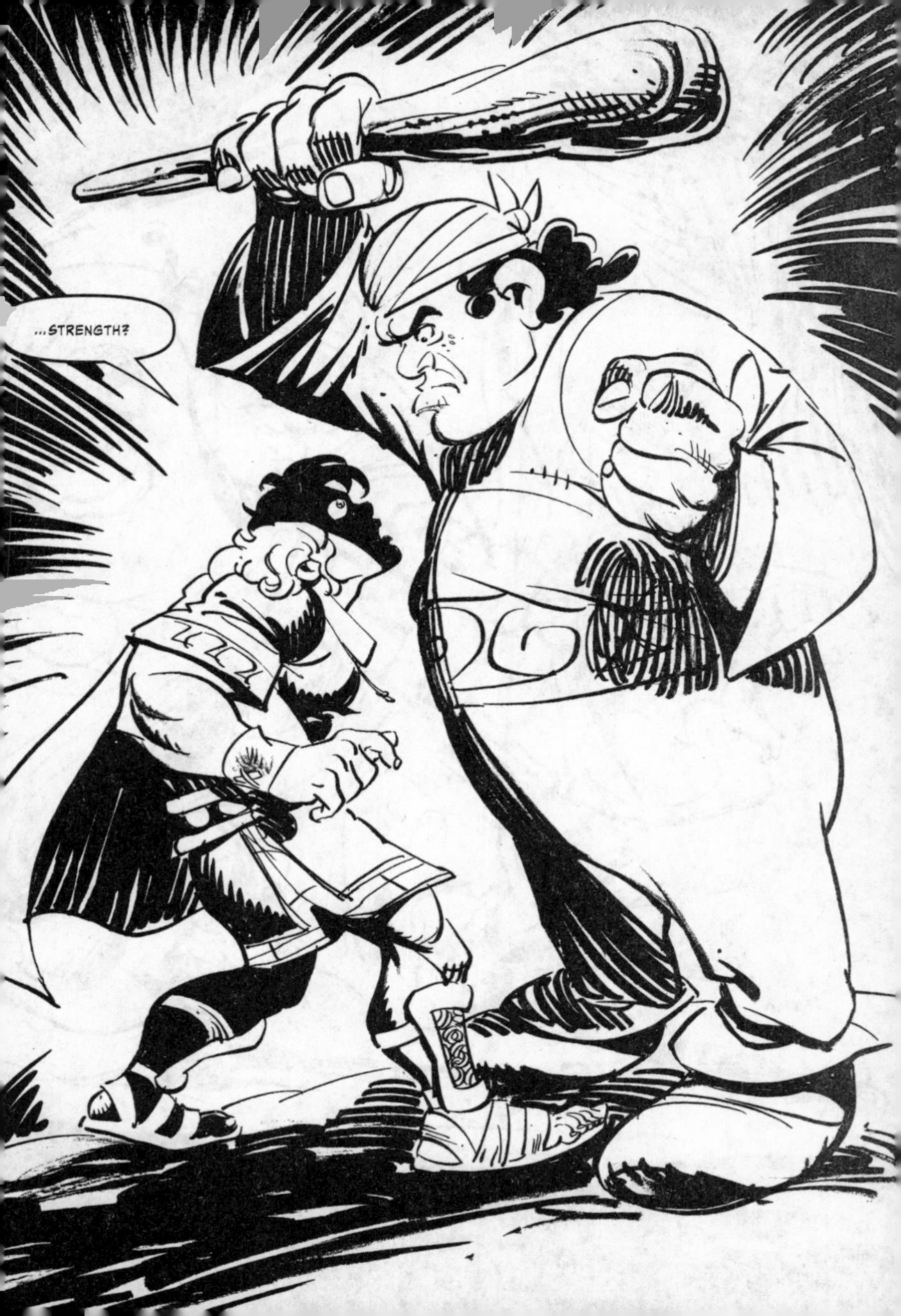

...STRENGTH?

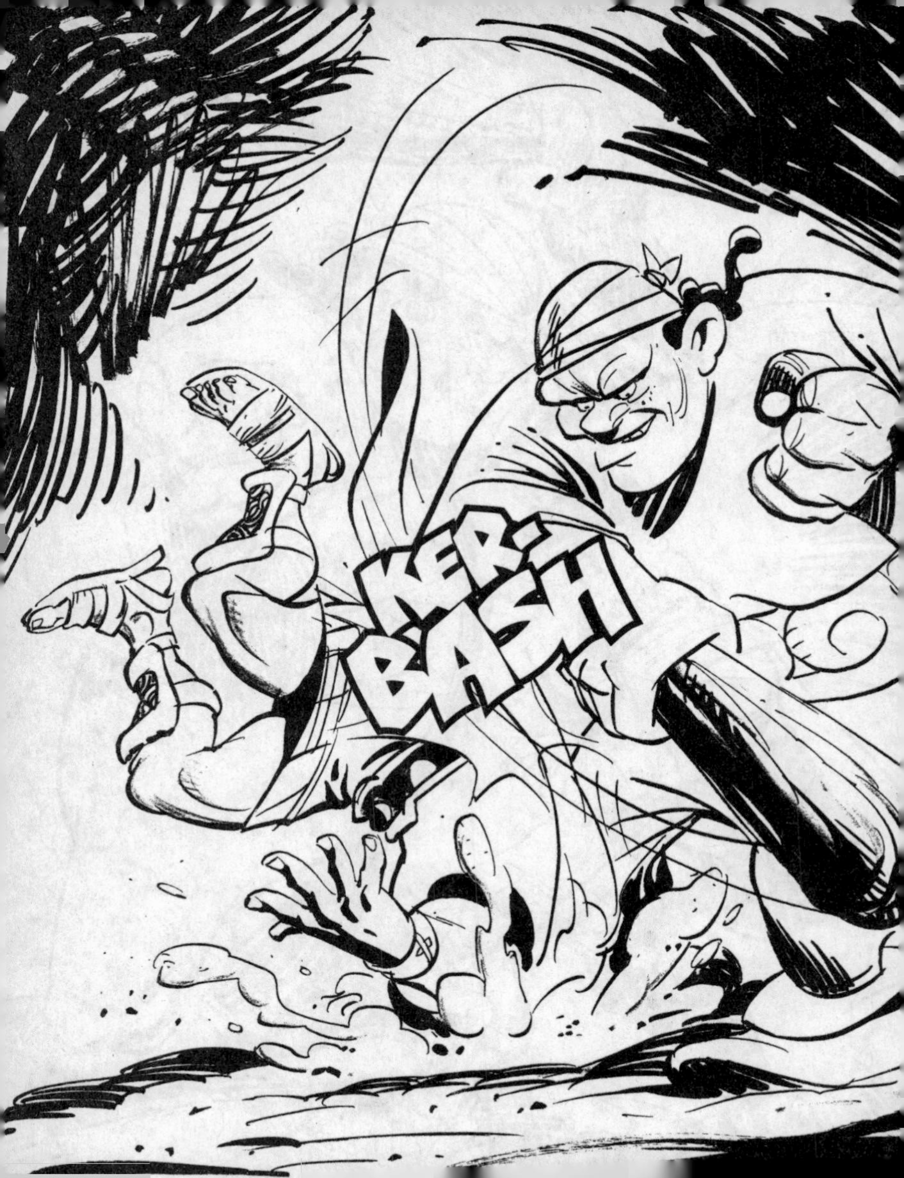
KER-BASH

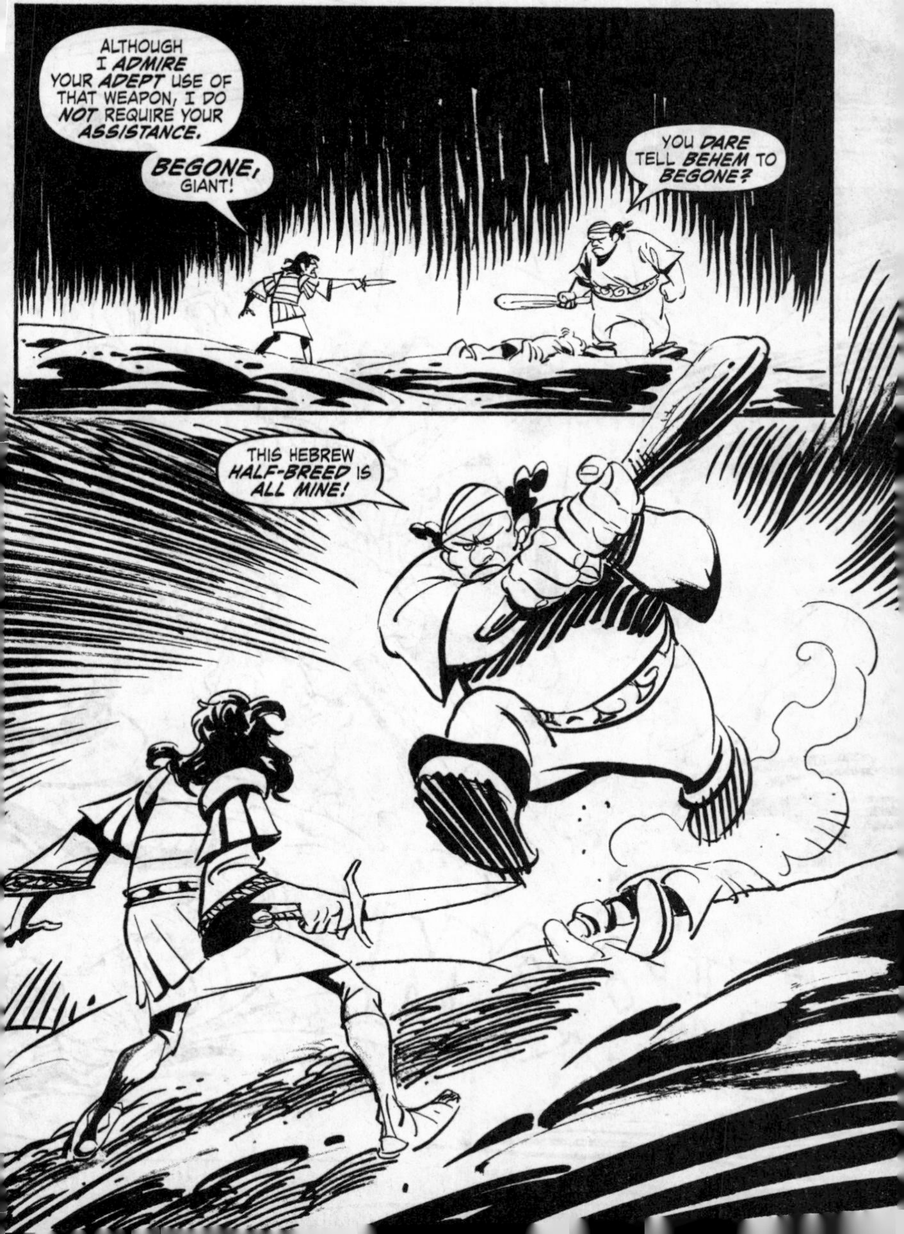
ALTHOUGH I ADMIRE YOUR ADEPT USE OF THAT WEAPON, I DO NOT REQUIRE YOUR ASSISTANCE.
BEGONE, GIANT!
YOU DARE TELL BEHEM TO BEGONE?
THIS HEBREW HALF-BREED IS ALL MINE!

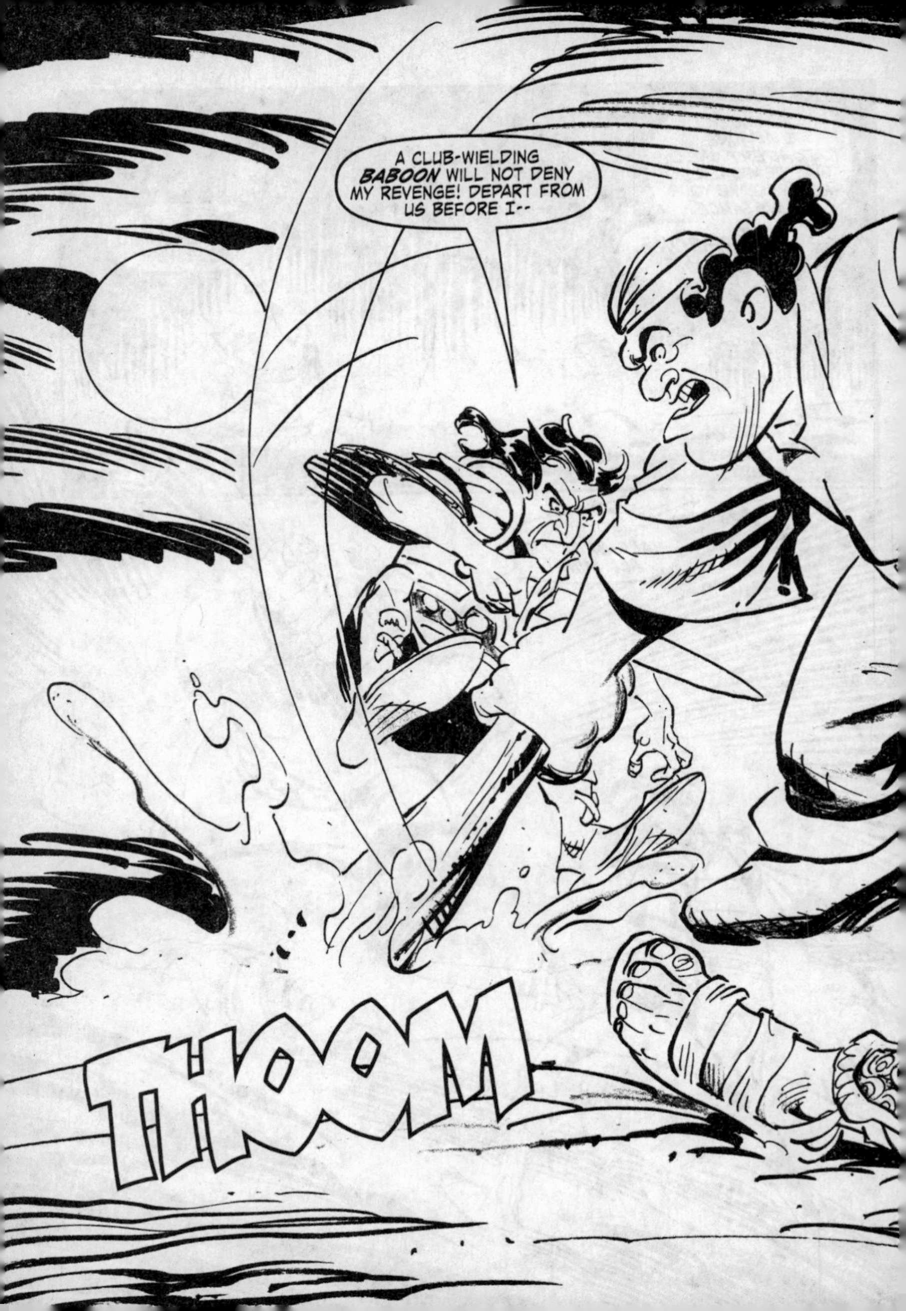
A CLUB-WIELDING *BABOON* WILL NOT DENY MY REVENGE! DEPART FROM US BEFORE I--
THOOM

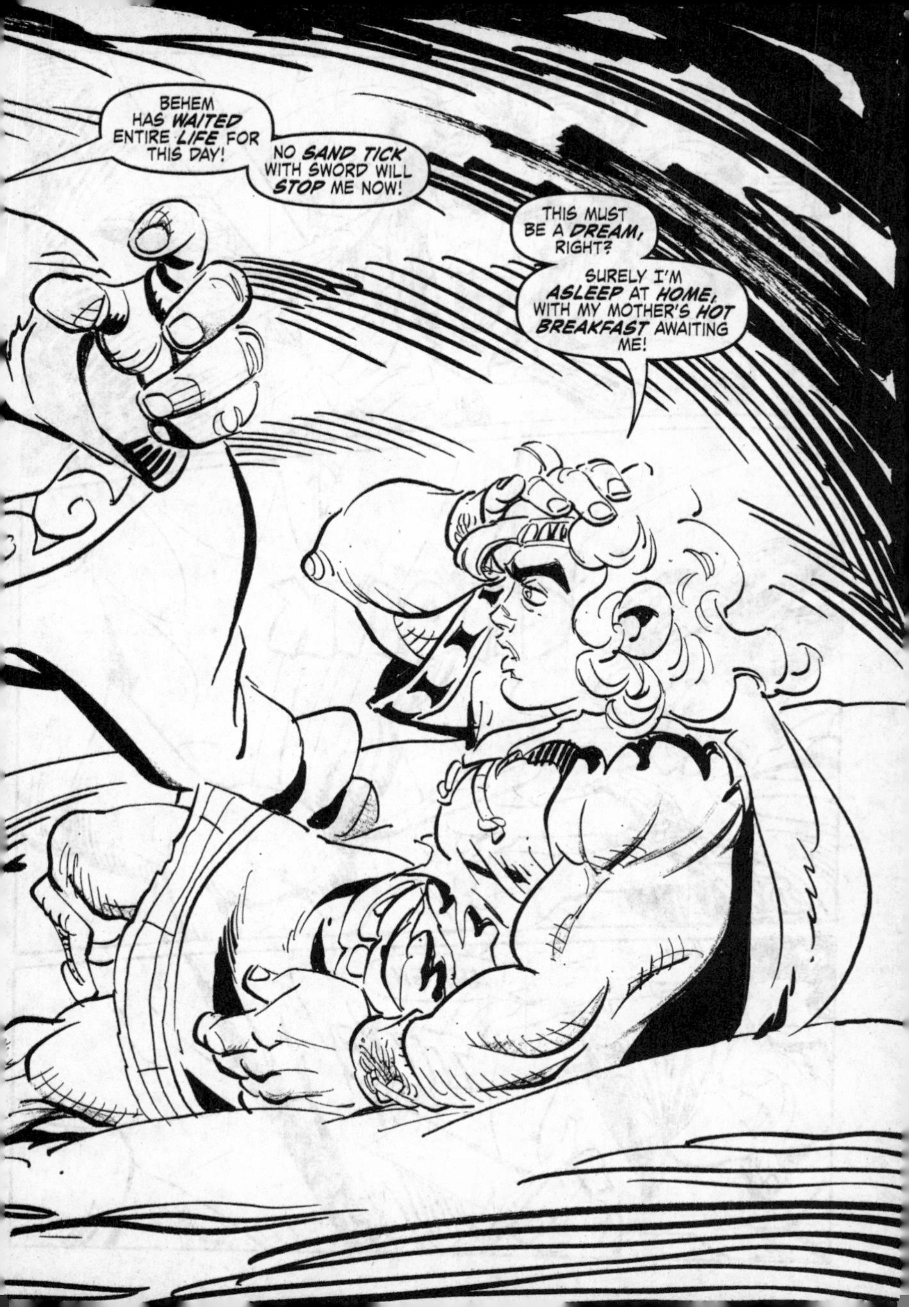

BEHEM HAS WAITED ENTIRE LIFE FOR THIS DAY!
NO SAND TICK WITH SWORD WILL STOP ME NOW!
THIS MUST BE A DREAM, RIGHT?
SURELY I'M ASLEEP AT HOME, WITH MY MOTHER'S HOT BREAKFAST AWAITING ME!

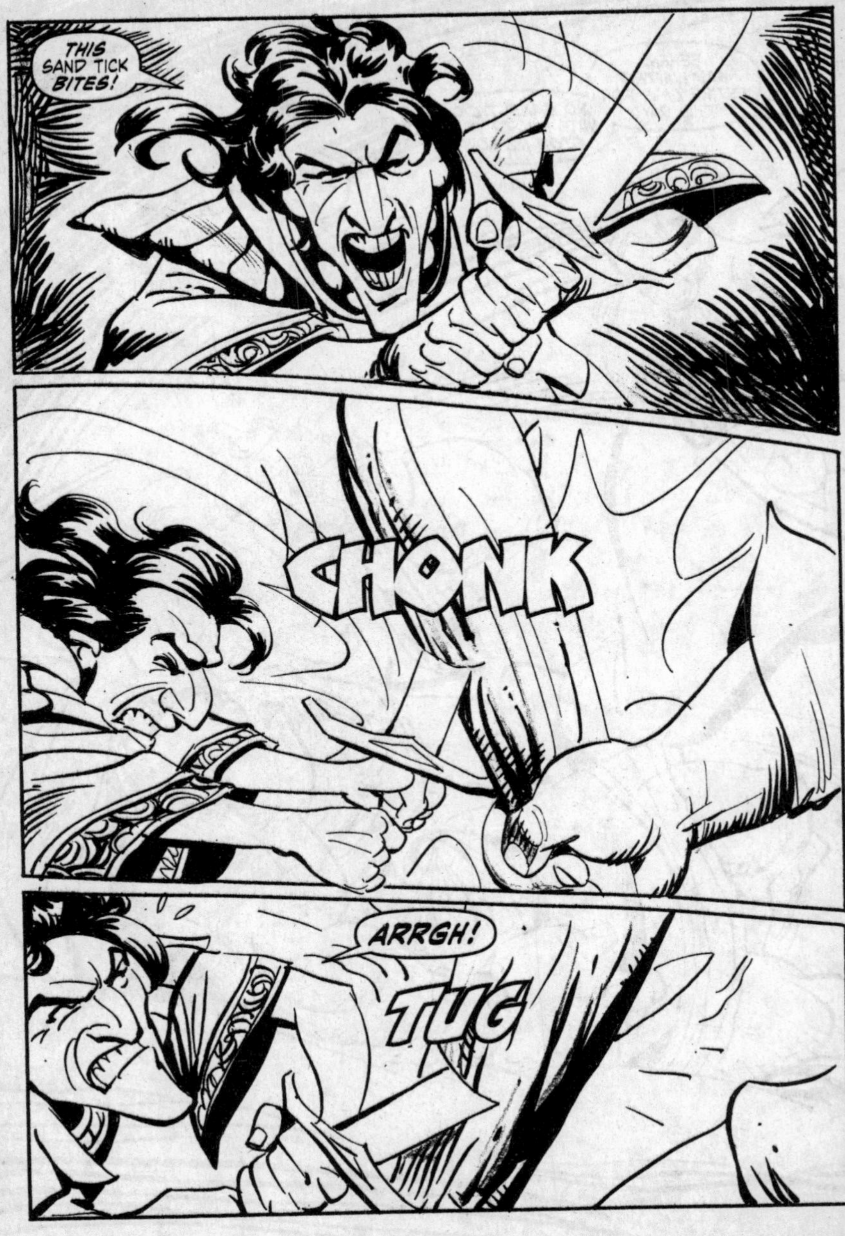
THIS SAND TICK BITES!
CHONK
ARRGH!
TUG

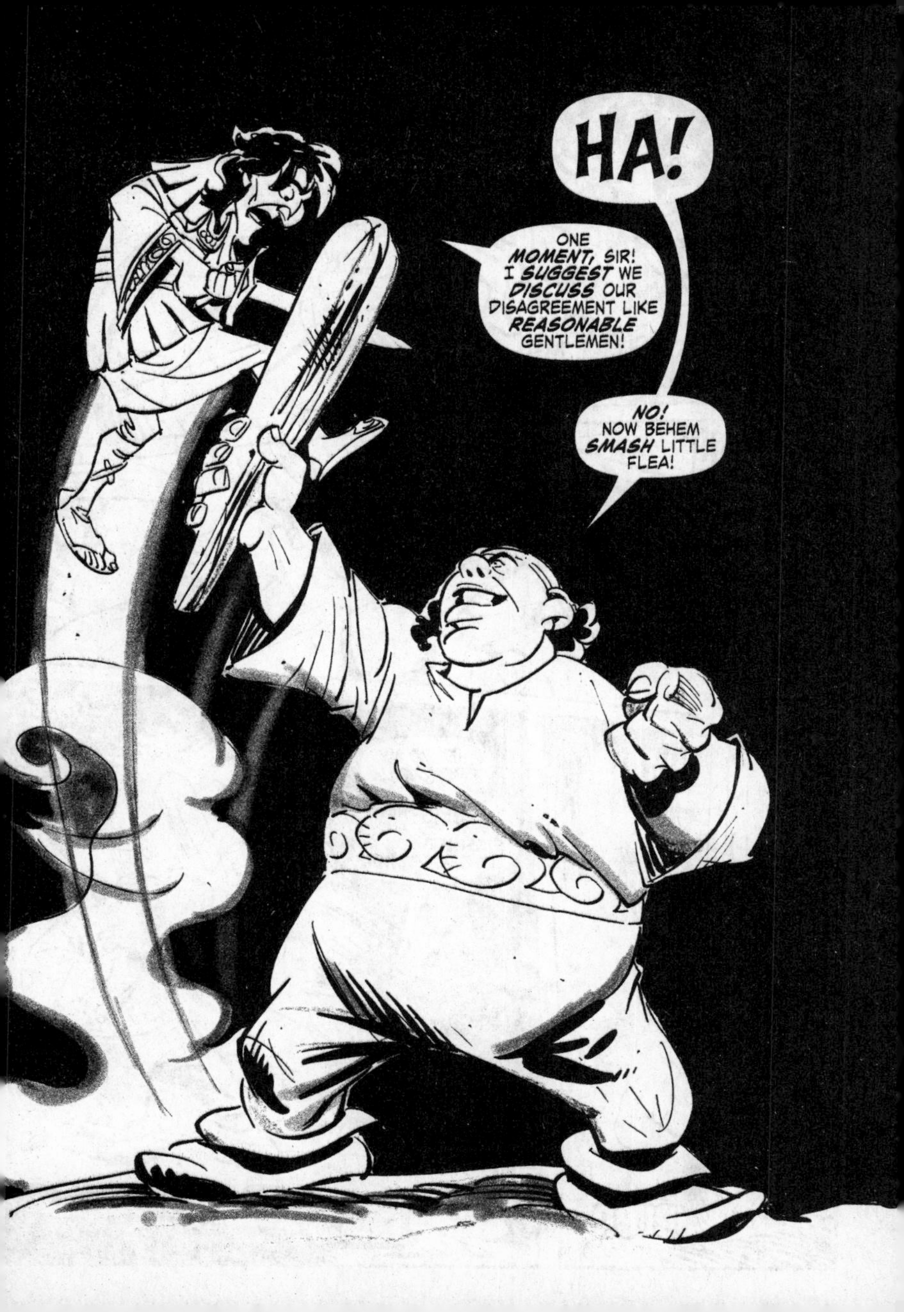
HA!
ONE MOMENT, SIR! I SUGGEST WE DISCUSS OUR DISAGREEMENT LIKE REASONABLE GENTLEMEN!
NO! NOW BEHEM SMASH LITTLE FLEA!

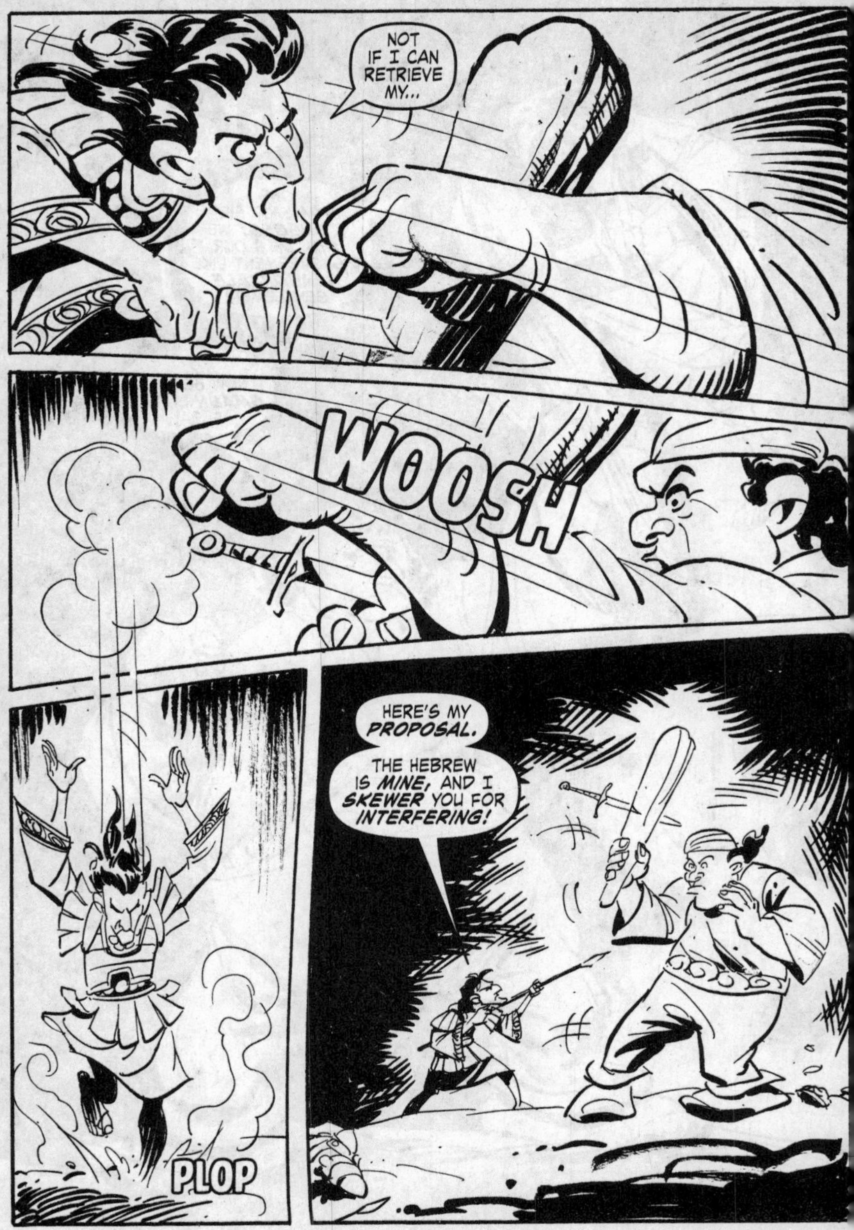

NOT IF I CAN RETRIEVE MY...
WOOSH
PLOP
HERE'S MY *PROPOSAL.*
THE HEBREW IS *MINE,* AND I *SKEWER* YOU FOR *INTERFERING!*

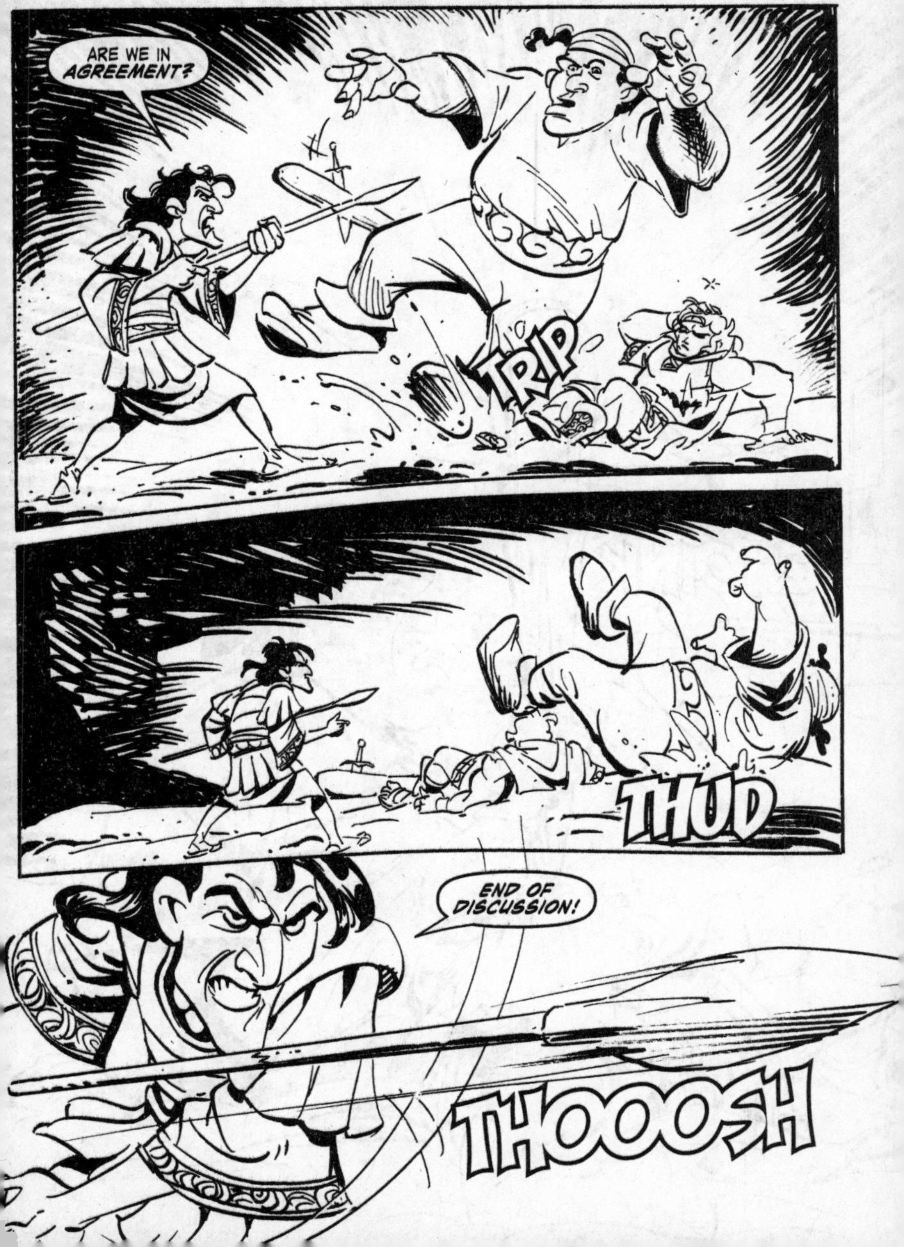
ARE WE IN AGREEMENT?
TRIP
THUD
END OF DISCUSSION!
THOOOSH

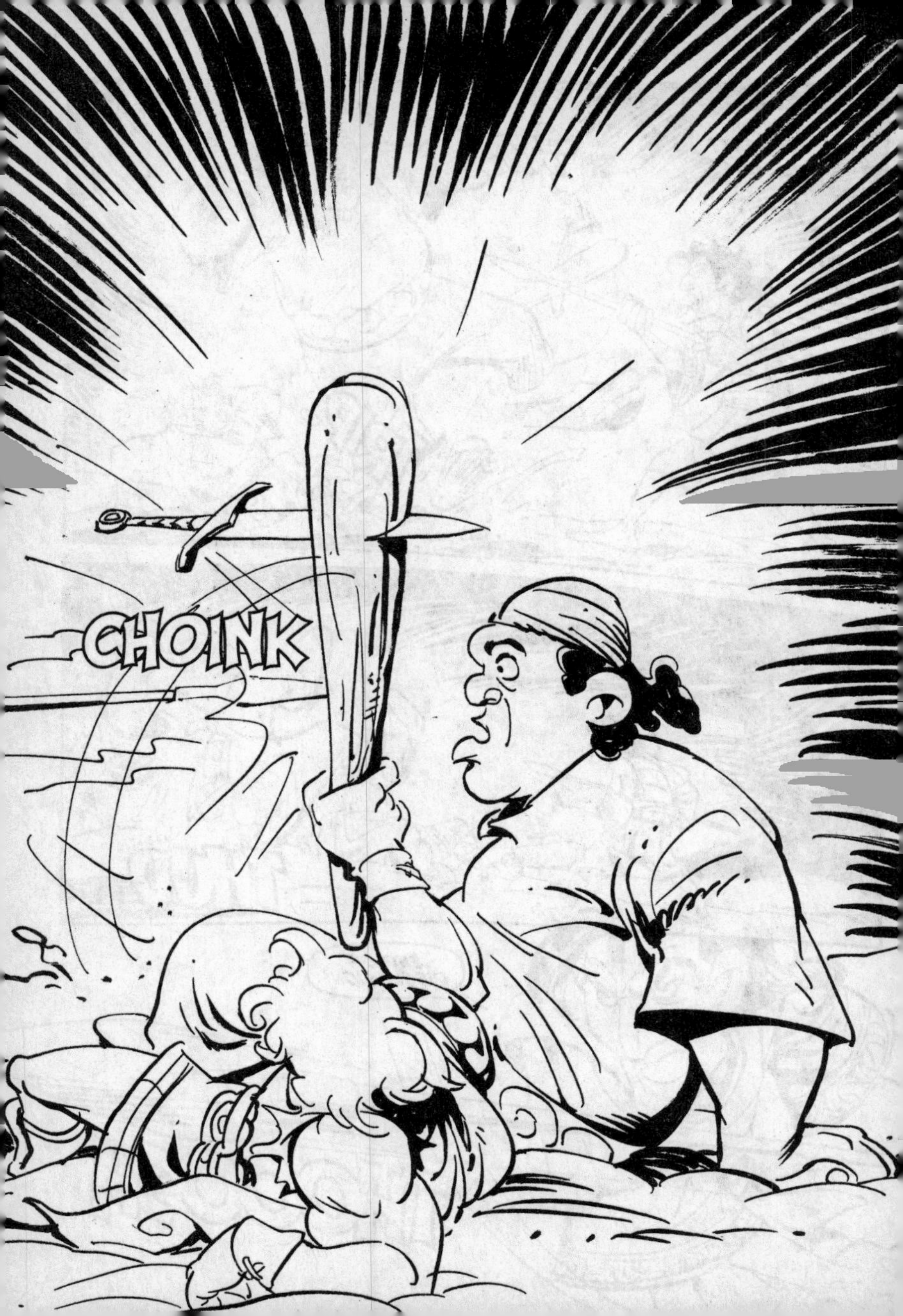
CHOINK

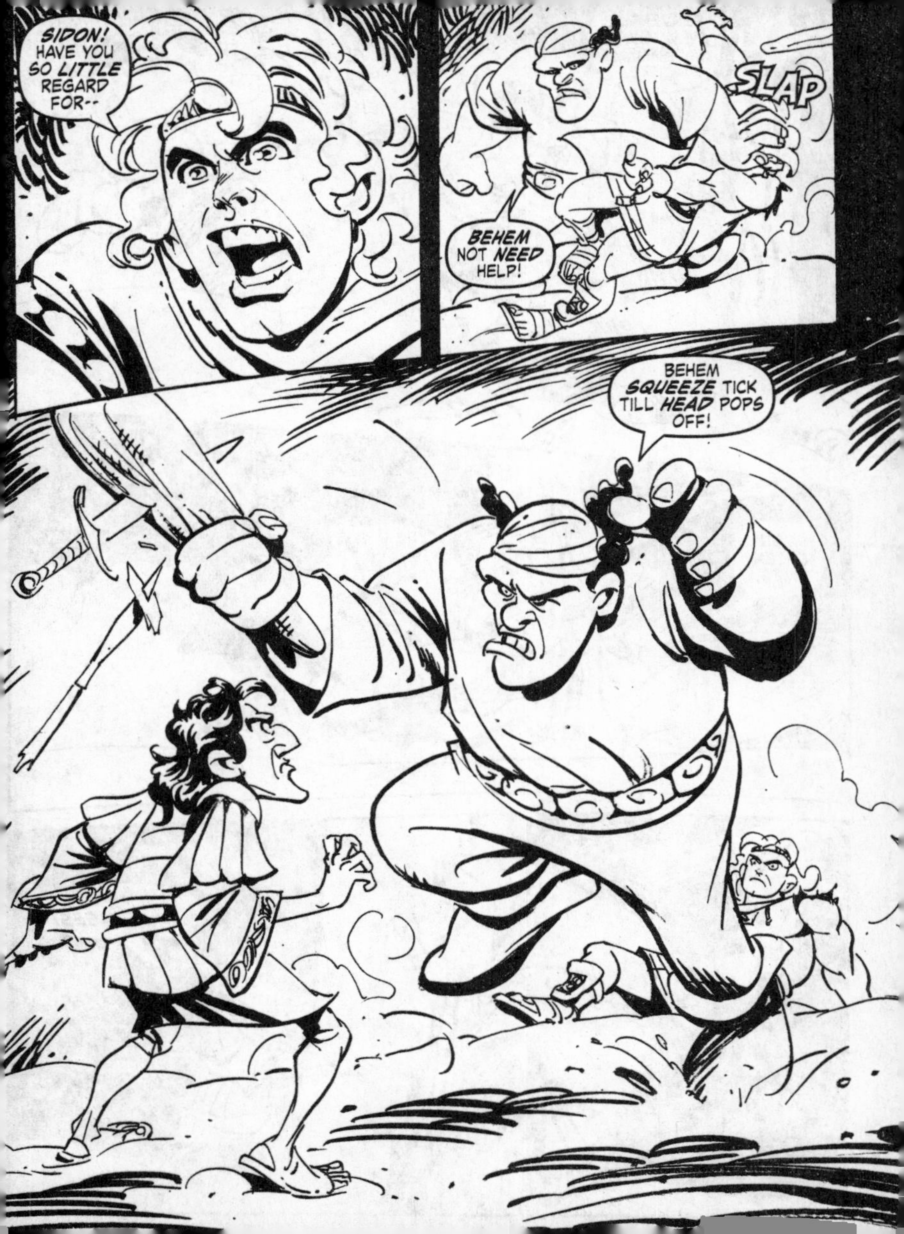
SIDON! HAVE YOU SO LITTLE REGARD FOR--
SLAP
BEHEM NOT NEED HELP!
BEHEM SQUEEZE TICK TILL HEAD POPS OFF!

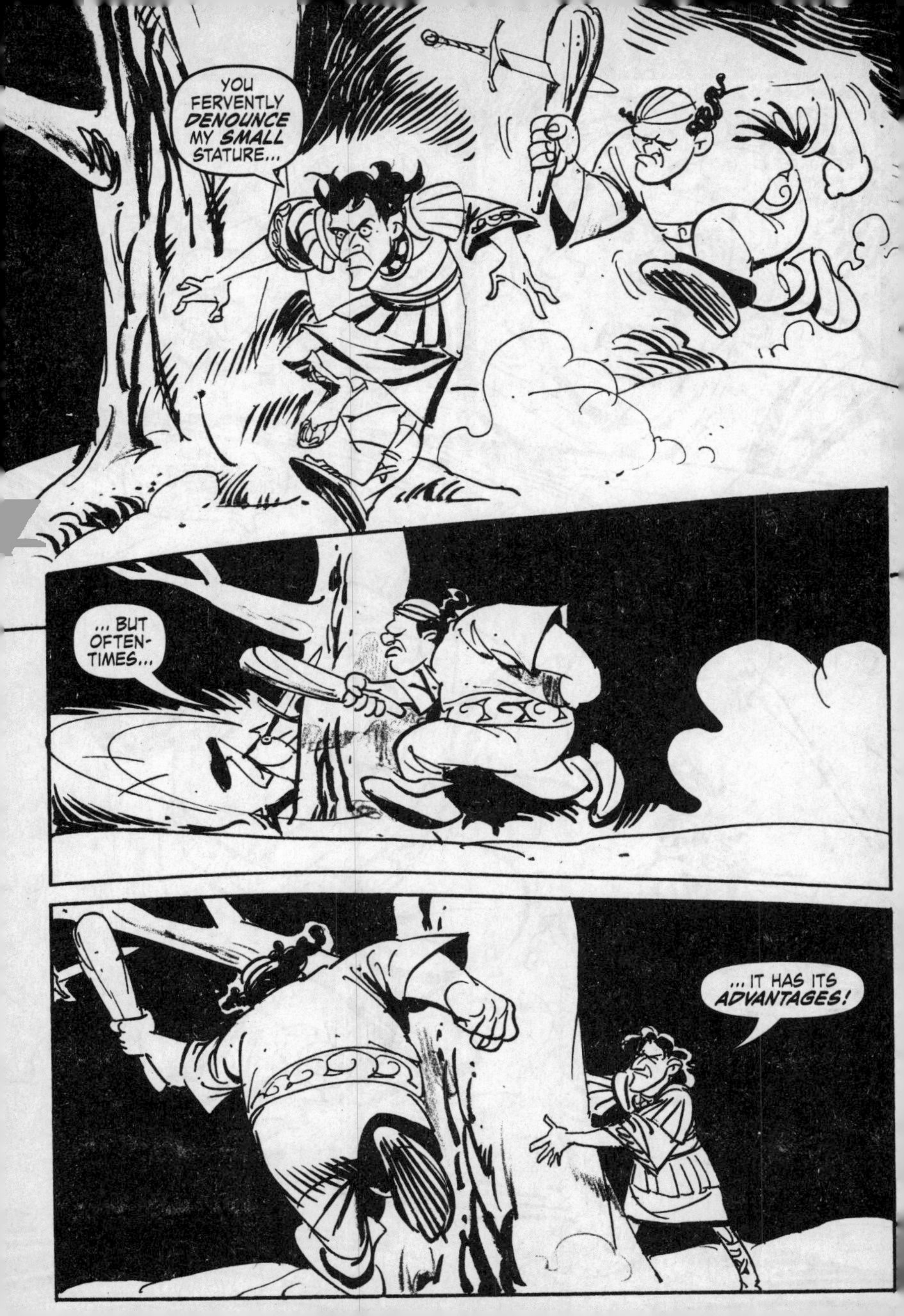
YOU FERVENTLY DENOUNCE MY SMALL STATURE...
... BUT OFTEN-TIMES...
... IT HAS ITS ADVANTAGES!

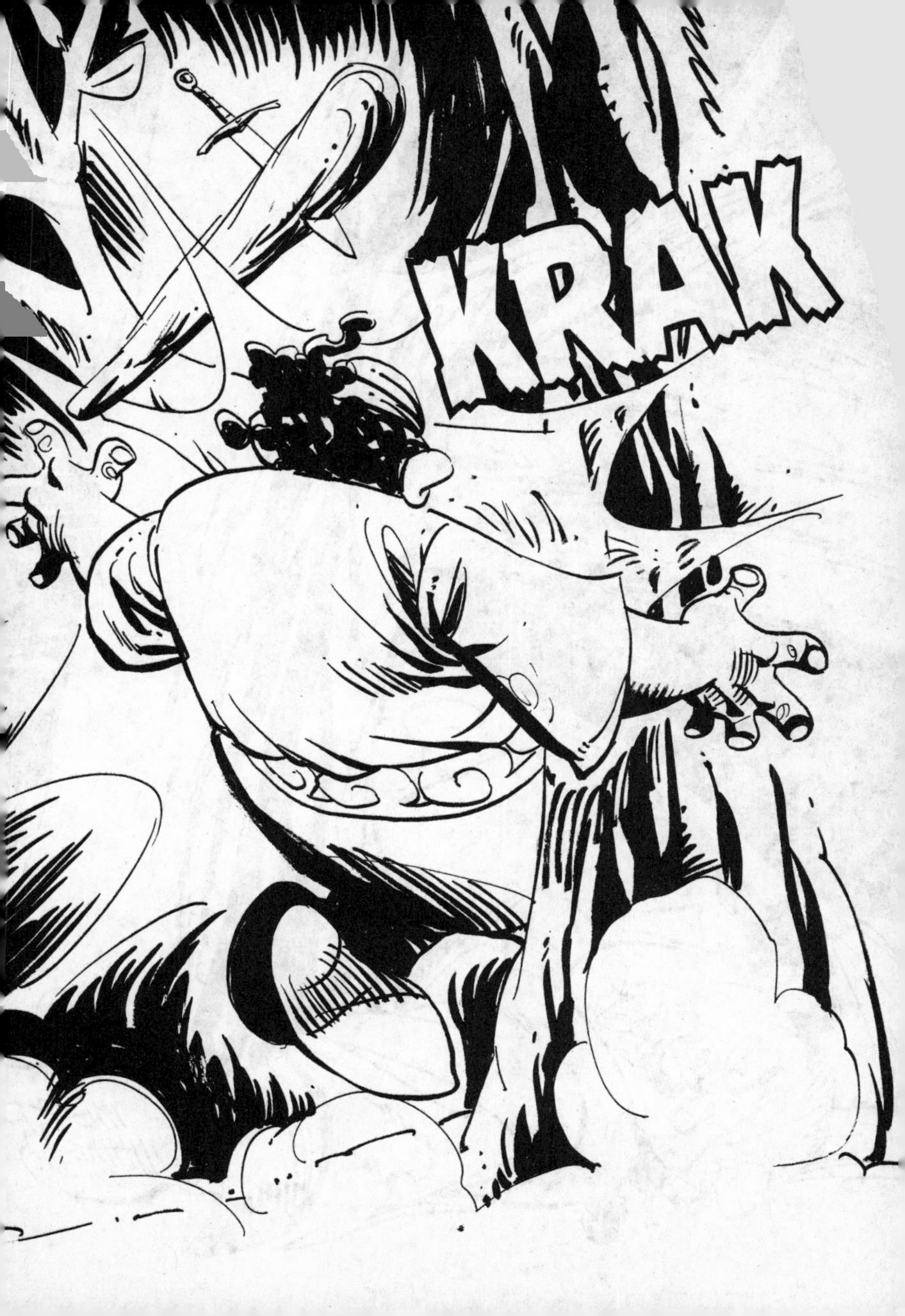
KRAK

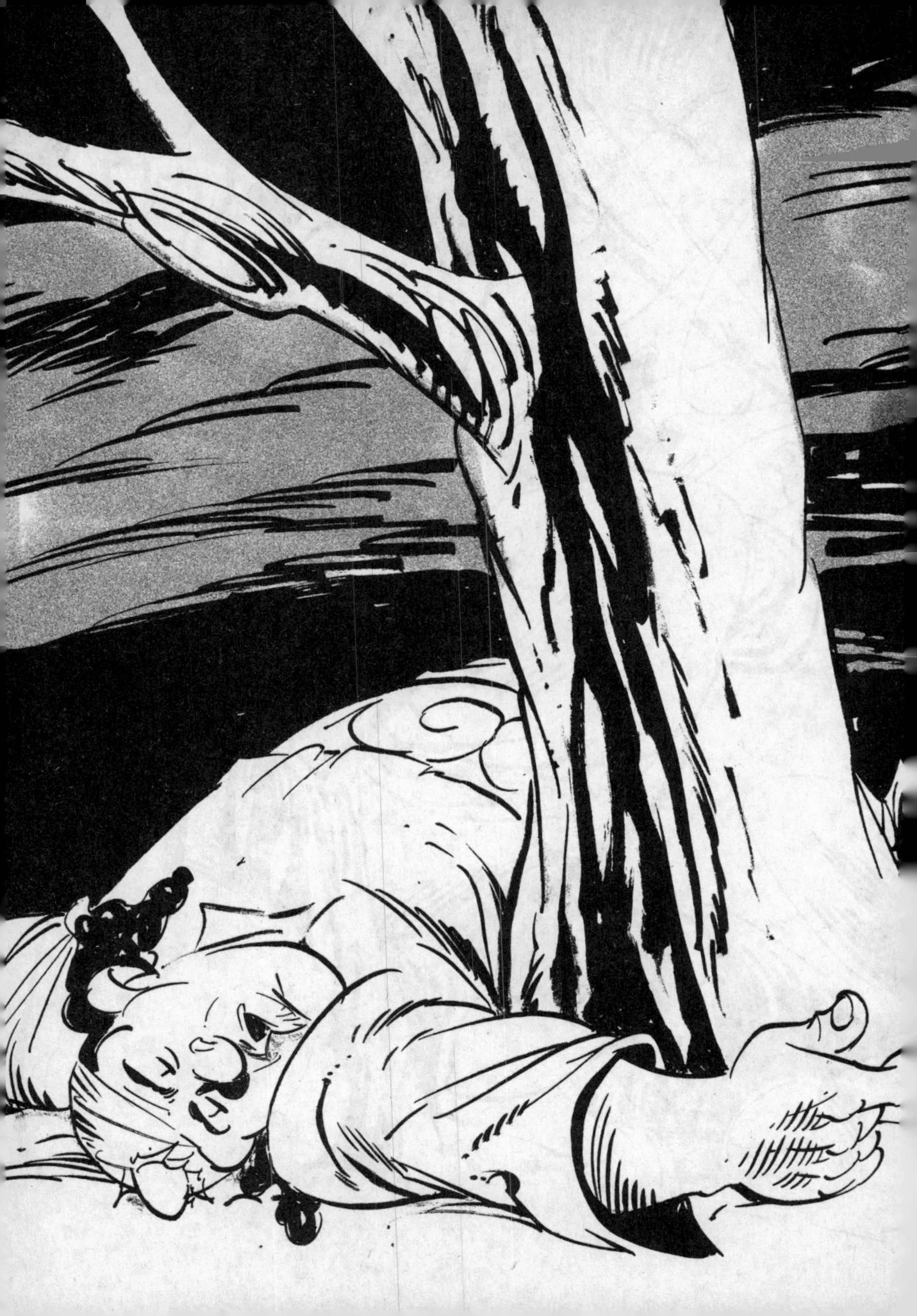

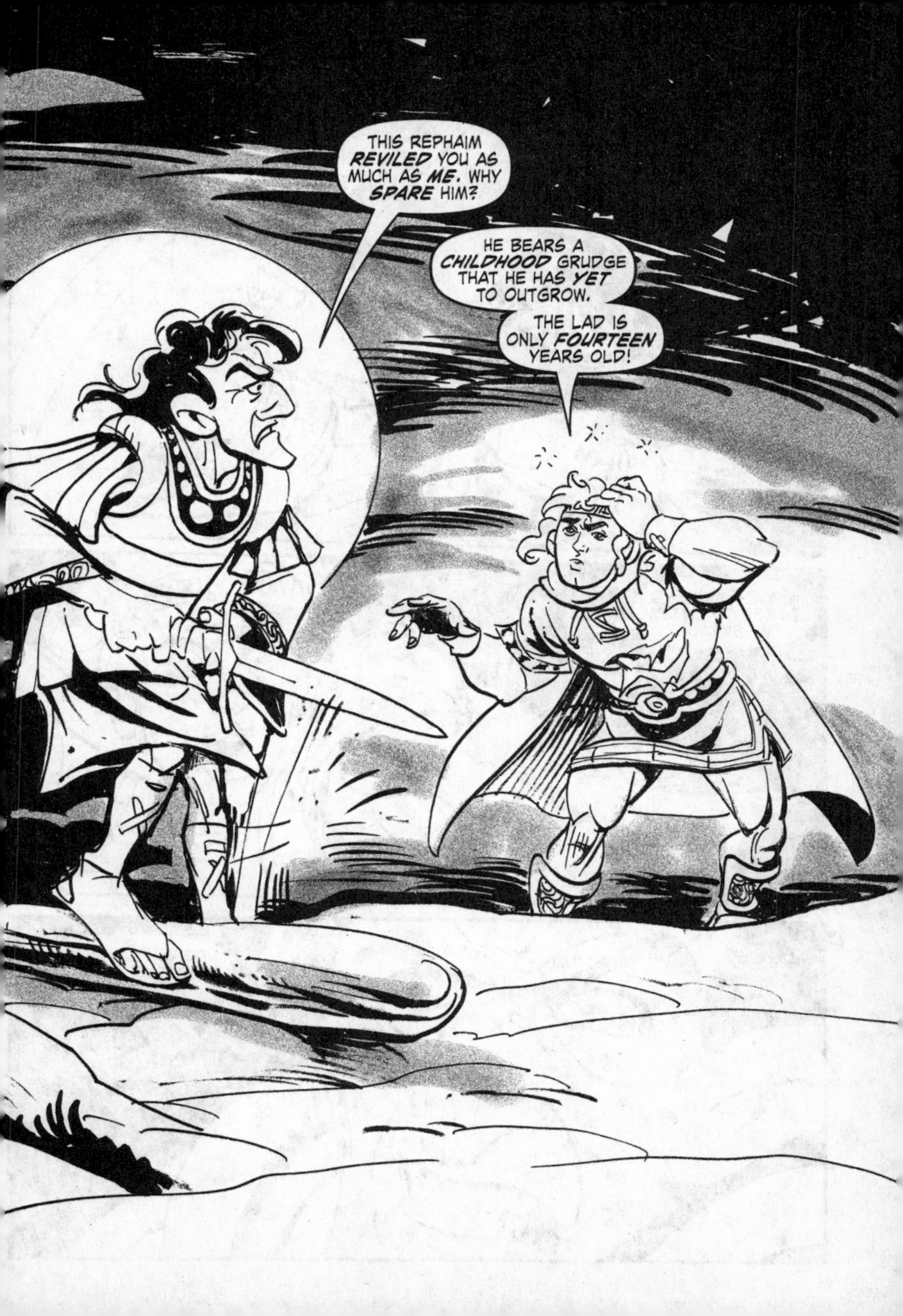
THIS REPHAIM **REVILED** YOU AS MUCH AS **ME**. WHY **SPARE** HIM?
HE BEARS A **CHILDHOOD** GRUDGE THAT HE HAS **YET** TO OUTGROW.
THE LAD IS ONLY **FOURTEEN** YEARS OLD!

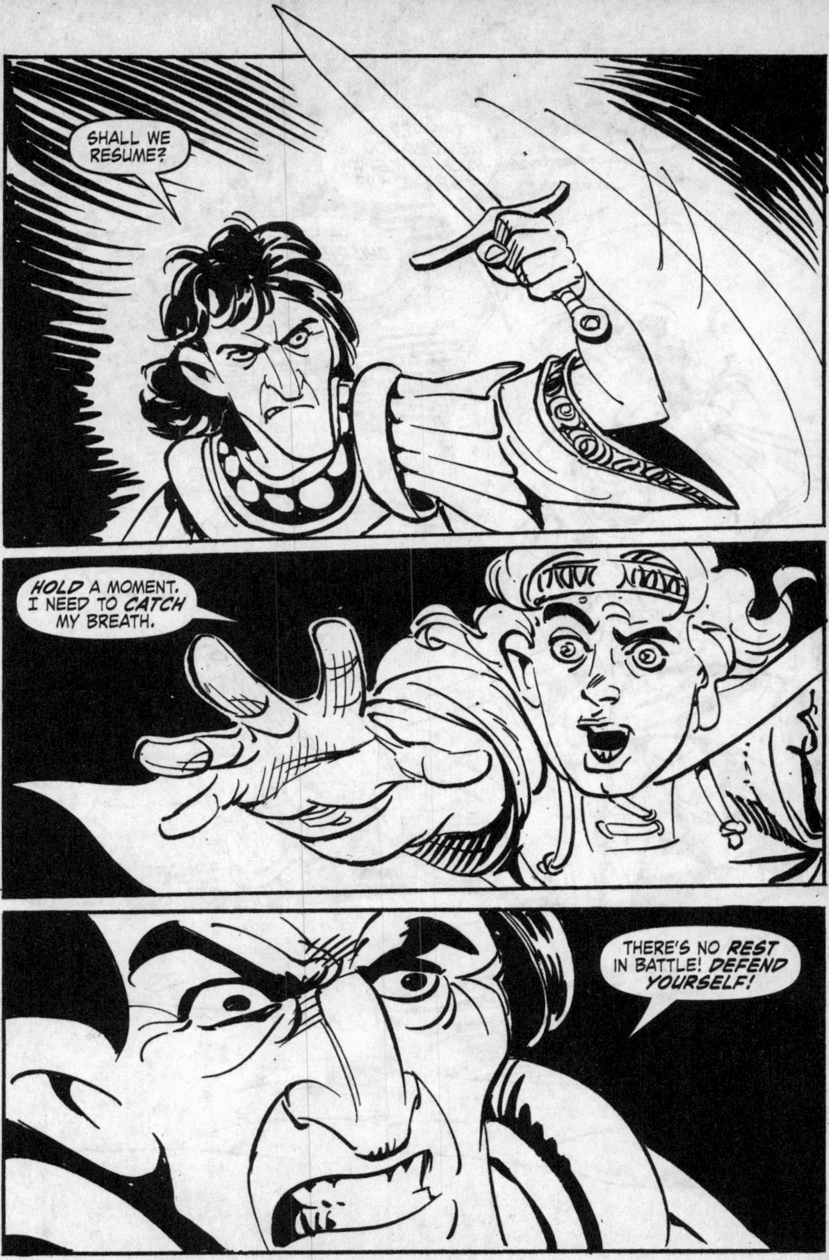
SHALL WE RESUME?
HOLD A MOMENT. I NEED TO CATCH MY BREATH.
THERE'S NO REST IN BATTLE! DEFEND YOURSELF!

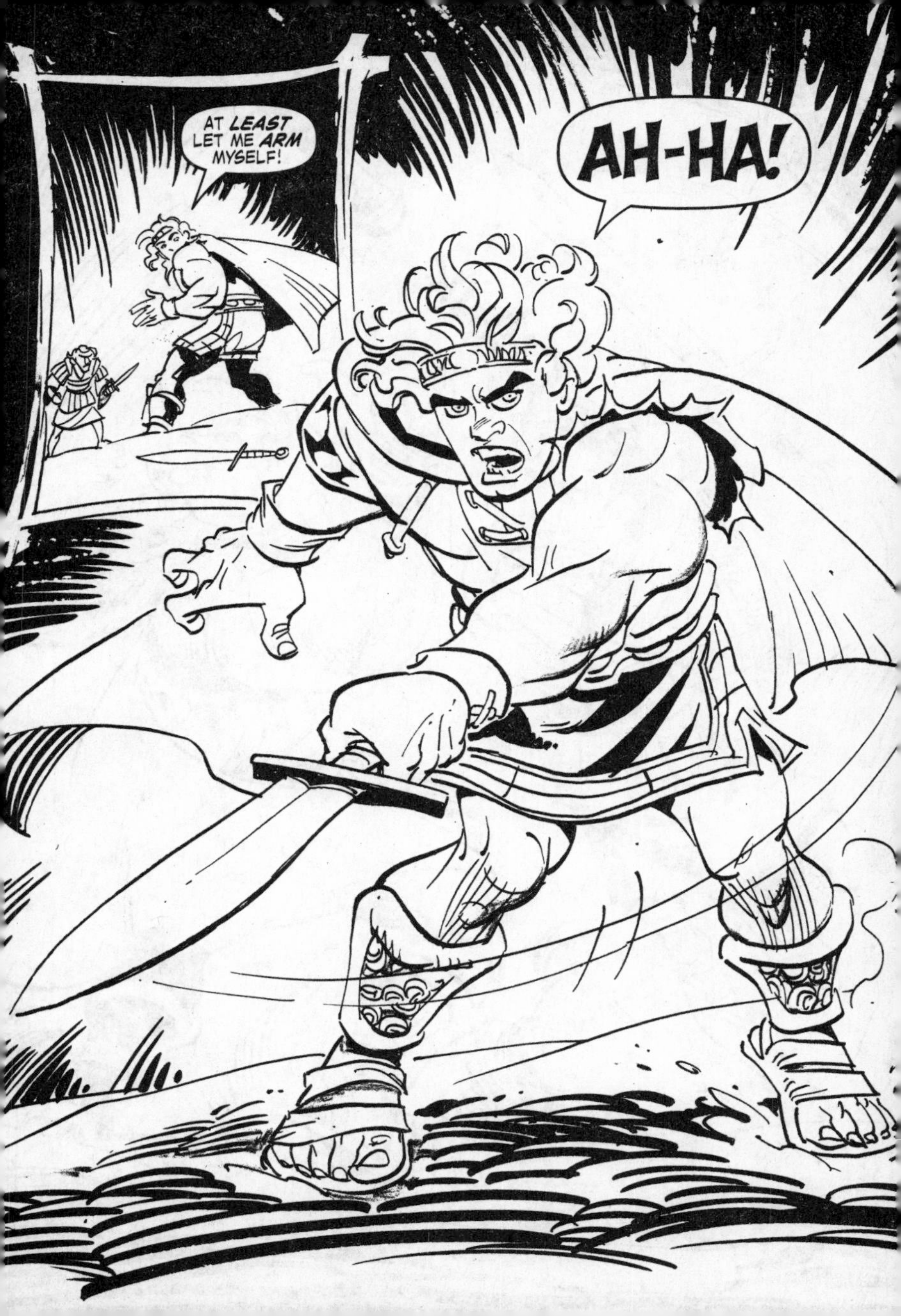
AT LEAST LET ME ARM MYSELF!
AH-HA!

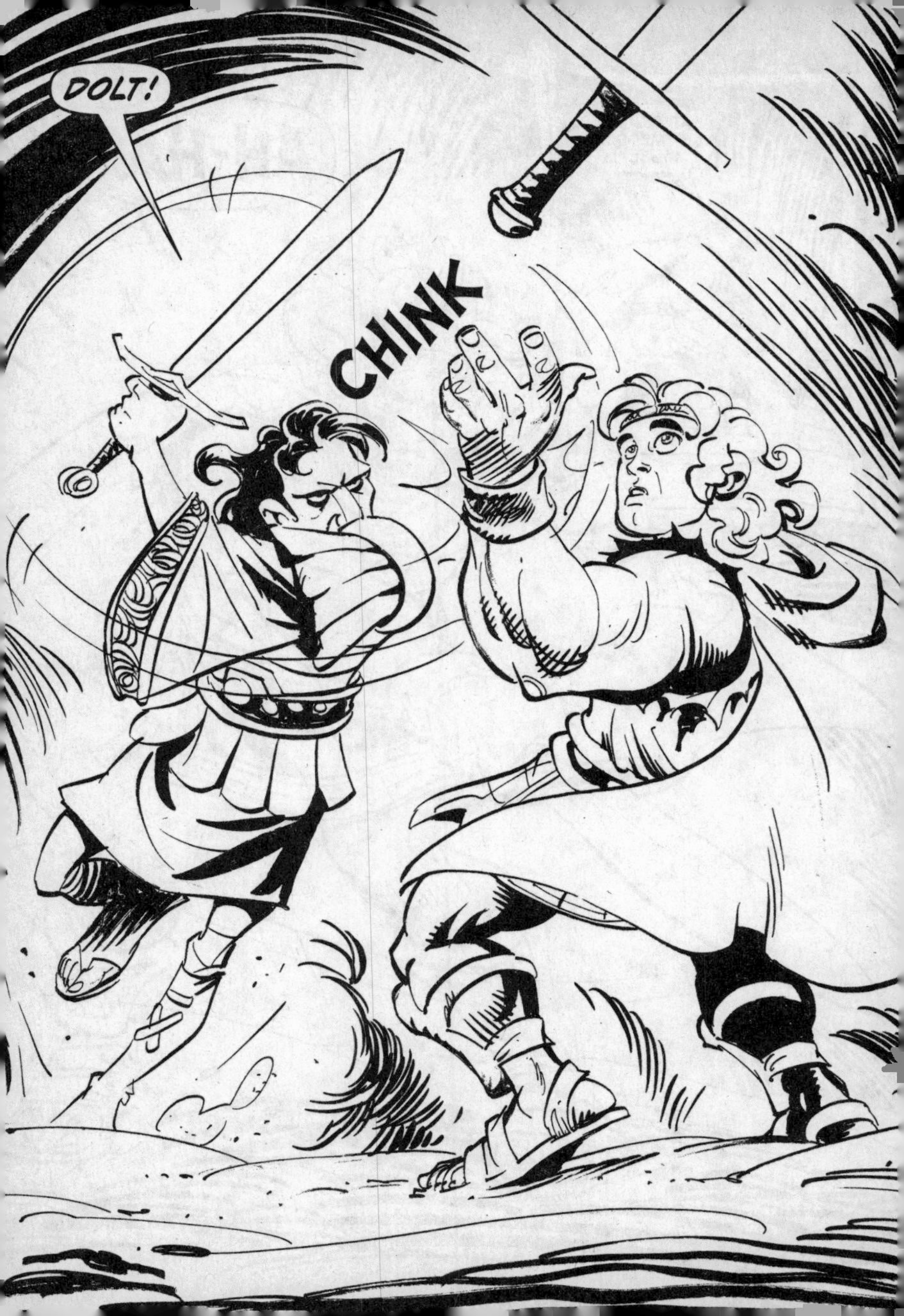
DOLT!
CHINK

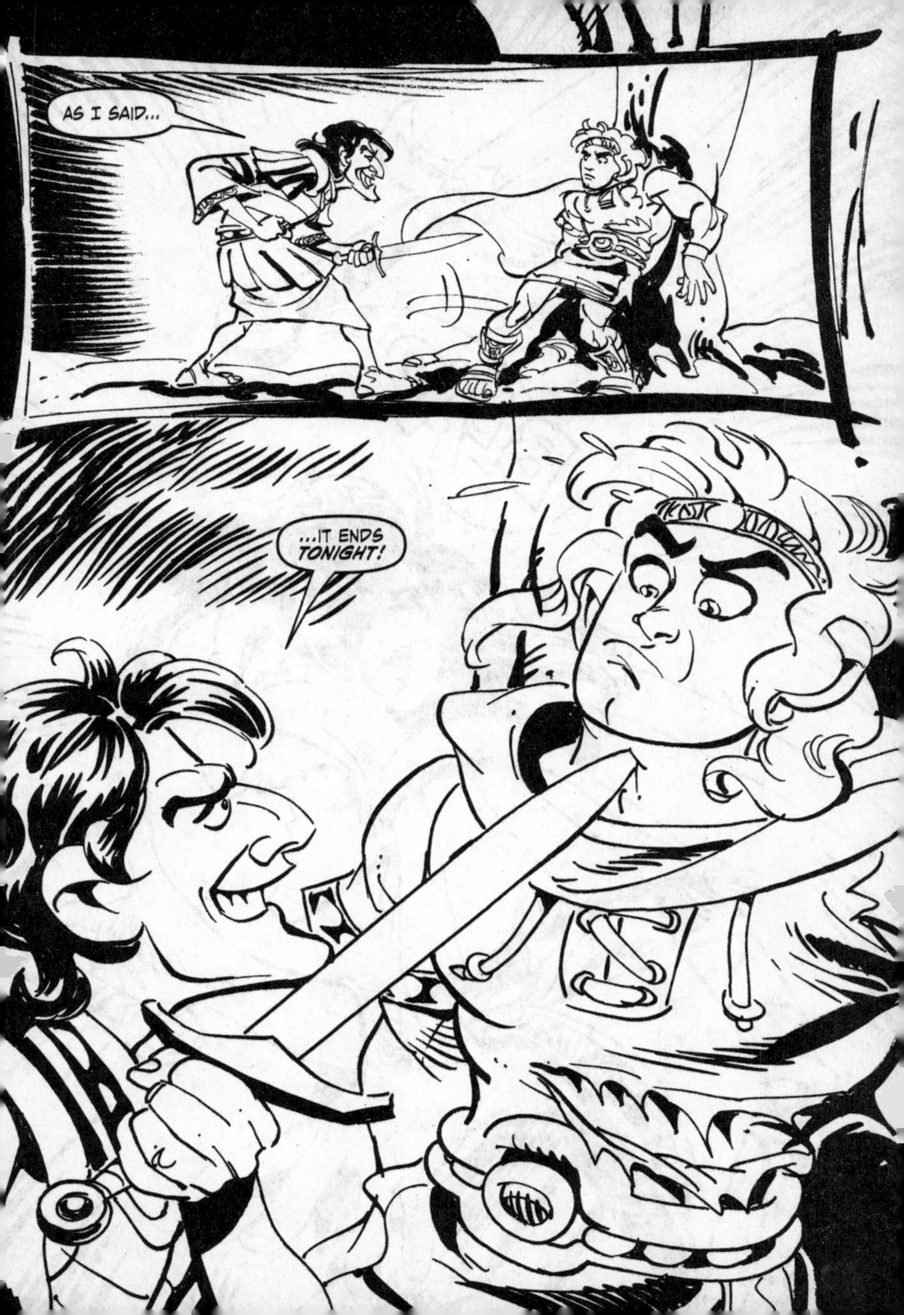
AS I SAID...
...IT ENDS TONIGHT!

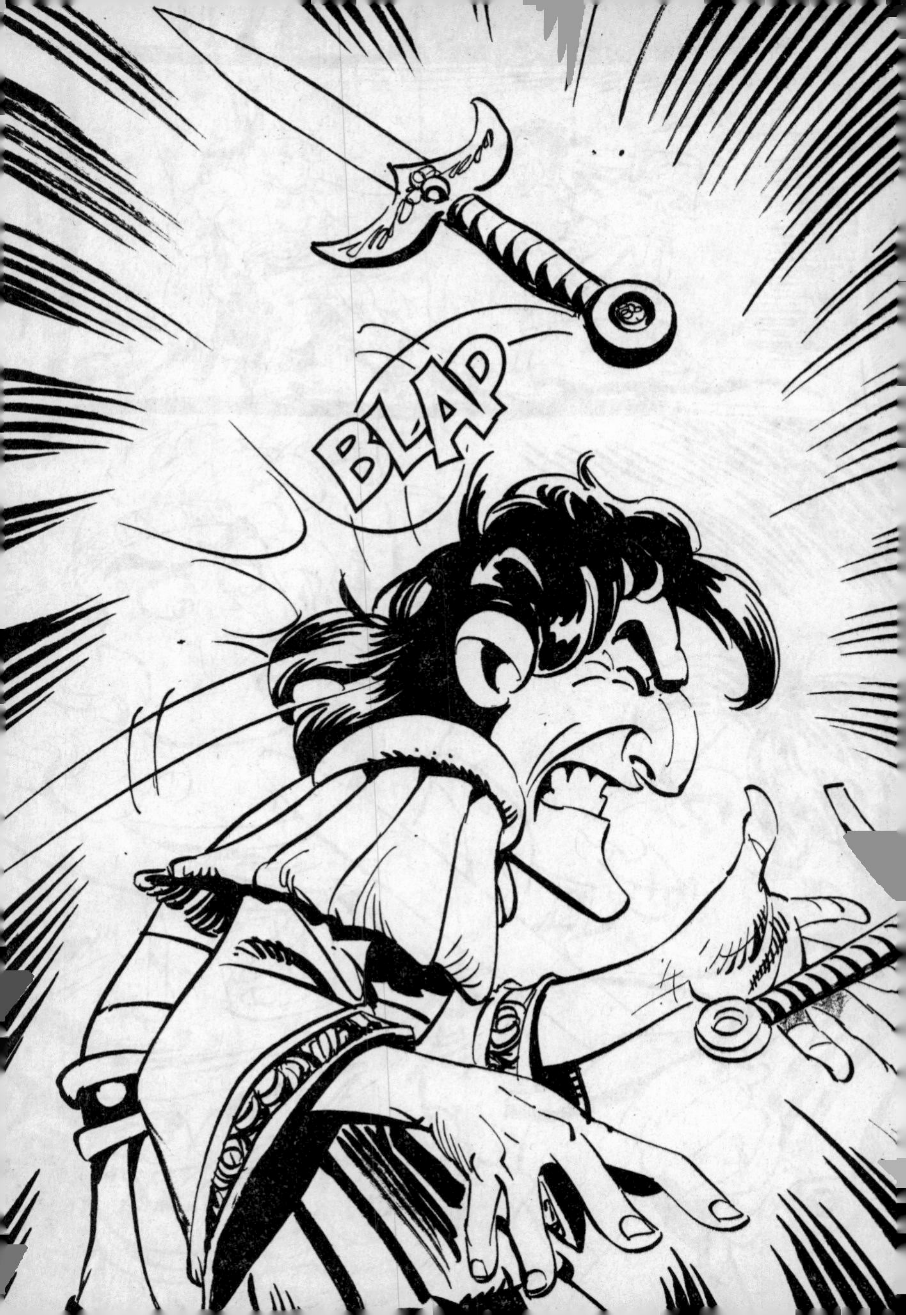
BLAP

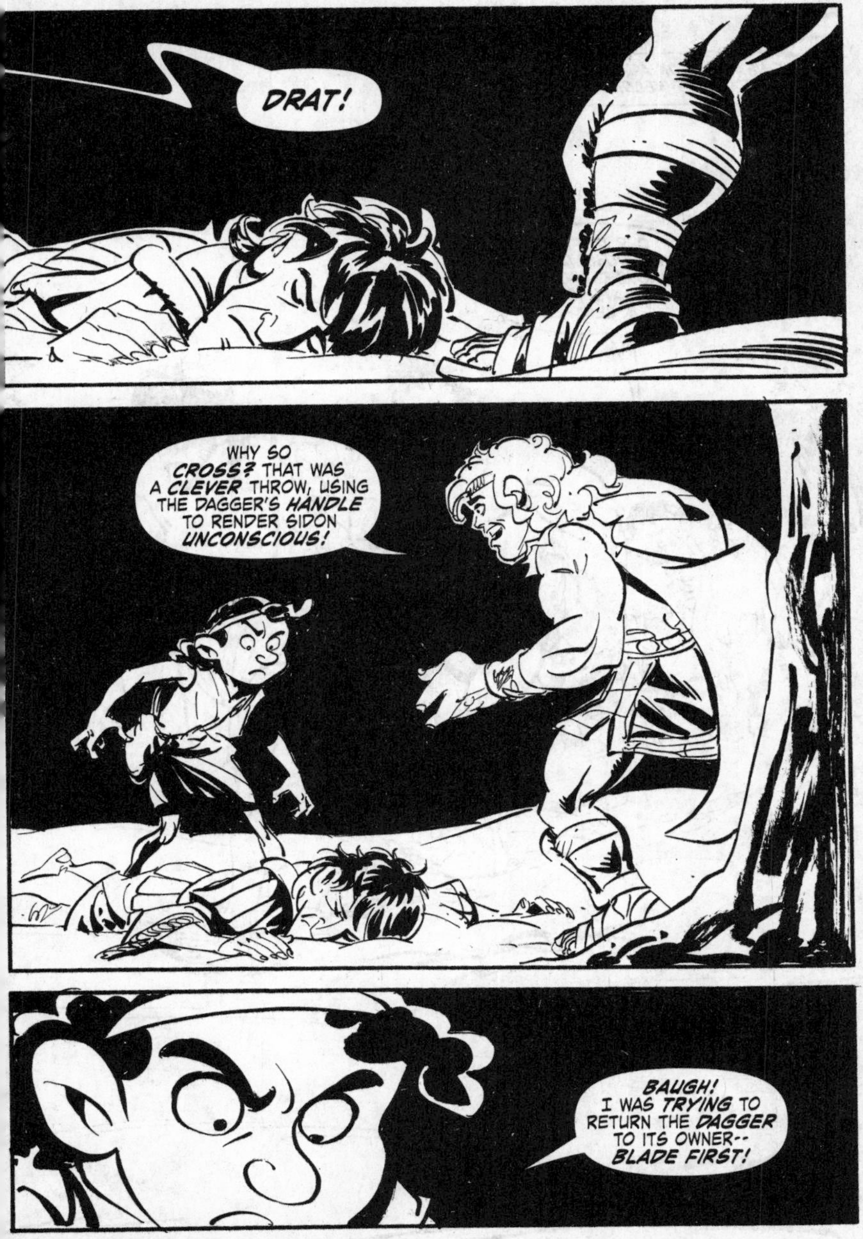
DRAT!
WHY SO CROSS? THAT WAS A CLEVER THROW, USING THE DAGGER'S HANDLE TO RENDER SIDON UNCONSCIOUS!
BAUGH! I WAS TRYING TO RETURN THE DAGGER TO ITS OWNER-- BLADE FIRST!

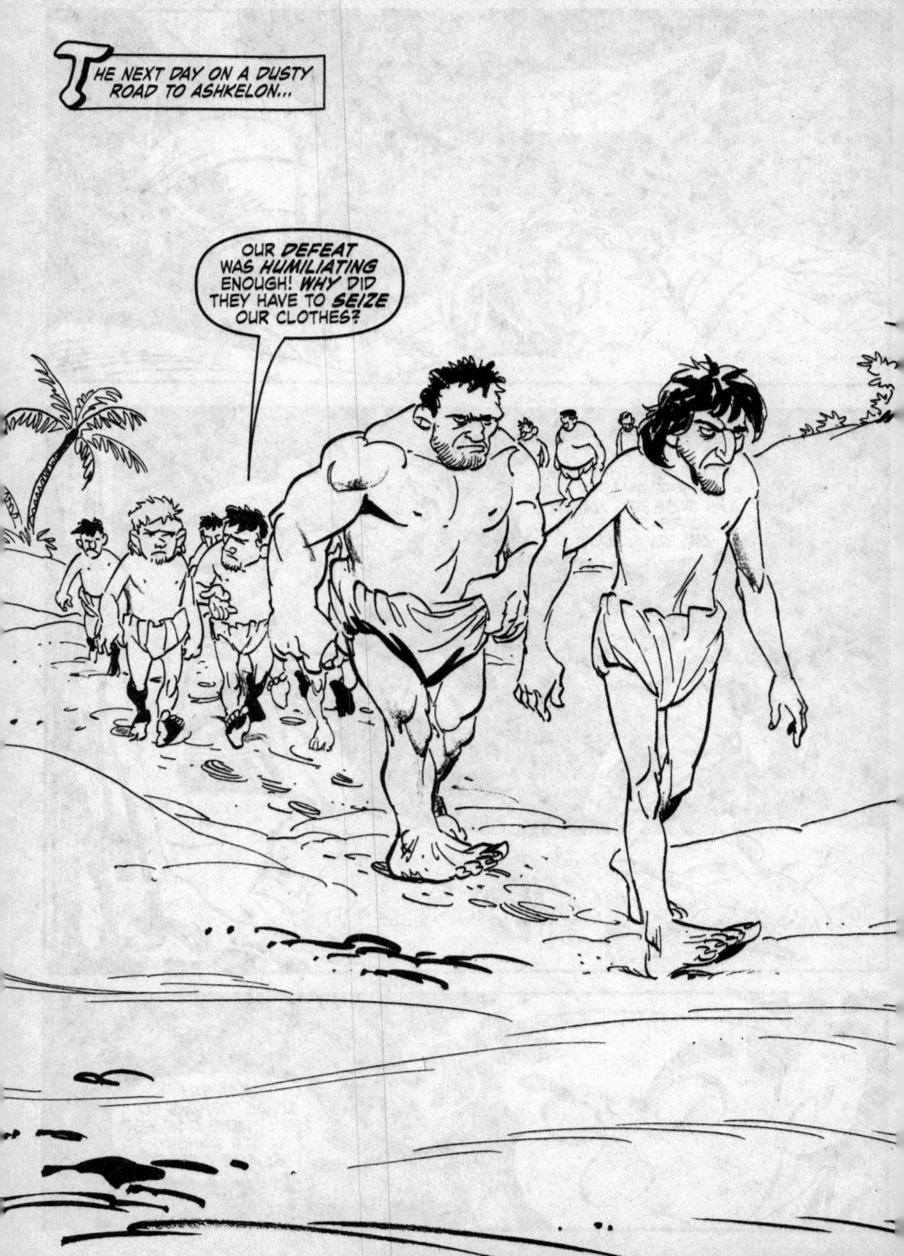
THE NEXT DAY ON A DUSTY ROAD TO ASHKELON...
OUR *DEFEAT* WAS *HUMILIATING* ENOUGH! *WHY* DID THEY HAVE TO *SEIZE* OUR CLOTHES?

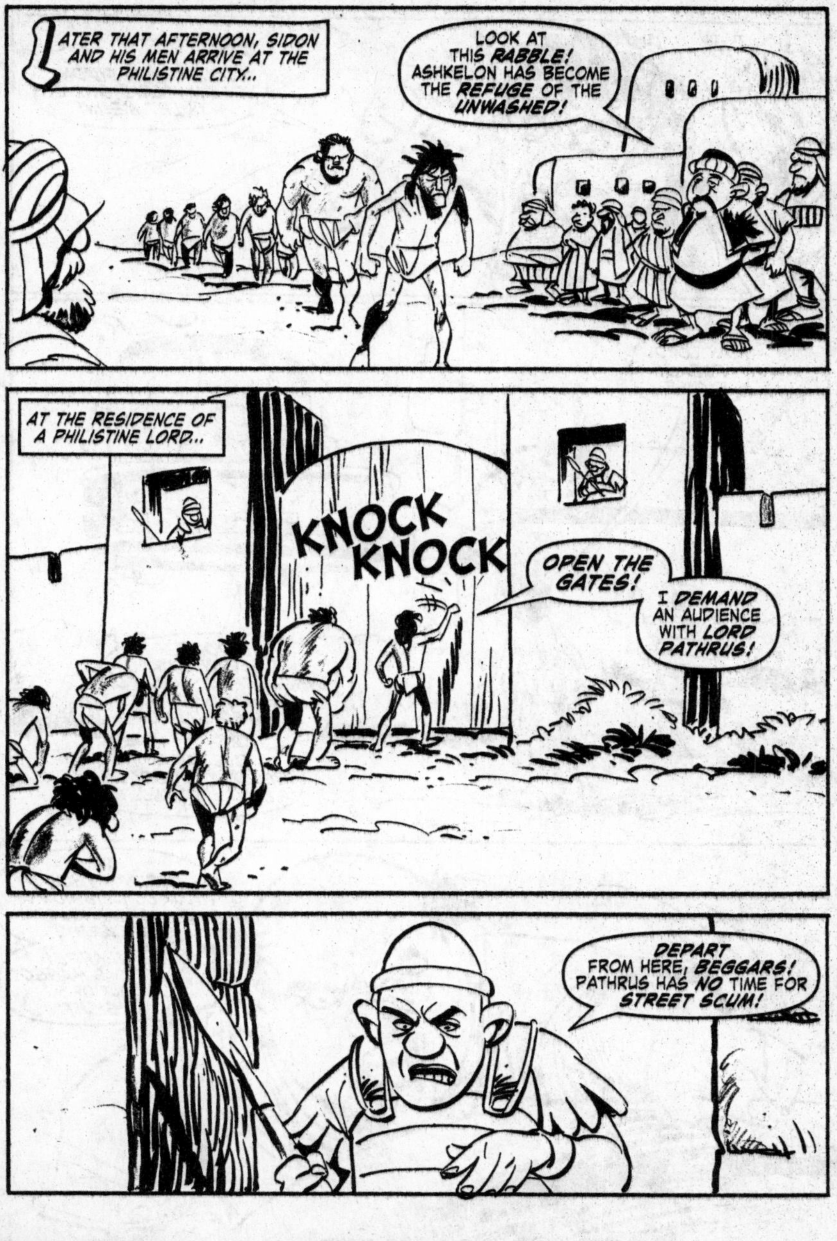
LATER THAT AFTERNOON, SIDON AND HIS MEN ARRIVE AT THE PHILISTINE CITY...
LOOK AT THIS RABBLE! ASHKELON HAS BECOME THE REFUGE OF THE UNWASHED!
AT THE RESIDENCE OF A PHILISTINE LORD...
KNOCK KNOCK
OPEN THE GATES!
I DEMAND AN AUDIENCE WITH LORD PATHRUS!
DEPART FROM HERE, BEGGARS! PATHRUS HAS NO TIME FOR STREET SCUM!

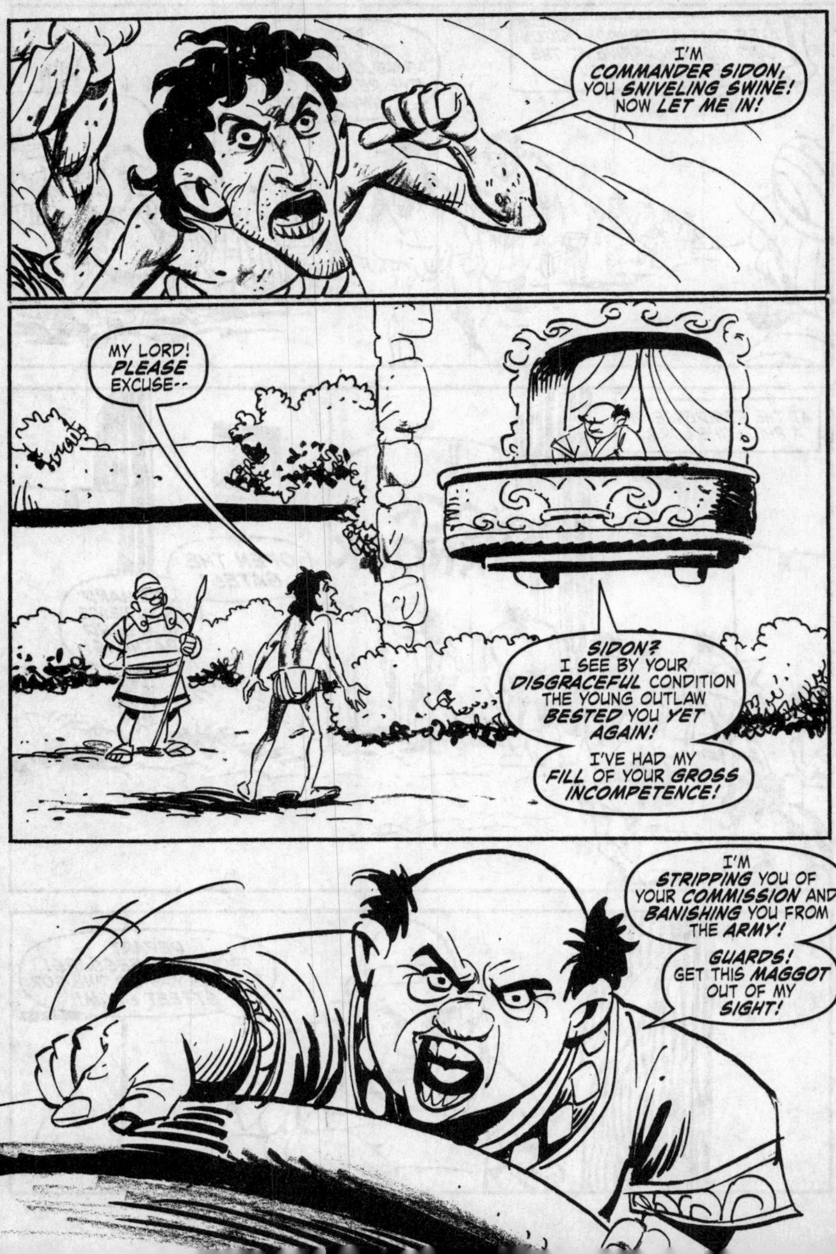
I'M COMMANDER SIDON, YOU SNIVELING SWINE! NOW LET ME IN!
MY LORD! PLEASE EXCUSE--
SIDON? I SEE BY YOUR DISGRACEFUL CONDITION THE YOUNG OUTLAW BESTED YOU YET AGAIN!
I'VE HAD MY FILL OF YOUR GROSS INCOMPETENCE!
I'M STRIPPING YOU OF YOUR COMMISSION AND BANISHING YOU FROM THE ARMY!
GUARDS! GET THIS MAGGOT OUT OF MY SIGHT!

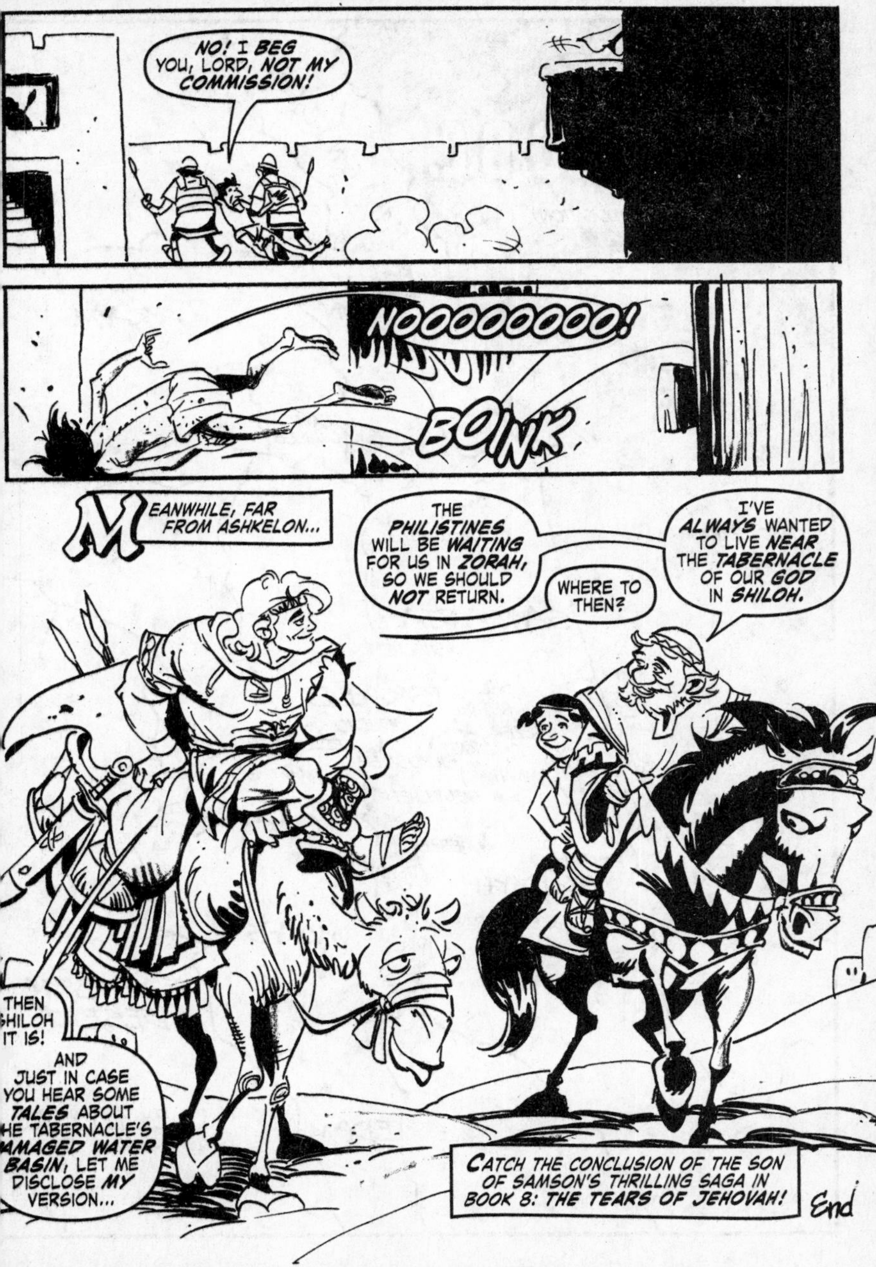

NO! I BEG YOU, LORD, NOT MY COMMISSION!
NOOOOOOOOO!
BOINK
MEANWHILE, FAR FROM ASHKELON...
THE PHILISTINES WILL BE WAITING FOR US IN ZORAH, SO WE SHOULD NOT RETURN.
WHERE TO THEN?
I'VE ALWAYS WANTED TO LIVE NEAR THE TABERNACLE OF OUR GOD IN SHILOH.
THEN SHILOH IT IS!
AND JUST IN CASE YOU HEAR SOME TALES ABOUT THE TABERNACLE'S DAMAGED WATER BASIN, LET ME DISCLOSE MY VERSION...
CATCH THE CONCLUSION OF THE SON OF SAMSON'S THRILLING SAGA IN BOOK 8: THE TEARS OF JEHOVAH!
End

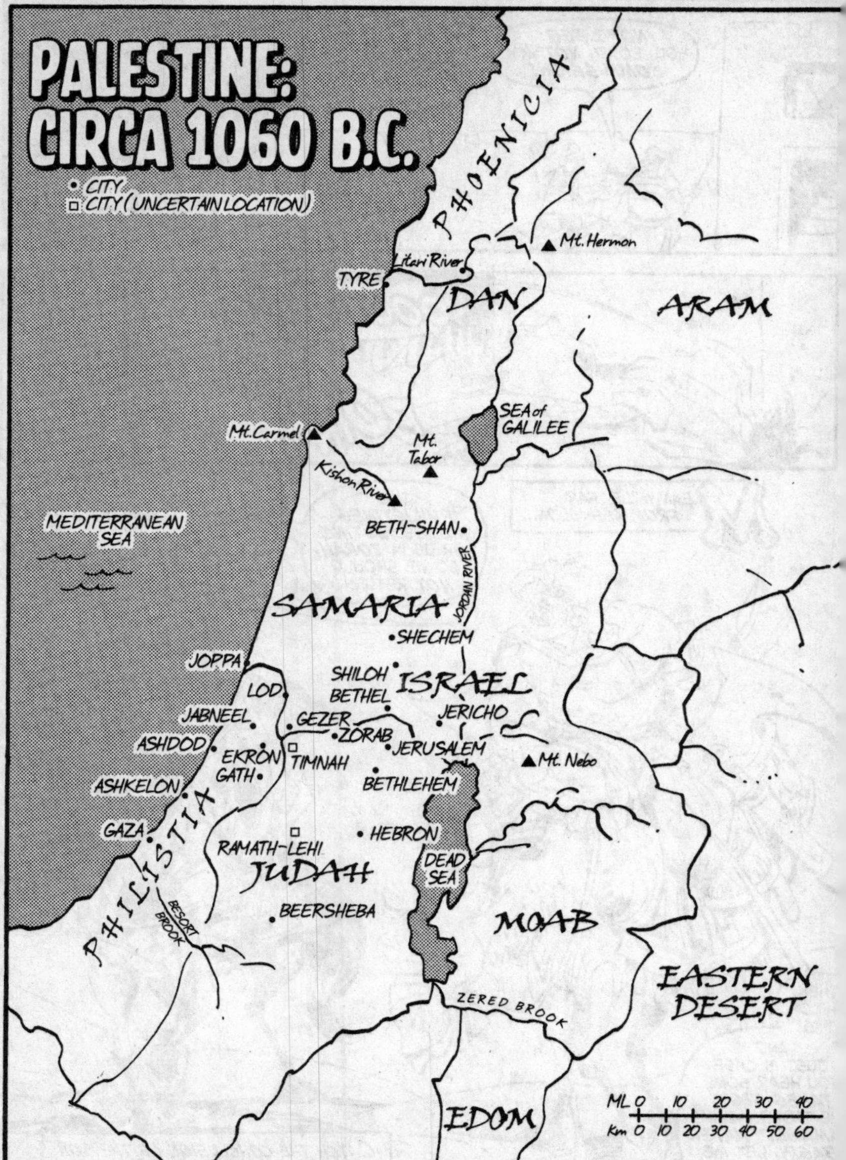
PALESTINE: CIRCA 1060 B.C.
• CITY
□ CITY (UNCERTAIN LOCATION)
PHOENICIA
Mt. Hermon
Litani River
TYRE
DAN
ARAM
SEA of GALILEE
Mt. Carmel
Mt. Tabor
Kishon River
BETH-SHAN
MEDITERRANEAN SEA
JORDAN RIVER
SAMARIA
SHECHEM
JOPPA
SHILOH
BETHEL
ISRAEL
LOD
JABNEEL
GEZER
JERICHO
ZORAB
ASHDOD
EKRON
TIMNAH
JERUSALEM
Mt. Nebo
GATH
ASHKELON
BETHLEHEM
GAZA
HEBRON
RAMATH-LEHI
DEAD SEA
JUDAH
PHILISTIA
BESORT BROOK
BEERSHEBA
MOAB
EASTERN DESERT
ZERED BROOK
EDOM
ML 0 10 20 30 40
Km 0 10 20 30 40 50 60

BRANAN

STANDING SIX FEET TWO INCHES AND WEIGHING TWO HUNDRED FORTY POUNDS, THE EIGHTEEN-YEAR-OLD SON OF SAMSON HAS INHERITED HIS FATHER'S INCREDIBLE STRENGTH. RAISED BY HIS PHILISTINE MOTHER, BRANAN NOW TRAVELS THE ANCIENT LANDS OF PALESTINE, RETRACING THE LEGENDARY DEEDS OF THE FATHER HE NEVER KNEW.

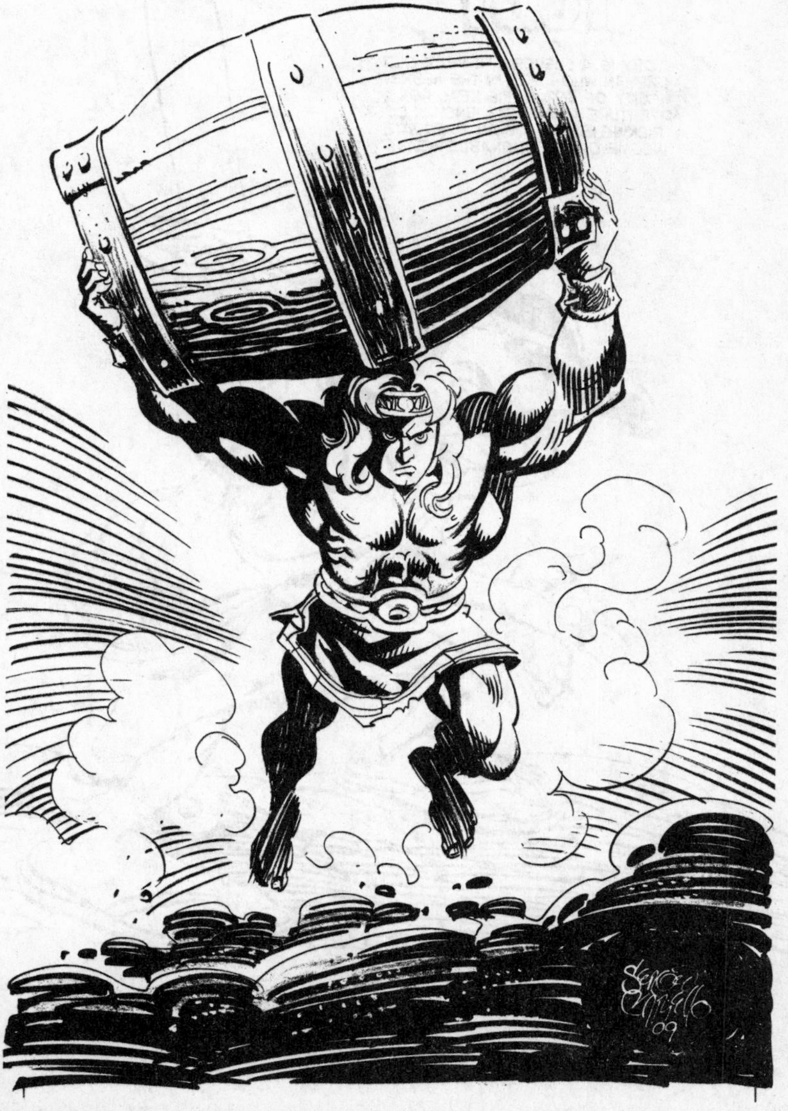

TOBY

TOBY IS A CLEVER TEN-YEAR-OLD ORPHAN WHO LIVES IN THE HEBREW CITY OF ZORAH. HIS ZEAL FOR ADVENTURE AND PROFICIENCY IN LOCK PICKING EARNS HIM AN ADEQUATE INCOME OF QUESTIONABLE MEANS.

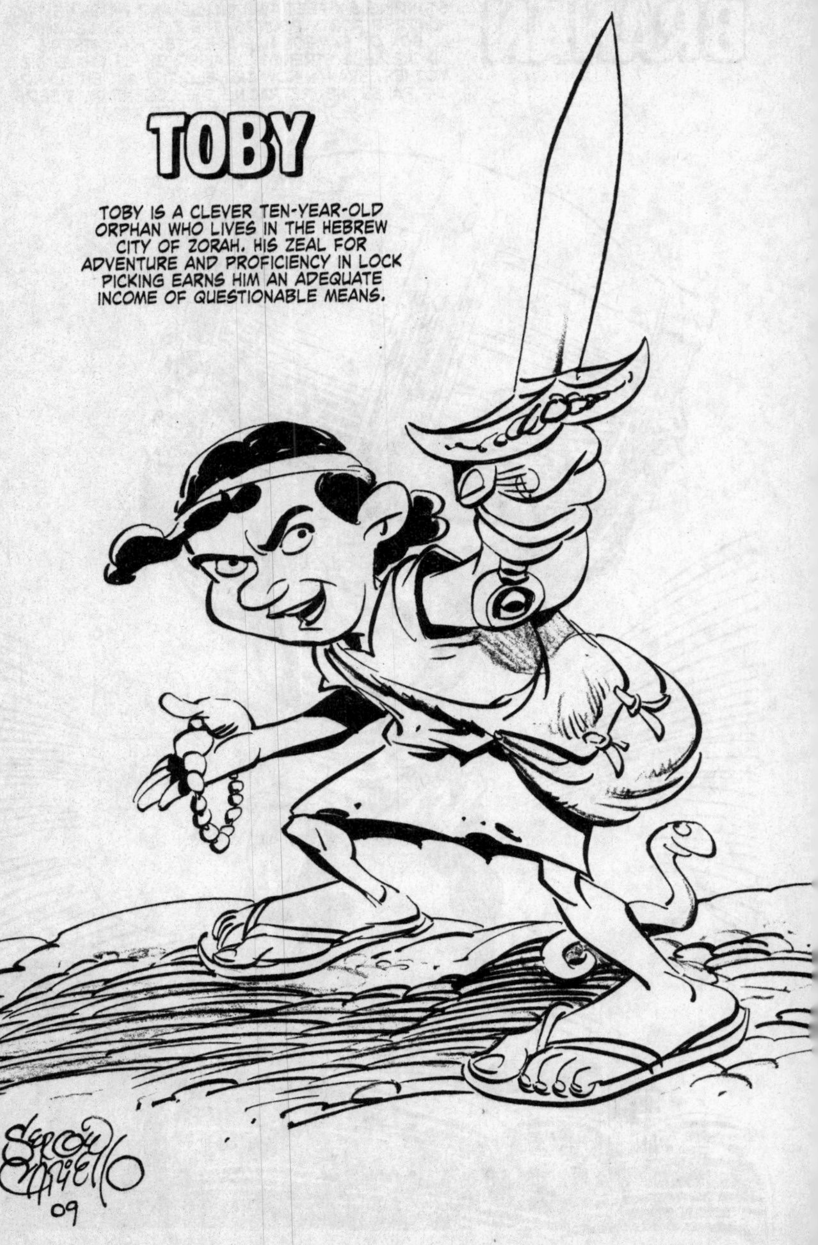

COMMANDER SIDON

A COMMANDER IN THE PHILISTINE ARMY, THE FORTY-YEAR-OLD SIDON IS A VETERAN OF NUMEROUS MILITARY CAMPAIGNS. WITH A LEAN SIX-FOOT FRAME, SIDON IS FORMIDABLE IN BATTLE AND A MASTER OF DIVERSE WEAPONRY. HIS CONTEMPT FOR THE ISRAELITES IS A PRODUCT OF HIS DARK AND BITTER HEART.

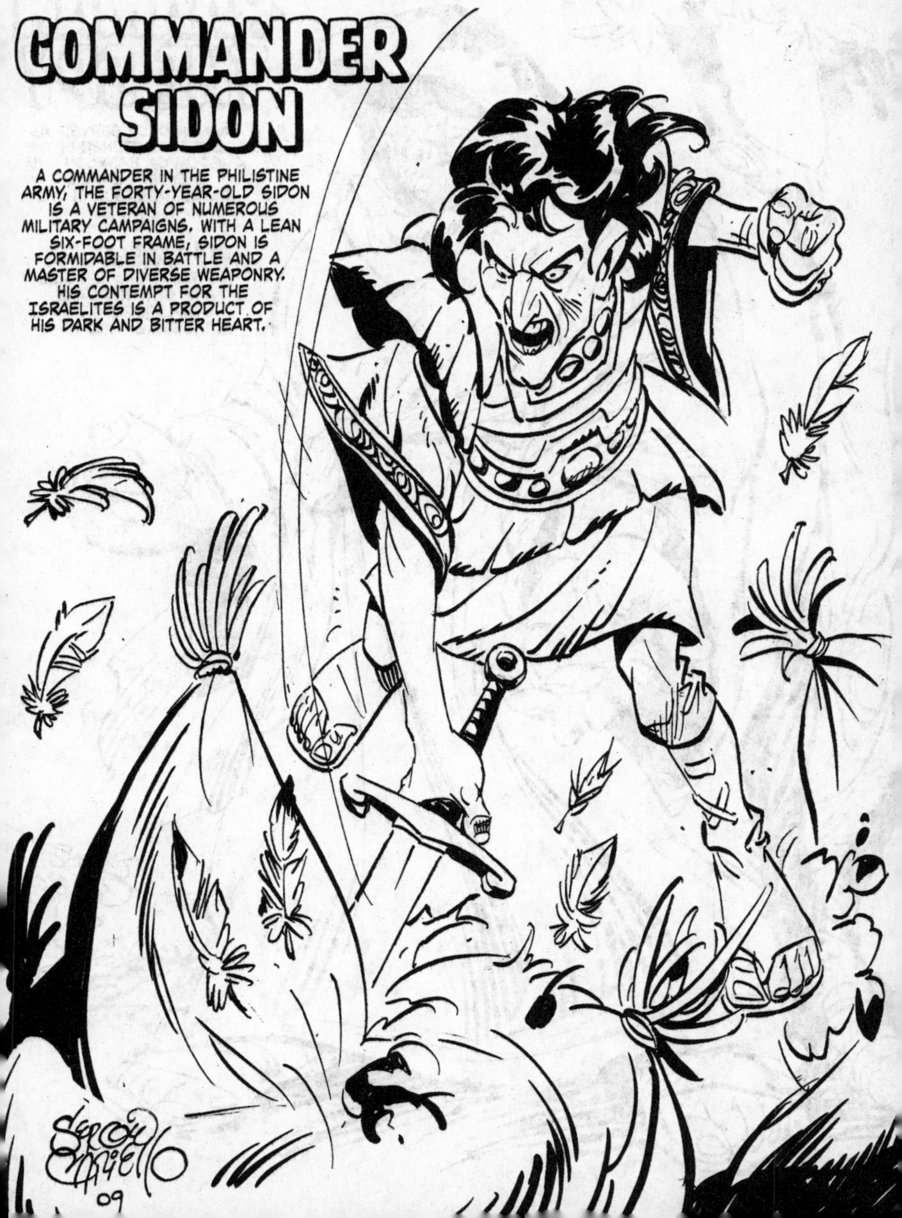

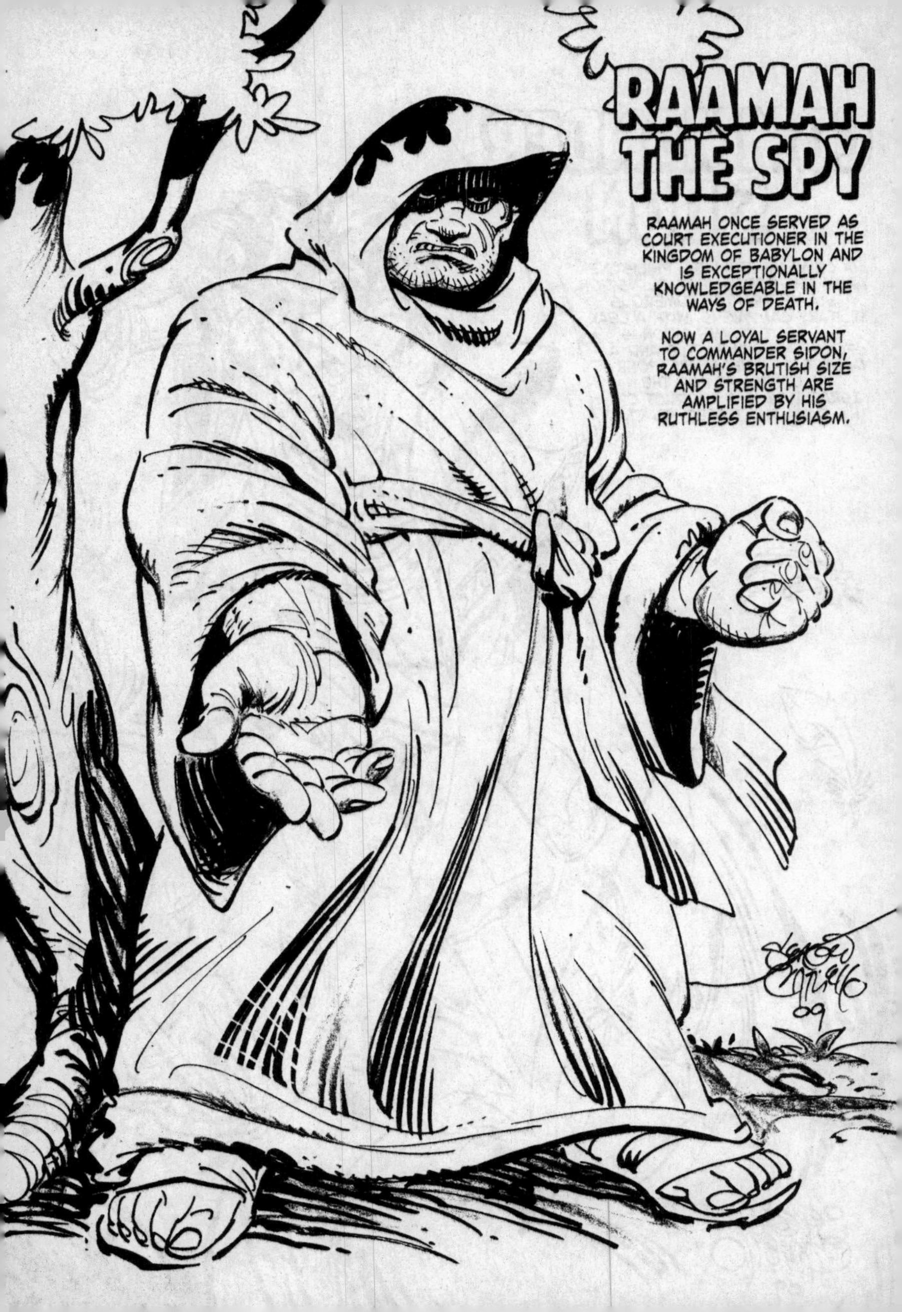
RAAMAH THE SPY
RAAMAH ONCE SERVED AS COURT EXECUTIONER IN THE KINGDOM OF BABYLON AND IS EXCEPTIONALLY KNOWLEDGEABLE IN THE WAYS OF DEATH.
NOW A LOYAL SERVANT TO COMMANDER SIDON, RAAMAH'S BRUTISH SIZE AND STRENGTH ARE AMPLIFIED BY HIS RUTHLESS ENTHUSIASM.

MANOAH

FATHER OF SAMSON AND GRAND-FATHER OF BRANAN, MANOAH RESIDES IN THE CITY OF ZORAH, WHERE HE IS BELOVED BY HIS FRIENDS AND NEIGHBORS. THE ONLY KNOWN RELATIVE TO BRANAN'S FATHER, MANOAH IS AN IMPORTANT CONNECTION TO BRANAN'S HERITAGE.

(TO LEARN MORE ABOUT MANOAH, READ *JUDGES 13-14:9.*)

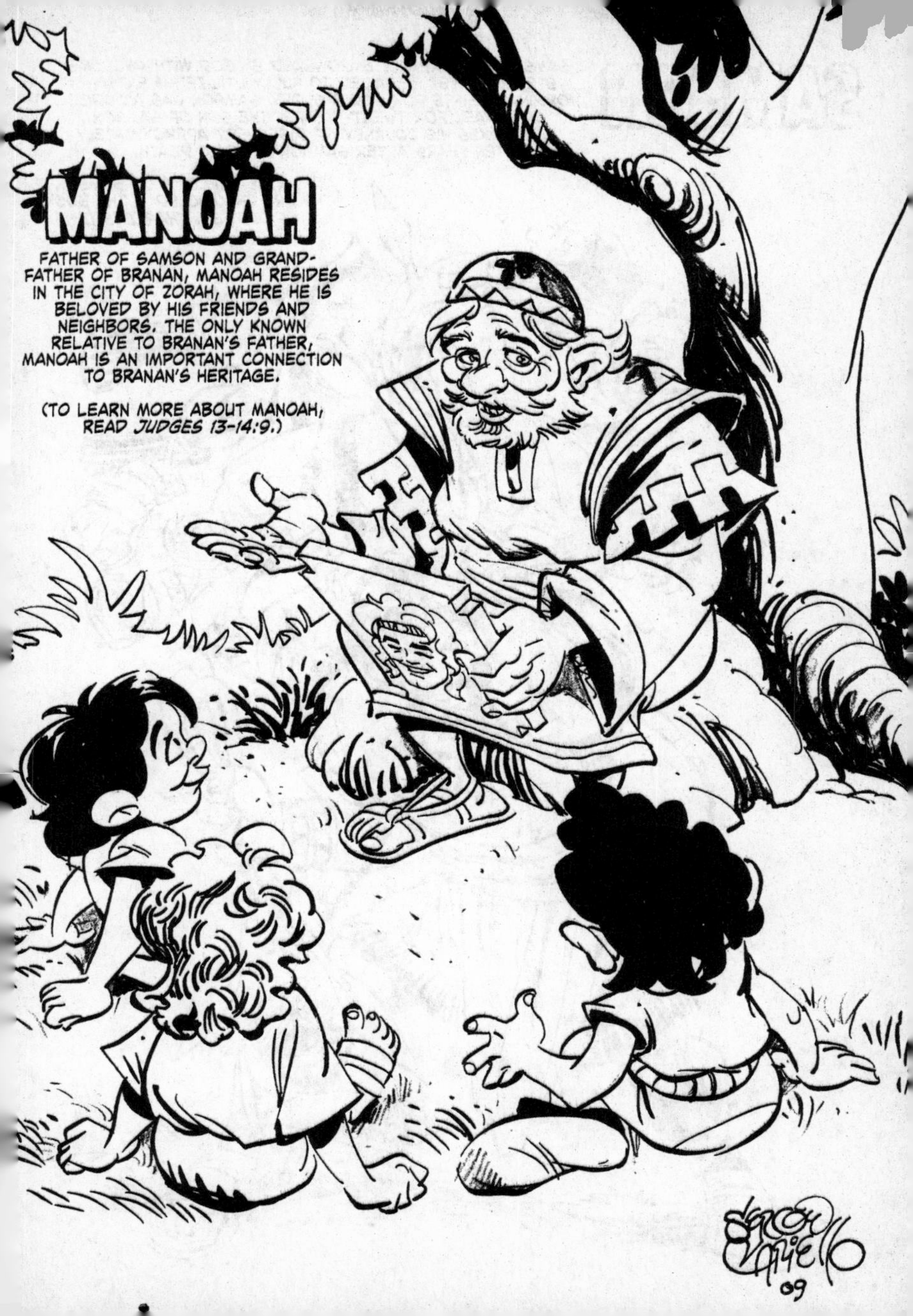

SAMSON

SAMSON WAS GREATLY EMPOWERED BY GOD WITH AWESOME STRENGTH, YET HE FAILED TO FULLY UTILIZE HIS EXTRAORDINARY GIFTS FOR GOD'S GLORY. SAMSON WAS A JUDGE OF ISRAEL FOR TWENTY YEARS. THE SON OF SAMSON UNDERTAKES HIS JOURNEY OF DISCOVERY APPROXIMATELY TEN YEARS AFTER SAMSON'S HEROIC DEATH.

(THE EXPLOITS OF SAMSON ARE CHRONICLED IN THE BOOK OF *JUDGES*, CHAPTERS 13-16.)

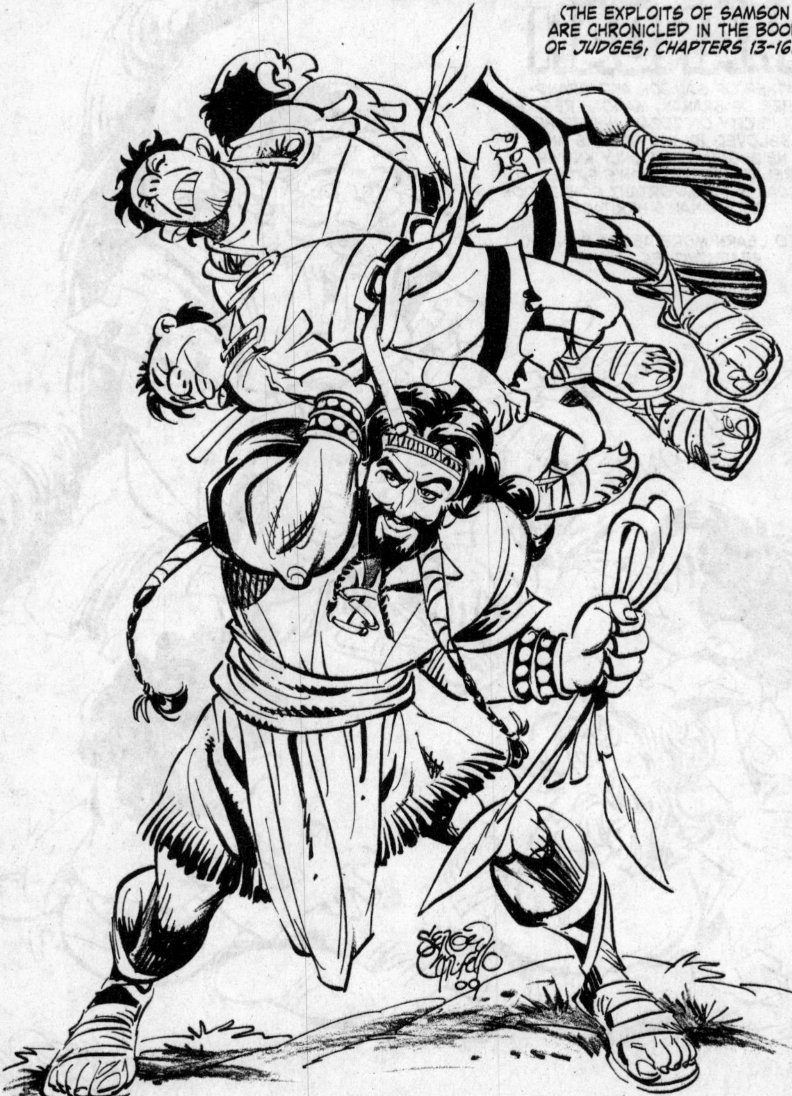

Kingdoms
A Biblical Epic

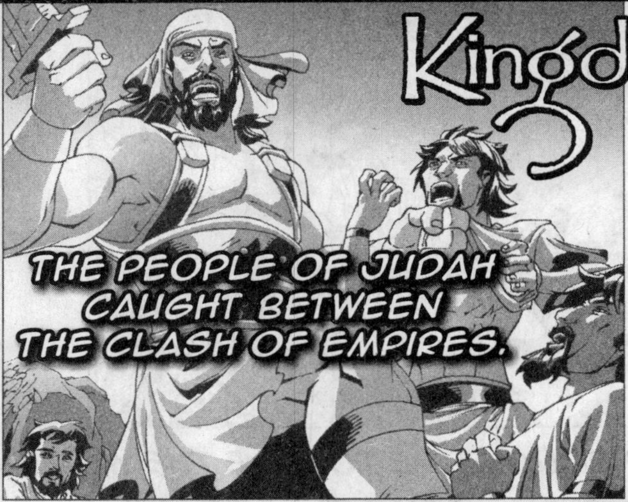
THE PEOPLE OF JUDAH
CAUGHT BETWEEN
THE CLASH OF EMPIRES.

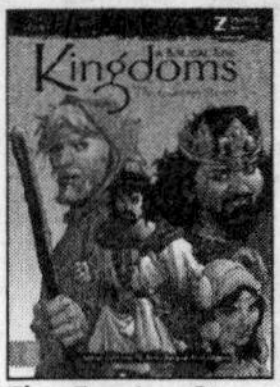

The Coming Storm
Available Now!

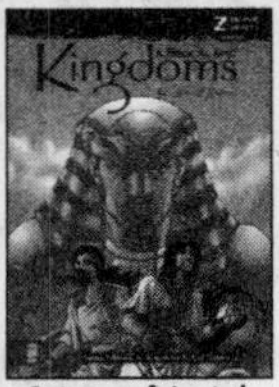

Scions of Josiah
Available Now!

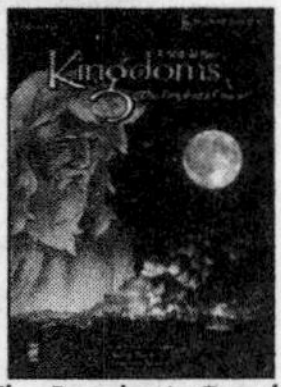

The Prophet's Oracle
Available Now!

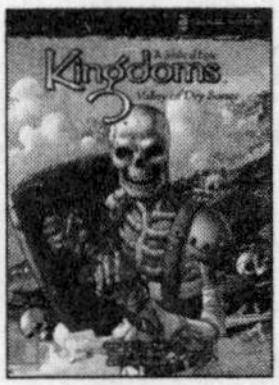

Valley of Dry Bones
Available Now!

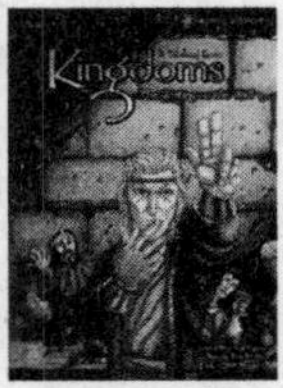

The Writing on the Wall
Available Now!

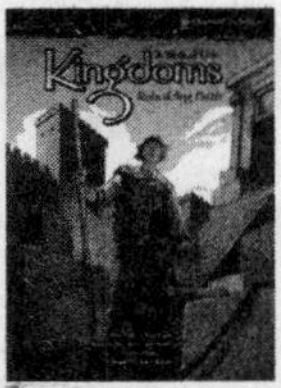

Rebuilding Faith
Available Now!

AVAILABLE AT YOUR LOCAL BOOKSTORE!

VOLUMES 7–8 COMING SOON!

LAMP POST

ZONDERVAN®

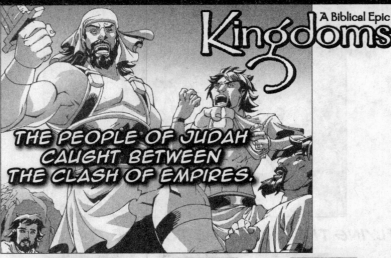

Hand of the
Morningstar
WHA-AAM!
IN THE BATTLE BETWEEN GOOD AND EVIL,
IT'S HARD TO TELL WHO'S ON WHICH SIDE.

Advent
Available Now!

Resurrection
Available Now!

Confession
Available Now!

Emergence
Available Now!

Indoctrination
Available Now!

Alliance
Available Now!

AVAILABLE AT YOUR LOCAL BOOKSTORE!

VOLUMES 7–8 COMING SOON!

ZONDERVAN®

We want to hear from you. Please send your comments about this book to us in care of zreview@zondervan.com. Thank you.

Grand Rapids, MI 49530
www.zonderkidz.com

ZONDERVAN.com/
AUTHORTRACKER
follow your favorite authors

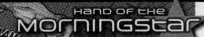

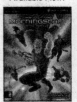

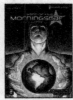

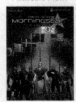

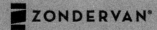

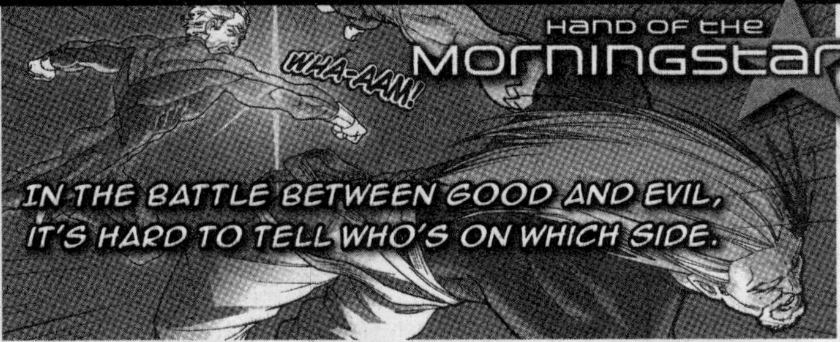

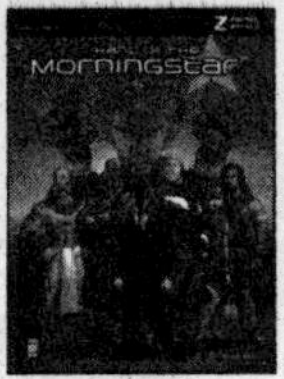

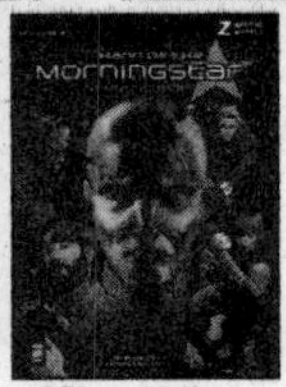

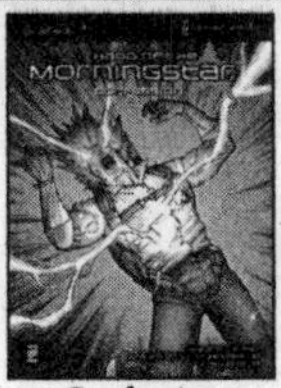